CARTEL PUBLICATIONS
PRESENTS

"Some women are not fit to be mothers. And Harmony Phillips is the worst of them all"

RAUNCHY

T. STYLES

ESSENCE MAGAZINE BEST SELLING AUTHOR OF BLACK & UGLY

Book One of a Trilogy
The Making of Mother Monster

CHECK OUT OTHER TITLES BY THE CARTEL PUBLICATIONS

WWW.THECARTELPUBLICATIONS.COM

Library of Congress Control Number: 2010936906
ISBN: 0982391374
ISBN 13:9780982391372
Cover Design: Davida Baldwin www.oddballdsgn.com
Editor: Advanced Editorial Services
Graphics: Davida Baldwin
www.thecartelpublications.com
First Edition

Printed in the United States of America

RAUNCHY

BY T. STYLES

What's Up Fam!!

It has been a wonderful two full years in business. Within those 2 years, The Cartel Publications is stronger than ever and growing. We are extremely excited about the direction the company is taking and we know you too are just as excited. Although we are ever evolving, we will ALWAYS bring the same fire that we promised from our first published novel, "Shyt List"

Now, on to our current book by Ms. T. Styles. First and foremost, all bullshit aside, T. Styles has a body of published work, not to be fucked wit', that goes without saying. Not only that, she is finally, in my humble opinion, being recognized as one of the best to write it in her field. Recently, she was named as being one of the Top 50 Urban Authors and her latest novel proves she is here to stay. With that said, I am happy to introduce to you, "Raunchy". This novel is everything the title means and more. We do not recommend you read this one while sneaking as it will have you yell out loud in disbelief and disgust! Trust me, this one will turn your stomach and keep you wanting more, so get ready.

Aight ya'll in keeping with tradition, with every novel you all know by now we shine a spotlight on an author who is either a vet or a new comer makin' their way in this literary world. In this novel, we recognize:

"Florence Scovel Shinn"

Mrs. Scovel Shinn is a Metaphysical writer who gained fame in her 1925 self-published novel, "The Game of Life and How to Play It". Her teachings, although started decades ago, continue to inspire and uplift today. I personally have benefited from Mrs. Scovell Shinn and recommend all of her writings to anyone in need of guidance.

On that note Fam, I'ma leave ya'll to it! Go head, call out sick from work, go grab your favorite snack and get ready to read one of the best novels of the year!

Be easy!

Charisse "C. Wash" Washington
VP, The Cartel Publications

www.thecartelpublications.com
www.twitter.com/cartelbooks
www.facebook.com/publishercharissewashington
www.myspace.com/thecartelpublications
www.facebook.com/cartelcafeandbooksstore

ACKNOWLEDGEMENTS

I hate this person…Harmony Phillips. I hate her because she hates back…because she can't be anything different than what she was taught to be. Still, I feel for her, like I feel for all of the women, who lay with a man, producing a child minus any love or compassion. I'm resentful of people for bringing kids into this world only to fin for themselves, yet I understand how it happens. I understand how one bad seed begats another one. I understand how unless we learn to love ourselves, and work to be stronger parents and people, keeping all those out of our family business who may mean us harm, we are doomed.

So I acknowledge all the mothers who do their best because their hearts are in the right place. I acknowledge those who don't know enough to raise a child, but have the wisdom to ask someone who does.

To you I say, Thank you.

T. Styles, President & CEO, The Cartel Publications
www.thecartelpublications.com
www.facebook.com/authortstyles
www.myspace.com/authortstyles
www.authortstyles.blogspot.com
www.twitter.com/authortstyles
Or you may call me on my Fan Line @ 202 656-TOYS

DEDICATION

I dedicate this book to great mother's everywhere.

"Why should my life change just 'cause I got kids? Shit…I brought them in this world…what more do they want?"

-Harmony Phillips

PART ONE

PROLOGUE

Summer of 1976
Fort Washington, Maryland

"Harmony! Harmony…Wake up!" Estelle Pointer yelled at her five-year-old daughter as she slept peacefully in her bed. Flopping down on the edge of her expensive sky blue canopy bed, it rocked violently. "You hear me, girl? Get up now!" Her breath reeked of her favorite poison, tonic water and vodka.

The long blue silk dress Estelle wore was soaked in sweat and her light skin wasn't painted in makeup like it usually was, instead she was frantic and angry.

"What's wrong, mama?" Harmony asked as she rubbed her eyes to see her mother clearly. Her soft curly black hair was pulled tightly back into a floppy ponytail, and a few loose curls rounded her angelic face. Her cheeks were rosy red, like always when she was excited for any reason. "Is daddy hurt?"

"Don't worry about that shit, hussy! Just get your fuckin' ass up…we moving tonight!" She screamed throwing the covers off her body. The cold air attacked her naked legs. "Go put some clothes on and meet me outside in fifteen minutes." When Harmony appeared motionless she said, "Do you hear me, girl?" Harmony nodded quickly. "Don't make me fuck you up! Outside in fifteen minutes!"

She wanted to obey Estelle by doing her best to rush downstairs, but what about her things? Although very young, she had a jewelry box full of diamond earrings, gold bangles and gold necklaces. Like Estelle, she'd become accustomed to luxury, and she wanted to know if her mother had a plan for her personal things as she was sure she had one for her own things.

"Ma,…What about my things?" Harmony asked before getting dressed. "I don't want to leave without my jewelry."

Estelle turned around and smacked her in the face. "Bitch, you heard me! Get dressed!"

Harmony jumped out of bed as quickly as her body could move, while her mother disappeared into the darkness of the house, slamming the door behind her.

"I hate her!" She thought aloud.

She didn't care what that bitch had to say, she was taking her fucking jewelry. Since she hadn't dressed herself before, because it was the nanny's job, she didn't know what to wear. So she chose to keep her pink pajama pants on and put on a white t-shirt. Then she stuffed her jewelry in her panties.

"I'm not ready yet. So stay in your room." Estelle said reentering. "I'll be back for you in ten minutes." She closed the door again.

"WHAT ARE YOU DOING, ESTELLE?! LEAVE MY DAUGHTER OUT OF THIS!" Cornell Phillips yelled.

Harmony knew what was happening without Estelle saying a word. From the argument she overheard earlier between her father Cornell and her mother Estelle, she knew that he was caught cheating with his Spanish mistress, the beautiful Irma Cruz. What Estelle didn't know was that Harmony favored Irma more than she did her, and had been with Cornell to visit her in L.A on many occasions. It was their little secret and she liked it that way. Besides, Estelle was too busy spending Cornell's money on million-dollar shopping sprees to notice his infidelities.

When Harmony was half dressed, she was startled again when her father crept into the room and locked the door behind him. Cornell's honey-colored complexion was reddened and his neat processed wavy hair was now scattered all over his head. Even though his hair was in disarray, he was strikingly handsome.

"Open the door, mothafucka! You ain't got shit to say to me or my daughter no more! Go back to that bitch!" Estelle yelled banging on the door.

KICK! BANG! KICK! Were the sounds heard against the door. "Estelle, give me a minute with my daughter! Just one damn minute!"

"Go back and stick your dick in that bitch," she persisted.

Cornell shook his head in disgust at how she was talking around Harmony.

Silence.

"You didn't stick to the plan!" She cried leaning against the door. "Why didn't you stick to the plan?!"

"Fuck you!"

"I'm tired of your shit, Cornell!" She stood up straight. "I'm not riding with you no more! Do you hear me…I'm not taking your shit no more!"

The yelling scared Harmony and Cornell was trying to spare her as best he could.

"Come here, princess," he continued sitting on a chair in her room. Estelle quieted down but he knew that she was a hateful bitch and was undoubtedly doing something to get back at him at that very moment.

Harmony rushed toward him and he spoke in a heavy whisper, her light skin was flushed from all the excitement. But every time she saw his face she felt safe because he treated her like a princess. Up until that point, life had been a dream and somehow she knew all would change.

"I gotta give you life in a hurry, princess, because you might not see me again."

"No, daddy."

"Just listen…Whatever your mother says about me when you leave, don't believe her. You hear me? I want you to remember our good times together, and how much I love you. And when you meet someone, if he can't afford you, I don't want you wasting your time on him."

"Daddy, I'm scared." Harmony began to sob uncontrollably until he caressed her back softly.

"I'm sorry but your life is getting ready to change and you need to be ready." He paused. "I'm gonna send somebody to bring you something. When you meet him, he'll talk to you alone. Don't worry, you can trust him."

"But you said never to trust anyone."

"I know, but we don't have a choice."

"But where is mama taking me, daddy? What about my things? I don't wanna-"

"You'll probably go over Shirley's house." He interrupted, speaking of her grandmother. "And you betta never trust that old bitch 'cause she'll smile in your face and stab you in the back the moment you turn around." The idea of her nana being so hateful frightened her. "Be smart, princess. It's important that you always do a good job in school and be smart, don't be anything like Estelle."

"You said you'd never leave me. And now you makin' me go with mama." A short jolt of unease pierced her stomach.

"There ain't shit we can do about that now, princess! I need you strong!" He said wiping his own tears away this time. "I'm sorry I exposed you to this lifestyle...because now the bar is set high for you, and you'll always want more. But always remember that when you're in pursuit of money, that you should never sell your soul."

"Okay, daddy."

He smiled weakly although his heart was breaking by the second. "Listen, before you go I have to tell you somethin' 'bout Estelle. She's..."

"POLICE! OPEN UP!" Loud knocking on the bedroom door scared Harmony and rattled her father. He stood up straight and shoved her toward her white bedroom closet door. She fell on her knees scraping them terribly.

"Get in the closet, and close the door! No matter what you see, don't come out here!" He said grabbing her up by her arms.

"Daddy, no! I'm scared."

"Harmony Phillips, you do what I say this instant!" He opened the closet door. "Now get in that closet and don't come out! Do you hear me?"

"Yes, daddy."

Whenever Cornell called her by her full name, he was serious, and she knew better than to disobey him. So she ran into the cold dark closet and looked through the wooden slits. Cornell could see the shine of her eyes against the dim light in her room and he stepped back and smiled.

"I love you," he whispered. She waved and wiped away the last few tears that crept upon her face, they were useless and she knew it. She'd made a promise to be strong and that was exactly what she was going to do, no matter what.

"OPEN THIS DOOR NOW! WE HAVE YOU CORNERED!"

Seconds later, the bedroom door came crashing in and five police officers wrestled Cornell to the floor.

"STAY DOWN!" One of the officers yelled striking him on his head with his Billy club. "Don't move!"

The other four officers joined in the abuse and struck Cornell multiple times in the face, neck and upper body.

"We finally got your ass," one of the cops said. "We have the dope and everything right in your house. You see, you not as smart as you thought you were."

"Get that mothafucka! Don't let him get up!" Estelle yelled, walking into the room. Her jaw flexed and her eyes formed tiny slits. She wasn't the slightest bit upset at how the officers were treating her long term boyfriend...the only thing on her mind was revenge. "He got all kinds of drugs and money underneath the house too! And me and my baby ain't no nothin' 'bout it either!" Then she directed her attention to Cornell. "And just so you know, nigga, you ain't neva seein' your daughter again! Ever!"

"Bitch, I will kill you first! She ain't even..."

"Shut the fuck up," an officer said hitting him again.

Seeing the violent officers hurt her father, and hearing Estelle's evil threats about never seeing her again, Harmony rushed out of the closet and hit one of the policemen on the leg with her tiny fists. She figured if she helped him, that her father would be able to escape and they could leave together. But the officer kicked her off and she tumbled against the blue wall hurting her head. Enraged and not thinking straight, Cornell mustered up enough strength to tackle the officer to the floor. Once in his grasp, he gripped his throat tightly. Spit escaped his mouth and his hair was drenched in sweat. It took all four officers to attempt to pull Cornell off of him.

"You fuckin', cracker! I know you just didn't hit my baby girl! I know you ain't that fuckin' crazy!"

Veins popped out of his forehead and neck as he continued to crush the officer's windpipe. Seconds later, the officer's eyes rolled up in his head and he was no longer able to fight him.

For as long as Cornell had been selling and transporting drugs in DC, Maryland and New York, he never took a life himself until now. Sure he handed down orders for hundreds of men to be killed, but never had he done the work himself until that night. After all, Cornell was a boss and bosses rarely got their hands dirty. Too bad for him that his first blood drawn, belonged to a white Maryland, police officer.

Being so close to death, his mind raced briefly to the past. Cornell was not a man who regretted much, but he did regret the day he participated in a high stakes Poker game. Had he not, maybe he would not be in the predicament he was in, but at the same time, Harmony may never had been in his life either. And he loved her more than life.

Seeing their partner's body go limp, one of the other officers shot Cornell in the shoulder and he dropped to the floor.

"For your sake you betta hope he's alive, nigger!" He said pressing his foot heavily on the fresh wound to keep Cornell penned to the floor. The other officers rushed to their partner one by one making the same determination, that he was dead.

"Mam...you better get your daughter out of here." One of them said giving her an evil glare. Then he leveled a dark look at Cornell. "I don't think either of you will want to see what's gonna happen next."

Harmony's jaw dropped when she saw the blood escaping her father's body. She contemplated hiding in the house until everyone left. Her favorite place was a crawl space under the stairs and sometimes the large basement. She figured after the cops left, she could still be there with her father. She didn't understand the repercussions of killing a white police officer.

No sooner than that thought entered her mind, Estelle grabbed her by the arm and whisked her away. Harmony's body was pulled down the beautiful spiral staircase, through the foyer with the large crystal chandelier hanging from the ceiling and into Estelle's blue Mercedes Benz, with the engine running. Police cars sat in the elegant stone driveway and blaring sirens indicated that more were on the way. Estelle didn't want to be anywhere near them.

"Mama, please! We gotta help daddy!" She was crying hysterically.

"Ain't nothin' we can do but help ourselves!"

Estelle removed a bottle of vodka from her purse, opened the back door and threw her bag inside, it landed on the floor. On the back seat sat a large duffle bag filled with so much money, hundred dollar bills peaked from the sides and floated softly to the floor.

"Get in the car! Now!" Estelle yelled at Harmony. "We got to get out of here!"

"But I don't wanna leave daddy!"

"Get in the fuckin' car you spoiled, little bitch!"

Harmony wiped the tears from her face and quickly opened the passenger door. Once inside, she put her seat belt on and waited for Estelle to enter the car, too. When she did, Harmony looked at her hoping she'd explain why the police were in their home, and more importantly, why she allowed them to shoot her father. Instead of giving Harmony answers, Estelle twisted the cap off the bottle of the liquor, downed half of it, and pulled out of the driveway.

"We're stayin' with mother for a couple of days. And you betta stay out of her way when we get there, too."

"Yes, mam."

"What did your father say to you?" She paused. "Huh? Did he tell you anything about me?"

"No, mama."

"You betta not be lying to me!"

"I'm not, mama."

Harmony swallowed hard and looked out ahead of her. Everything in her spirit wanted to know what was going on, but she also knew questioning her mother could be bad for her health.

Looking at the sign that read, "Thank You For Visiting Concord Manor", as they exited the multi-million dollar mansion, she felt faint. At Concord she had everything, including friends and a father who cherished the ground she walked on, now she would have nothing.

"Ma." She whispered filling her tiny chest with enough air to handle Estelle's response.

"What?!"

"Why did the police hurt daddy? Is he...Is he...Dead?"

Irritated, Estelle pulled erratically off the road and threw her car in park. "You wanna know the truth?"

"Yes, mam."

"They hurt him because he is a fuckin' drug dealer! He hurt a lot of people and now he has to pay for his actions! That's why!"

Harmony could hear her father's voice in her mind say, 'Whatever your mother says about me when you leave, don't believe her.' She wondered if he was talking about being a drug dealer. Harmony knew her father was far from an angel, but she also knew her mother had shit with her too. She was young, but she knew for a fact that Estelle was fully aware of what Cornell did for a living. She remembered seeing her on numerous occasions packaging the powder Harmony knew as Sugar on their kitchen table.

"But…I thought you knew what daddy did. I thought you said it was okay because what he was doin' he was doin' for us."

Estelle's lips pressed tightly together and her brows creased. Then she looked at Harmony and said, "Hussy, if you ever tell somebody that shit, I will kill you. You betta neva repeat that shit again, you understand me?" She yelled, squeezing her forearm so strongly she could feel the bone. "I will kill you."

"Okay…Mama."

Estelle slowly let her go and said, "I didn't know 'bout none of that shit he got goin' on back there! But I'm glad I found out. We don't want to be anywhere near there when they lock his cheatin' ass up!"

In that instance, as if it were even possible, Harmony hated her more. She couldn't understand why she was always so moody and most of all, so fuckin' fake. One minute Estelle would be boasting to her friends and family about how beautiful her daughter was and the very next minute she'd tell anyone who would listen that she was a spoiled and ungrateful red bitch. Now she had committed the ultimate crime as far as Harmony was concerned, by turning her back on Cornell.

After Estelle finished yelling at Harmony, she pulled back into traffic and drank some more vodka. On the sly, Harmony examined the beautiful Benz she was driving, the diamonds in her ears and the rings on her fingers. She knew immediately that her mother was a liar. But what could she do? And what could she say? She didn't have her father to protect her anymore.

While her mind was on her father, the jewelry in her panties dug at her undeveloped mound. She was about to ease some of the jewelry out when Estelle redirected her attention toward her again.

"Harmony, I know you only care about your damn daddy, but you gonna have to get use to the fact that I'm all you got. So you best start showin' me some respect. If you don't, I ain't got no problem puttin' you in one of them foster homes I hear about all the time. Maybe then you'd learn to 'ppreciate me." She paused looking over at her with an evil glare. "So what's it gonna be? Tell me now, 'cause I'll get rid of you with the quickness. Ain't but one pussy can be in charge at a time, and it damn sure ain't yours."

"I'm gonna try and do better, mama."

As if nothing happened, Estelle smiled and placed her hand on her leg. "Good. Drink some of this, it will make you feel better."

Harmony's eyes widened at her mother's offer. She had never touched alcohol a day in her life and was told many times by her father to leave it alone. But since it made Estelle feel better about her betrayal, she decided to see what it could do for her, too.

Taking the bottle slowly, she moved it to her lips, the bittersweet smell made her uncomfortable. But wanting to forget her problems, she closed her eyes, and poured a lot into her mouth. It burned the inside of her chest and she wanted to spit it out, but it was too late, it had gone down her throat.

"Yuck!" She said wiping her lips with the back of her hand. "That's nasty."

Estelle laughed, took the bottle back and said, "Yuck now, but feelin' betta later. Trust me." Then she drank some more herself. "Keep sipping on this, and you won't give a fuck about shit else!"

Within a few minutes she noticed her mother was right. Suddenly her problems seemed somewhat insignificant. Sure she didn't want to go to her grandmother's house, which was smack dab in the middle of Southeast Washington, DC. But unfortunately, she didn't have a choice. Now as she sat quietly in her seat, she felt warm and tingly all over. It would be the beginning of one of the biggest downfalls in her life. And soon so much violence, hate and deceit would fill her life that she would be unable to remember this moment.

What did Cornell have to tell her about her mother that he couldn't finish saying? She remembered. And what would he be sending me later?

She shook her head again in an attempt to forget everything about the night and then she remembered last summer at her grandmother's house. Suddenly she realized there was something to smile about after all, and his name was Jace Sherrod.

GRANDMA MONSTER

2 Months Later
Southeast, Washington D.C.

Shirley Pointer owned a medium sized brick house on Central Avenue in Southeast Washington DC. And although it was in a bad neighborhood, it was furnished from head to toe in expensive furniture. Each room had a huge TV and the bathroom had a small TV bolted to the wall. Everything Shirley owned was a compliment of Estelle trying to win her mother's love, but you'd never know it to hear Shirley tell it. She made it sound as if her fat ass had bought everything on her own when the bitch didn't even have a job.

It was eight o'clock in the morning and Estelle and Harmony were busy in the small green kitchen preparing for Shirley's fish fry, which was nothing more than a drunken fool party.

"Harmony, hurry up over here with those potatoes! I know you can move faster than that, girl! We got way too much to do for you to be lollygaggin' around."Yelled Estelle from the stove.

Harmony wasn't trying to ignore her mother but she was ear hustling and could've sworn she heard the phone ring.

"I'm not accepting no collect calls," said Shirley before hanging up.

Could it have been her father? Harmony thought. She hadn't heard or seen his face in months and she missed him terribly.

"Harmony, what you doin'? Get your ass over here!"

"Oh, I'm sorry, ma!"

Harmony straightened up, lifted the large blue bowl of raw potatoes off the brown kitchen table a few feet from the stove, and walked them slowly over to Estelle. One wrong move and the potatoes would have toppled to the floor, angering Estelle even more.

Estelle yanked the bowel out of her hands and dropped them into scolding hot water. Droplets plopped on Harmony's arm, burning her skin.

"Ouch!" She yelled rubbing the area that burned. "That hurt!"

On instinct, Estelle smacked her so hard in the face that her loose tooth fell from her mouth and bounced on the floor.

"Didn't I tell you to be quiet?" Estelle pointed her long finger in her face. "Now you gonna have your nana come in here hollerin' and screamin' and shit. And I'm not hardly tryin' to hear her fuckin mouth." Everything Harmony did angered her and it was apparent that there was no love between them.

Shirley Pointer, with her large robust body came barreling into the kitchen swinging her meaty arms back and forth. Her dark skin was ashy and her eyebrows were pulled together in anger.

"I know ya'll not crazy!" She yelled, her lips pressed closely together. The old smooth black bullet wound on her face glistened against the ceiling light. "What the fuck is goin' on 'round here?! And why the fuck is ya'll makin' all this noise in my house? If Preston was here, I'da throwed both of ya'll's asses out on them streets."

Preston was her boyfriend of two years who only came over when her refrigerator was full and her attitude was nowhere to be found. He could put up with a lot of things...but fussin' and cussin' was not one of them.

"Sorry, mama! Harmony done fell and knocked a tooth out of her mouth. You must've heard her when she yelled." She said picking it up off the floor. In Shirley's presence, Estelle acted like a scared child.

"What you mean?" She said walking up to Harmony. She squeezed her jaws forcing her mouth open. After examining Harmony's tooth, she pushed her away using her jaws, causing her to stumble backwards. "You sure you ain't hit this child? You never did have much in the way of patience when it came to kids."

"No, mama. It was all her grown ass!"

"Well, I'ma have to ask your daddy for some money to get this fixed. The next time he call collect, Estelle, accept it, and tell him we need some money to fix her mouth."

"He don't want to talk to me and he's locked up."

"And he won't have to talk to you. But he still got a child here and access to money, too. I guarantee it."

Harmony knew neither her tooth nor her hands would see any parts of the money if Cornell bothered to give it to either one of them slick bitches.

"How it happen anyway?"

"She was tryin' to help me make the food for the party tonight when she fell on this here stove and bust her mouth open. Ain't that what happened, Harmony?"

Harmony was in so much pain she wouldn't dare say anything to the contrary.

"Yes, mam. That's what happened."

"Well I don't care, if ya'll don't get it together there's gonna be problems. You ain't got your little maids waitin' on you hand and foot in Concord Manor no more. You in my house now, and 'round here, everything has to be cared for personally, including my peace and quiet!"

Shirley waddled back in her bedroom and Estelle continued about the meal nervously. It was easy to bully Harmony, but when it came to standing up to her mother, she failed miserably.

All Estelle's life Shirley belittled her and made her feel as if she could never stand up to her brother Charles, who was locked up for raping his seven month baby girl, killing her instantly. In Shirley's mind, Charles was a good man who was put in a terrible position by his wife Carmel. To hear her tell it, had Carmel bathed her own baby, instead of asking Charles to do it, little Debbie Pointer would still be alive today. No...in Shirley's mind Estelle could never measure up, no matter what she did, including giving her all of the money she'd stolen from Cornell.

Although Shirley Pointer ridiculed her only daughter, this bitch was far from an angel. In fact, Estelle was a product of her freak-whoreness. Many years ago, before Estelle was born, Shirley was supposed to be working for the Whitesdales, a wealthy white couple in Maryland. She was the family maid, yet she gave extra special attention to Todd, Mrs. Beverly Whitesdales's husband.

At the time Shirley was very beautiful with her wide smile, large breasts and cooking skills, which could put the meanest beast under her trance. But her real skills were in the bedroom because Shirley had sucked and fucked her way into some of the most prestigious homes in DC and was the rich white man's secret. In fact, they shared her amongst themselves, no man being allowed to keep *her longer than a year. But when Todd got greedy, and extended his time to two years not being able to part with the way Shirley wrapped her mouth around his dick, one of the husbands in the secret club got mad since he was next, and secretly told Mrs. Whitesdale.*

At the time Shirley was four months pregnant by Todd and barely showing when Beverly walked up to her in the kitchen and shot her in the head. The bullet didn't enter her skull and took no more than a few months to heal. But the gig was up because none of the wives wanted her in their homes. So she lived off of welfare most of her life and officially sold pussy from time to time to make ends meet. But on January 16, 1968 her hardships ended all together. Because it was the day that her beautiful daughter Estelle, went to a cabaret and met DC Drug lord Cornell Phillips.

Five hours after Harmony's tooth was broken, Shirley's large brick house was packed with every cousin's uncle who got an informal invitation. Moochers, greedy bastards and fake friends didn't mind filling every available seat and floor space in the house. And Shirley made sure her white Cadillac and Estelle's Benz was washed and sitting in the front of the house to represent luxury.

"Estelle…Bring me some more gin! And some ice, too!"

Estelle who was already running back and forth for her mother and her friends sighed heavily. Had she thought with her mind and not her heart, she would have never betrayed Cornell. At Concord Manor she lived like a queen, and now outside of the rings on her fingers and jewelry around her neck, no one would know she was once a hustler's girlfriend although never a hustler's wife.

"Okay, mama." She said. "Just give me a second to check on the ribs in the oven."

"Gin now, the food later!"

Estelle sighed and said, "Okay, ma." She fixed her drink and handed it to her and was on her way back to the refrigerator.

"And be careful with that fridge. You know it's so stuffed with food that I had to put tape on it." She bragged.

"Damn, Shirley! Ya'll really are doin' good 'round here." Lola said. "You need another daughter?" She laughed heartedly, before slapping her knee.

"Bitch, I ain't happy with the one I got. What I looks like takin' in more?"

"I heard that, look at her...she ain't so upitity now though is she?" Lola laughed, looking at Estelle.

Estelle heard Lola but tried to block her out. It was a mistake to give Shirley all of her money because out of the fifty thousand she'd stolen from Cornell, she only had a couple thousand left.

●━━━━━━━━━━━━━━━━━━━━━━━━━━━━━━━━━●

In the room, Harmony lie on the bed in tears, wishing her life was different. Wishing she could have warned her father that her mother was working with the DEA. But she knew nothing about what her mother put into work two weeks after learning about his continued involvement with Irma. Now because of Estelle's jealousy, Cornell was locked up, partially blind and confined to a wheel chair. The officers had beaten him so badly after Estelle and Harmony left, that they thought he was dead. In fact that was their chief aim and it angered them that unlike the successful murder of their partner, Cornell Phillips was still alive. They compensated for their failure by beating him regularly in prison. Almost every bone in his body had been broken and no matter how hard his lawyer fought, there was nothing he could do to have him moved. He killed a white man and a white police officer. In society's eyes, they were two different circumstances, both of which carried heavy penalties.

ROOF, ROOF, ROOF! Harmony looked out of the window at Shirley's dog Dingo. Kalive Miller, Kreshon Myter and Paco Carry taunted the dogs by throwing rocks at its face.

"Roof, Roof!" Dingo barked at them viciously. "Roof, Roof, Roof!"

Knowing the dog was liable to jump over the gate and chase them was why they taunted him. Already young, they lived dangerously.

"Get your black asses away from my animal!" Shirley yelled, breaking away from her party. "I'm tired of you little niggles fucking with my dog!"

The boys ran away laughing the entire way. When Shirley went back inside, Dingo continued to bark wildly at Harmony who was still staring at him through the window. Although she hated Dingo, she despised her mother even more.

As she moved around on the makeshift bed on the floor, because the room was used for Shirley's clothes and shoes, she wished she were back at home.

"I wish she were dead! I wish she were dead! I wish she were dead!" Harmony chanted over and over. She wanted nothing more than to laugh over her mother's grave and she prayed for the day her wish would come true.

"Harmony! What you doin' in here?" Estelle asked entering the room. She wiped the sweat from her brow and held the door open.

"Oh...uh...nothin', mama." Harmony shot up straight.

Estelle knew something else was on her mind so she walked into the room and sat on Harmony's makeshift bed. What she was really trying to do was catch her breath from all the running around Shirley had her doing.

"Sit down with me." Harmony sat. "You're still mad at me, aren't you?" Tears welled up in Harmony's eyes but she didn't want to admit to her feelings. "Don't worry. You can tell me the truth." She said softly. "You blame me for what happened to your father...don't you?"

Harmony nodded and whispered, "Yes...I'm still mad."

An angry disposition took over Estelle and she slapped Harmony in the face. She already knew how Harmony felt but wanted her to lie. She wanted somebody, anybody to be on her side and she hated Harmony for not choosing to be that person.

"Well come out here with me!" Estelle stood up and Harmony rose too. "I done told everybody how pretty you are and they can't even see you."

"Here comes the fake shit," Harmony said under her breath, following behind her mother.

"What you say?" Estelle asked turning around.

Harmony stopped in her tracks, wondering if she could have heard her over Diana Ross' song, "Do You Know Where You're Going", blasting over the speakers in the living room.

"Nothin', mama. I didn't say nothin'." She said still stewing over the slap.

"Well come on then, I need you to help me put the snacks on the table. Them niggas done damn near ate us out of house and home! What kind of shit is that anyway? Half of them bastards ain't even bring shit."

Harmony didn't know what her mother wanted from her, but she had no intentions of chiming in on her complaints. She had problems of her own and they all involved Estelle. Harmony followed Estelle to the kitchen and they each grabbed a plate filled with cheeses and crackers, when the doorbell rang.

"Somebody gonna get the door?!" Yelled Estelle. Her hands were full and she wasn't in the mood to be running to the door, and trying to replenish the food table at the same time.

"Yeah, you!" Shirley yelled, half drunk. "Now hurry up for who ever out there leaves! And bring me some more gin!" A cigarette burned in an ashtray next to her and the leather bound phonebook she carried everywhere sat on her lap.

"Fuck." She said under her breath.

"You want me to put the stuff on the table, mama?" Harmony asked standing behind her with the platter directly below her chin. The smells of cheese wafted in her nose and stank.

"No! Follow me to this door first. I wanna show you where I want everything to go before you fuck shit up." Harmony looked at her with an evil glare on her face.

Estelle walked slowly to the door trying not to drop the food. Balancing the tray in one hand, she opened the door with the other. Outside there was a beautiful Spanish woman standing before her with hate in her eyes. Estelle recognized her, immediately.

"What…are you doing here?"

"You ruined his life, you jealous bitch!" Wearing gloves, Irma Cruz raised the .45 she was carrying and blasted half of Estelle's face off. When her body dropped, Irma saw Harmony standing behind her, brain matter all about her face and fluffy green dress. Hearing the gun blast, Harmony's face held an evil stare, one that Irma would never forget.

"I…I…I'm sorry, Harmony! Please forgive me." Irma dropped the gun and took off running.

THE PROMISE

6 Months Later

Six-year-old Harmony lay on the floor with the door closed. Her favorite large teddy bear lie under her body. Using its nose, the largest and firmest part of the teddy, she rubbed her vagina over and over on the stuffed animal's face. Like many young children, she had already discovered masturbation. And felt all kinds of chills run through her body before her uncle Charles came into the room and ruined it all.

"Harmony, what are you doing?" He said softly, closing the door behind him.

Charles was a handsome man with deep-set eyes and dark chocolate skin. Yet his winning smile hid his sly and cunning ways. He had gotten out of prison for raping and killing his baby girl and already he was up to his usual tricks while staying with his mother.

"Oh…uh…nothing, uncle Charles. I was just…uh…just." Harmony jumped up.

Charles smiled and walked deeper into the room. "I know what you were doing, and it's okay."

"You not going to tell nana are you?" Harmony asked with wide eyes.

"No. I'm not. It'll be our little secret. But I want you to do something for me, too." He paused. "And I'll teach you everything you need to know.

Harmony didn't have a positive woman in her life, to talk to about what was happening. She was young, vulnerable and afraid and Charles preyed on every minute. After a while, he managed to convince her that it was okay to explore her body, just as long as she explored it with him.

Many days later, Harmony sat still in the room, with her nose pressed firmly against the cold dirty window, staring at Jace. Life at Shirley's had become unbearable. Charles had just left her room and molested her again, telling her had she not explored her body on her own, he would not be doing those things to her. And that it was all her fault. She believed him. She could still feel his hot breath against her ear, and his rough calloused hands all over her young body. If only she could befriend Jace, who her uncle forbade her to speak to, life might be worth living.

"Harmony! Come here!" Her nana yelled from the bathroom. Harmony stole one last look at Jace before seeing what Shirley wanted. Ever since Estelle went and got herself killed, a blessing Harmony was grateful for, Shirley treated her like a slave and it pissed her off. "Harmony, don't make me call you again!"

She looked at the bathroom door where Shirley was and thought about ignoring her. But the last time she did that, Shirley punished her for the entire weekend by making her stay in her room. Charles took full advantage of that time, too by fondling her every day of her punishment.

"You got your welfare check already, Lola?" Shirley said in the bathroom on the phone to her friend. "Well let me see if mine here, too."

"Yes, nana." Harmony said, standing at the open bathroom door. Steam crept from the tub and carried with it the smell of soap, dirty pussy and cigarettes.

"Bitch, what took you so long to answer me?" She asked.

"I didn't hear you." She lied.

"I see you gonna make me start puttin' my hands on you. Where is Charles?"

"He went to the store."

"Well go outside and get my mail. I'm expectin' my welfare check. Lola already done got hers."

"Okay, nana." She said in a sweet voice, although rolling her eyes when she wasn't looking.

With a chance to see Jace's honey colored skin, curly hair and cool disposition, she grabbed her coat, bolted out of the door and ran down the steps. The cold air attacked her body because it was the middle of December. Out of the corner of her eyes she could see the way Jace's wavy hair shined under the winter sun and couldn't get over how cute he was. Kali, the neighborhood menace was out there, too. Jace Sherrod was cut from the same cloth as Harmony, they both grew up in lavish homes headed by notorious drug dealers. He was speaking to Brittany, the neighborhood freaky girl. Harmony wondered if Brittany was doing all of the things to Jace her uncle had taught her to do to him. She felt if she could be friends with Jace, she could make him feel good like she did her uncle, and maybe he would like her more.

After grabbing the mail, she slowly walked back up the steps with her back-faced to Jace. She was hoping he'd see her and call her name, before she was forced to speak first. Maybe the kiss they shared, when their fathers gambled one night, would reenter his mind like it did hers. But when he remained silent, giving Brittany his undivided attention, she knew she'd have to speak first.

Turning toward him, her back faced the door, she said, "Hey, Jace." And waved. Jace waved back but his swag wouldn't allow him to do much else. He was a boy of few words and that both confused and appealed to Harmony. "You gonna be out all day?" Harmony continued. Brittany rolled her eyes and put her hands on her hips.

"Maybe." He said hunching his shoulders.

"Can I bounce the ball with you later?"

"Where your uncle at? I thought you couldn't talk to boys."

"It's fine," she said feeling bolder. "I'ma give my nana the mail and I'll be right back so we can play. Okay?"

"Aight." Jace smiled.

Harmony made a decision that no matter what, she would do whatever she could to see him. She was tired of being bored, lonely and scared. She needed some fun and was willing to take the chance. Even if it meant making her uncle, "smile again". Which was the phrase he gave his molestation. Already she was learning the power of seduction.

With a plan hatched in her mind, she was preparing to give Shirley the mail when she was met with jab so strong that she was knocked down the steps. The blow caused her to fall face first into a pile of Dingo's dog shit. Who as of yesterday was nowhere to be found.

"You okay?" Kalive asked. He had a crush on her, but she never noticed him. Kali's large body and stern look told her he would knock Shirley on her back if he could.

"Get your fat ass from out in front of my house!" Shirley told the boy who hadn't budged an inch. "And Harmony, get up these stairs!" She yelled from the top of the steps wearing only a towel, which partially exposed her stomach that was ripped to shreds because of her pregnancies.

When Shirley was gone, Kali helped her off the ground. "Thank you." Harmony said once on her feet. "I 'ppreciate it, Kali." She was panicky not knowing what Shirley would do to her once inside.

"You aight? You want me to go inside with you?"

"Yeah, I mean no, I'll be fine." She said rubbing her face.

"Is it true, what your uncle makes you do in there?" Kali asked from nowhere. Just like most kids, he could be uncouth.

"What you mean? My uncle is real nice to me."

"Oh…okay. I won't say nothin'. Just askin'."

She hadn't told anybody about what Charles did to her and she was nervous. Harmony was unaware that since Charles, a known sex offender had come back to live with his mother Shirley, that the neighborhood had been buzzing about the things he may be doing to her. But none of them, not one of them, cared enough to call the police.

Tasting the blood in her mouth, she grabbed the mail and walked up the stairs. When she looked to see if Jace was still there, her heart broke when she saw he wasn't, however, Kalive was. With the mail in her hands, Harmony walked inside. Now the bathroom door was closed and she knocked softly.

"Come in!" she screamed. Once inside Shirley said, "I should've known what was taken you so damn long! You just like your mother, a whore in the makin'. Now put the mail on the back of the toilet bowl, and get over here and wash my back!"

Harmony placed the mail down, walked deeper into the small yellow space and knelt to her knees. The funky, fishy smell inside the bathroom caused her stomach to churn. She saw the red washcloth floating around in the tub, and witnessed the water turning from a grungy grey to dirty yellow. The bitch had pissed in the tub.

"Why you takin' so long? Wash my back!"

Harmony grabbed the washcloth and dunked it into the toilet-bath-water like she was told. It took everything in her power not to throw up on her back.

"That's enough of that." She turned and looked at her. "What you been in here doin' with my son?"

Harmony's eyes widened. "Nothin', nana."

"I don't believe you!" She said wagging her finger in her face. "Now you tell me the truth, or I'ma call the police and have you locked up. And you won't neva be able to see that little boyfriend of yours across the street."

Harmony didn't know what to do, part of her wanted to tell the truth. If she did, maybe his sexual abuse would stop.

"He…he makes me kiss his thing and he puts his hands between my legs and stuff."

"So you in here havin' sex with my son?"

"No, no, nana! He made me do it."

All of a sudden, Shirley eased out of the water like a Loch Ness monster. Water dripped from her body as she placed one foot outside of the tub, followed by the other. Harmony backed up against the door before Shirley sat down on the edge of the tub with her legs wide open. The lips on her vagina hung like two slabs of brown chitterlings.

"Get over here," she said. "Now!"

"What?"

"Harmony Phillips, you heard me. Now get over here right now. I want you to lick it for me." Looking at the large woman before her, Harmony felt faint.

Why were all of these things happening to her? All she wanted was her father and to be happy. And now it seemed as if life had turned its back on her and she was all alone, in a house of monsters.

When she didn't move quickly enough, Shirley walked over to her, grabbed her by her hair and pulled her toward the tub. She slid easily on the floor because it was completely wet. Shirley she sat back on the edge of the tub and said, "Don't make me tell you again. Lick it."

With tears in her eyes, Harmony put her mouth on her inner thigh instead, in an attempt to fool Shirley. It wasn't working. Shirley knew the feeling she was going for, after all, she had gotten Estelle and Charles to lick her vagina many times when they were her age.

Pulling her pussy lips back, Shirley exposed her pink clit and said, "There, lick right there."

"Please, nana. I...I don't want to do this!"

SLAP!

"Lick there!"

"I...I feel sick." Harmony said not being able to fathom doing something so pathetically gross to her grandmother. "I...I feel like I'ma throw up."

Shirley got mad and slapped her again. "Lick, there! Now!"

"No, I don't want to do it."

Shirley hit her a third time so hard, she knocked her out.

Two Hours Later

When Harmony came to, she was outside in Dingo's nasty brick doghouse. Between being frightened that the animal would come back and kill her, and the temperatures reaching freezing points, she prayed to die in her sleep. Shirley didn't bother to give her a coat and she was placed there until she decided to do what Shirley wanted. Days went by with no food or water, and Harmony developed a heavy cough.

Finally on day three, Charles came to her with a hard peanut butter and jelly sandwich and a glass of milk.

"Here...eat this," he said nestled inside of his heavy coat, staring down at her. Harmony grabbed the sandwich and drank the milk quickly, fearing he would take it back from her at any time.

He watched her eat the sandwich crouched inside knowing she wanted an offer to come inside and warm up. "You ready to come in now?"

"Yes," she coughed. "Please."

Charles took her to the bathroom and ordered her to take a bath. When she was done, she walked into her room and he was there waiting. It wasn't long before he fondled her again. The loud coughing didn't appear to bother him one bit. With her legs open, he dug into her vagina deeply.

"Uncle Charles," she whispered. "That hurts."

"So what you want me to do, stop?"

"Yes."

"You know how to make me stop?" She shook her head no. "By acting like you like it. When you do that, I can cum quicker."

"What's cum?"

"You see the clear stuff that come out of my joint, when you touch it?" He taught.

Just the thought of his semen made her disgusted but she knew exactly what he was talking about. "Yes. I remember."

"Well when you act like you like it, like by havin' a smile on your face and stuff like that, then I cum quicker. And then I will leave you alone."

Harmony thought about what he said and didn't see any other way out. Both her grandmother and uncle wanted their way with her. She thought about telling, but didn't know any other adults she trusted or who would listen. And if someone were to take her away, where would she go?

"Listen, you gotta do what you gotta do to be aight, Harmony. You gotta give people what they want from you, so they'll like you more. And more than anything, you gotta do what you gotta do to survive."

"But...Daddy said if I'm smart in school, I'll be able to take care of myself. And maybe he'll come back and help me."

"Your mama is dead and your daddy is probably dead, too." He said with a scowl. Normally he played it cool when dealing with her but he was getting anxious and needed her mentally broken if he was going to do the things that he wanted to do to her body.

"My daddy not dead. He in jail."

"Even if it's true it don't matter. Nobody wants you back. They not even trying to find out who killed your mama." Harmony knew who Irma was but decided not to tell anyone. "Listen, right now, you live with me and your nana and we both know what we want. The question is, do you?"

She thought about it for a minute and said, "Yeah...I wanna be friends with Jace. I wanna be able to go outside and stuff like that," she coughed.

Charles frowned but soon realized by reasoning with her, their time together would be more pleasurable for him.

"Well if you wanna be friends with Jace, and you wanna go outside, you gotta do anything me and your nana want."

"I really don't want to do what nana wants. It's too, nasty."

Charles smiled and said, "You won't even notice after a while," then he appeared to mentally go somewhere else. "I didn't."

"I can't do it. I won't do it!"

"Then get ready to go back outside to live in the doghouse. And be ready to stay there for the rest of your life."

Harmony finally understood her options. Putting her guards down, after pleasing her uncle that night, she knocked on Shirley's door and pleased her, too. And so the cycle continued for months at a time. Where she would use her body, to get what she wanted in life. This was also how she learned to become a woman.

One day while playing outside, she remembered what her uncle said about knowing what she desired out of life. Sure her and Jace were friends, but she wanted something more.

"Jace, do you like Brittany?" She asked him sitting on his back door step.

"She cool, why?"

"Do she do stuff for you?"

"What you talkin' about?"

"You know, kiss you, and touch your stuff?"

"Naw…not really." He said. "But she dresses nice and smells real good."

That hurt and she knew he couldn't say the same thing about her. So she started asking Shirley and Charles for money. First she'd ask for money for the ice cream truck, then it was money for new clothes. She learned how to please Shirley and Charles so well, that they soon gave her everything she wanted, including alcohol. Day after day, she would suppress what she felt inside, until she thought her feelings didn't matter anymore. Her impressions of life and people were distorted and her reasoning was way off. In the end more damage had been done to her young mind than could ever be repaired.

One afternoon while preparing to go see Jace outside, a white man knocked on the door. Shirley answered and he asked for Harmony, claiming to have known her father.

"Come in." Shirley told him.

The stranger walked inside with an envelope in hand and said, "I'd like to speak to her alone." Harmony knew instantly that this must be the man her father told her would come and visit. "This is private." He continued.

"If you don't speak in front of me you can just turn around and leave. This here is my house."

"I see," he started adjusting his tie, "well, my name is Terrace Strong, and I'm Cornell's lawyer." He spoke calmly.

"Cornell?" Shirley said sarcastically. "We have done everything we could to get in touch with that fool, after all, I am lookin' afta his daughter you know."

"I do."

"Do you?" She paused. "'Cause as you can see, she don't want for nothin'. Where you think the money is comin' from? Off trees?" Shirley continued, speaking of the new clothes Harmony was wearing, that she had licked her ass to get. "And now he wants to reach out?"

"Mam, I'm not here to argue with you. I'm here to tell Harmony, and you, that Cornell is dead." The words hit Harmony like a ton of bricks and she dropped to the floor. Hope was gone the day her uncle entered her room, but hope was lost now. "Now, he asked me to give her something, and that's what I'm here to do."

"So them cops finally got him, huh?"

The man did not respond. Instead he nervously handed Harmony the envelope, and said, "He loved you very much."

Shirley snatched the envelope from her and counted five thousand dollars. "I know you not tellin' me this all he gave me to take care of her?"

"He didn't give YOU anything. The money belongs to Harmony." And just like that, he walked out the door.

Harmony had the swollen envelope filled with money in her hands for less than a minute before Shirley took it from her. However, Shirley was onto something, his lawyer managed to take everything from Cornell before his dying day. In the end leaving Harmony with nothing for her future. Once a millionaire Cornell Phillips died with not a penny to his name.

"Well, looks like he wasn't such a dead beat after all." Shirley said tucking the money in her bra. "And don't worry girl, you keep takin' care of me like you do, and I'll keep takin' care of you."

In a daze, Harmony shuffled her bare feet across the dirty kitchen floor and poured a glass of grape Kool-Aid from the refrigerator. Then she took a chair, pushed it in front of the fridge, climbed on top of it and grabbed the bottle of vodka from the freezer. Hopping off the chair, she poured it into her drink and swallowed it all. Having developed a tolerance for liquor, when the Kool-Aid mixture was done, she poured another glass of vodka straight before drinking it all. And just like that the trials and tribulations of Harmony Phillip's life began.

PRESENT DAY

Green Door – Adult Mental Health Care Clinic
Northwest, Washington DC

"So talk to me, Ms. Phillips, tell me at what point in your life, did *everything* else change?" Mrs. Christina Zahm, asked jotting down notes on Harmony's health chart.

"What do you mean when did everything else change? My life has been fucked up from the very beginning. Haven't you been listening to me?"

"Yes I have." Christina said putting a few loose strands of her brown hair behind her ear. Her white skin flushed from the heat in the room. Although it was summertime, the air conditioning was broken and no one had bothered to repair it yet. "And I know you know that I have been listening. But why bring kids into this world when you knew you hated yourself?"

"Because I was raped as a child, I don't deserve to have children?"

"I'm not saying that. It's just that, well, from what I read in the paper, you were so brutal with your children."

"I was."

"But why subject innocent children to a life so cold?"

"So...everything is my fault now? I told you my life story...and how I was brought up and after everything it's still my fault? What about those who were supposed to protect me?" Harmony said pointing at herself. Her body frail from years of alcohol abuse, and her face loaded with hate lines.

"Harmony, I don't mean to place blame. But in order to get down to the heart of the matter, I need to know the why's to some of my questions. It is through the why's that I can help you over these hurdles so that we can make a change."

"By change you mean you'll stop me from drinking alcohol? Or help me love my kids?"

"I mean we can help you change your life and everything about it. And when your life is changed, you'll be so much happier. And maybe even repair the relationship with your children."

"They don't want me and I don't want them." Harmony said looking down at her worn out tennis shoes.

"When they see you've changed, they may."

"You blame me don't you?" Harmony said with raised brows. "You blame me for what happened to all of those people."

"I don't blame you for anything." Mrs. Zhan sighed. "I've already said that. So how about we start over. Tell me about your teenage years."

"How early?"

"Take me back to your high school days. Let's start there."

PART TWO

SUMMER OF 1988

Southeast, Washington, DC
Harder...Stronger
Jace Sherrod

The basement in me and my aunt Karen's house was dim, but bright enough for me to see five members of my seven-man crew. The only light in the room sat above the pool table makin' it look greener than it actually was. The silence was heavy and my men were starin' at me. But I was lookin' at the nigga Bam on the pool table, tied up like a fuckin' hog, with rope binding his ankles and wrists together behind his back. A red sock was stuffed in his mouth and duct tape held it in place.

When Paco moved a little, I looked at him and then all of my men. I knew what they wanted from me, but I wasn't ready to bring it like that. I wasn't ready to kill.

"How much longer you think we should wait?" Paco, the getaway driver of my crew asked. "I mean, it ain't like we can let him go. We gotta do somethin'.."

Paco was light skin and shorter than the rest of us, but girls thought he was cute so he stayed with a different broad with him at all times. The only time he didn't was when we had meetings.

"We gonna wait until I say we move." I said sternly. "Now shut the fuck up you fuckin' up my concentration."He huffed a little but then leaned back against the wall with the rest of my crew, they all had guns in hand ready.

To be seventeen, Paco was the best nigga to have behind a steering wheel when you was in a jam. He had dreams of being a Nascar driver and even hired Grand, Kali's uncle to teach him how to race. I had to give it to the nigga, he was pretty good at it, too.

The only thing with Paco was he was too anxious and too impulsive to take anything seriously. So that was his downfall.

When I looked at my TAG sports watch I wondered what was takin' Kali so long. He had one job to do and he was fuckin' late at doin' it. But ten minutes later, he came walkin' downstairs with a little girl wearing a blue dress and his cousin Vaughn who I hated. Like always, he was wearing a brown leather strap on his back wit' a silver hatchet inside. His favorite large army green duffle bag was in his other hand. He slept from place to place and most of the shit he owned was in the bag. He tossed it to the floor when they reached the bottom step.

Kali maintained his hold of the girl by her forearm until she shook him off and ran to her father on the pool table. Me, Paco, Kreshon, Herb Dayo and Sick Sense all stood up straight and moved toward him. This wasn't in the plan so what was she doing here? And why was this nigga Vaughn wit' him?"

"Vaughn, get the fuck up out my basement, cuz." I said.

"Nigga, what?" He said gripping his tool.

My men closed in on him and Vaughn looked at us like he wanted to bust off. But he wasn't that stupid.

"Cousin, I'ma be upstairs." He said to Kali, gritting on us. "Let me know when you ready to roll." Kali was already explosive but Vaughn was his detonator.

When he went upstairs, I addressed my attention to Kali.

"Fuck is up, young?" I said lookin' at the kid. "You was 'sposed to bring his partner the nigga that ganked us. Why you got shawty? And what the fuck Vaughn doin' wit' you?"

"He drove the car for me to get away."

"You know I don't fuck wit' that nigga." I reminded him. "So now he know all our business?"

"He family, J. He ain't sayin' shit."

"Fuck that what's up wit' the kid? And where is Star?"

"I couldn't find him." Kali said.

The seven-year old girl hugged her father around the neck as we waited on Kali's response. Although Bam's mouth was bound, I could tell by the way his body jerked that he was crying. He ain't like seeing his kid here no more than we did.

"Daddy, what's going on? Why did they take me from school?" She sobbed. "Why won't they let me go? I want my mommy."

Bam, who we kidnapped a few hours earlier, looked at us with pleading eyes. But this shit was his fault. Had he and Star not hit our stash house, he wouldn't be in this situation.

"Yo, bitch, shut the fuck up, 'fore I put somethin' to your ass." Kali yelled at the girl. "Screamin' all up in my man's crib. I'm sick of hearin' your mouth."

"You don't tell me what to do! You don't tell me to do no-thin'!" She screamed back.

Enraged, Kali rushed up to the girl and smacked her in the mouth with the butt of his gun. Blood splashed all over the dress she was wearing and dampened the rug. Now, her DNA was every-where!

"Who the fuck is you talkin' too?" He said aiming his gun at her head. The barrel pressed firmly against her temple. He talked to her as if she was a nigga on the street who just shorted him of his money. "I will blow your mothafuckin' head off."

I couldn't believe what I was seein'. I was already havin' a problem killin' a nigga who was in to me for twenty grand, but kil-lin' a kid was out of the question.

"Kali," I whispered walking up behind him, putting a hand on his shoulder, "you need to put that shit down, man. You not 'bout to kill no kid in my crib."

The little girl was shaking scared and Bam was trying to get himself untied and off the table. He was doing a pretty good job of it too, until Paco hit Bam on the head with the back of his gun. The rest of my men provided cover.

"This little bitch been givin' me and Vaughn shit since we got here." He said, still aimed, the gun shaking in his hand. One wrong move and she would have a bullet in her head.

"Kali, put the fuckin' gun down!" I yelled. "Now!" Kali looked at the little girl and then at me.

"Herb, you on it?"

"You know it," he said holding his .45 automatic in position in case I needed him to smoke Kali.

Kali looked at him but listened to me. "I'm not gonna ask you again, man."

Finally he lowered his weapon and tucked his gun in his waist. The little girl held onto her mouth and judging by the way her jaw shifted, I knew it was broken.

"So you were really gonna shoot me?" He asked Herb Dayo.
Herb put his gun back in his waist and remained silent.

"What the fuck is goin' on, Kali?"

"I'm sorry, man. I...I took shit too far wit' the kid." He said pacing the floor.

"You always sayin' how I be fuckin' up, and then I go fuck up again." He continued bashing himself like he normally did. "I don't know what's wrong wit' me. It's like, I be meanin' to keep shit one hundred, but when shit don't go my way, I lose it!"

"Kali, what the fuck is she doin' here?" I said bringing him back to what was important. "And where is Star?"

Somebody told the nigga we was on the way, so he left town. And then I remembered you and Tony Wop talkin' 'bout Bam havin' a daughter. So I found out what school she went to, picked her up and brought her here. This nigga gotta give us our product now."

"We been torturing this nigga for a hour, and he still say he ain't got shit." Herb Dayo said. "I gotta believe he tellin' the truth."

Herb was light skin and good with washing money. He was older than us, especially me and Kali who were only seventeen.

"Bringin' the kid here was stupid!" Sick Sense said. "And I know somebody saw you."

Sick Sense had good senses, hence the nickname. But like most niggas he had his downfalls. He smoked a lot of weed but was good with scoping out scenes. So before we made a move we sent him in to check things out first. We did that every time we moved a stash house until last week. Had we done it, Star and Bam would not have gotten us for our product and money. Sick's other downfall was that he was an ugly nigga who hung wit' faggy Barry from 58th, although he think we ain't know it.

"Naw, they'll probably think it's somebody out Maryland. Or that dude who be rapin' and killin' them kids."

"Nigga, you kidnapped her with a hatchet on your back! I know somebody saw you." Paco persisted.

"Kali, ain't nobody gonna make a lotta fuss if a dope boy come up missin', but a kid is a whole 'notha story." Kreshon added.

Kreshon was tall, linky and sly. He had some shit with him, I just couldn't put my finger on it. But he was good with collecting the money from the soldiers on my squad, on time all the time, so I kept him around.

"I know for a fact ain't nobody see me."

"How?" Sick Sense added. "You fucked up before and we had to clean up behind you. You ain't 'bout to get me in no shit again."

"And what about fingerprints? Did you touch anything?" Herb Dayo continued.

"No..I don't think...um, I can't remember."

"Well I'm with Sick." Herb Dayo added. "You ain't 'bout to get me in no shit either."

"If you a member of this crew, and you gettin' from this crew then you already in some shit." I said looking at my men. "All of you. We in this together." When I heard or saw no more objections I redirected my attention to Kali.

"Go upstairs and make sure that nigga Vaughn not in my house." I told him.

"I'm sorry, man. For real."

As he was walking up the stairs Herb said, "We gotta get rid of that nigga, Jace. He a liability."

Kali's footsteps stopped and we all looked at Herb crazy. If Kali heard him it could cause a serious fight on top of everything else we had going on down here. But when he continued to walk up the stairs, I knew he didn't hear him.

With Kali gone I took the tape off of Bam's mouth and tried to talk some sense into him.

"Please...Let me daughter go! Please don't hurt her no more."

"I don't wanna hurt her, but I need to know where my product is. You stealin' from me made shit hot with my peeps and now I owe. Where my shit and I'll let you go. Both of you."

"I don't know." He sobbed. "On my life I would tell you if I knew."

I looked at my men and knew we were all thinking the same thing. He was telling the truth. Problem was, it ain't matter. I put the tape back on his mouth and tried to get my mind together.

If I didn't kill this nigga, and his kid too, I was gonna lose respect from my squad and my pops. I never took a life before, and I ain't wanna start today. I decided to walk away from the situation for a moment and consult with the one person I could always count on.

SOUTHEAST WASHINGTON, DC

Five-Year Pussy Plan
Harmony Phillips

We had been in class for a minute and already I was irritated. And fuck Woodson High School, fuck the student body staff and teachers. I'm all about getting mine and school was blockin' my style. That's why I told people it was my last day even though they thought I was bullshitting.

I was sitting between Constance and Trip, two chicks I kicked it with every now and again when for real all I wanted to do was get out of class, get a bottle of vodka, smoke and fuck. But the clock was taking its sweet time to tick by.

"Did ya'll hear about that girl...The one who was kidnapped from school the other day?" Constance asked. "They saying some dude took her when she went to the bathroom."

"From where?" I asked going through my MCM bag.

"I think it was from Nalle Elementary."

"Damn! How did he do that?"

"I don't know...but they testing for fingerprints now." Constance continued opening her book bag.

"Ya'll coming to my party right?" Ebony asked standing over top of us when the bell rang for class to began. "It's gonna be like that."

I peeped the gold hoop earrings with the word Princess in the middle she was wearing. My daddy use to call me princess all the time and they reminded me of him.

"Nice earrings." I said.

"Girl, my father gave them to me. I swear that man loves me to death."

I felt a hollow emptiness in my stomach and tried to push it down. I didn't know what the feeling was, all I knew was that it hurt.

Ebony lived in Northwest D.C. and should not have even been going to our school. But her cousin went here, and she was so pressed to be near her that she used her address.

"Ebony, I realize you want to start your birthday early, but class has started. So please take a seat," the teacher said. A few people laughed and then eventually settled down.

"Ya'll going to Ebony's cookout this weekend?" Constance whispered. "She said she gonna have mad smoke there, too."

Constance was kinda cute, short and light skin with a lot of freckles on her face. She kept her hair slicked back with a rack of gel in it. She had big titties and a loud mouth to go with it. And because she couldn't talk low, she stayed getting us in trouble with the teachers at school.

"If her party is anything like her party last year, you know I'm in there! And I ain't got no more money for no smoke either!" Trip laughed.

Trip was average looking but she always knew where to score money for some smoke, which is why I kept her around. At the same time she was also a backstabber, which is one reason I couldn't kick it with her all the time. Although she was only seventeen, she had a three-year-old son by her boyfriend Paco named Evan. I had to give it to them though, they made a cute baby together.

"Ya'll talking all that shit knowing good and well Kreshon not gonna let you go nowhere, Constance and Paco would kill your ass if he caught you at another party, Trip." I laughed. "So I don't even know why ya'll faking."

"Bitch, fuck Kreshon! He just better keep that money rolling for we have serious problems." Constance said.

"Why you say that?" I asked.

"Because lately he been holding out. Talking 'bout he ain't got this and he ain't got that. At the end of the day, the money is all I give a fuck about."

"Sure."

"Okay, and I got a feeling he cheating, and if he is, he may get smoked by the gun under my mother's bed."

"She got a gun?" I asked.

"Yep, and I know how to use it, too."

"Yeah right." She bragged. "A bitch with a gun is not to be fucked with."

Constance and me gave each other five and looked to see if the teacher saw us, she didn't. Although I was feeling what she was saying, I also knew that she was in deep when it came to her feelings for Kreshon. She just loved perpetrating the worse fraud in front of us.

"Bitch, you ain't hurting no Kreshon!" Trip said. "You so far up that nigga ass you can see his intestines."

"Fuck you...I'm all the way serious about that shit!" Constance yelled as usual. "I'm getting *sick* of Kreshon's ass."

"And I'm *sick* of you interrupting my class," Mrs. Duncan said. "Now if I have to ask you to be quiet in my classroom again, I will send you to the principal's office! Do I make myself clear?"

When she turned around to refocus on the blackboard I said, "Why you gotta be so hot all the time, Constance? Stay getting niggas late."

"Fuck her." She said a little lower, not doing a good job of whispering yet again. "She just a hating ass bitch."

I shook my head and said, "What ya'll 'bout to do when class let out?" I scribbled some shit on the paper in front of me, to pretend I was doing school work when I wasn't.

"You ask us that same question every Friday and every Friday you don't plan to do nothin' with us until later on at night." Trip said.

"You act like you want me to fuck you or something."

"Bitch, you know what I mean," Trip continued. "Why bother asking if we ain't gonna hook up?"

"I be asking ya'll what ya'll doing for later. Just 'cause I don't get up with ya'll right when we leave don't mean nothing."

"Well I don't know about Trip, but I'm going to my aunt's house to wait on Kreshon."

"Why you gotta go to your aunt's house to wait on him?"

"Because my mother don't want me being with him no more. Talking about he too old and shit. He ain't but five years older than me."

"I feel you. What you and Kreshon gonna do when ya'll get up?" I continued.

"He 'sposed to be giving me some money to buy some gear for the cookout tomorrow. You know I gotta look fresh." Constance said. "But before I do any shopping though, I got to drop Brittany off a little dough to do something for me."

"Weird Brittany?" I asked. "When you start fucking with her?" Even though I was the one Jace chose, whenever we would fight, like now, she'd stick her nose into our business.

"She not too bad." She said. "She just don't like a lot of people. But trust me, Brittany be havin' the dirt on everybody."

"What she gonna do for you?" Trip continued.

"I'll tell ya'll later." She said holding back.

I didn't care what she did with Brittany to tell you the truth, just as long as Brittany stayed out of my way. I think she was fucking my boyfriend, Jace and she better hope I didn't catch her.

"How much Kreshon giving you tonight?" I asked.

"He said about two hundred, but I'ma see if I can get more from him." Constance bragged. "Trust me when I say the wells have been dry lately. The nigga owe me big time tonight though."

"At least you know where your money coming from." I added. "Me and Jace still beefin'."

"I can't tell ya'll beefin'. You stay with fresh sneaks and gear. Like when you get them new Princess Reeboks?" Trip asked.

"I been had 'em."

"Bitch, you ain't been had them." Trip said.

"Girl, yes I have. And Jace said he really cutting me off this time. Saying he tired of my split personality. He sound like a fool."

"Well you do you have a split personality?" Constance added.

"I ain't no more moody than the rest of ya'll bitches." I said. "And some of ya'll take moodiness to a whole notha level, by back-stabbing your friends."

"Like who?"

"I don't know, you said you fuck with Brittany. How do I know you don't be tellin' her the shit I be telling you? Knowing she been wanting my man since day one."

"'Cause I wouldn't do that."

While she was lying, I tugged at the seat of my pants. I think somebody burned me I was fucking on the side but I didn't know who and I didn't know what I had.

"Yeah, well you better not." I warned her. "Because I got some shit on you, too." I paused. "I don't want ya'll telling ya'll boyfriends my business either. They do work with Jace you know."

"Girl, you already know I ain't tellin' Paco shit." Trip said. "And even if somebody did tell him your business, Jace is too blinded by you, girl."

When I turned around to fake on my work some more, I saw Constance look at Trip out the corner of my eye. Sneaky bitch. Bitches stay keepin' up shit.

When the bell rang I jumped up and said my goodbyes. I was almost out the door until the teacher called me. "Harmony, let me talk to you for a moment."

I rolled my eyes, turned around and said, "Mrs. Duncan, I really have to go. My ride is probably outside waiting on me right now."

"It'll only take a minute, Harmony. Please." I stomped toward her desk hoping she'd say never mind...But she didn't. "I hear today is your last day in school, is there any particular reason why?"

"I'm not like the other kids in this school, Mrs. Duncan. Most of them come day after day believing that education can get them far in life. But I know the truth."

"And what's that?"

"That the only thing that matters in this world is dick and pussy." I figured if I could be as nasty as possible, she'd leave me alone.

Her face frowned up and she said, "You don't think education is important?"

I looked at this green bitch and said, "Fuck no."

"Harmony, watch your language."

"Mrs. Duncan, this is me, and you wanted to talk to me so I'ma give it to you how you need to have it. So here it is...If it ain't making me money, or helping me bust a nut, than I don't need it and that goes for your so called education, too."

"Harmony Phillips, I can't believe what I'm hearing coming out of your mouth. What about the money education can make you in the long run?"

"Fuck a long run. I need money now!"

"Harmony, if you don't have a proper education, you're in for a hard life."

"A hard life? *A hard life?*" I laughed. "Let's see…My mother was killed in front of me, my father was murdered in prison, my grandmother and uncle have raped me for years at a time, and I have a drug dealer for a boyfriend." I paused. "So tell me, how much harder can life get for me?" I continued leaning on her desk. "How much harder, Mrs. Duncan?"

Silence.

"I…didn't know."

"How could you? You assumed that education can save the world when it can't. But I'm smarter than you in some ways, because I know the truth. I needed someone to be there for me then and they weren't. And now, I don't even know who I am anymore." I stood up straight and said, "Have a nice day."

"Harmony, wait!" I stopped. "Here, take my number. If you need someone to talk to…Let it be me."

"I'll take this, but it's too late for me, Mrs. Duncan. Do yourself a favor and go save somebody else."

●━━━━━━━━━━━━━━━━━━━━━━━━━━━━━━●

After I finished with Mrs. Duncan I bolted out of the building. I went four blocks up the street and opened the backdoor to an abandoned house I found six months back. It was my little getaway, and the only place I could go to escape from the world. I invited a few people over sometimes, but mainly it was all about me. Kinda like the crawlspace I went into all the time when I lived at Concord Manor. Even after all these years, I missed Concord and hoped that one day I'd be able to go back there, even though I couldn't.

When I got to the house, I went into the basement and turned on a lamp I brought from my grandmother's house and waited patiently. I loved Fridays, because it was the one-day I was sure to get fucked real nasty. Sex with my boyfriend could get a little weak at times when he had shit on his mind and today I needed a release.

There was an old couch and old leather chair inside the basement. I threw my book bag off, pulled my jeans down followed by my panties. My pussy started itching badly so I sat on the couch, opened my legs and scratched it as hard as I could without making it too raw. There was a slight smell, too but I didn't know what it was and figured I'd take a bath later to get rid of it. I had the strange itch for fifteen days straight and it was starting to really bother me. I also developed strange sores on my hands and my feet and figured it was from allergies. But what was I allergic too?

When I saw *him* pull up outside, get out of his car and look around, I opened my legs wider and stretched out on the old couch. Hearing his footsteps made me anxious. But not because I liked him, but because I knew when I was done, I'd be satisfied sexually. Having sex was my way of giving back to the community. At least that was how I looked at things.

When he walked down the steps he said, "Damn, shawty. You ready for me already ain't you?"

He dropped his jeans and then his boxers like they were on fire." I was actually getting ready to take care of myself." I lied. He liked to hear that kind of shit.

"Oh for real?"

"Naw, I'm just playing," I giggled. My other appointment was in an hour so I had to hurry.

"What it do, cutie?" He said. "You been here long?"

To me, Kreshon was real cute with a baby face and he was tall as shit. He always dressed good and smelled nice, too.

"You know it's never long whenever I'm waiting on you." He smiled at me and stroked his dick to a thickness. "You gonna suck it for me first?"

"What you gonna give me if I do?" I didn't need the money because I knew eventually Jace would be calling me back to make up. I used the money as an excuse to get what I really wanted...*FUCKED*. But today money could come in handy. I needed it to get some new gear and a bottle of vodka. "Because you know I like to have nice things."

"How much you askin' me for, Harmony? Just come out and say it."

"I need some clothes, Kreshon. So I'ma need a lot."

He looked at me like he could read me and said, "How much is a lot?" His jaw flexed a little.

"Two hundred."

"Fuck...I can't give you two hundred!" He yelled, his voice gruffer than before. I hated nickel and dime hustlers because they never had enough. "I gotta give Constance some money to go shoppin' later. And I know you already know that."

"So, she more important to you than me?"

"She's my girl, Harmony. And your friend."

"And Jace is your friend, too but that don't seem to stop you from fuckin' his girlfriend!" I said raising one eyebrow and poking my lips out.

"Jace is my boss…Not my friend."

"Do *he* know that?" A smirk spread across my face.

"Shit between us is just business." He said seriously. "Nothin' more nothin' less. And if it was, I wouldn't even be fuckin' with you."

"You keep believing that shit." I laughed.

"I'm serious."

"Humph. Well, I wonder what he'd say if he knew what we did to each other in this house. He probably would have Tony Wop kill you or somethin'. You know how hard he be tripping over me. Matta fact, maybe I should call him."

Silence.

He grabbed me by the neck and I smiled. "You can't hurt me. Nobody can hurt me."

"You real fucked up in the head ain't you?"

"The money. Give me the money."

"I can't do it." He said seriously. "I can't give you two hundred dollars when I know you can ask your man. That nigga got way more bread than me."

"You know what," I said gathering my clothes. "If she's so much more important to you than me, then you can go fuck her instead. I'm outta here."

I put back on my jeans and grabbed my panties. I knew he was going to stop me because there was no way in hell Constance could fuck him better than me. He and I both knew it. I was still faking my way back up the stairs when he said, "Wait!"

I turned around and placed my hands on my hips. "Waiting ain't gonna give you none of this good pussy but money will."

"It ain't about the money is it?" I was shocked at his question. "You just want to see how far I would go for you. What I would be willin' to give up."

"You know what," I said trying to throw him off my trail. "Maybe we shouldn't see each other no more. Shit is getting too serious anyway."

The confidence was drained from his face. "Why...Why you sayin' that?"

"I just think we need to slow all the way down."

"Harmony, I was just fuckin' wit' you." He said walking up to me, taking my panties out of my hand. "You know I can't be wit'out you."

"Then act like it, nigga."

"You can be cold as shit, Harmony." He reached in his pocket and pulled out two hundred dollars. "What I'm gonna tell, Constance?"

I tucked my money in the pocket of my jeans. "That's your problem not mine," I told him. "But in a minute you not about to give a fuck."

I bent down, took him into my mouth, put a lot of spit on his dick and gave him an extra sloppy blowjob. Spit ran down the sides of his dick and I jerked him off simultaneously.

"Ahhh, damn, Harmony. Do that shit!" Kreshon said.

"You like this, daddy?" I asked looking up at him.

"You know I like that shit. Keep it nice and wet. More spit, baby."

"You taste so good."

"How in the fuck you learn to suck a dick like this?"

"From my uncle."

"What?!" He said looking down at me.

"Just playing." I continued giving him the business.

He told me over and over how bad it was to have sex with Constance. How she wasn't as nasty as me. After I finished giving him a blowjob to die for, I bent over and let him fuck my wet pussy. He was falling deep and I loved it. I loved feeling needed. Out of all the things Uncle Charles told me he was right about sex. It was so much easier to control people, when you had something they wanted. I made sure every time Kreshon left me, that he remembered the difference between me and Constance. I could not be forgotten or mistaken for another bitch when I been fucking all my life.

"Kreshon."

"Yes, baby." He said with his eyes rolling up in the back of his head.

"I don't want you to love her more than me. I want you to be all mine. You know I'ma leave Jace soon right…Like we talked about?"

"Yes, baby."

"But you gotta make more money first so we can be good. You gotta be able to take care of me."

"I can't wait, girl." He said fucking me harder. Even if he was lying, for the minute it felt good to be wanted. "I hate stringing Connie along when I don't even fuck with her like that. I love you."

"I love you, too." I said feeling an orgasm coming over me. Whenever a man begged…I mean *really* begged, it was such a fucking turn on. It didn't take me much longer after that to bust my cum all over his dick. He gripped me tighter and filled my pussy with his nut. And just like that, I was done and so was the fantasy that I would be leaving Jace for him. Besides, right or wrong, Constance was my friend and I wasn't going to give up our friendship for a public relationship with Kreshon And what about Jace? Naw, he could never have me on a solo tip.

When he was taken care of, I put my clothes on, gave him a kiss on the cheek and rushed to my next rendezvous. I met him in the same place every Friday too, in his car, behind a row shopping center. So when I saw his white van, I got inside and we pulled closer to the trash can. We both looked around to make sure no one was looking and I eased my jeans off.

"You were late today," he told me with an unexpected crinkly grin. "I thought you weren't trying to fuck or somethin'."

"You know that ain't it." I smiled.

"You been fuckin' somebody else?" He asked me. "Other than Jace?"

"Paco, what difference does it make? We're together now."

"What's up with you?"

He was blowing the hell out of me. I moved a little in my seat and said, "Paco…What is up with you? You acting kind of weird."

He smiled and said, "Why you always so horny? I ain't never met a chick like you who had to do it all the time."

I hated this question and I hated that he kept asking me. I didn't know why I was so horny all the time. I didn't understand why I felt the need to be sexual. I didn't understand a lot of shit about myself.

"You know what, I gotta go." I said moving for my jeans.

He laughed and said, "I'm just fuckin' wit' you." Then he took the jeans out of my hand and put them back on the car floor. "I had a long couple of days."

"What happened?" I said although for real all I wanted was sex.

Unlike Kreshon, Paco loved to tell me about what was going on with Jace and business. I knew more about the business then Jace thought I did.

Paco sighed a little and said, "You and Jace still not talkin'?" He avoided my question.

"No." I sighed "And he's not answering my calls. So for real, I don't even want to talk about him. But what happen with you? Why you out of it?"

He looked at me and said, "Your boy Kali went crazy and did some shit that may get us all late."

"Like what?"

He looked me over and said, "What you mixed with?"

"What?"

"I said, what you mixed with?"

"Black. I mean…My mother was light-skin and mixed with white but I'm not mixed with too much of nothing I don't think." I said rubbing his dick in his jeans. "Why?"

"You look Spanish. Especially your hair and stuff."

I heard that all the time and my answer was always the same. I was what I was and that was pretty much it.

"So what did Kali do?" I said stroking him to hardness.

He looked at me and I knew he was trying to tell if he could trust me or not.

"He kidnapped a kid…The one that's been on the news all the time. The one that's missing from that school."

"The girl from Nalle?"

"Yeah."

I knew Kali could be crazy but this was different.

"Trip just told me about that today," I said. Whenever I mentioned Trip's name he always got uneasy. I could never tell if they were really feeling each other or not.

"You don't be talkin' about me with her do you?"

"Not so much."

"Look, I don't want you tellin' nobody about the shit with Kali either. This is between you and me. Okay?"

"Got it." I smiled. "So do you wanna keep talkin' or do what we came to do?"

I climbed in the back seat and let him bang me from the back. My pussy felt so raw and itchy that I started to change my mind. But all I thought about was sex. Sex when I was eating, sex when I went to sleep. Sex when I woke up. So I let myself go and didn't stop until I came and it felt so fucking good.

When we were done, and he busted off in my pussy too, I had him drop me off at Landover Mall. I was there for two hours and I burned the mall down. I bought five cute shirts, two pairs of Liz Claiborne blue jeans, a new crimping iron and two bottles of hairspray. My hair was soft and long so I had to put extra spray in it to keep the crimps from falling out. I was going to look too cute for the cookout tomorrow even though I was so broke, I didn't have enough money to catch a cab home. But I hitch-hiked a ride and within fifteen minutes was home.

When I was home I took the bags in the house and hid them from my grandmother. I was going to hit her up for some money too and I didn't want her to know what I'd gotten from other folks. With my gear in order, now I was going to have to get some money from somebody else for a bottle. The doorknob was in my hand and I was almost out the door when the phone rang. It was Constance.

"Girl, he's fucking cheating on me! I can't believe it! I told you I didn't trust Kreshon's ass. What I'ma do?" She cried. "He's gonna dump me!"

"Why do you say that?" I sighed. I wished she hurried the fuck up! I just fucked two niggas back to back and I needed a drink. "Cause you know that ain't the case. He would never cheat on you, girl."

"It is true!" She yelled. "Number one he never came to my aunt's house and when he finally called me later, he said he didn't have the money for me anymore. I don't know what to do if we not together."

"I thought you said it was all about the money? So if he ain't giving it to you, get another nigga."

"You know I was just talking shit. If he leaves me, Harmony. I'ma kill myself."

"Don't do that, girl. He ain't worth it," I paused. "But look, I'm 'bout to roll. I'ma hit you when I get back."

I slammed the phone down and shook the call off. I realize I probably sounded insensitive, but if I didn't get something to drink, I was gonna blow. Plus she was bringing me down and I didn't need it. Why should I care about her feelings when I had feelings and needs of my own? I needed somebody to want me, all the time, and it's too bad that one of the people who does that for me happens to be her boyfriend.

After I got off the phone, I went back outside and fanned a few fat ass bugs out of my face. I hate fuckin' Cicadas! Every seventeen years, them big ass bugs hatch and start botherin' niggas. What's their purpose anyway? All they do is roam around, make noise, leave wings all over the streets and irritate the hell out of me.

If you ask me, they remind me of the bitches at my high school. Walkin' around all day swingin' their hair and teasin' boys. If that's your thing cool, but don't get mad at me when I put out. Unlike them bitches, I got a five-year "Pussy Plan". To fuck Jace until he can't get enough, have the son he wants, and be set up for the rest of my life.

On the way to the liquor store, I got a couple of dollars from one of Jace's friends. I was on my way to get a pint of vodka from A&B Liquors on the corner because they didn't bother me about my age. After I bought my liquor and drank half of it I saw two older chicks I kicked it with from time to time standing on the corner. One called herself Nut and the other Cherry and nobody knew their real names or even cared. They fucked for money and as far as I knew they were good at it.

Cherry was dark skin, short, petite and real pretty. But what I always noticed about her was her wide eyes and naturally long lashes. The funniest thing about her was her parents. Them mothafuckas cursed each other out every day. I think because of it Cherry is used to drama and loves a man who beats her, at least that's what I hear anyway.

Nut has a honey complexion but she's real tall and shapely. She wears honey colored contact lenses and her hair in a golden brown bob. I don't know much about her past, except that she was raised in foster homes.

"What's good, Spanish fly?" Cherry said smoking a cigarette. She was talking to me but looking at the cars behind me waiting for a trick to pull up. "You ready to come out here and make some money?"

"I told y'all I'm not Spanish and I'm good on the money tip. Jace takes care of me so I'ma leave that raunchy shit to you."

They both laughed. "Jace takes care of you, huh?" Cherry smirked.

"Yeah...Why you say that?" I frowned.

"'Cause we be seeing him riding 'round with another girl in his *new* car all the time." Nut added.

My stomach felt like bowling balls were in it and I was off balance.

"A new car?" I repeated.

"Yeah...And a new girl to go with it." They both laughed. I didn't.

"Stop lying." I said. "You always starting shit."

"Aight, Spanish Fly." Nut said. "You gotta believe what makes you sleep better at night. But it's like I told you, you been getting a rep for yourself around the hood. You better slow down if you wanna keep your little boyfriend."

"Yeah, that may be why he got a new broad." Cherry added.

"This from a girl who's selling pussy on the corner?" I said.

"Yeah...But I know who I am and what I do?" She said. "Besides, ain't shit wrong with selling pussy." Then Nut grabbed the paper bag out my hand and drank the rest of my vodka. I thought about the two dicks I sucked today and smiled. "I am what I am and niggas who need my services respect that. But when you throw that thing around for no reason like you be doing with these little niggas 'round here, people don't know where you're coming from. So they can't trust you. And if they can't trust you, they can't respect you."

First off this bitch made me mad by drinking the last of my liquor. That was supposed to last me for the rest of the day. Second of all I was tired of people talking about me when for real, they didn't know shit about me.

"Can you please tell me why you just drank my shit, Nut?"

"Cause ain't shit free over here, including schooling young bitches on the game. 'Cause raunchy or not, sooner or later we all have to know who we are and why we do the things we do. For us it's about the money. For you it's something else. And sooner or later you have to figure out what it is."

"You better listen, Spanish Fly," Cherry laughed.

I was still salty about my liquor when a man in a small white Ford pulled up. Wearing thick-rimmed black glasses, he looked like shit. He kept wiping his head with a paper towel and his eyes moved to the left and right rapidly. I knew right away he was off.

"Rodger, what you doing here this early?" Cherry said walking up to the car. "You usually come at night."

"Something ain't right." Nut said out of earshot of Cherry. We kept looking at the car suspiciously but hung back a little.

"Why you say that? If he here to give her money what difference does it make what time he comes?" I whispered to Nut.

"You don't understand. Rodger's nasty ass is different."

"How?"

"He likes to wait until she's fucked at least five niggas, which is usually at night, so he can lick her pussy afterwards. He don't even like to fuck her, just jerks off while he's doing it."

"What the fuck?!!!!" Both Cherry and Rodger looked over at me and I covered my mouth.

"Nut, I'm 'bout to roll out with Rodger real quick. I be right back." Cherry said walking toward us.

"I don't know, Cherry. Something don't feel right with him today. He kinda look off."

We all looked at him and he kept patting his head with a paper towel. But sweat still poured down his face and he was looking all around him. He was acting like someone was out to get him.

"Girl, he always look weird. I'll be fine." She laughed. "Plus you know Rodger pays good money. We only going up the block. I be back." She jumped into the car and pulled off but Nut kept her eyes on the car until they turned into an alley and it was out of view.

"You okay?" I asked her. "You think he gonna hurt her or something?"

"What?" She snapped.

"Ughhh, I said are you okay?"

"Yeah. And stop getting into grown folk business." Her eyes remained in the direction Cherry went.

"Grown folk?" I laughed. "First of all we talking about whoring. And second of all you only 4 years older than me. So how is that grown folks business?"

"I'm still older than you." She told me.

I was about to respond when people started screaming from up the block. It was in the direction Cherry and Rodger went in. I wondered where all the commotion was coming from until I saw a crowd form. All of a sudden Cherry came limping out of the alley holding her hand between her legs. Blood poured from her body and she looked shocked. Then Rodger barreled out of the alley in his car almost hitting two kids riding bikes in the process. We both ran up to Cherry who walked a few feet before falling on the ground.

When Nut reached her, she got on the ground and held her closely. I'd never seen them this upset before and I could tell that these two whores had more love between each other than my own mother had for me.

"I told you not to trust him!" Nut cried out through her tears. "Why you ain't listen to me?" She lifted Cherry's head and placed it on her lap. "Somebody call the ambulance!" She screamed to no one in particular.

"I already did! They on their way?" An older black man yelled. "Is she okay?"

Nut ignored him and said, "What happened, Sasha? What he do to you, huh? Did that sick bitch shoot you?"

At first I thought she said the wrong name until I saw she was looking dead into her eyes. Go figure, Cherry's real name was Sasha.

Cherry looked like she was about to pass out as blood exited her body. "I think...I think he cut my pussy with...A blade or somethin'. You think I'm gonna die? I don't wanna die."

We both looked at each other in horror as the ambulance pulled up. They put Cherry on a gurney and Nut jumped in with without saying goodbye to me. That was a whole lot of action for one day.

I was left walking home by myself with no liquor and a fucked up picture in my mind of Cherry with a lot of blood over her body. My mind was racing in the heat when a new white beamer, with paper tags pulled up on the side of me. The music pumped from the stereo system and the tinted window rolled down.

"Harmony, let me holla at you for a minute?" Asked Jace. He parked on the curb and I tried my best not to jump all over his dick. Shit, he just got a red Audi a few months ago and now he pushin' a Beamer!

"Why you ain't been answering my calls, Jace?"

"Get in the car, Mony."

As the years went by he got cuter and it didn't hurt that his father Rick who lived in Los Angeles put him on in a major way. He didn't see his father regularly and his mother died when he was a baby. She was stabbed while breast-feeding him in a public park in L.A. When they found her slumped over, Jace was under her body with her breast in his face. He almost suffocated to death.

Still Jace was the kind of nigga who no matter what, when he came into a room, you had to turn around to look at him. And Shirley gave me one piece of advice that I thought made sense. She said, 'Harmony, never get with a man who looks better than you. Get an ugly man, one who would love you more than he does himself. That way he'll never leave you.' And although I hated her with a passion, I took that message to heart.

I walked over to his car and said, "You gonna give me a ride home?"

He smiled, leaned over, opened his car door and said, "Stop fuckin' around and get in."

I ran my fingers through my long black hair, wiped the sweat off of my forehead and onto my ripped acid wash jeans. Then I strutted smoothly toward his car and got inside. I felt nasty after having sex with Paco and Kreshon and needed a shower so I hoped he didn't want to fuck. Usually we had make-up sex after we broke up but that would have to wait today.

"Why you look like you been up to somethin'?" He asked me.

I wonder if he could see my day's nastiness and I tried to look innocent.

"I just came from hanging with Nut and Cherry in front of A&B. And one of Cherry's Johns stabbed her between the legs. It was a mess. "

"Why were you with them anyway? I thought I told you I ain't want you hangin' with them no more."

"I don't hang with them, Jace." I said irritated. Knowing he could care less about them I said, "So what's up? Why you ain't been answering my calls? And who is this girl I hear you're running around with?" The cool air from the air conditioner dried my sweaty face.

"You too moody and I'm sick of that shit."

"Jace, I'm not moody, I just be havin' a lot of shit on my mind." Silence.

"I'm movin' to Los Angeles for a while. So I'm tryin' to make shit right with you before I leave. I don't know how long I'ma be gone for either, I got some shit to take care of. "

I swallowed hard and my eyes widened. My breaths were quick and I felt jittery. Was I losing my boyfriend, like this?

"Does this have somethin' to do with the girl ya'll kidnapped the other day?"

He stopped driving, threw the car in park and looked over at me. "What you talkin' about?"

I was so scared about losing him to L.A that I hadn't thought about the most important point. That I wasn't supposed to know about the kidnapping. My mouth had gotten me into trouble and I couldn't lie because it was too far-fetched for me to mention a kidnapped girl, and most of all that he was involved. I had to think quickly.

"Uh…Baby, I want to tell you something, but I don't want you to get mad."

"Harmony, who told you about a kidnapped girl?"

"Uh…Some police came to my house today. And asked me if I knew anything about a kidnapping. I think they investigating you or something. They wouldn't tell me more though. What's going on?"

I tried to look into his eyes but he was wearing a pair of dark Versace shades.

"What did you say?"

"Nothing…Because I don't know nothing."

"Look, if they visit you again, call me. I'ma be at your house later on to pick you up. I gotta handle some shit right now though."

"Jace, is it over?" I asked when we got to my house.

We both glanced over to see Kali standing by my door, waiting. It was so normal to see him at my house, that I don't think Jace thought too much of it. Kali and me were cool before Jace even became my boyfriend. But there was something in Jace's eyes that told me that today something was different. I figured it involved the kidnapping.

"How close are you two?"

"Who…Me and Kali?"

"Who you think I'm talkin' 'bout?"

"We pretty cool, but ain't nothin' going on if that's what you mean."

"I don't know if I'm all the way good with you keepin' time with one of my friends."

I loved his jealousy. "You want me to stop talkin' to him or something?"

As I was talking to him, he was looking at Kali. Eventually he walked over to the driver's side window and said, "What up, Jace. Everything cool?"

"Harmony, let me rap to him for a minute."

"Okay. I love you." I said.

When I walked to the house I walked slowly. I wanted to hear as much as I could before he pulled off.

"Did you mention anything to anybody?" Jace asked him.

"Naw. Why?"

Both of them looked at me and he said, "We'll rap about that later. But don't forget to meet them people I asked you to meet later. Page me when you're done and I'll scoop you up."

"Bet." Kali said backing away from the car.

"And you betta be ready in a couple of hours." He told me.

I hoped Jace didn't mention me knowing about the kidnapping to Paco because he would go completely off. How could I be so fucking stupid?

When I walked toward my house, Kali walked with me and we watched Jace pull off, before he gave us one last look. Kali and me had a weird relationship because he was like a bodyguard to me. But his heart and soul belonged to Cherry. Even he got cuter over the years but he was still an average dude. Kali lost most of his baby fat and he had a honey colored complexion with really dark eyes. They resembled black marbles.

"What you and Jace talkin' about?" He asked out of nowhere.

"What?" His question was weird.

"Was he talkin' about me? Or blaming me for somethin like he always do?"

His eyes got wild like Rodger's. "Kali, you tripping now. I'm 'bout to go inside."

Like a light switched off he said, "Well you need anything before I leave?"

He always asked me the same question and there were plenty of times I ran him all around town when I had the munchies.

"Can you buy me a bottle of vodka from A&B?"

"Yeah...But before you go in, I gotta ask you something."

"What?"

"If something were to happen to Jace, would you be cool?"

NERVOUS ENERGY

Jace

It had been four days since the kidnapping and between the heat, which was unbearable, and Kali's recklessness I wanted to blow. I talked to my cousin about the matter and he told me I had to kill them both, the girl and Bam. But before I made a move, I had to be sure there wasn't another way.

Girls were outside in less than nothing and all Kali talked about was how they were setting themselves up while we drove in my car. All I wanted to talk about was the girl who was still tied up in my basement with her father.

Kali took his hatchet off his back and set it on the floor to get comfortable.

"I'm tellin' you, nigga, that's why bitches be gettin' raped and shit. Look at half of the shit they be wearin'." He pointed to a shawty with a pair of purple tight ass shorts on.

"Fuck is you talkin' 'bout, young?" I frowned.

"You heard me. Bitches be comin' outside in less than nothin' and then they wonder why niggas be plottin' on takin' that pussy. If you wear shit like that, you deserve everything you got comin'. A stiff dick." He laughed grabbing his.

"Nigga, fire that shit up. I ain't tryin' to hear all that other shit you spittin'."

Silence.

"Hey, J," he paused inhaling the bob, "let me ask you somethin'."

"Shoot."

"Why you let Herb D talk reckless to me the other day? I heard the shit he said. Now I'da been wrong if I sliced him wouldn'tve I?"

"What are you talkin' about?"

"So you gonna say you didn't hear him say you should get rid of me?"

"I heard it but I also think you took shit too far by kidnapping that kid. Now Herb talked a little off beat, I'll give you that, but you had some of that shit comin'."

"You always takin' Herb and Sick's side when we be beefin'. That's fucked up."

"Nigga, you fucked up." I said looking at him seriously. "What are you, my bitch or somethin'?" I said accepting the bob. "I ain't 'bout to sooth your feelings and shit."

He laughed, and said, "So what you gonna do? You want me to handle that situation in your basement? 'Cause you know I ain't got no problem with it."

"I don't know what I'ma do yet. Tony at my crib, and I'ma rap to him 'bout it when we get there. But you makin' a move without thinkin' put me in a bind."

"You know I ain't mean for shit to get this heavy right?"

Silence.

"Kali, are you sure you didn't tell nobody about that shit?"

He was silent for a moment and said, "Why would I do that? If I say somethin' I'm the one they gonna come lookin' for." He paused. "Naw, I ain't say shit to nobody."

Something was off with Kali and people told me he was border-line Bi Polar but I didn't wanna believe them until now. I also knew telling him about the cops visiting Harmony could put her in danger. So for now, I was gonna keep that information to myself.

"J, don't worry about shit. For real, I got you." He paused pulling on the bob. "And I wouldn't jeopardize the operation.

You always jeopardize the operation. I thought.

"If they come lookin' for me, I'm takin' the rap." He said. "And as far as I'm concerned, none of ya'll niggas were involved."

When my father called on me to build his operation in D.C., I couldn't be more ready. Finally I would be making that serious paper. But wherever there was money, there were risks. And one of my risks was having Kali on my team.

But I hated living the way we were before my pops asked me to open up a shop in DC. Don't get me wrong, my aunt Karen was good to me but before the call we were living regular. The money Rick sent her she used on mortgage and private schools. I could've called him and asked him for a little more dough, but I didn't want her thinking I didn't appreciate her putting it all on the line for me. But I always had a strong desire to hustle, just like my father. Although, unlike my father, murder was not my thing and I don't think it would ever be. That's where niggas like Kali came in but taming him was out of the question.

"I want you to lay low for a while." I told him. My pager went off and I saw it was Paco. The code was '287' which meant to meet him at his house. I figured he had some info on Star so I wanted to hurry. "Outside of the niggas in the room that day," I said looking at him again, "don't talk about the situation to no one. You got me?"

"I got you."

We pulled up at my house and I saw Tony's Forerunner, which meant he was already inside my house. But my aunt Karen wasn't home. I'll be glad when I get my own crib to keep this drama out her house.

"Go in and get Tony for me. Hurry up 'cause Paco just hit me and wants us to meet him at his crib. I'ma be out here waitin'."

"Aight. But I left my bag in your house the other day. I'ma have to scoop it before we leave." He said before dipping into the house.

The street was wet and my cousin's car was shiny so I figured he had just washed it. I waited for fifteen minutes before my cousin Tony Wop walked outside *without* Kali. By the look on his face, I could tell he was shocked to see me out front.

"What you doin' here?" He said walking up to my car. "I just got a page from Paco, he got some info on Star. I was just grabbin' somethin' out my truck real quick before I hit you."

My heart raced because I already knew what was going on. Kali was in my house alone, with Bam and his daughter. "You ain't see Kali?"

"Naw." He paused. "Where he at?"

"In the house, man."

"I must've been in the bathroom when he came in."

I got out of the car and approached my house. Before I reached the door, Kali bolted out of it with a crazed look on his face and his green bag in his hand. Tony and me approached him and I couldn't ask what I already knew.

"Kali, please tell me you didn't do nothin' stupid." I asked.

"I told you, I got you? So it's done."

CRAZED HOMIES

Jace

Right before I walked into my house, Nut walked up on us. The three of us looked at her and I'm sure guilt was written all over our faces.

"Why ya'll lookin' all crazy and shit?" She said.

"Fuck you want?" I asked. I needed to get back in the house to see the mess Kali left for me. I also wondered how much of our conversation she overheard. "How long you been right there?"

"I just walked up. I came for Kali." She said, her body covered in dry blood. I figured she was here to tell Kali about Cherry. So much shit had happened, that I forgot to tell him myself and I wondered did Harmony tell him either.

"What you want?" Kali asked.

"Some nigga cut Cherry. She's at the hospital and the doctor saying she might not make it. She could be bleeding to death right now!"

"What?" Kali said walking closer toward her putting his bag down next to him. I could tell just like that, he'd already forgotten about the two corpses he left in my basement. "When this shit happen?"

"Earlier today, Harmony was there. She ain't tell you?"

"Naw," He paused. "Look, Jace, I'ma get up with you later. I gotta see what's up with my peoples."

I started to say fuck his people and that he needed to help me clean up the mess I know he made in my basement but the look Tony gave me told me to let him go ahead.

"Aight…But hit me the moment you get back. We got a lot to rap about."

After he left, Tony and me went into the house and went downstairs. All I can say is I couldn't believe the mess he had made in a matter of minutes. Bam's face was smashed in partially with my aunt Karen's old typewriter and a broken pool stick was lodged in his neck. Blood was everywhere and it looked like a horror movie.

I went into the corner over top of the tin Redskins trash can and threw up. When I thought I was done I threw up some more. My stomach tugged and pulled against itself as I released all of my meal for that day.

"Yo, this kid is sick, Jace. This don't make no fuckin' sense. He killed this nigga without makin' sure we had all the information we needed first. Kali ain't playin' smart, man."

I stood up straight threw my fist in my left hip for support and wiped my mouth with the back of my hand. Then my arms dropped loosely beside me.

"Where's the girl?" I asked calmly.

He looked at the scene and ran around the pool table. Then he looked in the closet and then under the pool table again.

"What the fuck he do to her?" Tony asked.

"He took her out of here. In that bag." I said not even realizing I knew the answer to my own question.

"But the nigga said he not even goin' home first. What he gonna do, run around the hospital with a dead body in a green army bag?"

I looked at him. Although he hadn't been around him more than me, he already knew what type dude he was.

"FUCK! THIS NIGGA GONNA GET US LATE!"

"You tellin' me somethin' I already know." I said pacing the floor with my hand over my head. I wanted this shit to be over, all the way over. And I knew had I just had the strength to give the order, not even necessarily pull the trigger, we woulda had a chance to clean up our own mess. Now this nigga was running around town with a dead girl in his bag like he was Freddy Krueger or something. Or alive girl, with him you could never tell. "Get the crew on the phone and tell them to get over here."

Tony made a few calls and when he was done, we sat in silence for a minute and looked at the work Kali put in.

"I know this is too late to ask, but where you get this dude from?" He paused. "Because the more I think about it, the more I think he may need to stay the fuck from around us, cousin."

I sat down in a chair in the room and said, "Since we was younger I knew Kali was a killer. But he ain't start out like nobody you know." I paused.

"Well how did he start? By butchering old ladies?"

"I'm serious. Back in the day, on the block, it seemed like every other month our neighbor's pets kept comin' up missin'. Like, somebody would walk their dogs one day, and the next day they'd be gone." I paused, trying not to look at the body.

"One day, I saw Kali lookin' at Dingo, my girl Harmony's dog from across the street." I paused. "That dog use to bark her ass in the house every other day. I'm talkin' about vicious ass barkin' like if it got off the leash or somethin', it would kill her."

I could tell Tony wanted me to rush the story but I needed to take my time. It was like I finally understood something I already knew, that this nigga was off. Way off.

"That night I was outside, sneakin' one of Karen's beers, I saw Kali grab Dingo the dog by its neck and pick it up in the air." I demonstrated the way he had Dingo with my hand. "Now I don't know how tightly he had this dog's throat, but it wasn't barkin' no more, cuz. Just whimpering loud enough for me to know it was scared."

"What happened to the dog?"

"Fuck you think, nigga?" I said. "I ain't never see that dog again."

"Stop fuckin' around."

"Nigga, I'm tellin' you the truth. Look around us."

We both looked at the blood and Bam's body.

"Well what happened after that? What he say he did to the dog?" Tony said like a child listening to scary story.

"I stepped to him about it a little while after that. At first he ain't wanna tell me, and even tried lyin', but I told him I'd seen him already. Eventually he kept it real and told me he killed it."

"Where was his peoples while he was killin' animals and shit?"

"He lived with his grandparents. They were old as shit and died a few months after that. Then he moved with his moms who was on that shit, and we kinda lost contact after that. But he moved back in the house that his grandparents lived in now. 'Cept for he don't like to be there alone, so he'll stay over here, or over his cousin Vaughn's."

"How many dogs did this bitch ass nigga kill?"

"Can't be sure...But at least ten."

"Why in the fuck would he kill a dog, man? That's some bull-shit."

"I'm just tellin' you what I know. He heartless and I don't know a nigga on earth like him, not even Russ, Rick's muscle." I paused. "Think of the place you'd have to be mentally to do some shit like that. Or to do some shit like this?"

We looked at Bam's body again.

"Whatever happened to the old fashioned days of just bustin' a nigga in the head?" I said feeling my stomach churning again. "Naw...He gotta go all Jason Voorhees and shit."

"Whoa."

"At the time when I asked him why he killed all them dogs he said, *'Would you rather it be some mutt or some nigga you know instead?'* I never forgot that shit."

We both looked at the dead body before us and swallowed hard.

"What's up with his cousin Vaughn? Why you don't like him?"

"'Cause he listen to anything that nigga tell him to do. And even though he said it was his idea to grab that girl outta school, I got five hundred that say the nigga Vaughn told him to do that shit."

"But Kali do anything you tell him to do, too."

"I know, but I ain't gonna lead him astray." I said. "The nigga Vaughn like to turn him against me. Like trying to get my own dog to bite me or somethin'."

"Damn, I feel you."

A second later, Paco, Herb Dayo, Sick Sense and Kreshon came in and walked down the stairs.

"WHAT THE FUCK?!" Kreshon said.

"THIS NIGGA SICK!" Sick Sense added.

"You tellin' me?" I said.

"What made him kirk out like this?" Paco asked.

"I don't know...Before he did this shit we were in the car tal-kin'. I sent him in the house to get Wop, and the next thing I know, all this shit happen."

"Man...Why he do the nigga like that?" Kreshon asked.

"I don't know but I do know my girl said some cops showed up at her place askin' questions," I said. Paco and Kreshon looked at each other and then at me. I wondered what that meant. "So they on to something but I don't know what. She said they were askin' her about the kidnapping."

"Why would they go to her house?" Tony said. "She ain't connected to this shit in no way. Right?" He asked me.

"Man, maybe they did see him take her. We all know Harmony and Kali cool." Paco said.

"Or, maybe he told her and she told on him." Kreshon added.

"Listen, that's my girl, and bet not nair one of you niggas disrespect her again. She may have her shit with her but she still my girl and my future wife."

Kreshon and Paco looked at each other again.

"Why ya'll keep lookin' like that? You got somethin' you wanna tell me?"

"Naw, man." Paco said. "I'm just fucked up about all of this."

"Me too and I know somethin' not right with this cop situation."

"Right, it don't make no sense that the cops would go to her." Tony said. "You sure Kali ain't tell her, man."

"I ain't sure that he didn't tell her but I do know she ain't no snitch. She maybe sneaky but she not no snitch."

"Maybe he told on himself," Paco interrupted. "You see he not all the way right."

"I'm not sure what happened. But I do know we don't want them knockin' on this door next. So I need this shit cleaned up quick. Then call somebody you trust to have them take out this pool table and burn it. I don't want it trashed, I want it burned. We don't need mothafuckas findin' it and liftin' our prints." I paused looking at all of them. "Whatever you do, don't tell nobody 'bout his shit. If you got a mind to talk about it, then there's enough niggas in this room to feed that need. Outside of that, this shit stays here."

"Got it." Kreshon said.

"So what's up wit' Star?" I asked Paco. "You get anything on him?

"He scared shitless. He must've heard that Bam was missin' and decided he ain't comin' back. But we found out where he is anyway."

"Where is he?"

"In Baltimore. I got somebody watchin' his house right now. Whenever you want to get 'em, we can move."

I paused for a while and looked at the murder scene in front of me. Truthfully I didn't know if I could take another situation like this happening again. And if we picked up Star, I was going to have to give the order.

"Jace, sooner or later you gonna have to get blood on your hands." Tony said.

I looked at my men and I knew what they wanted from me. I had seen this look on their faces a lot lately. They weren't sure if they could respect me as a leader if I couldn't give the order to kill. And it wasn't even like hustlers were automatically murderers…It was just that my father was a stone cold killer. He was vicious and cold and they expected me to be the same way, but I wasn't.

"Have him picked up and taken care of." I said, unable to say the word.

"I'll put the call in when we leave here." Paco said. "But what about our product? We don't have the money to pay Rick off."

"Have them do what they have to do, to get him to talk. If he don't talk, take care of him. I'll just have to tell my father what happened and get more product. But either way…Either way," I paused. "I want Star killed."

Paco smiled and said, "I got that."

Five minutes later my aunt Karen came home and my crew was still downstairs. She never came downstairs so I wasn't worried about her walking in on a crime scene in her house. That's why we knew we could keep them here. She respected my privacy and I respected hers. We stayed out of each other's way.

Tony and me helped clean up as much as possible, then we went upstairs to kick it with Karen while they did the rest. I didn't want to risk her suddenly deciding to come into the basement, even though it wasn't like her.

Before me and Tony went upstairs, I pointed my crew to the tools necessary to hack up the body. This included trash bags, hacksaws and bleach. I'm glad I didn't have to see that part of it and to be honest I wanted the shit over and done with before I went back downstairs.

My aunt made us some food and when she was done, she just stood in the kitchen staring me down. She had been upset ever since she found out her brother Rick had sent for me to go to L.A for a little while. She was wearing a sky blue long dress that looked like a bag and it had silver threads throughout it. Her natural locks were covered in the same material as her dress. Since my mom was murdered, Karen was the closest person in my life to a mother.

"What up, auntie? Why you in my look space?" I said chewing a piece of a biscuit.

"'I'm in your look space because I'm scared for you."

"I know you not about to say nothin' about me goin' to L.A again, 'cause my mind already made up and it's a done deal."

"You know I don't want you to leave, but I'm worried about something else now."

"Like what?"

"I had a dream about you last night."

Tony and me looked at each other because she always had dreams she claimed were premonitions. Some came true and others didn't.

"And what happened in your dream this time?" I asked sarcastically.

"You gotta stay away from that Harmony girl, she's bad news."

"I can't do that. That's my shawty." I said still eating. "Maybe your dream wrong."

"I'm never wrong. Never!" She shouted hitting the counter with a closed fist. Everything on top of it shifted a few inches. "Now I need you to take me seriously."

When I saw the anger and love in her eyes, I stood up and walked over to her. Then I placed my hands on her shoulders and felt the anger go away. Paco and them were banging pretty loudly downstairs, and I hoped she wouldn't ask me what they were doing. Judging by the thumps, I had a feeling they were taking down the pool table.

"You gotta stop worrying about me. I'm good. And you usin' them rock claws to fuck up your kitchen counters ain't gonna make shit no different." I winked. "Relax, auntie. Harmony is good for me and I'm good for her."

She smiled and said, "Just be careful."

"You know I will."

"I don't know what I'd do if someone took you away from me. If I was ever gonna have a son, you would be it."

"What you talkin' about? I *am* your son." She hugged me, walked into her bedroom and shut the door.

"Whoa," I said sitting back at the table with Tony. "She was serious as a heart attack that time."

"Yeah…She ain't feelin' her at all."

"She never liked her…But I don't know why. Harmony good peoples." Tony remained quiet. "What?"

"Cuzin, you better watch her. I been hearing niggas sayin' she get around."

I knew niggas wanted to fuck Harmony so I wasn't even trippin' off of the rumors. She would never cheat on me. Anyway, I was fuckin' the girl Brittany on the side.

"Niggas always talkin' shit when they wanna fuck your girl. They just mad 'cause they can't fuck mine."

"I don't think they know they can't fuck her."

"Slow up, Tony." I said putting my hand out in front of me. "Like I said, that's my shawty."

Harmony wasn't innocent but she definitely wasn't guilty either. The main problems I had with her were her moody ways and how she tried to use sex to get me to do what she wanted. Don't get me wrong, it was good, but I didn't like that about her because we could never talk out our problems. Whenever we had an argument, she'd throw pussy at me and I usually took the bait. But I didn't this last time and I know that fucked her up. We had gotten into an argument about her uncle, and how she don't need to be doing what this nigga say all the time. When the next thing I know, she slapped me in the face. The whole thing was, I was agreeing with her. It's like she got split personalities sometimes.

I was about to go check on things downstairs when the phone rang. I jumped up, looked at the caller ID box and saw Rick's number. People always asked me why I called him Rick instead of dad or some shit like that, but to me Rick held more respect than the word "father" ever could.

"What up, Rick?" I said.

"I just got word that Massive has been spotted in DC."

I can't lie, my pressure went up a little because I knew for a fact that if he was here, he was here for me. "Do you know where at in DC?"

"No. Just be careful, son."

When he hung up I knew he was serious because he never called me son. My father was a ruthless coldblooded killer and yet when it came to Massive, I sensed fear. Not because he was scared of him, but because he was scared for me. Massive was the reason my father moved me to DC in the first place.

When I was younger, Massive was in to my father for ten thousand dollars after losing in a High Stakes Poker game. From what Karen told me it was Rick, Cornell, Massive and a few other players at the table that night. My father loves gambling and has lost and gained millions doing what he loved. Anyway, Massive lost that night and was in to Rick and Cornell for a lot of cash. I don't know what he offered Cornell but he offered Rick one of his custom made Porsches, which was way over the amount owed to cover his loss. But Rick made a living off his reputation so he took the nonpayment of his debt as a sign of disrespect.

So Rick waited a few months and did nothing to Massive. Massive would call him every day to thank him for giving him more time, promising to make good on the debt. He knew what my father was capable of and figured if he was still alive, all was forgiven.

When Massive finally came up with the money, his daughter was graduating from high school. Rick accepted the money although in his mind it was a day late. So he attended Massive's daughter's graduation and the moment Massive's daughter crossed the stage to accept her high school diploma, Rick had her gunned down in front of her friends and family. But Rick underestimated how far Massive would go to get revenge, and because of it, I would never have the luxury of being safe, just as long as he was alive.

"What Rick say, Jace?" Tony asked seeing the concern on my face.

"He said Massive in town."

The look on Tony Wop's face told me what I already know. "You got it bad this week, cousin."

"Tell me about it."

"I don't know when it's gonna happen, but you not gonna be able to fully live your life until you take care of this nigga, Jace. You gonna have to do it yourself, too."

"I know. But how do you catch somebody who can't be caught?"

"Seems to me that you 'bout to find out."

D.C. GENERAL HOSPITAL

A Crazy Kind Of Love
Kali

When Kali walked into DC General Hospital Center to see Sa-sha "Cherry" Miller, he was going for different reasons. Their's was a peculiar kind of relationship and both of them had sick upbring-ings, which caused them to connect on strange levels. But it was Kali who thought that by holding onto her, Harmony, Jace and Vaughn, he could recreate the makeshift family he never had.

Cherry enjoyed Hybristophilia, a paraphilia that involved loving men who participated in violent crimes. She couldn't find a more perfect match in Kali because he enjoyed Coprophagia, a paraphilia that involved being turned on by the eating of human feces as well as Sadism, a paraphilia that involved inflicting pain on another. To-gether they were a match made in hell.

When he stepped toward her hospital room, with the green army bag clasped tightly in his hand, he saw her hooked up to cords through an open door. Off the brake, his dick got hard. He loved how she was almost brought to death, yet somehow managed to survive. Her eyes were closed shut and she looked like she was in a peaceful sleep.

He walked deeper into the room and said, "Cherry..."

"What the fuck are you doing here?" Mary Miller, Sasha's mother, yelled walking up to him. He didn't see her based on where she was sitting. Although she was older, she was just as beautiful as Cherry.

"Yeah, son. I thought I told you to stay away from our daugh-ter." Bobby Miller added.

"And I thought I told ya'll to suck my dick." He said looking between them with hate in his eyes. "Now if Sasha wants me to leave her alone, then I will, but until then get the fuck outta my face with that shit." He walked around them and toward Cherry's bed and dropped his bag on the floor. It made a loud thud but no one paid it any mind.

"And I don't want you to leave." Cherry said in a weak voice. She opened her eyes fully and said, "Mom...Dad...Please give us some privacy."

"You so fucking ignorant and stupid!" Mary yelled. "Don't you see the hate in this boy's eyes? Are you that fuckin' blind?"

"Ma, please! This is between me and Kali."

"But he's gonna kill you! Are you that desperate for some dick?"

"No, ma, I get plenty of dick at work, remember?"

"Oh my sweet, Jesus!" She said walking closer to her bed. "You are going straight to hell!" Her finger wagged back and forth in Cherry's face. "Why would God curse me with such a selfish bitch?"

"Come on, honey." Bobby said pulling Mary away by her fragile elbow. "If she want us gone, then we should just leave."

"Get your decrepit hands off of me, you weak bastard." She shook him off. "You should be beating the shit out of this boy right here instead of wrestling with me."

"Bitch, I'm 72 years old! What you trying to do...Get me killed?" He paused. "So you can cash in on my life insurance policy or something?"

Once again Bobby and Mary turned a situation that was not about them, into one involving them. This was the reason Cherry was so messed up to begin with.

"Nigga, if I wanted you dead you'd be dead by now...You halfway walking anyway, shiny black, mothafucka!"

"Bitch, get your shit and come on!" He picked up her purse and pushed it into her chest, forcing her to hold it. "Pussy so foul it stunk up the whole damn room." He said helping her toward the door. "No wonder she wants us to leave."

"Fuck you, ya no dick having mothafucka!"

"It's time to go, you bent over backwards, bitch!" Bobby said stealing the last words.

People on the outside of the room gathered around when they heard the commotion. Mary and Bobby fussed and cussed all the way down the hall and onto the elevator. When they were gone one of the orderlies peeked into the room and said, "I feel so sorry for you." He shook his head. "They must give you the blues."

"Nigga, get your faggy ass from out in front the door before I break your back." Kali said. The orderly got out of dodge with the quickness.

Cherry shook her head and said, "I'm so embarrassed. Why do they always have to cut up?"

"I don't know why, but they been like that forever and ain't never gonna change."

She smiled and said, "I know but sometimes I wish my life could be different."

"Wishing's for fools, Cherry. Take the life you got and deal with it. You'd be better off that way."

"I...I can't believe you came."

"I ain't beefin' with you no more."

"I'm sorry about what I said about you and Harmony. I like her, and I know ya'll gonna always be cool. But sometimes I get so jealous at ya'll's relationship though."

He walked over to her, took his cap off and said, "So what happened to you?" He paused. "Tell me everything."

"Well I was servicing a client."

"Yeah but how?"

"Kali, I don't want to go into detail. It's too gross."

"Just tell me and stop fuckin' around."

"Why do you like to hear these stories?"

"Would it make you feel better if I didn't like your lifestyle? Didn't you tell me you loved that about me? The fact that I wanted to know everything about you where other niggas didn't?"

"Yes."

"Well stop tryin' to make me feel fucked up about it. And tell me what happened."

She sighed and said, "I have a real sick ass client. He likes to...He likes to eat my pussy after I've had sex with other men. Normally he comes at night," she said taking a deep breath. She was still a little weak from all of the pain meds she was on. "But this time he came during the day. We pulled up in the alley, I lifted my dress and he started eating my pussy. Then he whipped out his dick and started jerking off." She paused like she was about to cry but her sorrow turned to pleasure when Kali pulled out his dick and started beating off too.

"What are you doing?" She asked knowing full well what he was doing. She loved playing the martyr...It made sex better. "Somebody could come in here and see you."

" I'ma be quick," he frowned. "Now go 'head...Finish telling me."

"O...Okay. So he pulled his dick out and started jerking off." She stared at Kali who was jerking his dick harder. "Then he stopped and looked up at me while he was eating my pussy and all of a sudden he looked angry. Normally I'd pretend to be enjoying the act but this time I didn't, there were too many people outside and it was daytime. I was more concerned with getting caught than anything so I guess he got mad. I saw him messing around in his pocket but I didn't see the blade in his hand at first. When I finally did, it was too late because he pressed me up against the car door and cut what the doctor says is my femoral artery. I could've bled to death."

"Awww shit! Awww shit!" Kali said as he nutted in his hand before wiping it on the bottom of her sheet. "Damn." He zippened his pants.

"Kali, sometimes I don't get you."

"What's there to get?" He said sitting in the chair next to her bed as if nothing just happened.

"I could've died and that shit turned you on?"

"I know you could've died, but I'm still here ain't I?"

"But you should be concerned about my health too, not just try-ing to bust a nut." Kali stood over top of her and stared down at her. Then he cracked his knuckles. "No...please don't. Please don't do it again."

Whenever she begged him not to, he knew she wanted him to do the exact opposite. She would pick fights with him just to get smacked and he gladly obliged.

"Bitch, shut the fuck up." He smacked her in the face hard. "You ain't nothin' but a slutty whore!"

"Please...Please stop, Kali. Don't hit me again," she smiled.

He smacked her harder and again she smiled, licking the blood that fell in the corner of her lips. Seeing her pleasure, he knew what she wanted so he walked over to the door and closed it. Then he took one of the chairs in the room and pressed it against the doorknob so no one else could get inside. When the door was closed he took off his pants and on the hospital bed, made her suck his dick. When she was done he made her repeat the same actions four more times. And then he gave her the best fuck of her life. Stitches and all.

DIRTY OLD BITCH

Harmony

My grandmother is such a bitch! When I got home earlier today she was in the house running her mouth with Lola from up the street. All they ever did was run their fucking mouths and worry about everybody else's business but their own. I wonder if Lola fucks her granddaughter like Shirley makes me fuck her.

"Hi." I said dryly, looking at Meleny's baby, which was on the couch with them. It was crying and being loud. "Where is uncle Charles?"

"He's not here. I don't know, why?"

"No reason."

"Anyway, I'm glad you here, Harmony. Meleny needs you to watch her baby tonight." Shirley said. Two liquor glasses sat on the floor and Shirley's phonebook sat next to them. "So I hope you ain't got plans."

"Well I do got plans tonight, so I can't watch her."

"Just what the fuck do you have planned tonight?" She placed a bottle in the baby's mouth silencing it for a little while. "You 17 years old and all you do is rip and run the streets with them two hoes. The least ya can do is hang 'round here and do somethin' of meanin' for a change. 'Specially since the teacher called me today saying she had to talk to me about something. Do you know what she want?"

"Naw," I said hoping Mrs. Duncan wouldn't tell her about the rape. All I needed was drama at my crib even though I wasn't scared of Shirley anymore.

I laughed and said, "I don't know what she wanted with you and I don't give a fuck either."

"Well it bet not be no bullshit." She said drinking some liquor. "But cancel your plans, I need you to babysit. Make yourself useful."

"I make myself useful all the time," I said licking my lips. Shirley looked at Lola wondering if she caught on. "Or have you forgotten. Maybe we can tell Lola what I do for you around here."

"Harmony! Stop it!"

"I'm not watching no baby that smell like weed." I paused. "Tell Meleny's fry making ass to leave McDonald's and take care of her own kid." I said walking toward my room stopping at the wall. "Anyway, why can't you watch it?"

"Cause we 'bout to go down Mary Miller's house and play Gin Rummy. She's in a bad mood and a baby may make shit worse."

"Again it is not my problem."

"And I'm not sayin' it is! But the least you could do is help me out."

"I said no. And since Mary Miller's daughter is one of the whores you claimed I be running around with, then I know you know she's in the hospital. So I doubt Mary will be playing Gin Rummy with anybody tonight."

"She just called me to tell me to come over. You don't know so much after all."

"Well I ain't watchin' it anyway." I said turning the corner to go into my room. "I don't care what you two bitches talking about out there! Trying to use up my weekend and shit! If she can't get a babysitter, she shouldn't have a baby!" I paused. "Wait 'til Charles get back?"

Ever since I had gotten older, he didn't bother me anymore. But he did spend a lot of time out of the house and I wondered who's child he was bothering now.

"NO!" Lola jumped in. "I mean...Not for nothin', Shirley, but I can't have him watching my grandbaby."

Shirley rolled her eyes at Lola and said, "He ain't like that no more."

My grandmother was straight tripping. Whenever I asked her for something she never came through for me unless I made her feel good and I'm her flesh and blood. And now she wanna ask me for something?

"Harmony, this will really help me out," she continued walking into my room.

"And that makes me want to say no even more!"

"This is ridiculous! I do everything around here for you." She had a serious face as she ran that bullshit down to me. "I put food on the table, a roof over your head and everything."

"You collect welfare, Shirley. And I hoped you saved up because when I'm eighteen, I'm getting my own place and you won't be able to draw welfare off of me no more."

She stomped out in an attitude and I spent the next thirty minutes trying to put on the right outfit to hang out with Jace tonight. I turned on the radio and New Edition's "If It Isn't Love", played from the speakers. I danced around a little before settling on an off the shoulder yellow shirt, a black mini skirt and my yellow Jellies to wear. Then I smoothed on some strawberry lotion, blew dried my naturally curly hair straight and crimped it all over. When my hair was done I decided to do my face so I put on some blue mascara, red blush and some clear lip-gloss. I looked really cute even though I normally didn't wear makeup.

I was about to go into the living room when the phone in my room rang. It was Paco. "Harmony, did you tell anybody about what we talked about?"

Him telling me what happened with the girl put me in more shit than I wanted to be in. "Paco, I gotta go, Jace gonna be here soon."

"Answer the fuckin' question!"

"I didn't tell nobody nothing. Okay?"

Silence.

"If I find out you lyin' to me, shit could get real ugly."

He was threatening me, which was something he'd never done before, and I was scared. "I'm telling you the truth."

He hung up without responding and I thought about what I'd gotten myself into. I should've never said anything to Jace about the situation. And Jace must've said something to Paco, which was why he was calling me tonight.

Needing a buzz, I walked into the kitchen and opened a bottle of Shirley's gin downing half of the bottle. As the liquid warmed my chest, I started to feel better immediately. When all of a sudden I realized Shirley and Lola were too fucking quiet in the living room. *Fuck are they doing in there?* I thought. When I walked into the living room to see what they were up to, I saw the baby laying on the sofa by itself sleep.

"Shirley!" I yelled walking around the house. "Shirley, I know you didn't leave this thing in here with me!"

She didn't answer because she wasn't there! Dirty old bitch! Before I called her name I knew she was gone because her leather phonebook was not there. She didn't go anywhere without that book.

I looked on the refrigerator and saw a few of the frequent phone numbers she used under a purple refrigerator magnet. Lola and Meleny lived together and their number was on the paper so I dialed theirs first. The phone kept ringing and all I could think about was that there was no way in hell I was giving up a night with Jace for a night with a baby. Selfish maybe, but at this point I didn't care.

A few seconds later, the baby started crying so when I couldn't get in contact with Lola or Meleny, I called Mary.

"Mary, this Harmony. Is Shirley there?"

"Not yet. Why?"

"Well when she get there, tell her this baby she left will be still here *left* waiting on her."

"Harmony, that's awful! You can't leave a baby in the house by itself."

Click.

Don't blame me. What everybody should be asking is what kind of grandmother is Lola.

I was still waiting on Jace when my phone rang again. "Harmony, it's Trip, have you talked to Constance?"

"No, why?"

"She's been crying all day about something and she won't tell me what. Maybe you should call her."

"Okay, I'll call her now," I lied, just to get her off my phone.

"I feel so bad..."

The sound of my phone clicking in her face interrupted her sentence. I looked over at the baby and it was playing with itself. Good for it because I couldn't stand baby girls.

I sat impatiently at the window and waited for Jace's car to pull up. It was exactly twenty-two cars later before I finally heard his music. I put the baby on the floor so it wouldn't roll off and then I rolled out. And the moment I opened the door and saw his Audi, my pussy throbbed.

"What up, J?" I said getting into his car. I loved the smell of a new car mixed with a vanilla tree air freshener.

Jace looked fly as usual with his designer jeans and Polo t-shirt. A gold chain just big enough hung from his neck and the name Jace was spelled out in diamonds. Boy did I love his style.

"You smell good." He said looking at me with his hazel eyes. Then he looked carefully out of his side view mirrors.

"Thank you. You do, too." I said pulling on my yellow shirt so that it hung off my shoulders.

With me rushing tonight, I didn't have a chance to bathe but I did take a whore's bath and wiped my pussy.

"Harmony, you talk to Kali?"

"How come every time I see you, you asking me about Kali?"

"We been tryin' to find him since he left to visit Cherry at the hospital. Now I can't find this nigga nowhere."

"Naw, I haven't seen him since earlier."

"This nigga is gettin' on my fuckin' nerves."

I was tired of talking about Kali and wanted to talk about me. But after his question he didn't say anything for a few more minutes. I crossed my legs and just like I always did and tried to think of ways to get his attention.

"So what we 'bout to do?" I asked.

"Sit back and relax." He said without looking at me.

"I'm saying...Where we going, Jace? You can't even tell me that?"

"You got somewhere else to be?" He asked looking over at me.

"No. I'm just..."

"I'ma take you back home if you keep runnin' your mouth." He looked at me seriously. "Anyway I don't know where we rolling right now. I got some shit on my mind and I started not to even pick you up."

"Why did you?"

"'Cause I said that I would and I always keep my word to you." A minute later, he turned the air conditioning up and said, "You cold?"

"Naw."

"Hungry?"

"Yeah."

When a black car pulled up next to us at the light, he jumped a little and looked around like he was looking for someone. But who could it be? His father's reputation rung bells and I knew people knew better than to fuck with him.

"Is everything cool? I mean...Why you keep looking around? Somebody after you or something?"

"Why you ask me some shit like that?" He said gritting on me. "Fuck wrong wit' you?"

"Jace, I'm trying to talk to you. You said you wanted to hang out but you ain't talking to me. Are we back together or what!!?" I yelled. "Say something...Anything!"

Silence.

"Did the cops come back again? To your house?"

"What cops?" I asked not knowing what the fuck he was talking about.

"The cop you told me came to your door." He steered his wheel and looked over at me suspiciously. "What...You was lyin' or somethin'?"

"No...I didn't know what you was talking about at first because we weren't even talking about cops."

"Well how many cops you got comin' to your house?"

I wish Paco never told me about this shit because now it was coming in between our relationship. "He didn't come back, Jace." I sighed.

"What was his name?"

Think quick, Harmony. "I can't remember. I left his card at the house."

"Don't forget to give me his information later."

"Okay." I paused. "Now can you start answering some of my questions? Are you seeing somebody else?"

"Naw."

"You sure?"

"Yes."

We took brief looks at each other and I knew he didn't trust me anymore than I trusted him. "Can you tell me why you're acting so strange? And why you going to L.A?"

"My life 'bout to change. Shit already changing...And I need to see if you serious 'bout ridin' with me or not."

"I'm not scared of the drug life. Or have you forgotten my father died in the game?"

"Your father died because he murdered a cop. There is a difference."

"Yeah...He killed a cop to protect me and his family." I put him back in his place. When it came to my father I could be serious. "But he also ran everything that came in and out of DC and I know you know that. For a while your father used to work for mine."

"Yeah but my pops don't work for nobody now." Jace looked out of the window again and turned back to me.

"So what we playing, 'your father ain't better than my father', now?"

"You took it there not me." He focused on my face for the first time.

"Even when you mad you pretty. That shit be fuckin' me up 'bout you."

"Thank you." I smiled.

"But why you got all that bullshit on your face. I like you better natural."

"Start acting right and you can have my face however you want it."

"I'ma have your face anyway I want it now." He said turning me on.

We were still talking until I saw McDonald's golden arches. Why we have to come here? I got a little nervous because I didn't feel like seeing Meleny's ass and she worked here. If I was with Jace that meant I wasn't at home watching her baby. It wouldn't matter that I never agreed to babysit.

"Why we comin' here?" I asked. "Can't we do Burger King or somethin'? Any place but here."

"I wanted to take you somewhere else but it ain't gonna work out tonight. So it's McDonald's or nothin'."

"Well, let it be nothin'."

"Well I'm hungry." He said checking his pager. "We ain't gonna be here long. The line is short anyway."

When we pulled up in the Drive Thru window and Meleny wasn't there I exhaled.

"Welcome to McDonald's how may I help you?" A cute light skin girl asked smiling in his face. If I thought she was pretty I know Jace did, too. "Oh...Ain't your name, Jace?"

"Why?"

"'Cause you look familiar." She said smacking her lips after every world. "That's all."

"Well don't worry about who I am. Just take my order." He carried the shit out of her and I loved it. "You sure you don't want nothin'?" He asked me again.

The look on the girl's face turned from conniving to mad when she saw me in his passenger seat. Too bad...So sad, bitch, this rich nigga's all mine.

"Yeah...You can get me a Big Mac, fries and a strawberry shake." I said.

"Aight, get her order and give me a Hamburger, no cheese with Big Mac sauce and a large fry. Oh...Add a Coke too."

"'Ahn...Ahn, you can't get a Hamburger with Mac Sauce. You gotta get a Big Mac if you want all that."

"Well I don't want a Big Mac. Now get me what the fuck I asked for."

"But I can't, Jace. That's not how we make 'em."

"I don't care how they make 'em for everybody else, put Mac sauce on my shit."

"I NEED A MANAGER!" She screamed turning around.

She was being so ridiculous and he was too. Just when I thought it couldn't get any worse, Meleny brings her skinny ass to the window. Her tag said manager and I tried to hide my face.

"Oh...Hey, Jace. I didn't know...," she paused, stooped down a little to look further into his car and said, "hold up, where my baby at, Harmony?"

"Bitch, what is you talking about?" I said trying to ignore her.

"My mother said you were watching my baby tonight. So why ain't she in the car with you?"

PRESENT DAY

Green Door – Adult Mental Health Care Clinic
Northwest, Washington DC

"Wait a second, why would you leave a baby in the house by itself?" Christina Zhan asked Harmony.

"Because it wasn't my kid! Fuck was I supposed to do?" Harmony said raising her voice.

"You don't see anything wrong with leaving a baby in the house by itself?"

"No." She said seriously. "If I did I would not have done it."

"So you were very promiscuous when you were coming up, why?"

"It was one of the first things I was taught. How to have sex. From the time I was a little girl."

"Just so you know, masturbation is very common in children and I'm sorry you had someone around you, who took advantage of that."

"I'm sorry I was born."

Silence.

"But why give yourself to so many people, when it was obvious Jace loved you?"

"I don't know. I felt like…I felt like if I gave myself to as many people as I could, that they would want me and make me feel good about myself."

"What was Kalive's relationship with you about?"

"Me and Kalive were the same. He had a fucked up life and so did I. I think that's why we were so close. At first anyway."

"At first?"

"Yeah...Things started to change between me and him pretty quickly."

"Do you know why?"

"No. Plus I was too busy worrying about my own problems."

"Where was your uncle during all of this?"

"You know, it would take me a long while to find out where he was. And when I did, it was almost too unbelievable to be true."

Christina shook her head in disgust and said, "Continue with your story.

SUMMER OF 1988

Southeast, Washington, DC
McDonalds
Harmony

"Bitch, I'm not your babysitter." I yelled at Meleny who was looking at me like she was crazy. "You betta get outta my face with all that shit and go talk to Lola's ass!"

"Listen, all this shit you doin', you can save for another time. Now take your stupid ass in the back and get my food." Jase yelled.

"NuNu, go make his shit right quick!" Meleny told the light skin cashier. "I'm 'bout to call my mova and find out what's going on with my baby. And if I find out you did somethin' to her, I'ma fuck you up, too!"

"Fuck you and that weed-smellin' baby!" I yelled as she was walking away.

We waited in the drive thru for two minutes and I could feel my stomach rumble. I hated that if she stepped to me, I would be forced to fight.

"Let's go to another drive thru, Jace. It ain't that serious."

"We can do that if you scared."

"I'm not hardly scared."

Five more minutes passed when I glanced in my rear view mirror. Meleny was leading a pack of six girls and they were moving quickly in my direction.

"Jace, we gotta problem." I told him.

He looked out of his back window and shook his head. "Fuck is wrong with this chick?" He said as the girls approached the passenger side.

"Step out the car, Harmony."

"Girl you betta get outta my face."

"My mova said you left my baby in the house by herself!" She said rolling her sleeves up. "Fuck wrong with you? What kind of person would do some shit like that?"

Without waiting on my response, she flung my door open and grabbed me by my hair pulling me outside. I was landing wild blow after wild blow until her friends started hitting and kicking me all over my body. I heard Jace try to get out, but the drive thru-window blocked him in.

"Fuck!" I heard him say. "I don't have time for this shit!"

Everything happened in a matter of seconds. Then I heard, "Get the fuck off of her." Jace had eased out through the passenger side door.

I was on the ground, balled up covering my head and face. Suddenly everybody stopped hitting me and then I heard their footsteps go away. When I turned around, I saw the gun in his waist.

"Get the fuck in the car, Harmony."

I got inside and he did too. The line at the drive thru was backed up but no one cared because of the show.

"Here's your food, Jace," NuNu said before we pulled off. "Sorry 'bout the confusion."

He shook his head and pulled off. "Please tell me you ain't do some hateful ass shit like leave a baby in the house by itself." A cop was to the right of the drive thru and he was giving someone a ticket. "The fuckin' cops were right there. What if they saw that shit?"

"That bitch lyin', Jace! What I look like doing something like that?"

We were on our way onto the street when a long black limo blocked our path. When the door opened, I saw an older black man with an orange Hawaiian style shirt and some shades on step out. He looked powerful and threatening all at once. Jace appeared uneasy and gripped the handle of his .45 a little tighter.

When he stepped out, he slowly approached my side of the window and said, "I don't mean to bother you, but I'm a little lost. Can you tell me where Kennedy Street is?"

After I told him where he needed to go and he got back in his limo, I was finally able to breathe.

"Is somebody trying to kill you?" I said looking at the limo pull off.

"You safe, so leave it at that." He paused. "Let's go get a room."

"Can we stop and get something to drink first?"

"Yeah..."

Five minutes later we ended up at a cheap motel not too far from McDonald's. When we walked into room 456 it smelled musty and old. Jace flipped the lights on to look around before looking out the window. Then he drew the curtains closed and sat down on one of the twin beds and gave me my food.

"Sit down." He told me as he sucked down his fries with one breath. Then he started chewing his hamburger.

"They put Mac sauce on it?" I asked eating my food, too.

"Fuck you think?"

I laughed. "It must be nice to always get what you want."

"I wasn't even worried about that shit she was spittin'. She was gonna give me my food. She probably was runnin' all that shit 'cause she saw you in my car. You know how bitches are." He paused. "How's your face?"

"It's fine." I said touching the place they hit me. "That bitch is so dumb! She really act like I was her baby father or something."

He took two more bites of his burger and it was done. "Yeah, she was trippin' hard but I hate to see chicks fight. It's not classy."

"So you saying I don't have no class?"

"You got to answer that question yourself, Harmony. I'm speaking 'bout fightin' in general and I'm tellin' you what I like. If a dude wanted to see a chick all fucked up in the face, he'd fuck another dude."

I laughed.

"What?"

"Nothing, you funny." I said.

He smirked and said, "Take your clothes off and get in the bed."

I love how he was carrying it because after the shit with Meleny, I needed to be fucked badly. I was about to take my clothes off until I felt something oozing in my panties.

"Give me a second, I have to go to the bathroom." I said taking my purse with me.

"Do you."

When I walked into the bathroom, I was disgusted at how grungy everything looked. Sitting on the toilet, I looked in my pink panties and saw a lot of discharge but no blood. I took one of the hard white washcloths, and ran some warm water on it. Then I softly rubbed the smelly discharge away. After I was done, I dug in my purse for my pint of vodka. Downing most of it, my chest was warm and I was finally able to relax. So much was running through my mind...Paco telling me about Kali, Jace acting weird, Meleny and her weed smelling baby and the possibility that if I fucked Jace tonight, I could possibly burn him. But alcohol is amazing, because after five minutes later, nothing really mattered.

WIDER

Jace

Shit was coming down hard on me. I'm doin' more at seventeen then most niggas do in their forties. When I left my house today, I saw to it that the pool table was gone and Bam's body was missing. Herb Dayo's father owns a funeral home, which specializes in disintegration so we were able to get rid of everything with blood on it, including the rug. I already arranged through Kreshon's people to have new carpet put in the house along with a new pool table. There was no way I could see staying in that house and getting my aunt mixed in my business. I had to move.

With Massive trying to kill me and Kali not answering any of my calls, I had a lot on my plate. What did he do with the girl's body and was her kidnapping going to be tied back to me somehow?

When she came back into the bedroom from the bathroom, she wasn't wearing any clothes and my dick got hard. When it came to the sex, she couldn't be fucked with and she knew it. I wondered how it was possible for her to be so experienced and so young but she never wanted to talk about it. And for real I'm not sure if I wanted to listen.

"Lay down," I demanded, making a spot on the bed next to me. She looked disappointed and I wondered what I said wrong. "Now what's up?"

"Nothing...I just thought you were gonna tell me how I look." She walked over to me and got in the bed. Throwing her clothes on a chair.

"Harmony, this is how I am and you should know by now that I don't do a lot of talkin'. But you do look sexy. You know that."

"I guess I'm feeling this way because I don't know if we're back together. You not telling me nothing. It's like you avoiding me."

"We better than back together and I'ma leave it at that." I paused. "Now get under the covers."

"Better than back together?"

She wouldn't let up. "If shit work out, I want you to move in with me at my new place. When I come back from L.A."

"For real?!!!"

"Yeah...Now get under these covers and open your legs." She did. "Wider."

I ran my hands over her breasts and between her legs. Then slowly I eased into her pussy and she felt so fuckin' good. Easing out of her I pushed my dick back in deeper and was immediately sucked into her wetness. Harmony bucked her hips wildly and bit down on her bottom lip. Her nails met the skin on my back and we were fuckin' like we never fucked before. This was the best part about breaking up, the making up.

"Mmmmmmmm. I miss you so much, Jace." She told me.

I was working the fuck out of her pussy when all of a sudden...I felt a lot of heat on the shaft of my penis. I thought I was tripping at first so I continued to move in and out of her but slowly this time. But the feeling wouldn't go away and the sensation got worst so I slowed down all together.

"I don't feel good to you, Jace?" She said opening her eyes. "Am I doing something wrong?"

"Yeah you feel good to me."

"You sure? 'Cause you not moving like you were when we first started."

"I said yeah, aight?! Stop trippin'."

Could she be burning that bad, where I would find out right away? Or was I burning her? After all, I did fuck Brittany earlier this week and we ain't use a condom. I wasn't sure and was about to stop until I saw her crying.

"What's wrong?" I asked stopping my motions. "Am I hurtin' you or somethin'?"

She wiped the wetness from her face and said, "No. But I know you been with somebody else, Jace, and it feels...It feels like you not responding to me no more. Like you don't like me or some-thing."

She sounded fake but I couldn't be sure. "That ain't hardly true. You know I'm feelin' you."

"Yes it is true." I couldn't stand to see her cry so I tried to focus on fucking her now and deal with everything else later. Plus I ain't never heard of no nigga being able to tell if a chick burned him or not right away.

"Listen, I was trying to let you get yours off first but if you con-cerned about me gettin' mine, that's exactly what I'm gonna do."

So I closed my eyes and tried to focus on her warmth. Her legs widened and I pushed deeper into her pussy. But the sensation was getting too bad and I decided I didn't give a fuck about her feelings anymore. Something was up.

"Harmony, somethin' ain't right with you." I said getting off of her body. When I got up, I went into the bathroom.

"What...What you mean?" She asked sitting up in the bed.

"My dick burnin' like shit. Have you been fuckin' somebody else?" If I found out she was cheating I don't know what I would do to her.

"What?" She paused. "Fuck no! Why would you say that?"

"Because I ain't never experience no shit like this when we fucked before."

"Well maybe It's somebody else you fuckin'. What about the girl I hear you be rolling around in your car with?"

I leaned out of the bathroom, wiping my dick with a warm washcloth. "Yo, get your shit together. We 'bout to go."

"I ain't going nowhere until you tell me what the fuck you mean."

"Aight then, stay here. But if you don't have your shit on when I get ready to leave, you gettin' left."

She picked up the bible next to the bed and threw it at me. I ducked. "Fuck you! You the one cheating on me and now you try-ing to blame me!"

"If that woulda hit me I woulda dropped your ass!"

"I hate you, Jace!" She cried getting out of bed. "If you wanted to break up with me you shoulda just broke up with me! No need, to lie!"

The moment I was about to tell her how I really felt, two niggas kicked open the motel door.

"Ahhhhhhhh!!!" She screamed cowering in the corner.

I rushed for my gun but realized I left it in my car. "Get on the floor, nigga! Now!" One of them said to me.

After the two of them came in, I saw a third man. It was the nigga from earlier at the McDonalds. I should've went with my instincts and shot him when I had a chance. Now it was too late.

I GOT YOU

Harmony

I couldn't stop crying in the pitch-blackness of the trunk. They smacked me around a few times, but Jace was beaten so badly, that his face was covered in blood and he was almost unrecognizable. As the car, which held us, rolled over DC's bumpy streets, my head knocked against everything within the dark trunk. The pain I felt was overpowering. It angered me to know that the man I'd given directions to at the McDonald's was there for us after all.

"Jace, can you hear me?" I whispered, hoping the kidnapper wouldn't hear my voice. "Jace, please get up. I'm afraid."

When he didn't respond I figured I had to get us out alive because he wouldn't be able to do shit. I felt my surroundings with my hands, which were tied behind my back, and tried to see as much as I could with the light peeking in from the sides of the trunk. A long time ago my father told me that if I was ever kidnapped and thrown into a trunk, that I should try and knock the keyhole out and stick some material through it, to alert people driving behind us that I was inside. And if that didn't work I should use my fingers instead. I was just a kid when he told me that, but I never forgot anything he said to me, even if I didn't always listen.

Since my arms were duct taped behind my back, I felt some sort of long hard tool on the right of me. I placed my body on top of it and it felt like my back would break in half. Then I rubbed the tape on my wrists over and over on the edge of the tool until it was half-way torn. I could feel blood oozing from my back and hands, which was making it harder for me to cut the tape. But eventually I got myself free.

Once free, I started to untie Jace but I didn't want to make too much noise, so he would have to wait. Focusing on the keyhole, whenever we rolled over a bump, I took the tool out and knocked it against the keyhole. For each bump we hit I did the same thing over and over again, until the keyhole became loose. Now I had more light shining inside from the streetlights outside. And then it dawned on me, the car was riding differently. There were more turns, which meant we were in a residential area and on our way to never being found again. It was truly now or never.

For a moment we drove without any jolts from DC potholes and I needed the noise to hit the keyhole so that the sounds would go undetected. So when the road got bumpy again, I banged harder on the keyhole and the car stopped completely.

"What the fuck?" I heard someone mumble from the front of the car.

Oh no! He heard me! I tried to position myself like he had me, but I knew it wasn't going to work. I was completely wet from my blood and sweat trying to set myself free. When the trunk opened, I squinted because the lights were blinding and all I could see was my abductor's silhouette. I knew it was over so I decided then and there to just give up. But the moment I did, I saw cop lights behind the car. But the kidnapper was so focused on me that he didn't see them.

"What you doing back here, bitch?"

"Fuck you!" I screamed as loud as I could. "Help!!!!! Help!!!!

He stole me so hard in the face, I felt my teeth clank together. "You're gonna wish you ain't try no slick shit with me, bitch."

"Who's gonna wish they ain't try no slick shit?" The cop said walking up behind him. The kidnapper slammed the trunk shut and I banged on the inside of the trunk hysterically.

"No one, officer," the kidnapper laughed. "I was just talking to myself."

"Where are you going?"

"I'm just on my way to visit my sister."

"Well what's that banging inside your trunk?"

"Uh…Nothing."

"Oh yeah? Well open it up, I want to see for myself."

"Officer, this really isn't necessary."

"Open the trunk, sir! I won't ask you again!" The officer yelled.

It was silent and I was nervous. Something was about to happen but what? Knowing this was my last chance, I kicked the trunk several times again and yelled, "Hellllp! Hellllp! We're in here!"

There was a brief silent period before I heard the officer say, "He's going for a gun!"

"What the..." I heard another voice say followed by a hail of bullets.

I knew then that whoever wanted me or Jace, wanted us badly enough to kill a police officer. When the trunk door opened, I knew our fate would be revealed. Court was held in the streets, and this was the verdict.

I saw a shiny badge and exhaled when I saw the officer's face. He put the gun on his holster and said, "Are you two alright?"

●━━━━━━━━━━━━━━━━━━━━━━━━━━━●

We were in the hospital for two hours before I saw six people walk up to Jace's room in a hurry. The only one I recognized was Kali and Tony Wop. Tony's muscles peeked from the sides of his shirt and he talked smoothly. His accent was different from a DC accent because he was from L.A.

"You alright?" Kali asked me blocking my view of Tony. He's such a hater.

"Not really. I got cuts on my back and wrists. My head hurts pretty badly too, but I'm alive. I can't believe all this shit popped off tonight." I said looking around him at Tony.

Kali adjusted the leather strap he had on his back and said, "At least you safe," he said looking into my eyes. I never understood why he went around town with a hatchet. Part of it was creepy, but the other part was bold and it kinda turned me on. "Don't worry 'bout nothin' else though. I got you."

"Kali, where were you earlier? Jace said he was looking all over for you."

"Let me deal with that. I'm just glad you're alive. When I heard some niggas kicked that door in, I almost lost it."

I didn't know what Kali meant by the way he was looking at me. Plus he was fucking Cherry, so why was he all in my face? Don't get me wrong, I ain't got no problem fucking what I want, but him and I will never be like that.

Tony all of a sudden walked up to me and said, "I'm sorry you got mixed in this shit tonight but I 'ppreciate you gettin' my peoples out of that shit alive. I heard 'bout the keyhole thing too. That shit was smart." Kali looked at him as if he had just violated by speaking to me and all I could think about was the way Tony would feel inside of my pussy. I thought about fucking 24/7 and tonight was no different. "But are you aight?"

"Yeah...She fine. I got her." Kali interrupted.

What the fuck was he doing? I thought. Tony looked at him and then at me. "I'm talkin' to her, cuz." He said mean mugging him.

"Yeah, but I was just tellin' you that I'ma make sure she aight."

"Yeah but that wasn't the question. And I wasn't even talkin' to you, homie." He paused. "But we do have a conversation due."

"What convo you gotta have with me?"

"We'll have it soon. Don't worry 'bout that shit." He said looking at me as if I had just violated a private meeting. "With my cousin bein' down, I'ma be the one lookin' after things."

"Whenever you ready." Kali said back.

The two looked at each other with harsh stares and I decided it was time to bring the attention back to me so I said, "Is Jace gonna be alright?"

"Yeah...We cut from the same cloth. Don't worry 'bout him. You just take care of yourself." I knew right then he was as attracted to me as I was to him. "Well let me get back to my cousin. Kali, I'ma holla at you," he paused pointing his finger at his chest, "later." He walked away giving him one last boss look.

When Tony left, Kali said, "Go wait for me in the lobby, I'ma take you home. You shouldn't be out here this late at night anyway."

"Can you please tell me why you acted like that just now? You acting like I'm Cherry or something."

"What are you talkin' about?"

"What am I talking about? You were acting all possessive and shit. I don't like that, Kali, people could get the wrong impression."

"Hold up, you're worried about someone gettin' the wrong impression? Of you?"

"What the fuck is that supposed to mean?" I asked putting my hands on my hips.

"Harmony, go wait in the lobby and don't make me say it again." He said pushing me toward the elevator. "You don't need to be over here with all these niggas anyway."

I was tired and after the night I had, really didn't feel like arguing. "The next time you want to boss me around, be sure you're putting money in my pocket."

"You gonna make me tell you again to go wait in the lobby?" He asked ignoring my statement. He was acting real crazy and didn't look the same.

"Hurry up." I told him before walking away. "I ain't waitin' all day."

I was a few feet away from Jace's room when Karen's overweight fat ass stepped in my path and said, "What are you doing here?"

"Jace is my boyfriend, Karen." I said. "And I was kidnapped with him."

"This is probably all your fault, I don't trust you. Stay away from him."

"I'm not trying to hear none of the shit you spittin'. But if Jace wants me to leave him alone, that's between me and him."

She looked at me like I shitted on myself and walked away. Tony walked over to her hugged her and they walked into Jace's room. But before she turned the corner she made sure to look at me again. She had a major issue with me and I knew right then that after the problem we had in the hotel, the only way to get Jace to stay with me was to trap him into a pregnancy. So I was gonna do what I had to do.

———————●———————

Kali and me were driving in silence for about five minutes before he said, "You know I don't know what I would do if someone hurt you right?"

"Kali, why are you acting like this all of a sudden?" I said looking at him from the corner of my eyes.

"I don't know. I guess I was always feelin' you. But you was so worried about Jace." He paused. "When I'm the one who *has* and will kill for you."

"Kill for me? When?"

"Remember that dog? The one you were scared of all the time?" he paused. "I did that for you. And I'd kill anybody else for you if you needed me to. All you gotta do is say the word."

To tell you the truth, I always believed he had something to do with Dingo missing but I never had hardcore proof until now.

"How is Cherry?" I asked skipping the subject. "You go visit her yet?"

"Yeah…She cool."

Silence.

"You shouldn't be so serious about me, Kali. Plus I don't want Jace thinking the wrong thing about us. I already don't think he's feelin' our friendship."

He was silent until he said, "Jace my man and all, but he's not loyal like I am. He lets people come in the way of our family, like he don't care about me or somethin'. Sometimes I feel like I gotta put him outta of his misery, for his own good."

"You're scaring me now."

"Don't be scared," he said staring out in front of him. "I would never do anything to hurt Jace, unless I felt like he'd do something to hurt me first."

"He's my boyfriend, Kali. You gotta remember that. And I don't want nothing to happen to him."

"How would you feel if something happened to me?"

"Bad. Real bad."

"Who would you want alive more, me or Jace?"

"Kali! Stop asking me questions like that!"

Kali was scaring the hell out of me. His questions and responses were all over the place and I didn't know where he was coming from.

"You not in any pain are you? That bruise on your face looks bad."

"The doctor said I'll be fine, so I'll be fine." I paused. "And since when do you care about bruises on somebody's face? Seeing as though you beat up on Cherry on a regular."

"Now who's in who's business?" He said. "And just so you know, Cherry like when I fuck her up. So I ain't doin' shit she not in to." He was telling me something I already knew but didn't understand.

When we pulled up to my house he said, "I'ma walk you inside."

"I guess there's no way I can convince you not to huh?"

"No." He said following me.

When I opened the door to my house Shirley was sitting on the couch looking at TV until she saw me. She stood up and said, "WHY THE FUCK WOULD YOU LEAVE THAT BABY IN HERE BY ITSELF!"

"I told you I wasn't watching that weed smelling baby!" I said putting my keys on the table by the door. I didn't bother telling her what happened to me tonight because I knew she wouldn't care.

Shirley stepped closer to me and said, "You need your ass kicked for that shit."

"And who gonna do it?" I said with my hands on my hips. She looked at me and then at Kali. "Shirley, get the fuck out of my face." I continued walking around her.

She looked as if she wanted to hit me. And I don't know if the look in my eyes or the look in Kali's told her it would be a dumb move.

When we got to my room I tried to organize it a little bit because my clothes were everywhere due to trying to look cute for Jace tonight. At least I didn't have to worry about Shirley's stinky ass clothes being in here anymore. I finally got the room all to myself, one of the gifts she gave me for, *'taking care of her'*. The good thing about it was when I got with Jace I didn't have to do those things any more.

"Okay, Kali, I'm in my room and I'm fine now. So you can leave."

"You gonna take a shower?"

"Why?"

"Cause I want to make sure you're in the bed safe before I go." He said standing in the middle of the floor. Then he looked out of the window as if the man who had kidnapped me earlier was still outside. I knew he was in the hospital though because the cops shot him up pretty badly.

"Okay...Well I'ma take a shower. You can stay until I get out."

"Aight." Kali looked around everywhere, and I realized then he'd never been in my room before. "Your room looks just like I imagined. Real pretty, like a girl's."

"Kali, why did you use to watch over me so much?"

"You needed me. To protect you."

"What made you think that?"

"Because I know what Charles use to do to you." He said picking up a Polaroid picture in my room of me, Trip and Connie.

"I don't know what you're talking about."

"I know you don't," he smiled slyly.

"Well you can sit down, Kali." I paused grabbing my baby blue nightgown out of my dresser. "You don't have to stand up looking all creepy and shit."

Kali sat on the edge of my bed and I hopped into the shower. The water felt good moving over my body and hair. For the first time since everything happened, reality hit me that I almost died. My father told me that loving money meant being prepared for anything and I finally understood what that meant. I was always a strong person, able to deal with whatever, but lately shit wasn't going my way and I hated it. As I was crying to myself, Kali walked into the bathroom and I wiped the suds away from my eyes.

"What are you doing in here?" I cried trying my best to cover my naked body with my hands. "Get out!"

"Harmony, please...Let me take care of you. That's all I wanna do."

"But I don't want you in here, Kali!" I said wiping my tears. "Now please leave."

"Let me hold you and if you want me to leave after that, I'm out. I promise."

Kali took his shoes and t-shirt off and stepped into the shower in his jeans. I saw scars all over his body that resembled dog bites.

"What happened to you?" I asked seriously touching one of the scars. "You were bit by a dog or something?"

"Don't worry about that." He said rubbing my face. "Let me worry about you."

"I don't know about this, Kali. Forreal." Thoughts of how he acted earlier ran through my mind. He was obsessive and unpredictable and that scared me. If we had sex, and I put it on him, who knew how he would act then.

"Please, I just want to make you feel good. Let me do this for you."

I finally understood that he worshipped me and I knew then that Kali could come in handy. When he stood behind me, he massaged my shoulders and I immediately felt safe. His large hands massaged my body with tenderness and care. Then he took the washcloth and washed my pussy but it was raw and itchy so I took the rag from him and did it myself. My stomach started fluttering and I decided then that I wanted to fuck him. Whenever someone showed me attention, I wanted to take things to the next level and I never understood why.

"I was doing it too rough?" He asked me.

"Naw." I smiled wiping between my legs. "You weren't too rough."

His jeans were soak and wet and he looked so sexy with the water running all over his body. "You want me to leave?" He asked looking up at me.

"No, you can stay."

He took off his jeans and then his boxers and I saw his large dick standing before me. "Can I kiss you?" He asked me.

"Kali, I'ma be real with you, if you want to be with me like this, then you have to be able to keep it between me and you. I love Jace in my own way and don't want to lose him. Can you understand that?"

"I got you." He said seriously.

"You sure?"

"Yeah. I got you." He smiled.

That was his favorite saying, 'I got you.' But I think only he knew what that really meant.

"Well you can kiss me."

When he kissed me I was surprised at how soft his lips were. While I fell into his kisses, he parted my legs and entered my wet pussy. I wanted him to bust off inside of me, because if Jace didn't cum tonight, it would be hard for me to pass a baby off on him later. I needed to get pregnant within weeks of us having sex, because I wasn't sure if Jace would want to fuck me again. My mouth opened and I loved how he felt. The slickness of my juices surrounded his dick and I hoped he wouldn't get the same irritation Jace had earlier. When he appeared to be enjoying it so did I.

"Can I fuck you in your ass?"

"Huh?" I said wiping the water out of my face.

"I want to fuck you in the ass. You gonna let me?"

"Uh…Yeah, but don't cum in my ass. I want you to cum inside of me."

He turned me around and didn't enter me right away. Instead he bent down, took two fingers and slipped them into my asshole. Then he took his fingers out and sucked them. He did it again and again and I thought it was so weird. What exactly was he into?

"You used the bathroom today?" He asked me looking up at me.

"What?"

"Did you take a bowel movement today?"

"Earlier…Why? You smell something?"

"Naw."

But he seemed to be disappointed. So he stood up and he fucked me in the ass for a while before turning me around and reentering my pussy. I had to admit, he was the right size and I liked that about him. I was caught up in the feeling and had my eyes closed for most of the time but Kali appeared to not look away from me once.

"I'm feelin' you, Harmony." He said seriously. He lifted me up so that my legs surrounded his waist and my back pressed against the wet shower wall.

We were so caught up into the moment that I didn't hear Shirley enter the bathroom.

"HOLD UP! I KNOW GOT DAMN WELL YA'LL NOT FUCKING IN MY HOUSE!" Shirley said moving the shower curtain open, exposing our nakedness.

I jumped down and stepped outside the shower. Kali didn't bother to cover his naked body. "BITCH, GET OUT OF HERE!" I yelled walking toward the door to push her out.

"HARMONY, IF YOU WANT TO FUCK SO BAD, YOU BETTA GET YOUR OWN PLACE!"

"Shirley, get the fuck outta here before I go off!"

"I'M SERIOUS!"

"Oh…It's okay for me to lick you and suck Charles's dick for all those years but if somebody else wants to be with me and make me feel good, it's a problem?"

Silence.

It was the first time I'd ever talked about what she and Charles made me do out loud to her with someone else in the room. Embarrassed, Shirley finally walked out of the door. When she was gone Kali looked at me strangely.

"What did you mean *'lick you'* and *'suck Charles's dick'*?" He asked seriously.

"Kali, I don't want to talk about it. Okay?"

"Alright, but whatever happened between ya'll, is not your fault. I wish I could kill everybody who takes advantage of kids when they can't help themselves." He appeared to go somewhere else in his mind and I kissed him softly on the chest bringing him back to reality.

"Let's just worry about us. Okay?"

He lifted me back up and I wrapped my legs around his waist. His hand rested on the wall for support as he drilled into my pussy over and over again. As he pushed deeper into my cave I felt my body shiver. Who would have ever thought that Kali and me could be like this together? He was in sync with me and I was in sync with him.

"Mmmmmmm, you feel so good," I told him.

"I wish I could stay inside of you forever." He placed both hands on the wall and I wrapped my legs around him tighter. He pushed in and out of me over and over and I could feel his throbbing dick.

"I'm...I'm cuming, Harmony. Damn your pussy feels so good."

"It's okay to cum inside me," I told him. "I'm on the pill."

And then he did it. He released himself inside my pussy. I hoped this worked for my plan and I hoped Kali wouldn't be too weird afterwards. I guess only time would tell. And before long, that's exactly what it did.

IT'S ALL ABOUT THE MONEY

Harmony

I had been calling Jace to check on him every day. Tony told me he was feeling better but couldn't explain why he hadn't accepted my calls. I was starting to hate him for leaving me to deal with this kidnapping alone. And I was also hating him acting like we weren't together anymore. If that was what he wanted, he should at least be man enough to tell me.

After I was kidnapped I forbade anybody to talk about it around me. That went for Constance and Trip, too. Ebony is another nosey bitch and at first I wasn't going to even go to her cookout, but she begged me so I changed my mind.

'It Takes Two', by Rob Bass and DJ E-Z Rock blasted on the speakers and she had food for days spread out on the tables.

"Ya'll come in and make yourself comfortable," she said when we got there. "I'm gonna be roaming around but call me if you need me."

I tried to spot my next money prospect since Jace was blowing me off. I decided I was done fucking my grandmother and my uncle for a few measly bucks. Nothing but nickel and dime hustlers was there and I was irritated. I needed longer money if I was going to be set up the way I wanted. Why can't Jace just answer his phone? Then I wouldn't have to go through this.

"Ebony, before you leave, who got some smoke?" I asked. "I'm trying to get high tonight."

"Are you okay, Harmony? I know you been through a lot. Is Jace good?"

"Ebony, I'm not trying to talk about that. I'm asking you if you got some smoke."

She frowned a little. "Girl, you know how it is. Just mingle a little and see who got what. You know how stingy people are 'bout they shit though."

"So you don't have nothin'?"

"Naw. I'm fresh out."

She was lying and I knew it. When she bounced off I looked at her walk away. That northwest DC boogie ass bitch was so fuckin' fake. Everybody kept saying how pretty she was just because she had brown eyes and long hair when I thought she was just average. My shit went down my back so she couldn't fuck with me. She kept acting like she was so much better than everybody else when for real her house was no bigger than my grandmother's.

At about seven o'clock, I was drunk as shit and feeling good. Her house was filled with people running in and out of every room. And since she had so much going on, I had already plotted on taking the gold hoop earrings I saw her with the other day at school. I didn't really want them, I just didn't want her to have them.

When somebody brought in some vodka I drank half of it down and started to feel real light and horny. Maybe I would kick it with Kreshon later like he asked me too since Jace was still ignoring my calls.

"I thought you said it was gonna be some smoke here?" I asked Constance again.

"Girl, I hate when you drunk. You keep asking the same shit over and over again. You heard what Ebony said."

"Well ain't shit here but beer now." I said.

"That's 'cause you drank everything else." Trip laughed.

"I'm serious." I said swaying a little. I think I might've hit my limit after all. "I want to get high."

"Well I can't help you," Constance said tugging at the seat of her pants. "But you need to sit down, girl. You 'bout to fall."

"Fuck that," I told her. "I need a hit. I'm thinkin' about trying something harder. Like crack."

Trip and Constance looked at each other and then at me. "What?" Trip said.

"Girl, you been gettin' extra drunk lately," Connie said. "Maybe you should push back a little."

"Damn, Shirley!" I laughed.

"I'm serious. You need to chill out. You know you had too much when you start talking about smoking crack."

"Girl, please! Fuck that. I'm a grown ass woman. And I was just fucking with ya'll anyway."

I scratched my hands because the sores on them had gotten worse. When I did, Trip looked suspiciously at my hand and grabbed it.

"You know Paco got that same rash on his hands and feet. He allergic to something and he don't know what."

He has the same rash? I thought. *What the fuck is this shit?*

I snatched my hand from her. "Yeah...I'm allergic to something, too, I have to get it checked though. My doctor's appointment tomorrow."

Trip dropped the subject when we noticed Constance tugging at the seat of her pants again. Since I had been suffering with the same problem lately, I figured she must've gotten the same shit I did. Who burned who I didn't know.

"Bitch, why you keep scratching between your legs?" Trip pointed out. "Don't tell me you burning."

Constance looked at us worriedly and said, "I gotta tell ya'll something."

"What?" Trip said.

"I think Kreshon *did* burn me."

My heart started beating until I remembered they had no idea I was fucking their men. Truthfully Trip should be scratching, too.

"Are you sure?" I added.

"Yeah. I think so."

"Paco been snooping a lot lately, too. But what really fucks me up is that we don't talk a lot anymore. And if you know Paco, you know he gossips like a bitch. So if he not talking to me, who he talking to?"

"He sure do run his mouth like a bitch," I laughed. "Sometimes you don't even wanna hear the shit but he tells you anyway. Next thing you know, you mixed into some shit you didn't want to be mixed in to."

Silence.

My drunkenness was getting harder to control. Lately I could never tell when I had too much to drink because alcohol was my everything.

"How you know so much about Pac?" Trip said.

"Girl, please. How many times you tell me Paco talk too much?" I paused. "I'm just listening to you."

"Oh...Yeah." She paused, still looking at me strangely. "I just hope Evan don't learn his father's ways and think it's okay to lie and cheat on your girl." Trip continued.

"I'm sick of cheating ass niggas," Constance said. "If Kreshon really is cheating on me, I don't know what I'ma do."

"Girl, just drop it." Trip said. "You say the same thing over and over again."

"I won't stop it. What I'ma do if he dumps me for another girl?"

"Wait, I thought it was all about the money," Trip continued. "I mean, that's what you said the other day at school anyway."

"It is all about the money. Well...Kinda."

"So what you plan to do, Connie? Ask him? 'Cause you know he not going to tell the truth if he is cheating." I said.

"I don't have to ask him." She whispered.

"Then how you gonna find out?" Trip said.

"Remember when I told ya'll I had to meet up with Brittany?" She paused leaning in to us. "Well, I paid her to follow him for me. You know somebody bought her a new car."

"So." I said.

"Anyway, she don't live too far from him. I had her follow him for me the other day and she got something for me already. She said when she come back in town she gonna tell me who he's fucking but that I'm not going to like it."

My heart dropped. If she *did* follow him on the day I was with him, then she would have seen me going into the house with Kreshon.

"When...When do she get back in town?"

"In three days. She said it's a friend of mine too. Who ya'll think it is?"

I knew I had to plant the right seeds in her head now. If Brittany told her I was fucking Kreshon this could cause problems for me and Jace. The friendship I was prepared to lose but Jace, I wasn't.

"Well I can't stand Brittany's ass," I told her. "Me and her got into it awhile back and she proved then she could be fake. So if I were you, I wouldn't believe half of what that bitch tells me. For all we know, she may be fucking him, too."

"Too?" Trip repeated.

Damn, I'm talking too much. This alcohol got me all over the place.

"Yeah, too! Brittany already said she caught him cheating so what's to say Brittany not getting up with him, too?" I said. Then I turned around to Constance and said, "I'm just saying, you got to be smart, Constance. You can't trust bitches. Anyway why she can't just tell you over the phone?"

"She want her money first."

"Humph." I said. "Be careful, you may be paying her for lies."

Trip said, "So did you go to the doctors yet, Connie?" Trip said bringing us back to the point. "To check on the itching? Maybe it's a yeast infection or something."

Bobby Brown's, *'My Prerogative'*, blasted from the speakers.

"No, I'm going tomorrow though. I'm scared, ya'll. If he fucking some nasty bitch and they gave me something I'm goin' the fuck off."

"Girl, just because you got something don't mean she nasty." I said.

Both Constance and Trip looked at me. "Why don't it mean she's nasty?" Trip asked. "If she's burning somebody, she's a hot ass mess."

"That's ya'lls opinion not mine." I stated.

I saw the looks they gave each other out the corner of my eyes. "Yeah...It is my opinion." Trip continued.

As she was talking the burning sensation between my legs got so bad, I needed to cool it off. The only thing that worked for me was a cold washrag. And since I wasn't at home, I was gonna have to use one of Ebony's instead.

"Hold that thought," I told them. "I got to go to the bathroom right quick."

"Go 'head." Constance said. "We gonna see if we can find some smoke. Some more people here now."

"Okay, well if you find some don't forget to hold a little something for me."

After I left them, I bypassed a few people hanging in the hallways. I couldn't believe she let all these people in her house. Half of them I know she didn't know. When I got to the bottom of the stairwell, I looked around and slowly walked up the stairs, stumbling a bit.

I went to the bathroom upstairs, and once inside, I locked the door. Her bathroom colors were burgundy and cream and it was real comfortable. I allowed my jeans to fall by my ankles, followed by my panties. When I was done I sat on the edge of her toilet and opened my legs. She didn't have any toilet paper in the bathroom so I grabbed a pink washcloth on the rack and wet it with cool water. Then I placed it between my legs and pressed firmly. The coolness stopped the burning sensation right away and I wanted to stay in here all day. It was settled, there was no way I'd be able to go around like this. I had to go to the STD clinic tomorrow to find out what the fuck I had. And then there was Jace...And Kali. Did I burn them, too? I guess I'd soon find out.

When I was done, I opened the door and looked down the stairs. I could see shadows but no one appeared to be coming upstairs. So I ran across the hall and went into Ebony's room. Once inside I closed the door and locked it behind me.

It would be fucked up if she came upstairs and couldn't get into her own room so I was going to have to act fast. She had posters of Michael Jackson, Janet Jackson and New Edition everywhere and everything was neat and in its place.

Where the fuck are your earrings? I said out loud. When I happened upon a small pink jewelry box I knew they had to be in there. Inside the box were her earrings and two other sets. I don't know why I wanted the earrings. I guess hearing that her father gave them to her, made me miss mine even more and I hated her for that.

Since I was in her room, I decided to see if she had any cash. So I went through her dresser, found a few quarters and stuffed those in my pockets. *Fuck! I know this girl got something else in here. Maybe she got something under her bed. Everybody keeps shit under their bed.* I took another look at the closed bedroom door to make sure nobody was coming, and then I lifted her mattress and found a stuffed envelope. Inside of it was five hundred dollars in cash and weed in a small plastic baggy. *Fuckin' liar!* She said she didn't have smoke! Since I was up on some weed and some money, I stuffed the earrings in the envelope and then I placed the shit in my panties and moved to leave. When I was younger, I use to see my mother steal from my father and hide the money in her panties. And 'til this day, it was my favorite hiding space.

There was no way I could stay in the party after this. I had to make an excuse to go home. When I walked up to the door, I put my ear against it. I didn't hear anyone on the other side. But when I opened the bedroom door I ran into Trip leaving the bathroom. She walked up to me and looked at me suspiciously.

"What...Were you doing in Ebony's room?" She asked. "She in there?"

"Girl, I'm not doing nothing." I closed the door and looked down at myself quickly to make sure the budge from the envelope was not showing between my legs.

"Nothing?" She repeated. "Do Ebony know you were in her room?"

"I was using the phone okay? It ain't that big of a deal so drop it." I walked down the stairs and she was on my heels and I could feel her suspicious eyes burning a hole in the back of my neck. "What is wrong with you?" I said before we went deeper into the party. I didn't want people to overhear us in case she got hot and loud.

"If you were using the phone then why you acting all strange?"

"I'm acting strange because of how you trying to carry me."

"I'm just asking you a question, Harmony. Don't act all crazy."

"Are you my friend or not?"

"Don't be dumb."

"Answer the question." I said.

"You know I'm your friend."

"Okay, then...If you think I was doing something else in her room say it, but don't keep beating around the bush."

"It's not that deep," she said. "Let me go find Constance."

"Yeah you do that."

After my beef with her I figured it was time for me to plant a few seeds in Ebony's head. I could tell that Trip was going to say something to Ebony and I wanted to beat her to the punch. Plus what if she called the cops? So before I left, I found Ebony and pulled her to the side. The edge of the envelope I stuffed in my draws was scraping against my pussy lips making them uncomfortable. I had to walk like I was bowlegged to prevent from doing more damage. But I figured I only needed a few minutes with her and then I'd be out.

Pulling her away from a fine as nigga I said, "Ebony, I got to tell you something," I looked around us before I started speaking. "I saw Trip come out of your bedroom, and she had something in her hand."

"What?" Her eyes grew wide. "What she have?"

"I'm not sure, but it looks like an envelope and some earrings."

Her eyes grew wide. "What the fuck are you talking about?"

"You heard me, girl. And I think it's fucked up because you let us in your house, and then she go pull some shit like this." Then I paused and said, "Now I was up there too going to the bathroom. But I want you to look in my purse right now so you know I ain't got shit. In case she tries to lie on me."

She really looked inside, which meant she didn't trust me either. Then I flipped open my pockets so she can check those too. A few quarters fell out and I told her she could keep them. Besides, they were hers anyway.

When she was done I said, "See...I ain't got shit."

"Why would she do some shit like that to me?" She said to no one in particular. "I would expect that from anybody but her."

"Anybody like me?"

"No girl."

Yeah whatever. I thought. *I can't stand fake bitches.*

"I don't know why she did it to you, but I would appreciate it if you wouldn't tell her I told you. You know she one of my best friends. But right is right and wrong is wrong."

"Thanks, girl," she said trying to separate herself from me. I knew she was going to check on her room and then check Trip's ass when she found out her shit was missing. "I appreciate it."

"Okay, I gotta go home. I'ma rap to you later."

"You leaving already."

"Yeah, girl. I don't feel too good."

"You are kinda walking funny."

"I'ma call you later."

I moved as quickly as I could with an envelope between my legs. Once at the front door I could see Ebony approaching Trip from of my peripheral vision. I was halfway out the door when I heard Ebony yell, "Trip! I gotta talk to you!"

I closed the door behind me and hot tailed home. I ain't want to be anywhere near the beef when the shit hit the fan. Bitches stay keeping up shit, thank goodness that ain't me.

ONE WEEK LATER

Rick Boss
Jace

The weather was hotter in California than DC ever could've been when I stepped off of Rick's private jet. But the wind provided a nice smooth breeze and rustled the leaves on the palm trees around the landing. The sky was an ice cold blue and fluffy white clouds were scattered lightly.

"Jace, you made it," Rick said walking up to me placing a heavy hand on my shoulder. He was wearing cream linen pants suit, with a pair of Louis Vuitton sandals. His head was bald and he covered his eyes with dark shades. Two men were on each side of him and they were conducting heavy surveillance of the area.

My father had the same complexion as me but his eyes were lighter and he was much shorter. I stood at about 6'1 while he only reached a little over 5'4. People said that was one of the reasons he was so ruthless, because he had a short man's complex but I couldn't be sure. Rick was mixed with Mexican and black while my mother was straight African-American and his Mexican heritage could be detected in his voice.

"We have everything set up for you back at the house." He told me. "You should be very comfortable."

Here it was, I was born in L.A even though my heart screams Washington, DC.

"What's up? What's on your mind?" He asked.

"I can't believe I'm from here. I can barely remember shit about it."

"Trust me when I say it was for your own good. I would not have sent you away for so long, if I thought you would be safe here.

But from what I'm told, you've made quite a life for yourself in DC."

"I'm doing aight."

"Come...We have much to discuss."

We walked to a white limousine and a white man opened the door for me and said, "Welcome to California, sir."

I nodded and stepped inside the limo, looking around inside. Moments later, the bodyguards piled inside with us. He seemed to have a lot of people around him all the time. Two bottles of Moet sat in buckets and I shared a bottle with my father. It didn't matter that I was only seventeen and would be eighteen in a month, to him I was now a man. As I sat in my seat, I thought about everything that happened and how I almost was responsible for Harmony's murder. Shit wasn't going the way I planned with us but fuck it, it was what it was.

I looked at his bodyguards again and saw that they seemed to be more interested in what was going on outside of the car, than they were with what was going on inside. It made me think at any moment someone would start firing at us.

"Don't worry, Jace. You're safe here." Rick said.

He must've seen it in my face. "I'm not worried." I told him remembering my ordeal a week ago.

We drove for ten minutes before we pulled up to his new house. I hadn't been there since I visited briefly last year. When we pulled up in the driveway, a fence and men in black expensive suits surrounded the large property. All of them were armed and wearing wired ear plugs in one ear. When the limo stopped a young Pakistan man in his early thirties opened the door and Rick got out and follow him.

"Welcome to California, Jace. We have been waiting for you. I am Ahmed, and I am here to see that anything you need is taken care of." He told me.

"Thank you." I nodded grabbing my bag.

As my father spoke to a few of his staff members off to the side, I walked through the large foyer covered in marble and gold. The ceilings had elaborate paintings on them and everything looked larger than life. Two men followed me and I got the impression that they were protecting me and not watching me. Even in the house my life was not safe. I had to find this nigga Massive and I had to find him soon.

To my right was a huge dining room, which could seat about twenty people, and to my left was a large entertainment room filled with large screen TV's and a huge stereo system. When I walked upstairs and saw six closed cherry wood doors. I stared at all of them wondering which one I would be in while I was here.

"Right this way, sir," Ahmed said walking up behind me before walking ahead of me to lead the way.

I didn't even know he was following us. If I was gonna run a successful operation, I had to remember to check my surroundings at all times. It didn't matter where I was since it was evident that for as long as Massive was alive, that he'd be after me. And although the man who kidnapped us was not Massive, but one of his flunkies, I knew I could never afford to let them catch me slipping again. When I walked into my room, I could tell it was recently designed for me. Everything smelled new and a large TV was on my favorite station, MTV.

"Please let me know if you'll be needing anything else." Ahmed said walking to the door. "I am here to serve you."

I walked deeper into my room and sat on the edge of the bed. It was the first time I had been alone since I'd been kidnapped. I made a call to Tony Wop to be sure my plans for my operation were in motion. When Tony told me that both Herb Dayo and Sick Sense were missing I got noid.

"We haven't been able to get a hold of 'em, man. Something's up."

"What about Kali?"

"He around…But you know that's your man, not mine. I deal with him when I have to."

"Well deal with him now. If Massive's involved, you need to be careful and Kali not afraid of doing what's needed."

"Do you believe him about the girl thing?"

"Not over the phone. I'll rap to you about that later."

"Aight…I know you got a lot to deal with, but call the girl Brittany when you get a chance. I ran into her at Karen's house, and she said she gotta talk to you. Said it was important."

"Aight." I said ending the call.

Then I called Brittany, a chick I fucked on the side every now and again. As a matter of fact, we had gotten together right before my trip to L.A.

"Jace, I been trying to reach you! We gotta talk!" She said hyped.

"What's up? Why you sound all extra?"

"Jace, are you still fuckin' Harmony?" I hated when she asked me that shit because before we broke up, she knew I was. "I need you to tell me right now."

"Jace, come downstairs. We're having a meeting." Rick called from the intercom within my room interrupting our call.

"I gotta go."

"Jace, wait!"

I hung up, hit the intercom button and said, "I'm on my way."

I don't know what shit she was on but it was a mistake calling her ass anyway. I was here for business, not to be rapping to no bitch. When I got downstairs, I saw a few men inside the large dining room. They all stood when they saw me enter, before sitting back down.

"Gentlemen, this is my son, Jace Sherrod." Rick said clapping his hands. They all clapped before stopping abruptly.

"Welcome, son," one man said.

"We've been wanting to meet you officially," said another. "Your father has told us a lot about you."

"Please introduce yourselves." Rick advised everyone.

I wondered how he could tell anybody about me, when he really didn't know me.

One man stood up. His skin was real light and his nose was so crooked it looked broke. "The name's Russ Gamber." He said pointing to himself.

"He's muscle." Rick said. "He makes sure I'm protected wherever I go before I get there."

"That's right, and it's because of me you still alive today."

"Awe, here he goes again sucking his own dick," one man said. The room erupted in laughter.

"Well it's true. I don't miss a thing, son. If there's a problem, I smell it miles away." He continued. "Trust me, around me your father is beyond safe."

"Yeah...Look at the fuckin' nose of yours. What else you gonna do with that thing but smell." Another man said.

"Or fuck a bitch with it! I heard it's bigger than his dick."

All of the men laughed again.

"Fuck you!" Gamber said.

Someone else stood up and said, "Anyway, son, I'm Sammy Batters. I run distribution." Sammy was shorter than my father and his skin was very dark.

"Sammy's the man who will have everything set up for you in DC." He paused. "You need anything for the business, you call on him first." Rick added.

As Sammy sat down, another man stood up." And I'm Leo Lips. I help Sammy with distro in California and I am in charge of meeting our connect."

Leo looked Spanish and judging by the tattoos all over his arms, I could tell he was either involved in gangs in the past, or still active. He also had a lot of tattoos of babies over his arms and I could tell he had a lot of children. Leo also seemed nervous and out of place and that made me uneasy.

"Other than me, Leo's the only one who has direct access to our connect. We are dealing with some Arabians who've found their way into the industry. But we may be moving over to the Russians soon. Right now, the Russians have lower prices." Rick said.

"So why not drop the Arabians and do what we have to do?" I questioned.

Rick smiled. "Look at my son, thinking outside the box already." He paused. "Let's just say that for now, I'm doing what's best for our operations. Sometimes rocking the boat unnecessarily can cause more problems than it's worth. You should run your operation the same way." He said leveling a serious look at me.

"I'm Chin Chu, I'm one of Rick's lawyers."

Chin was Chinese and had a serious glare on his face. Even when he laughed earlier his face expression remained the same.

"And I'm Terrace Strong, you met me before, a long time ago. I'm your father's other attorney."

"Oh that's right. You handled Cornell's daughter's estate. What did he leave her before he died? A million?"

Terrace looked at me and I knew then that she didn't get anywhere near that amount of money. "Yeah...About that."

"You still talk to her anymore, Jace?" Rick asked me.

"Not since that shit with Massive's peoples kidnapping us." I told him.

"That's right." He paused. "Massive...Well...That brings us to business at hand." Rick said preparing to take a seat. "So let's get right to it. We have a lot to discuss."

"Massive is planning something now and I don't know what."

"You may be right. Two members of my crew have gone unaccounted for and we can't get in contact with them." I paused. "The only thing is, I figured he'd leave DC, after the failed kidnap attempt."

"He'll do whatever he can to get at you. So it's quite possible." He paused. "Okay, these are the issues at hand. The DC market is growing rapidly. Crack is the drug of choice now and we are in every position to provide the choice. The problem is, Massive won't allow us to move smoothly. We've already lost five good men by his hands and although we've taken out his entire crew that doesn't make him more vulnerable. It makes him invincible."

"Why?" I asked.

"Because unlike me, son, he doesn't have anything else to lose. And if he hurts you, I don't know what I'm going to do." he took a deep breath and said, "So, I don't intend on letting him catch you."

The men moved around in their seats because Rick's show of emotion made them uncomfortable.

"Tony Wop is staying in DC to help you get things off the ground. I've taught him everything I know, Jace. When you're really ready to stand on your own, he'll release you to run things. Now the reason why I asked these men here today is because over the next few months, before you go back to DC, they will give you a few skills necessary to be the best in the drug game. But with my guidance you'll be even better than me."

"I appreciate the opportunity, Rick."

"I know you do, son. But there's one thing you have to do before we get started."

Everyone shuffled in their seats again and I knew something serious was coming my way. "What's that?"

"Russ, bring her out."

Russ went into another room off of the dining room we were in. Then he wheeled a Spanish lady into the living room in an office chair. Her hair was matted down to the sides of her face and her makeup was smeared all over her eyes.

"Who is she?" I asked standing up straight.

"Your first kill."

"What she do? I mean, why kill her?"

The men in the room looked at one another and I could tell I made a comment they weren't comfortable with. I guess questioning Rick no matter how unreasonable was out of the question.

Rick walked around the table and up to me. Then he placed his hand firmly on my shoulder. "Jace, I know I haven't spent much time with you. If I had, you would know better than to question my authority." I felt the seriousness in his voice. "So I'll answer you once and from here on out, you are never to question me again. Got it?"

"Yes."

"Good...The woman before you was a nobody, just some girl who sold her body to me for money. Now after meeting you," he smiled, "her life will have purpose, and meaning."

"And why's that?" I asked staring at the woman who was pleading to me with her eyes.

"She'll be the reason I can know that no matter what, you'll be willing to do what's necessary for our operation. She'll be the reason our bond will be strengthened. And she will be the reason that more than anything *you* will know that you are ready." He paused. "I heard about the situation in DC, Jace." He paused. "You know, with Bam and the kid."

I swallowed hard.

"You know your men will never respect you if you aren't willing to go the extra mile."

"I thought bosses didn't have to get their hands dirty. I thought all I had to do was give the right orders and watch the money roll in."

"All chiefs have at one time or another, been soldiers. You are no different." He said seriously. "Jace, your enemy will come to you in all nationalities...Both female and male, some young...Some old. And you have to be ready to make the hard decisions when the right times come. One of those right times is now. "

I looked at my father and then at the men around the room. He was right and I knew it. "Where's the gun?"

He smiled and said, "A gun is so impersonal. Here's a knife." He placed it in my hand. "Now kill her like you mean it."

LOCAL NEWS

Constance

Constance sat glued to the TV watching the local news. The news was airing a story about a brash outbreak of syphilis within the DC area amongst people under the age of 21. In less than two weeks over twenty people in the southeast DC area had gone to a free clinic for testing only to find out they had been infected. Although those were the people who had gone to the clinic, there were many more who didn't exhibit any signs, and were unaware of how bad things had gotten for them, too. The trouble was, the longer the disease stayed in their blood system without treatment, the worse things became. Before long, it would be untreatable and may even lead to death.

Constance thought about the news she had recently been given from the doctor that she too had contracted syphilis. Despite it all, what hurt worse was that Brittany had told her that her best friend had been sleeping with her boyfriend. She wondered, could it be true and decided to talk to Trip first.

Meanwhile on the other side of DC, at Ebony's house in Northwest, she was crying after learning that after doing her best to maintain a safe-sex relationship, that she had also contracted syphilis. She didn't know that had Harmony not sat her diseased ridden ass on the edge of her toilet seat, which was oozing vaginal secretions filled with the virus, and had she not followed behind her and sat on the edge of the seat by mistake too, that she would not have contracted the disease. How could she? Instead she immediately blamed her friend.

But Constance and Ebony were just two cases of those infected by Harmony's raunchy irresponsible wrath. Many others would be finding out that they were also infected. Although not everyone

would ever discover that she was involved many more would find
out in the months to come.

TWO WEEKS LATER

Southeast, Washington, DC
Bring The Pain
Harmony

All day my stomach had been bothering me. I tried everything I could to make it go away, but nothing worked. At first I thought it was the fact that I hadn't spoken to Jace in three weeks. But when the smells of certain foods made my stomach churn, I realized it was much more. I had to be pregnant. If only I could tell Jace, I'm sure he would take me back and we could work things out.

When my phone rang right before I left the house, I knew it was probably Trip, Ebony or Constance. They kept saying the same things over and over and I was tired of hearing it. When I did speak to them, Trip asked me did I tell Ebony she stole from her. And Ebony said Trip said it was me who stole her shit and all she wanted was her stuff back. While Constance called me to tell me that Brittany said that Ebony was fucking her man. I was wondering why Brittany didn't tell Constance it was me the moment she found out Kreshon was cheating or why she hadn't told Jace. Now it all made sense, he was fucking Ebony on the side, too and had gotten caught. Was I a little mad that Kreshon was with both of us? Yes. But I still didn't need any of the drama when all I wanted was Jace back.

I put on my gold hoop earrings, with the word Princess in the middle, courtesy of Ebony and was leaving out of my house on my way to the store when Kali pulled up. I could tell he was coming into a little money but knew he'd never make as much money as Jace. He parked and jumped out of his 300 ZX and a pair of Versace shades covered his eyes. The leather strap holding his hatchet still on his back.

"You aight?" He asked me after parking his car. Sometimes he was real nice and at other times he could be very mean. It seemed like any little thing could set him off. "You don't look too good."

"No...I been sick all week, I think I'm coming down with something."

"You want me to grab you somethin' to eat?"

"Naw. I *was* going to A & B store to get some liquor, but now I'm thinking about going back inside to lie down now. What you doing here?"

"I was tryin' to see if you wanted go see that Beverly Hills Cop 2, joint." He tugged at his baseball cap. I don't know if it was because we had been fucking ever since our first encounter in the shower or what. But for some reason, he looked cuter each time I saw him. It probably was the money.

"I don't know if I'ma be able to sit in no movie theater feeling like this, Kali. I'm fucked up."

"Well why you drinkin' then?"

"'Cause I do what the fuck I want to, that's why." I frowned.

"Fuck all that...I'm tired of doin' the same shit with you. I wanna take you out. If you can sit at home and get drunk by yourself, then you can hang out with me."

Although I didn't feel too well, I knew if I didn't go, he would get upset.

"You gonna buy me a bottle of vodka?"

"Yeah, but you need to be drinkin' ginger ale, too."

I rolled my eyes. "Okay, get me the ginger ale and the vodka and I'll go with you."

"Bet."

Before he left, I decided to bring up the kidnapping. The cops hadn't found the girl and I wanted to see where Kali's head was at. The only thing was, Kali never talked about the details of the kidnapping to me. At this point I had only heard it first hand from Paco, and secondhand from Jace. Truthfully, I wasn't supposed to know anything. But I figured if I could get him to tell me something, I would have something over his head, like he held the fact that we were fucking behind Jace's back over mine.

"Kali, you trust me, right?"

"Yeah...Why?"

"Because if you do, then I wanna know if you had something to do with…That situation."

Kali looked behind him and back at me. Someone was walking up the street and he let him pass before speaking.

"How could you know?"

"I just do, Kali."

"That ain't a good enough reason."

"Because I know you and I care about you." I said as believably as possible. "I could tell by the way that you were acting that something was up. Talk to me. You can trust me."

He looked down at his new sneaks and said, "I don't wanna talk about Charles…So I'ma leave it at that."

"Charles?" I said confused. "My uncle?"

"Isn't that what you were talkin' about?"

"No…" I paused. "I'm talking about the girl."

"Oh," he said walking a few feet away from me. "I…I thought you were askin' me somethin' else."

My heart was pumping wildly in my chest. "But why did you say something about my uncle?"

"No reason," he smiled. "And as far as the girl, I think you should leave it alone. Too many people know too much already."

"So I guess you don't trust me?" I said sitting on my steps. "I thought we were best friends, Kali. And ever since we've been making love, I thought we been closer. So if that's how you feel, that hurts me. A lot."

"We are close," he said walking up to me, sitting on the step next to my foot. Looking up at me he said, "I did what I had to do for me and Jace. So let's just say she won't be showing up at school no more. Ever."

I had something over his head now.

"I appreciate you protecting me, and Jace. You are so loyal," I said gassing him up. He started smiling and I couldn't believe how emotional he really was. It was evident that just like me, all he wanted was love. But unlike me, he did a bad job of hiding his feelings. "I don't know what I would do if I didn't have you."

"You don't have to worry 'bout that, because as long as you alive, you going to always have me in your life. You'll see…I got you."

There he goes again with that, *I got you*, shit. Every time he said it he gave me the creeps. And what did he mean by as long as I'm alive?

"You serious about the movies though?" He asked skipping the subject.

"I said yes, Kali. What time you gonna be back?"

"I'ma scoop you up in a couple of hours. You gonna be home right?" He said standing up and getting back into his car.

"Yeah...But if I'm not, pick me up over Nut and Cherry's house." He looked strange.

"Why you be hanging over there all the time?"

"Kali, don't nobody be checking for you or talking about you when I'm over there if that's what you thinkin'."

"Do she know we fucked?" He asked me.

"I won't tell her if you won't." I smiled. "So what, ya'll some kinda weird couple or somethin' now."

"I'll be back *here* later," he said with an attitude. "I'm not scoopin' you from her crib."

"Whatever!"

"Aight, I'ma check you later. But I hope you know you gonna have to stop that drinking shit soon."

"Why you say that?"

"Cause you pregnant. And if you really are, it's a girl. I don't want my kid lookin' all deformed and shit."

I was shocked because he said out loud exactly what I had known all along. Had I just fucked Jace and not Kali, Kreshon and Paco, I'd be on cloud nine. Because giving Jace a baby could set me up real good, I mean, what man wouldn't want a son? I wasn't even thinking about having a girl because I have too much style with me to raise a bitch. I knew out of this body could only come a boy.

"I don't know about all that. I'ma have to find out if I'm pregnant first."

"Well I'ma buy you one of them pregnancy test joints from Peoples Drug store. You need to know if you are 'cause you ain't gonna be able to drink no more. I'm serious 'bout that shit, Harmony."

I don't know what he talking about because pregnant or not, I ain't have no intentions on putting down the bottle. My grandmother told me she drank the entire time she was pregnant with my mother and she was okay.

"Whatever, I'll take the test tonight but just don't forget my liquor."

He smiled and said, "You know you 'bout to have my seed right?"

"Kali, if I'm pregnant, it could be Jace's. You know that."

To be honest it could have been anybody's, I couldn't be sure. What I was sure about was that Jace was my target. And even if Kali's blood did pump through my son's veins, Kali wouldn't know about it.

"I'm not even worried 'bout that shit. My nut too strong to take second place. If you pregnant, it's definitely mine. And like I said, it's a girl."

I felt like punching him in the face. Having a little girl was one of the last things on my mind followed by having his baby.

He was about to pull off when I remembered I wanted to ask him something. I missed Jace and wanted him to know that I was thinking about him while he was in L.A. Even if I had to stop fucking other dudes, I was willing to do that.

"Kali, have you talked to Jace?" I paused. "I mean…Did he even ask about me?"

Kali turned around and looked toward the front of the car. Then he turned back to me and said, "Why?"

"Because I wanted to see if he was okay. And how come every time I mention his name to you it's a problem?"

"What difference do it make how he is, Harmony? He not tryin' to see you."

"I don't believe you."

"He fucked you, had you kidnapped and didn't call you not one time to make sure you were okay. The dude ain't tryin' to be bothered…But I am."

"Have you forgotten that you are with, Cherry? You act like I'm your girl or somethin'."

"That's me and her business. And I ain't talkin' 'bout her right now."

Niggas kill me. Always want the world but jump on you if you want the same.

"You know what, I don't even care about what you and Cherry do." I said feeling a wave of nausea coming on. "And as far as Jace's concerned, he probably feels bad that I almost got hurt after that kidnap shit. So stop trying to come in between us. "

An angry glare came over his face and he said, "I don't know what happened between ya'll, but he made it clear that he ain't fuckin' with you no more. You need to move on."

"Whatever," I said waving him off.

"What is it, Harmony? The fact that he got money?" He jumped out of the car and dug in his pocket pulling out a wad of cash. "Here...Here you go!" He threw five hundred dollar bills in my face before they hit the ground. Some of the bills scratched me and stung. "Take it, since that's all you care about."

"What the fuck is wrong with you?!" I asked him.

"You an ungrateful, bitch! That's what's wrong with me." Then he started looking wild-eyed around him. He reminded me of Jack Nicholson in that movie, 'The Shining'. "You gonna have me do something I don't wanna do to you."

"You know what, fuck you." I wanted the money but I didn't want him to know it so I wasn't going to pick it up. I was on my way back inside the house when he came up behind me, grabbed me by my neck and pushed me to the ground.

"Pick it up! Bitch, I'm not fuckin' around with you!" When I didn't do it fast enough, he gripped my neck so tight it felt like it would break. I managed to finally get the money in my hand, but I scraped my knees in the process. "Now be ready when I come back to scoop you up. You gonna take that pregnancy test first and if you pregnant, you gonna stop drinkin'. Do I make myself clear? Don't make me fuck you up. Answer me!"

I was scared because if he could beat someone who could possibly be pregnant with his child, what else could he do? "Y...Yes. I'm clear."

He let me go.

"Don't make me come lookin' for you later tonight." He said walking back to his car.

When he was done with me, he jumped in his car and pulled off. Kali was changing and becoming more obsessive and I hoped my decision to give him some pussy wouldn't come back and haunt me later.

With a fist full of money, and a sore neck, I was about to call a cab to go to the liquor store. With everything that Kali was giving me, I needed a drink badly. But before I could go into the house and place the call, Paco pulled up. He had an evil look on his face, just as bad as the one Kali had just given me.

"Get the fuck in my car, Harmony." He said parking his Acura in front of me.

"Naw...I gotta go." I could tell he was mad and I didn't feel like dealing with him.

I ran into the house and into Shirley. She was drunk and mad that Charles had still not been home. Also, the school board was threatening to call child protective services because of the allegations I made about sexual abuse to Mrs. Duncan.

Glaring at me she said, "What kinda trouble you bringin' in here now?"

I locked the door and said, "Shirley, somebody wants to hurt me out there. I can't talk now."

When I moved toward my room she blocked me and said, "So, what you gonna do for me, if I let you stay inside?"

"What?" I asked confused. "What do you mean, *if you let me stay inside?*"

"Harmony, don't act like you don't know what I'm talking about. You haven't taken care of me for a while, so what you gonna do for me if I let you stay? Since you got the people at school in our business anyway."

"Shirley, fuck you!" I said attempting to walk around her.

Right before I could turn the corner, she grabbed me by my hair, opened the door and threw me outside. I banged on the door but she wouldn't open it. And when I turned around, I saw Paco standing before me.

"Do you want to walk to the car, or do you want me to fuck you up?"

"I'll walk." I said still angry with Shirley.

He pushed me inside of his car and walked toward the driver's side. Then he got inside and pulled off violently not talking for a little over a minute. To me it seemed like forever.

"Syphilis, Harmony? You gave me fuckin' Syphilis?" He said hitting the steering wheel.

"I don't know what you talking about." I lied.

I did have Syphilis and the nurse told me it was bad too. She said whenever there were sores on the hands and feet, like there were on mine, I had it for a while. She also told me I had the frothy green discharge because I had a sexually transmitted disease called Trichomoniasis. That would explain the odor and the itching. So did I burn him? Maybe or maybe not! But he act like he didn't want the pussy. Ain't nobody force him to fuck me raw. He really had a nerve considering he didn't bother to ask for a condom either. Fuck him, fuck his bitch and fuck his dick.

"You better go see Trip about that shit 'cause I'm clean."

"Bitch, stop lyin' to me! Tell me the truth! You gave me that shit didn't you? And it's 'cause of you I might've gave it to my girl."

"Trip told me you had sores on your hands and feet, too. So how I know you ain't give it to me?"

"Trip ain't got it...At least she didn't say nothing to me about it. So this problem is between me and you."

"You know what, let me the fuck outta this car!" I said pulling on the car door before he took my head and mashed it against the window while he steered the car with the other hand.

"You ain't nothin' but a, gutter bitch! A fucking stank hoe!" He continued pushing my head so hard, my temples throbbed. I was sure the glass would crack any minute. Then he stopped the car and said, "You better never let me see you walk these streets again. You hear me, bitch?!"

"Okay, just let me out!"

Between these niggas and Shirley, if I was pregnant, they were gonna beat this baby out of me.

"And just so you know," he continued, "a group of bitches talkin' about jumpin' you until they draw blood. Everybody know you throwin' around a diseased pussy! It don't sound like they fuckin' around with you either. And if I ever catch you out here, I'ma hand you right over to them. You better be glad I gotta go get my son." He said as spit escaped his mouth. He was beyond mad. "Matta fact, I'm not gonna even call you Harmony no more 'cause ain't nothin' about you harmonic. I don't know what the fuck your peoples were thinkin' naming you that. From here on out, your name is Miss Burns!" He screamed. "Now get the fuck out my car."

I hopped out before he could change his mind and realized I was stranded in the middle of nowhere. I was left alone trying to think about what I was going to do and suddenly, for the first time in my life, I realized that DC, the place I'd known since my father was murdered, was not for me anymore.

VICIOUS

Jace

I was riding in my limo, thinking about my eighteenth birthday when the car phone rang. I turned the Tupac tape down and answered. I had been in California for a month, and I didn't feel like the same dude. I was on some whole otha shit and seen a lot of things in my short time here. Rick's team made me look at life differently and I was ready to hustle and hustle hard. Knowing I could take everything I learned from L.A, back to DC and rule.

"Hello." I answered, sipping on some Moet.

"Jace, everything cool on our end. We ready to move on them spots you had us check out." Kali said. "Them niggas tried to come at us sideways at first, but after we put a few of them on their backs, they got with the program. Basically, southeast DC is yours."

I smiled and said, "You sure? I don't want no problems"

"I'm positive."

"Where, Tony Wop? Why he ain't call?"

"What, you don't want an update from me?"

"I ain't sayin' that, but you got other shit to be worried about. Like that shit at the zoo." I said referring to Bam and his daughter. Bam was burned and scattered over Hains Point in DC, but his daughter's body had never been found.

"And I said shit good. Don't worry 'bout it. Did anything come up yet?"

"Naw."

"I told you...I got you."

This nigga was fuckin' me up with this nonchalant bullshit. I was lookin' for the first chance to get rid of him, but I knew it wasn't now.

"What about Herb Dayo and Sick Sense? Any word from them?"

"Naw, homie. I think Massive had his fist on that shit."

When my pager went off, I knew it was my new girl Antoinette, a chick my father hooked me up with while I was here. She didn't ask a lot of questions and was more than happy to do anything I needed. She was much older than me but told me she never fucked anybody as good as me before and she even challenged my age. Antoinette was different than the bitches I usually got up with and I liked that about her. But I still did miss, Harmony.

"Aight, hopefully something will come up," I paused. "But what's up with, Harmony?"

"Not much. She still fucked up about you not callin' after the kidnapping."

After going to the doctors, and finding out she gave me syphilis, I knew I wasn't fuckin' with her no more. I couldn't get over the fact that she burned me. And what was really fucked up was that I gave it to Brittany. What kind of shit is that? I wouldn't even be asking him about her, had she not saved my life.

"I probably shoulda called her." I paused. "Is she okay though?"

"Uh...I been meaning to tell you...shit has changed with her since you been gone."

"What happen?"

"She pregnant. With some niggas kid. I think he live out Maryland or somethin'. But people sayin' she don't know who the father is. Shawty, loose booty. They callin' her Miss Burns and everything. Good thing you stop fuckin' with her."

"Pregnant by a nigga out Maryland, huh?"

"Yep."

"Fuck her." I said wondering if it could be possible for the kid to be mine even though I didn't bust that night. "She as good as dead to me."

"I feel you. Fuck that nasty, slut."

I laughed and said, "Don't tell her I asked about her either. I don't want her gettin' the wrong impression."

"It is what it is...But look, I'ma be real with you on some shit. She knows about the zoo. Matta of fact, she knew a week after the shit happened."

Silence.

"How she know, I ain't tell her shit then."

"Then?"

"I mean, I never told her about it."

"I don't know, but I think she told the zoo keepers too." I continued referring to the cops she said showed up at her house. "They showed up at her crib."

Silence.

"You there, nigga?"

"Uh…Yeah."

"Ya'll still cool?"

"We were, but I'm not sure about that shit now."

"Watch your back. I thought I knew her pretty good and I was wrong."

"I will."

"I know ya'll cool, but if I were you, I'd stay away from her."

"*I got you*." He said.

"What you mean *you got me*? I ain't tellin' you that for you to get nothin'." I said, knowing that *I got you*, usually ended up in murder.

"Naw…I'm saying it's cool." He paused. "You sure you okay though?"

I was really feeling Harmony but she had too much shit going on. "Never better, playa. I'ma get up with you later though."

When I hung up with him I addressed my attention to my driver. "Jessup, take me past Antoinette's house. I wanna get up with her before I leave."

"I'm right on top of it, sir."

⏺━━⏺

I was back in Washington DC and I was jive glad. Don't get me wrong, L.A was beautiful but I'm a city nigga and couldn't take being away from home for too long. Plus I had bought a nice crib out Maryland and was moving my stuff today.

Everything was in my place when I remembered I left a box of shoes at my aunt's crib. The moment I came back outside, I saw Harmony walking across the street. Even though she was reckless, she was so fucking pretty. But I let that shit hold me up for too long and now I was done.

"Jace," she said running across the street. "When you get back in town?"

One of the bodyguards Rick sent to protect me stopped her from approaching. Security was tight around me since Massive made it known that he wouldn't rest until he counted my bones. I would never be by myself until he was found dead.

"Don't come any closer, mam." Kevin told her.

Kevin was 6'4, darker than night and very muscular. He couldn't ride in certain cars because they were too small for him. He never said much but he always listened.

She looked at me and said, "Can we talk, Jace? Please."

"We ain't got shit to talk about. I'm busy right now." I said getting into my limo.

"Jace, please. This is important."

I looked at my bodyguard and told him, "We gonna talk in the car."

"No problem, sir. I'll keep an eye on things out here. Let me know if you need me though."

He put the box in the trunk and stood next to my window in case I called. When she climbed into the limo, I couldn't help but notice her beauty. I know she said she was black and that her mother was light skin but to me she looked like she was mixed with something else. I'd seen enough mix breed chicks in California to know the difference. She had Spanish in her blood whether she knew it or not.

"What you want, Harmony?"

"Did I do something wrong? I mean...Why haven't you called me?" The moment she opened her mouth, I could tell she was drunk.

"You been drinkin'?"

"Yes," she said under her breath. "Why?"

"Just askin', you can do whatever the fuck you want to. You ain't my girl no more."

"Can you tell me why you haven't called?"

"'Cause I had shit to handle in California, that's why."

"But you didn't even call to see if I was okay after we were kidnapped. You didn't even say thank you for saving your life."

"So you think you saved my life?" I told her pouring me a cup of Moet. "What that make you feel better or somethin'?"

"No! What would make me feel better is if you would talk to me."

Silence.

"We don't have nothin' to talk about but I will say, thank you for looking out. And then thank you for givin' me syphilis."

Silence.

"I...I don't know what you talking about."

"Harmony, niggas is calling you Miss Burns now. The whole block knows you a whore and I hear you got a hit on your head. You over."

"Miss Burns?" She said.

I didn't know if it was the first time she'd heard the name or not.

"Yeah, word got around that you burned half of DC." I could tell she was about to cry but I didn't care. "Now is there anything else, 'cause lookin' at you makes me sick?"

"Jace, I'm pregnant." She paused. "With your baby."

"What...How you figure it's mine?"

"I got tested, Jace. I'm pregnant and I'm having our baby."

Shit didn't add up. Number one, even though she think I busted the night in the motel, I didn't. Number two, Kali told me she was pregnant by some nigga in Maryland. Number three, even if Kali didn't tell me she was pregnant by somebody else, she was burning. So she had to have fucked somebody else other than me. This chick is raunchy.

"Yeah, but you get around. With the mileage you put on that thing, you don't know who baby it is. Plus somebody told me, the nigga who got you pregnant with live out Maryland."

"What? I mean...Who told you I get around? And who told you the baby was somebody's out Maryland?"

"You still not admitting to burning me, huh?"

"It wasn't me." She paused. "Can you really tell me that you didn't fuck somebody else, Jace? Be honest."

I couldn't tell her I hadn't fucked nobody else because I had fucked Brittany. But I didn't have syphilis before I got with her. And what about the sensation I felt when I was inside of her. Her pussy was loaded with niggas nut from niggas around the way.

"So you tryin' to tell me that you don't get around?" I said. "And that you not pregnant by some nigga out Maryland?"

"No, and whoever told you some shit like that is a mothafuckin' liar!"

I wanted to believe her but now was not the time. I needed to think things through alone.

"Look, I'm 'bout to bounce. I'ma holla at you later."

"I'm not leaving here until you talk to me."

"Look at you! You half drunk and you talkin' 'bout being pregnant! You don't think shit wrong with that?"

"And I'm gonna stop drinking for me and the baby." She paused. "But if you don't wanna be with me I don't care anymore."

"That baby ain't mine."

"I promise on my mother's life that the baby growing inside of me is yours."

"Put it on your father."

Silence.

I opened the car door and said, "Kevin, get this bitch outta my car."

"Jace, why can't you believe me?"

"Cause I ain't bust inside of you that's why." I paused. "How the kid gonna be mine when I ain't even bust?"

Before she could respond again, Kevin whisked her out of the car by her arm.

"You gonna wish you didn't treat me like this!" She cried. "You gonna wish it real soon."

When she was gone I thought about the follow-up appointment I had with my doctor tomorrow. And then my pager went off again. It was my cousin, so I picked up my car phone and called Tony Wop.

"Jace, they saying Massive is back in town man and he got a whole rack of niggas who's working with him. Their mission is to get at you."

Shit just got serious."

CONTROL FREAK

Harmony

I be glad when I get a car! 'Cause if I had one I would've been able to get to Kali's bitch ass quicker than my feet were carrying me. I knew he was the only one who told Jace I got pregnant by somebody out Maryland. He was always hollering about Maryland niggas this and Maryland niggas that. Since I was high off the alcohol, I was ready to step to him.

It took me awhile to find out where he was at and when I walked up on him he was in front of his old house, talking to Edge, Kreshon and Paco. Without the others seeing him, Paco made a slick neck motion with his hand.

"Kali, we have to talk," I said gripping him by the elbow. Trying not to look at Paco.

He faced me, looked me up and down and gave me a black look. "Give me a second," he said stepping away from them. "Why you coming at me all hard and shit?" And then he paused and said, "Hold up, you been drinking?"

"Fuck all that! Did you tell Jace a lot of dudes fucked me? And that I got pregnant by somebody out Maryland?" I tried not to look at Kreshon and Paco since I'd been with them on many occasions.

"Why the fuck you talkin' to Jace?"

"Answer the question!" I yelled holding my ground. "Why would you do some shit like that, Kali? I know it was you!"

"'Cause that's what I heard. Don't act like it ain't true either, Miss Burns." He laughed.

I looked over at Paco and Kreshon who were looking at me with hate in their eyes. Niggas kill me with the bullshit. They were acting like girls.

"Kali, you tripping hard." I said seriously. "Now you got him thinking he not the baby's father."

"He might not be."

"There is a chance he is, Kali. And you know that."

"You know what, there's a chance any nigga out here the father of that mothafucka. You go hard when it comes to the pussy and everybody know it now."

I looked at Paco and Kreshon. "Yeah, niggas out here talking about you." He continued.

"You know what, fuck you and fuck every nigga out here!" I threw my finger up at Kreshon and Paco. "All you niggas broke and busted and I don't need nobody to take care of me or my baby."

"Yes you do. That's the problem. You will never be able to take care of yourself 'cause you wasn't raised like that. You were raised to be a whore like your mother before she died. So be one, bitch, and stay in your place."

"Don't talk about what you think you know."

"You can't be serious. You get F's in school and you barely passed the eleventh grade. So don't act like you don't expect a nigga to look out for you 'cause you not smart enough to do it yourself and you will never be."

"I'm gone," I said turning around to walk away.

"Don't walk away from me." He said grabbing me by my arm. "And don't move. I'm not done with you yet."

"Boy, bye! I'm outta here." I said snatching away from him again.

"Harmony, if you move one more step, I'ma break your jaw." He said so seriously it sent chills up my spine. Then he leaned in and whispered, "And I know you told the cops about me, and when the time is right, I'ma kill you."

Silence.

"Now stay right there. If you move one inch, I'ma drop your ass. And you know I'm dead serious." He told me as he walked back up to his crew leaving me alone.

I felt like crying because if Jace told Kali, who he knew was capable of murder that I told the cops anything, he was over me. And my life was in danger. I felt powerless and my stomach churned. The sensation of nausea was coming over me again, and I had to pee.

Twenty minutes later, I was still waiting on him to tell me it was okay to go home but he didn't. My legs felt weak and I was tired, and while they leaned on Edge's truck, they made me stand in the middle of the sidewalk. When I tried to move for someone, he slapped me in my face and told me the next time I moved one inch, it would be worst. It was like he was getting a kick out of treating me badly.

"Kali, I gotta go to the bathroom." I said. I could feel the tingling sensation between my legs and doubted I would make it to the bathroom if I tried now. A bush was all I could make it to next to the place I stood.

"What you gotta do? Number one or number two?" They all laughed again.

"Kali, come on. Please...I really have to-"

"What you gotta do? Number one or two?" He yelled interrupting me.

"I gotta pee."

"Pee right where you are then. We ain't watching." He was still leaning on the truck. They all looked at me with smirks on their faces. And if I had a gun, I would've killed them all.

"Kali, please. Don't do this shit."

"Don't make me say it again." He said standing up straight. "Piss, and I want to see you do it, too."

I looked at all of them hoping there was at least one man among them who would say something in my defense but they all remained silent. So I pulled my pants down and tried to hide on the side of Mrs. Creston's overgrown bush.

"Naw...Don't hide. Piss right there in the middle of the block. I don't know what you hidin' for," he laughed. "Every nigga out here done seen that pussy." He continued looking at them. I knew then that they talked behind my back. "You shoulda thought about who the fuck you was approachin' before you stepped to me."

There was no getting through to Kali. So in front of them all, I released urine from my body in the middle of the sidewalk. It ran down my legs, dampened my shoes and rolled out into the street. When I was done, I pulled my pants up.

"Kali, I really feel sick." I said crying uncontrollably.

"Then throw up. But whatever you do, you better not interrupt me again."

"Why are you doing this?"

"'Cause, I'ma treat you like you wanna be treated, Miss Burns. You ain't nothin' but a smut!"

Kali was really showing off and there was nothing I could do. I hadn't eaten all day and was extremely hungry. But right where I was, I threw up. The smell of my urine and throw up made me sicker. The sky was now dark and partially hid the tears running down my cheeks. I hated Kali so much, that words could not express. Thinking he was going to let me go home now, I was seriously surprised when he made me stay still for another hour.

The temperature had dropped a little and a cold front was coming in. But because I was wet with from my own pee, I was cold and shivering. I felt like I was about to pass out until I heard loud base coming from stereo speakers. Kali and the rest of the dudes jumped off the car and looked behind me. It was then that I saw Jace's Beamer pull up. Kevin was driving and he parked the car, and opened the passenger door to let Jace out. When Jace walked toward us, he looked at them and then at me.

"We meetin' at my new crib in Maryland." He said looking at me again. Then his eyes wondered on the wet spot underneath me. "What she doin' out here?" Nobody answered the question. I guess the fact that I was once his girl still held some weight after all. "Answer the fuckin' question!"

"Man, this nigga made her piss right in front of us," Kreshon laughed like he couldn't wait. "This nigga's mad stupid."

Jace cut his eyes at Kali and without looking at me said, "Is this true?"

"Come on, J. You can't be still serious about this bitch. She a snitch."

A snitch? I figured he was talking about the cop story I told Jace which was all a lie. "Harmony, get in my car." Jace said, eyes still glued onto Kali.

"But...But I'm wet."

"Get in my car." He said evenly.

His bodyguard Kevin opened the back door for me. Relieved to be away from Kali, and happy because of the possibility of talking to Jace again, I sighed in relief. Jace said a few more words to them and whatever he said wiped the smile off of their faces.

When he got back inside the car, he sat in the front seat and said, "You aight?" He never looked at me though.

"Not really." I swallowed and said, "Where are we going?"

Kevin drove away and said, "I'ma take you home."

"Thank you." I paused. "But...can we talk, Jace? Please."

He sighed and said, "Harmony, what Kali just did to you was fucked up and I just told him about it. But that shit happened because you carry yourself like a slut. And I'm just glad I never made you wifey."

"What...What you mean?"

"You know what I'm sayin'." He said finally looking at me. "Ain't no nigga gonna *ever* make you wifey. You gotta recognize that shit."

I swallowed hard, "So there's no chance for us? Ever?"

Silence.

"Naw. Because I can't make you respect yourself and I can't take back all the shit you did."

"But it ain't true!" I said starting to believe my own lies.

"Even if it ain't, niggas believe so it makes it true."

"Jace, what...What if I'm right? And what if this baby really is yours? Won't you feel bad for how you're treating me?"

He hesitated a little and said, "If you pregnant by me, than the baby is gonna be good. But as far as me and you, we through."

I looked out in front of me felt Kevin's judging eyes on me. Then Jace's words played over and over in my head. *'Ain't no nigga gonna ever make you wifey.'* He must've forgot the saying...It's cheaper to keep her. But I was quickly going to make him remember.

OUT FOR ME

Jace

Me and Kevin were sitting in the doctor's office for a follow-up visit for the Syphilis I contracted from somebody. Although I went to Virginia to get treatment and to prevent from being spotted, I still saw a few dudes I knew from DC. Guess we all had the same idea and the shit didn't work. But I needed to make sure this shit was out of my system for good and then I could go on about my business.

I had a lot of shit on my mind, like the fact that this party my cousin was throwing for my birthday was in three days and I didn't even care. I was doing it for him and my aunt more than anything. After my brush with death, they were happy I was still alive, and wanted to celebrate.

"Mr. Sherrod, we're ready for you now." A white older nurse said to me. I walked up to her and she said, "Right this way."

"You want me to go with you?" Kevin asked.

"Naw, I'm good."

I followed the nurse and walked into a cold patient room, checked my Chopard watch and waited. Ten minutes later, a black male doctor knocked on the door. He was thin, older and his hands were manicured. Like he hadn't done any real work a day in his life. Once inside, he grabbed my chart off the back of the door and scanned over it. I noticed a gold chain with a cross hanging from his neck along with a pinky ring. With the chart in his hands, he closed the door.

"Have a seat," he told me. I sat on the edge of the hospital bed and looked him over strangely. Something about him was off. "So, how is everything going?"

"It depends on if this shit is out of my system or not."

"We'll see about that." He told me. "Drop your pants." I didn't like his choice of words but whatever. I dropped my pants. "Your boxers too."

I was naked from the waist down in front of another man and was very uncomfortable. He stepped away from me and looked around the office like it was his first time being there. And then he found a box of gloves, put them on and examined my penis. "So far so good, a little small, but not too bad."

"Fuck you just say to me?" I said mugging this dude.

"I'm just kidding, son." He laughed.

He lifted my penis by moving it from the left to right. I couldn't look at another man touching me so I kept my eyes on the ceiling until he gripped my dick and balls so hard, I would have rather died then to deal with the pain any longer.

"Do you know who I am, son?" He squeezed tighter.

"What...The...Fuck...Are...You...Doin', nigga?" I said very slowly and very carefully.

"Did you know I had a daughter, that I would have given the world for, ONLY TO HAVE HER TAKEN FROM ME BY THAT NO GOOD FATHER OF YOURS?!" He screamed.

I wiped the sweat from my brow, with the back of my left hand and tried my best to stop shivering. I even contemplated if I could hit him in the face hard enough to get him to release me. But the chance was not one I was willing to take.

"How...How did you know I was here?"

"I've been following you for a while. Just could never seem to get you alone. I have to give it to you, your security is pretty tight." He laughed. "And then it dawned on me, I was traveling with too many people," he continued maintaining the hold he had on my jewels. "It would be much easier to get at you if I was alone."

"Now what, nigga! Either shoot me, or get the fuck out of my face!"

At that moment, I didn't give a fuck anymore. The pain was blinding but just when I had given up, someone walked into the door.

"There he is!" The nurse said whom I had seen earlier. "He's not supposed to be in here." Two unarmed security guards grabbed Massive and wrestled him to the floor.

"You gonna see me again real soon, son." He said trying to get away. "Real soon."

When they took him out of the office I fell to the floor cupping my jewels. Kevin came rushing inside the room and said, "Please don't tell me that was who I think it was."

"Yeah...At least we know what he looks like now," I said breathing heavily.

"I'm 'bout to go shoot that nigga!" Kevin said preparing to leave me again.

"No!" I stopped him. "Now is not the right time. Just help me up, man."

He did and I no longer cared who saw me naked. All I wanted was the pain to go away.

Although Massive was taken away by security I already knew how it was going to end. He would probably have them both killed within the hour and escape. I knew there was no way he was going to let two unarmed guards take him into custody. But had it not been for the men being stronger than him, I would probably be dead. I was still trying my hardest to breathe when the nurse walked up to me.

"Mr. Sherrod, I'm so sorry," she said. "I didn't know he was in here."

Followed behind her was the real doctor. "Son, let me take a look at you."

Both the nurse and the doctor spent the next few minutes looking me over while Kevin stayed by my side. I knew then that I couldn't even go to something as private as a doctor's appointment without having Kevin right with me.

FUCK! I need this nigga dead like yesterday!

⬤————————————————————————⬤

After the doctor's appointment, I had Kevin drive me around a little before going home. Outside of a little bruising I was good and the disease was gone. Still, I had a lot of shit on my mind. From Massive being at my doctor's appointment to this shit with Harmony. Then there was the shit with Kali kidnapping the girl from school and Herb Dayo and Sick Sense still being missing. I really needed someone to talk too, it would be nice if it was my father.

Since I decided to operate DC's shops, I was seeing Rick regularly. It was the most I'd ever seen him for any period of my life. Normally his visits lasted a weekend before we were in business together, but now I talked to him daily. I know our relationship was different because we were in business together but I wished it didn't have to be that way. There were times when I dealt with regular shit in my life and could have used the guidance of a father. But that guidance never came.

When I finally pulled up at my crib, I saw cars everywhere. My house was jam packed with wall-to-wall niggas when I walked through my doors.

"Welcome home, sir. Your friends are still here." My maid said with a phone in her hand.

"I see." I said walking deeper into the house.

"But Harmony is on the phone, she said she wants to talk to you."

I really didn't feel like dealing with her but my relationship with my own father made me change my mind. If she was pregnant and the child was mine, I couldn't put it through what I been through.

"Tell her I can't talk now, but I'll have a car come get her later."

"No problem, sir."

<hr>

An hour later, Harmony was there and we went into a private room. Harmony wasn't showing yet and she still had her figure. For a moment I thought about fuckin' her but remembered the doctor's visit and said fuck it.

I sat on a sofa, and she sat next to me. "What's up, Harmony? What you want to talk about now?"

"I want to know if you're still mad at me? And if you had a chance to think about you and me having this baby together?"

"Yeah…I thought about it. And when and if it gets here, I'll be ready to make a decision then."

She frowned and said, "Whatever happens after this, is your fault."

"Fuck is that 'sposed to mean?"

She was just about to respond when Tony Wop knocked on the door.

"Come in," I said.

He came in, looked at Harmony and then at me. "I ain't know you had company."

"Yeah…What's up?" I said standing up.

"Everything set for your party at Newton's Mansion. And I got the paper from our soldiers in Southeast too. Where you want it?"

I got up and told him where to put it, then I came back into the room with Harmony. She was quiet at first before she started talking.

"So…Can we work on us or not?"

"I already told you, me and you never gonna have nothin' outside of a kid together."

"If you don't want me, I'ma hate this baby for the rest of my life, and raise it on my own." She pouted.

"You ain't raising shit on your own if the kid is mine," I said. "'Cause I'ma look out for both of you. But that don't mean I ever want to be with you again."

I gave her something to eat before getting rid of her so I could take a nap. But since everybody was at my crib, it didn't look like rest would come any time soon. Wanting to be alone, I bypassed a few of my friends and went upstairs. When I got to my room Antoinette was in the bed sleep. I looked at her sexy silhouette and wondered why I couldn't be happy with her. Easing into the bed I imagined that she was Harmony, and that we had the life that I always wanted us to have. And for the moment, shit was alright.

NASTY MOVES

Harmony

After talking to Jace and dealing with Kali, I was tired of playing nice, so I decided to make a few moves that would force me to have to leave DC for good. I didn't have much family outside of my grandmother and my uncle who had been missing for a while now. And I didn't know much about my father's side of the family, outside of an aunt who lived in Houston. But I had to get in contact with her, somehow.

I remember her coming by the house when I was younger, to borrow money from daddy that never came back. She used to bring me fake dolls that would always break the moment I touched them. His sister was a mooch and I knew hell would have to freeze over before she changed.

Her name was Angela Phillips and unless she got married that was going to have to be enough for me to find her. First I needed to visit old man Grand today because I needed his help with my biggest play yet. People were going to remember my name when I finally left DC. And I wasn't talking about Miss Burns, the nickname they tried to label me with either.

"You need to tell them bitches to stop callin' my house!" Shirley yelled. "Trip called here ten times already."

"Whatever, Shirley," I said ignoring her.

I picked up the phone preparing to call Grand, but Trip was on the line.

"Harmony." She said in a low voice. I hadn't spoken to her since she got all upset about what Ebony told her. "I'm not mad at you no more, okay?"

"Whatever, Trip. You believed something Ebony told you instead of believing a friend."

"You right and I'm sorry. But I can't talk about that now. Can you please come over to Constance's house? She talking crazy."

"Well call Kreshon. I ain't her man."

"Please, Harmony. She over here saying she gonna kill herself and shit like that. I can't stay with her because I gotta go pick up Evan from school."

I swear I didn't feel like dealing with any of this shit. "Alright...I'm on my way."

When I went into my room to get dressed, Shirley walked in. "You ain't been tyin' up my line have you? 'Cause I still haven't heard from my son yet."

"No," I said ignoring her again.

"Where the fuck are you goin'?"

"If you must know over Connie's," I said.

I threw my stuff on and went to Constance's house and knocked on the door. When I got there the door was wide opened and I let myself in. She was in the living room sitting on the sofa rocking back and forth. I felt like I should go back out but was nervous to do anything. Her hair was all over her head and she was sitting in her white dingy panties and a red fitted T-shirt.

"Where's your mother, Connie?" I said walking up behind the sofa. She was quiet and I walked deeper into the living room and then to the front of the sofa. That's when I saw the gun sitting on the couch next to her.

I turned around about to leave until she aimed the gun at me and said, "Sit down, Harmony." I reluctantly walked back toward her. "Sit over here, next to me."

Then she started laughing and I could finally see that her wrists had knicks in them.

"Do you know how to slit your wrists?" She asked with wide eyes. "Can you help me?" She smiled crazily.

"No, Connie...I don't know how." I said nervously.

"Then what are you doing here, bitch?" She asked. "Since I know you don't care about nobody but yourself."

"I do care about people."

"Then why didn't you answer the phone when I called? Why weren't you there for me when Ebony got with my man? Do you know that they're still together to this day?" She wiped the tears away and then gripped the gun tighter.

"Oh so what, you gonna shoot me now?" I asked looking at the gun pointing in my direction.

She was crying hysterically and said, "No, I'm gonna shoot myself."

I felt a little relieved but would have preferred if nobody got shot at all. And if someone did, I didn't want to be anywhere around when it happened.

"Constance, please stop tripping. Let me call, Kreshon."

"I did already," she said sobbing again. "He said fuck me. Can you believe that shit? After everything he did to me, he said fuck me!"

"Maybe if you call him a..."

POW!

"OH MY GAWD!!!"

I couldn't believe it. She actually shot herself right in front of me. I jumped up and backed into a table falling flat on my ass. Blood was everywhere and I never seen anything like it before. All I knew was that I had to leave and get as far away from the situation as possible, and that's exactly what I did.

Constance's suicide played over and over in my mind. She said her mother had a gun and that she knew how to use it but I always thought she was lying. I had to leave DC now more than ever before. I didn't even bother to call the cops because I didn't want them asking me questions. Plus if Kali or Jace found out, they might think I was talking to the police about the girl instead of Connie's suicide. So I went home to change to get the blood off of my clothes and then I would go to Grand's house. I knew he'd have some smoke and some liquor and that's all I needed right now.

I had been cool with Grand since I was a little girl even though Kali was his uncle. Now that I think about it, Grand told me a while back to stay away from his nephew but I never listened. When I was younger, Grand ran an ice cream truck that everybody loved to go to. But when I discovered that grown men preferred his treats more than kids, I found out what he really sold was weed. He got ten years in prison for his little scheme and decided it was best to sell shit out of his house. Lately he'd been doing more smoking than selling and I wondered how he even made a living.

Since Grand had a weakness for young girls, namely me, I decided to put on my tight jeans. But the moment I zipped them up, I felt nauseous all over again. This was my first time being pregnant so I was unsure if the nausea was going to last forever.

When my jeans were on, I put on the red low-cut Guess top he always complimented then I splashed on some perfume and looked at myself in the mirror. I was so thankful that my hair was way more manageable then my mother or my grandmother's. It was almost like a white girl's but a little curlier and thicker. Today, I decided to blow dry my shit straight so that when I moved, it would move, too.

I was on my way out the door when Shirley stopped me. "Your school called again. They're sending someone over about what you told that teacher."

"And?" I said pouring me a glass of ginger ale from the fridge. Afterwards, pouring vodka in my cup.

"Well you can't stay here if they cause me problems, Harmony."

I laughed in her face.

"Well I guess I won't stay here then." She must've been out with her mind if she thought I was pressed to stay in her funky ass house. "I'm out. I'll get up with you later," I continued leaving out the door.

It took me five minutes to walk to Grand's house. When I got there, I saw Kali and Jace talking to Kreshon a few houses over. I wondered if he knew about his ex-girlfriend yet.

"Hey, Grand!" I said when he opened the door, I took one last look at Kali who was still staring me down and closed the door behind me.

"Damn, girl. You looking good, and you got on my favorite top too. You must want something."

Grand was wearing a red lumberjack shirt and some blue jeans. It seemed that every time I saw him, he had more salt in his hair than pepper but he was still attractive.

"You know me so well don't you?" I said.

"I know you better than you know yourself."

I walked fully into his small house and sat down. A wooden table sat in the middle of the floor and weed buds were on top of it. Instead of a couch he had four leather recliners, two were black, one was tan and the other was off white. They were all banged out with smoke burns from years of abuse. Grand's house use to be the hang out spot back in the day but lately it had changed.

"What can I do for you?" He said sitting in the tan recliner.

I could smell weed and my stomach started to churn again. This pregnancy shit was getting on my nerves and it would be all for nothing if it wasn't Jace's baby. He made it clear, that either the baby was his or I would be assed out.

"I need you to help me find someone in jail, Grand. And don't tell me you can't help me because I know you know everybody."

"Who you want to find?"

"The one who kidnapped me."

Grand stopped what he was doing and stared up at me. "Speak up, Harmony. 'Cause you asking more from me than I know how to give."

Whenever Grand told me to speak up it meant he couldn't believe what I was saying.

"It ain't a whole lot to it, Grand. You have access to people in jail and I need you to access one for me. Now can you help me or not?"

He looked around his grungy house and looked at me again. "Who got on your bad side now that you want to raise the dead? I mean, didn't the man who kidnapped you also try to kill you?"

"I repeat, can you help me or not? I'm not about to give you the reasons for why I want to contact him. I just need it done."

"What are you...Seventeen?" He laughed. "You messing in a grown man's world now."

"I'm about to leave," I said standing up.

"Wait."

I turned around and said, "Listen...Your name might be Grand but you not my grandfather. What I need from you is what I'm asking you for." I continued touching the doorknob. "Save the bullshit for somebody else who will listen." I said preparing to leave again.

"I said wait. Maybe we can work something out."

I knew what he wanted so I walked back over to the recliner and sat down. Then I lifted my shirt up and took it off. Grand always worked better with a pair of titties staring in his face. Last year me, Nut and Cherry used to come over here all the time to smoke. He use to let us smoke as much weed as we wanted for free, just as long as when we did it we sat around his living room with our shirts off.

"Oh no," he said slyly. "I'ma need more than that this time, little lady."

Although I never fucked Grand, I had all intentions on doing whatever was necessary. "Then what do you want? To suck 'em or somethin'?"

He stood up and walked toward me. "Naw, I want *you* to suck 'em first. Then I know you know what I want."

Doing my best to read his mind, I took one of my breasts and placed the nipple in my mouth. Then I allowed my pink tongue to run over the tip. My breasts were sore from being pregnant but I couldn't let him know. I was going to have to endure the pain. Plus he was so attracted to me, that if I did have to fuck him, I knew he wouldn't last too long anyway.

"What you want with this person?" He said looking at me with lust.

"For now I just need you to get me the address. I think his name is Arnold Recaro." I paused. "Once I get the information I need, your involvement in all of this will be over. It's as simple as that."

"When you need it?"

"I need you to do this soon, Grand. It can't wait." I said massaging my breasts seductively. "Now can you do it for me or not? I'm tired of asking you."

"It depends on what you do next."

There was no need in wasting time. He wanted what he wanted just like I wanted what I wanted. All my life I had to give people what they wanted sexually, to get what I needed. So this wasn't new to me, just boring.

Five minutes later, I was riding Grand's dick in the tan recliner. He clawed at my back and the smell of cigarettes and weed on his skin made my stomach churn once more. Grand lasted longer than I thought and it was disgusting to feel his body which was covered in hair against mine. But just like that, it was over.

When we were done, he said, "Whoever did you wrong, you must really want them bad." He paused. "Because I been trying to get in them panties for a minute. And now, I finally got 'em." He paused and said, "I guess Kali really fucked up huh?"

He pulled his clothes up and grabbed a sweat towel that was sitting on the edge of the couch. Then he dabbed it all over his dark skin, leaving a few lint balls on his nose.

"Just do your part of the deal, Grand."

"Have I ever let you down?" He asked me.

"Never. That's why I came to you."

"Then I won't start letting you down today. Besides, if I do what you ask me to, you might give me some more of that sweet young thang."

"I doubt that, let's just do one thing at a time."

I was on my way out the door when I remembered I needed some information on my father's sister. I knew she use to be around here all the time because my father and my mother grew up in the neighborhood.

"Grand, do you know where my father's sister lives? She ever keep in contact with anybody around here anymore?"

"Who, Angel?"

"I thought her name was Angela."

He laughed. "It's sad you don't even know your own aunt's nickname." He paused. "We call her Angel."

"Well do you know where she is or not?"

"I haven't seen her since she moved to Texas. Why?"

"Just asking. Well I gotta go, let me know when you get the information I need."

I walked hurriedly up the street hoping nobody would stop me about Constance who I was sure was still slumped over in her living room. But I couldn't make it up the street without throwing up in somebody's yard. Eventually I made it home.

When I opened up my house door, two neighborhood niggas walked past me and left out the door. "What were ya'll doing in my house?" I asked the younger one.

"You betta ask your, grandmother." The older one said counting money.

When I walked further inside, I closed my door and my mouth dropped when I saw all my shit in the living room on the floor. My grandmother must've lost her fucking mind! When I went into my room, all of her tired ass shoes and clothes were back inside, like it was when I first moved in. Although I told her I was leaving, I know she knew it wasn't going to be today.

"Shirley! What the fuck is going on?" I asked looking for her throughout the house.

I found her in the kitchen with the phone in her hand and a cigarette dangling from her mouth. The worn out leather phonebook she kept with her sat on the table and a rubber band held it together because the pages were falling out. And then I remembered, she'd definitely have Angela's number in that thing somewhere. She had everybody's number. I was going to have to get it from up under her.

"What you mean what the fuck is going on? That's why I never liked your ass, you too damn grown."

"Whatever," I said.

"Come over here," she said her voice slurring. "Kiss me."

"Yuck! I'm not fucking with you again. Ever."

"Oh you not," she laughed.

"Fuck no!"

"Well if you don't, I might have a little information for the officer who came by today."

"What?" I said still mad about my shit being in the living room.

"That little girl was murdered and Trip said she saw you coming out of her house." I couldn't believe the lengths Trip would go through, to get back at me. Did she set this whole shit up? And if so, how did she know Connie would really kill herself? "Now I got to admit the truth to the cops. Unless…"

"Unless what?"

She raised up, took her panties down and sat back in her seat. "Get over here."

My stomach churned just thinking about what she was making me do. Again.

"Did you ever care about me?" I cried, mad at myself for hoping she did. As if her love would make what she wanted me to do a little better.

"Now! Or do I have to call the cops?"

I hated my life. More than anybody could ever wonder. Suddenly I started to wonder, if maybe Constance didn't have the right idea after all.

NASTY SHIRLEY

Harmony

I was the sickest I had ever been after my grandmother made me have sex with her again. I was sitting in the living room, which thanks to Shirley was now my new bedroom, when someone knocked at my door. When I opened it, I saw Kali staring at me strangely.

"What do you want?" I asked him as he walked inside. "I didn't say you could come in."

"Well I'm in now. And what I want is you." He had a brown paper bag in his hand and handed it to me.

"I thought you didn't want me to drink?" The bag had my favorite bottle of vodka inside. "And I thought you didn't have any more words for me."

"You want the bottle or not?" I kept it even though I knew I shouldn't. He wanted something from me but I didn't know what.

"Yeah." I said closing the door.

"Why you got your face all squinted up?" He continued. "You too busy for me or somethin'?" He talked to himself as if no one was in the room. "I'm sick of comin' over here all the time for you to have a fuckin' attitude."

"Well stop coming over here all the time then."

He balled his fists up and I backed up a little. "If I was Jace you'd be all smiles wouldn't you?"

"Kali, I told you I don't want to see you no more after the last time you called. Where is Cherry? You should be worried about her instead of me."

"I ain't goin' nowhere before I'm ready." He told me sitting in my living room on the couch. And why all your shit out here and not in your room?"

"Kali, please get to your point. I don't feel too good."

"So why you hangin' out with my uncle so much lately?"

"That's my personal business."

He looked down at the floor and said, "You been tellin' him about that kidnapping? You been tellin' him my business?"

"I don't want to talk about that shit no more. Ya'll got me tied up into something I didn't want to be tied up into."

"So you really ain't got no words for me, huh?"

It was like he was asking me questions he knew I'd have negative responses to. And even though I knew I shouldn't piss him off, I didn't care.

"Kali, I ain't got shit for you. You violated with that shit you pulled a couple of weeks back. You didn't care how I felt and I will never forgive you for it."

"You know what," he said standing up, "I ain't come over here about all that other bullshit, I came to see what you gonna do 'bout my baby when it's born."

Kali is sicker than I thought and his thoughts seem to run together. "You told me I fucked a rack of dudes and you even bought over a pint of vodka for me to drink today. So let me remind you...IT...AIN'T...YOUR...FUCKIN'...BABY! Okay?"

"So it ain't my baby, huh?" He said frowning.

"You heard me, now please get the fuck out of my house before I put you out." When I walked to the door, he took the side of his hand and hit me in the throat crippling me momentarily.

"Bitch, if you can take my money, you can make time for me." He said grabbing me by my hair. "When you gonna realize that I own you, huh? There ain't a place on earth you can hide from me."

"I...I...can't breathe." I whispered.

"One day, I'ma put a scar on that pretty little face of yours. Then every time you look into the mirror, you're going to remember me."

I was rubbing my throat so he could know I couldn't breathe, but the look in his eyes showed me he knew and didn't care. When he opened the door to leave, two cops were standing there. One of their tags said Robins and the other Mendez. I shot up, brushed myself off and leaned against the wall. Kali shifted nervously where he stood before stepping all the way back.

"Good morning, young lady. Good morning, sir," he said to Kali.

"Morning," Kali said.

"Is Shirley Pointer here?"

"Uh...Yes," I said feeling faint. I rubbed my throat some more and Kali sat down on the sofa, I guess trying to look normal. I wanted to tell the cops about the kidnapped girl then maybe they'd lock him up, so he could finally leave me alone. But what if they were here for me? Shirley said they came for me the other day asking questions about Constance.

Before I could think more into it, Shirley walked to the door. "Good morning. What can I do for you?"

"We have some information about the kidnapped girl. And your son."

Kali seemed nervous and adjusted in his seat. "And...What is it?"

"We found her body along with your son's in his car. They fell into an embankment in Virginia and died instantly. We're just letting you know that the case is closed."

"You're tellin' me...You're tellin' me that my only surviving child is dead?"

"Yes...And also that he was responsible for the kidnap and murder of the little girl from Nalle Elementary."

When I looked at Kali he smiled. He set all of this shit into motion and I knew the truth. But the cops evidently didn't. He was more dangerous than I could have ever imagined.

"Well, we just wanted to let you know, since we came here to question you about him the other day."

The other day? What did he mean the other day?

"You came here the other day?" I said with a sore throat.

"Yes. We did."

Shirley lied to me about the reason the cops were here just to get me to have sex with her again. Their visit had nothing to do with me...They were here for Charles.

"Well have a good day, mam," one of them said.

"We're sorry about your loss," said the other before they walked away. I closed the door behind them.

"Shirley, I thought you said the cops came for me that day? The day Constance was found dead!" I said following her into the kitchen.

She said, "My son just died, and you come at me 'bout some bitch who committed suicide." For the first time ever, I saw her cry. "Well fuck your friend and fuck you!" She said crying as she walked to her room.

I was filled with hate, rage and confusion. My life was so fucked up and I didn't know the first thing to do to get things to change. She didn't care about me, Jace didn't care about me, and I wasn't even sure if I cared about myself.

Kali walked up to me and said, "Don't worry, just like I took care of Charles for you...And that girl for Jace...I got you with your grandmother, too."

"NO! JUST STAY AWAY FROM ME!"

He laughed and walked out the door.

MAYBE MINE

Jace

My party was tomorrow night and I wasn't even feeling it. Ever since Harmony came over I felt like I should be doing more for her. If it was true that she was pregnant, and that the kid was mine, she would probably lose it without my help.

When I walked into my house, with Kevin followed behind me, I saw my crew in the kitchen.

"I just got back from the mansion you rented for the party. We wanted to make sure everything was good with security." Kreshon said.

"So was it?" I asked grabbing a beer.

"Man, you should see how many niggas Rick got surrounding that place." Kreshon said. "It's gotta be at least twenty mothafuckas, easy!"

"Yeah...Your pops not fuckin' around." Kali added. "'Specially after that shit at the clinic."

After I found out the work Kali put into the missing girl, I had a new respect for him. He not only got the heat off of us, he put it onto somebody else who deserved it. A convicted pedophile. If only I could find out what happened to Herb Dayo and Sick Sense.

"It's whatever to me...Just as long as shit goes smoothly." I said.

"I feel you," Kali added.

"So what's up with Herb Dayo and Sick? Anybody hear anything yet?" I asked.

"Naw, man. They mothers ain't heard nothin' from them neither." Kreshon said. "I think at this point the worst is what it is."

"Them niggas probably bailed out," Kali said. "I never trusted either of 'em."

Me and Kreshon looked at each other. This nigga lived in a delusional world.

"How was Connie's funeral?" I asked Kreshon. "Sorry I couldn't go, man. Had some shit to take care of in New York."

"I know. It was what it was," He said. "Still can't believe shawty off'ed herself like that."

"Me either."

When my phone rang my maid answered it. "Hello." She paused. "Yes, sir. He's right here. Jace, it's your father."

I got out of my seat and grabbed the phone. "Jace, something terrible has happened."

"What?"

"Massive set a bomb off in my house and my entire crew is dead."

"The whole crew?"

"Yep, everybody that you met when you were here. Except Leo Lips, he was in on it with Massive. My entire team has been murdered."

"I knew I didn't like him when I met him." I paused, angry I didn't go with my gut and tell him. "Are you okay?"

"Yeah...Just got to start all over. I'm thinking about getting out of town for now." He sighed. "Well, I'm counting on you more than ever. I have to lay low. For whatever reason, he wants my blood and everyone's who's involved with me."

"You killed his daughter, Rick." I said growing angrier by Massive's wrath.

Silence.

"I know, son. But it was business, not pleasure." He paused. "So are you ready to officially become a man?" Rick said to me on the phone. That was his way of saying happy birthday.

"I thought you said I was already a man."

"In my book you are. But I started helping my father out with the family business at twelve, so you're starting pretty late."

"Better late than never." I paused wanting to ask him a personal question.

"Is everything okay, Jace? You sound out of it." He laughed. "I know I laid quite a bit on you today, but I still want to make sure you're fine."

I was surprised he even noticed the something in my voice so I decided to take advantage. I looked at my crew and said, "Let me rap to Rick right quick. It's private." When they were gone I said, "Dad, I gotta ask you somethin'."

"You can talk to me about anything. What is it?"

"I...I mean can you...Well...Is it possible to..."

"Say it, son."

"Is it possible to...Get somebody pregnant...If you ain't bust?"

"If you ain't bust?" He repeated.

"Yeah. If you ain't bust inside them. You know, while fuckin'."

"Why? Do you think you got somebody pregnant?"

"I don't know...I mean...I fucked this chick but I ain't really..." I paused. For some reason it was hard for me to just say it to him. "I ain't cum."

"I got it. Well," Rick paused and cleared his throat, "you can still get her pregnant by the pre-cum, although it's somewhat unlikely. But I wasn't there so I can't really be sure. The best way to find out really is to get it tested when it's born."

"Okay...Well...Thanks, Rick."

"Not a problem." He laughed. "Be careful tomorrow, Jace. After the fire at my house, and then him getting away after the doctor's office, I know he won't stop."

"I know. But I'll be okay. You gonna be able to make it?"

"Naw, I can't get away. I have a few meetings in L.A. And then there's this high roller poker game I'm going to in Atlantic City."

I could count the times on my hands I've seen him for my birthday. And I guess I could add another year to the list. "It's cool."

He was always putting poker games before me. The story of my life.

"But remember to be careful, Jace."

"I got you. I'll hit you when it's time to discuss business."

HIT OR MISS

Harmony

Grand had gotten in contact with the kidnapper who was hesitant to talk to me at first, until I told him where Massive, who I found out was his boss, could locate Jace. And that was at his party. I gave him the address of his house, which I knew he'd have a harder time catching him, and the address to the mansion. After the collect call ended he sounded too happy to give the information to his boss. I also asked him would he have hurt me, if given the chance, and he said it's best to let sleeping dogs lie. So I dropped it knowing what that meant.

Lastly I found my aunt Angela's number in Texas from Shirley's phonebook. She wasn't too happy to hear from me at first, saying the rooms in her two bedroom apartment were filled with her two children. She claimed she barely had enough money from welfare to feed them and her boyfriend so taking in someone else was out of the question.

I tried telling her that I wasn't going to have to stay long, and that it would be just until I was able to find a place of my own, but she still wasn't having it. But when I told her I had a little money to give her for rent, which I didn't have yet, miraculously a room had become available. Bitches kill me.

Before I left, Paco called me telling me he was sorry about how he acted in the car. And to tell you the truth, I was glad I got the call. I was broke and needed some money and dick before I left DC. So if he could help me with both before I left, I'd be very grateful.

I was meeting Paco at a Burger King and was there for ten minutes when I saw him walk in with Ebony. What the fuck was she doing here? To make matters worse, I had on the earrings I'd stolen from her at her party and didn't have enough time to take them off.

When they got inside, they both looked around and sat in the seat directly in front of me. I didn't know what was going on but I knew whatever it was wouldn't be nice.

"So you fucking Paco, too?" I said.

"Bitch, I'm asking the questions." I laughed. "So you did steal my earrings after all, huh?" She said. Then she reached over and snatched one of them out my ear.

"Ouch!" I could feel my blood trickle down my neck. I touched my ear to see how much of my ear was ripped but it didn't seem to be too bad. However the pain was crazy.

"You want me to take the other one out, too? Or do you wanna give me my shit back?"

I took the other earring out and handed it to her. Paco didn't say anything, just stared at me wildly and I knew I was in danger. He said he would hand me over to whoever wanted to kill me, so I guess now was that time. I got up and was about to run out when her and Paco stood up and blocked me. It was a set up. How could I be so stupid?

"Sit down, bitch!" He told me.

"What is this about, Paco?" I asked him looking between both of them. "You said you weren't mad at me anymore."

"Bitch. you burned half of DC." Paco laughed. "You thought I was going to let you get away with that shit?"

"So what ya'll gonna do now? Jump me or something?" I laughed.

"You wish," He said. "Look outside."

When I looked outside I saw Trip, Meleny and five other girls standing outside of the door with closed fists and I knew they were all waiting on me. Some of the girls I knew, most of them I didn't but I was sure I'd fucked one of their boyfriends at one time in my life and they probably caught something because of it. Some of their men I fucked for money, most I fucked just because. Still, I knew I couldn't go outside because they'd kill me.

So I scanned my surroundings quickly and saw a white man by the counter with a security uniform on and yelled, "HELP! They're trying to rob me!"

"What?" Paco said. He and Ebony looked at the man and then back at me. "What the fuck are you talkin' about? Ain't nobody tryin' to rob your ass."

"If anything you the one who robbed me by stealing my earrings." Ebony added.

"What's going on over here?" The man said walking up to us. I was relieved.

"Don't listen to this bitch! She lyin!" Ebony said.

"Then why is blood all over her face?"

"She snatched my earrings out of my ear and he tried to rob me for my money." I interjected.

The security guard's friends I didn't see came from nowhere and grabbed Paco and Ebony. The man who approached first took the earrings from Ebony and put them in my hand and I saw the mob outside run away. I had gotten away and knew even more that DC was not for me.

"Those are my earrings!" Ebony yelled while being detained. "I want my shit back!"

"If they really are yours, you can take her to court." The guard said.

●━━━━━━━━━━━━━━━━━━━━━━━━━━━━●

The guard offered to drop me off at Grand's house. I wanted to be around somebody that wasn't always judging me. I would normally go to Nut and Cherry's but they seemed out of it after Cherry got cut. People said they were fucking with crack and that Kali was supplying them and I didn't want to believe it. But every time I called, they sounded out of it and I was starting to believe it was true.

When I got to Grand's house, I could smell the weed in the air and knew he was getting high. And since I was still having morning sickness, the smell was making me sick.

"Who is it?!" He screamed from the inside of his door.

"It's me, Grand. Open up."

"Who the fuck is me?!" He yelled. I heard his footsteps approaching the door until he finally opened it. It wasn't long before a devious smile spread across his face. "Well hello there."

I walked inside and sat down on the tan recliner. "I'm not fucking you again, Grand. So get that nasty ass shit out of your mind right now."

He laughed, closed the door and said, "I knew good luck wouldn't strike my old ass twice."

"It sure doesn't." I saw a bottle of vodka on the table and poured me a glass. I was glad he didn't give me the blues like everyone else did when I drank while pregnant. On second thought, maybe he didn't know I was pregnant. "I just wanted to say bye, Grand. I'm leaving for Texas tomorrow."

"So you really are doing it?" He said sitting in the black recliner.

"I told you. Ain't nothin' in DC for me no more."

"What about Jace? I thought you two would get married when the time was right."

"He put shit in perspective for me the other day...As long as he thinks I'm a whore, I will forever be a whore. And who wants to marry a person like that?" I said forcing my pain deeply into the pit of my stomach. It hurt too much to hear and understand the truth. That I had messed up my chances with the one person I really loved.

He took another pull of his weed and said, "So when you gonna tell me what you wanted with that jailbird? The one who kidnapped you?"

"It's best you don't know."

"You know that nephew of mine stepped to me and told me to stay away from you the other day." He laughed. "That boy's fucked up in the head and he don't even know it." I never told Grand about the things Kali did to me, mainly because I was too embarrassed. "Are you fucking him or something?"

"Not anymore." I paused.

"That explains everything."

"Hey, Grand, why is Kali...You know...So violent? Did something happen to him when he was younger?"

"That boy was doomed from the day he was born." He said firing up another joint. "My sister didn't just get high with him, she stayed high with him. When she was with his father Rufus, Kali at least ate two squares. But when Rufus got clean off the drugs, and she wasn't, he left both of them.

"Whenever she got high, she'd leave Kali with anybody who had a floor. But when she wouldn't come back for him for days at a time, people got hip to her shit and wouldn't let Kalive stay at their houses no more. So she started leaving him in this abandoned one bedroom apartment she lived in. But she had two dogs in that place too and they were just as hungry as Kalive."

"Dogs? Why?"

"She figured the dogs would keep people from coming in. She didn't care that her son was in there alone with them." He said shaking his head. "If my trifling ass sister Bernie brought Kalive food, and left him in the house with those hungry dogs by himself, they'd fight him for it and would eventually take it from him. Look at his body, he got bruises all over from dog bites."

I remembered the dog marks when we took the shower together. Damn.

"This went on for days at a time, until one day she came home after being gone for a month. And both dogs were dead. But one of them...One of them..." Grand paused.

"What?! Spit it out!"

"The boy ate one of them to survive."

"Grand, please tell me you lying."

"I wish I was, Harmony. But I couldn't play with nothing like that even if I tried."

Kali's life was way worse than I ever could've imagined and as long as he stayed away from me, I didn't care.

"What happened to his mother?"

"I don't know. People saying she moved out of the state, some people saying he killed her. No one ever really found out."

I shook my head and said, "He is really fucked up."

"More than you can imagine."

I kicked it with Grand for a few minutes and went back to house. When I got home, my grandmother was in the living room on the phone. Most of the things I was taking were neatly organized and stacked against the side of the wall. And reminded me of my decision to go.

"Look, talk to this damn teacher and tell her you were lying about what you said. She been callin' my damn house every day threatening to have folks come over here because of you."

I rolled my eyes, got on the phone and said, "Yes?"

"Harmony?"

"Yes!" I repeated with an attitude.

Silence.

"Harmony, I understand you'll be leaving to stay with your aunt in Texas soon. Is this right?"

I looked at Shirley and said, "Yeah...So what?"

"Well, what are you going to do about an education? You don't even have your diploma."

"There are schools there you know." I said, as if I had intentions on going to any of them. "I am enrolling there."

"Why don't I believe you?"

"I don't know, Mrs. Duncan."

"Harmony, if you don't go to school, how are you going to support your baby?" She persisted. "You need an education."

"Who told you I was pregnant?" I said already knowing it was Shirley's ass.

"That doesn't matter, Harmony. But I hate seeing young black women go down the road you're traveling. And you need...Help. If you were sexually abused, then we can help you."

"I thought you were sending somebody to come over here. To question my grandmother and her son." Shirley stomped around in place. "What happened to that?"

"I was told your uncle died and they believe he was the one who hurt you. People find it hard to believe that your grandmother could be so cold."

"This is why kids don't tell the truth! Nobody believes them." I hung up in that bitch's face.

"You so fuckin' pathetic!" Big Shirley said. "That's a damn shame." She continued getting some gin. "You really told people about what goes on in my damn house. And I want you out tonight."

"Shirley, come on now, I'm your granddaughter." I said. "Let me stay until tomorrow and I'll be out of here for good, I promise."

She frowned and said, "And you betta tell them friends of yours to stop callin' my damn house!"

"Shirley, considering what you have done to me and considering how you threw all of my shit out of my bedroom and into the living room...I should be able to have anybody call I want."

"When are you movin' again?"

"Tomorrow." I said.

"Good!" She said walking to the back of the house.

"Can you at least tell me who called?" I asked. "Other than my teacher?"

"Jace!" She said bending the corner.

"Jace?" I said running behind her. "What…What did he say?"

"I ain't no answering service, girl. Call him back."

I quickly ran to the phone but when I did, it rang. It was Shirley's friend Lola from up the street. "Lola, can Shirley call you back? I was about to make a call."

"Naw…She asked me to get a number for her. And I have it and need to talk to her now. Somebody owes her some money."

"Lola, I got to make a call. Can I have her call you right-"

"I know damn well you ain't about to redirect one of my calls!" Shirley came from behind me, going for the phone.

I rolled my eyes and said, "I'm just trying to call Jace. It'll be…"

"Bitch, give me my phone!" she said pushing me away. Shirley was very strong when angry even though she was old.

I didn't give her shit and the next thing I know, we were tussling for the phone. If Jace called me and couldn't get in contact with me, how did I know he would call back? I was leaving tomorrow and chances are he would think I was dodging his calls. No I had to talk to him and I had to talk to him now.

When Shirley had the phone in her hand, and was about to walk away, I kicked her in the back and she fell. I know it was fucked up that I had kicked my grandmother but I didn't give a fuck.

"Bitch, you gonna wish you didn't put your hands on me!" Shirley said from the floor.

"I put my foot on you, bitch! Get it right!"

"Fuck a day, I want you out of my house, tonight!"

She was right…We hated each other too much to last another night in here alone together. Somebody was going to die and it wouldn't be me. I gave all I was willing to give and didn't have anything left. She and her daughter took my father, and then I watched my mother murdered. I can still taste her blood on my lips. Then I lived in secrecy as my uncle and grandmother raped me for years of my life. I started to hate people, especially women, because all of them seemed to hate me.

"I just wanted to use the phone, Shirley!" I said placing it back on the hook to get a dial tone. The moment I did, it rang again.

"Hello?"

"Did you get my message?" Jace asked.

His voice sounded soothing and I wanted him to hold me. I decided after all of the drama I was in, if he gave me another chance, I'd be serious about him. And never cheat on him again.

"J…Jace?"

"Yeah. What you doin' tonight?" He asked.

"Nothing."

"I'm trying to see you."

"Okay," I smiled. "Can you come get me?"

"I'ma send Kevin to pick you up. Bring some overnight clothes, too."

I looked at my stuff on the floor and decided to take my most important shit. I knew Shirley wasn't letting me back in the house for nothing else. And I didn't wanna come back.

"I'll see you soon," I said with a big ass smile on my face.

"Good, 'cause we gotta talk about you…And us."

"Us?"

"Yeah…If you really are carrying my baby, I'm ready to be serious about you."

When I got off the phone with Jace, I was lifted. This was the one thing I realized I always wanted. A family. With a father for my baby, like I had before my father was murdered and taken from me. And now, there was a possibility of having a family again. But what about the call I put in? I had to get in contact with Grand now! Maybe it wasn't too late to stop the hit! The only thing is, his party is today!

ANGRY EYES

Kali stood outside of Grand's door for ten minutes before he knocked. He was grappling with whether or not he should step to him about Harmony. He decided to do just that because when it came to her he couldn't see straight and was blindly obsessed. Plus she had information that could put him in jail for good.

"What you doing out there, Kali?" Grand asked opening the door. He was preparing to go to 7 Eleven because he always got hungry after smoking weed.

"Can I come in?"

Grand hesitated at first but then stepped back and allowed him to walk inside. When they were both in, Grand locked the door and they sat down.

"What is it, son? I'm on my way out."

"Are you...Fucking Harmony?"

Grand swallowed hard, moved around a little in his recliner and said, "You know damn well that young girl ain't giving me no pussy. My luck ain't been that good since I hit the lottery for ten thousand that one year."

Silence.

"That ain't what I asked you, nigga. I asked you are you fuckin' her?" His eyes were wild and he was sweating.

"Come on, Kalive. What's this really about?" He said with a guilty look on his face. "Are you two together?"

Kali stood up, walked toward him and said, "I'm askin' the questions."

"Okay. Well...To answer your question correctly, son, I'd have to say, no, I'm not fucking her."

"How come I don't believe you?"

"Kalive..."

"Kali." He said cutting him off. "Niggas call me Kali now."

"Okay, well, Kali, she came over to ask me for a favor. That's it. You know she wouldn't be the slightest bit interested in me."

Just then his phone rang but he didn't answer. He didn't know it was Harmony begging him to somehow get back in contact with the kidnapper to call things off. But her youth didn't allow her to understand that once vengeance has been set into motion, there are no calling things off.

"What was the favor?"

"I can't tell you. She asked me to keep it to myself."

"So she's worth dyin' for?" He laughed. "You must be fuckin' her."

"I'm not, Kali. You my nephew and I wouldn't lie to you."

"Fuck that shit! The only thing that binds us is the whore I have for a mother." He said with as much anger as one man could hold. "Now, what did she have you do?"

Grand thought long and hard about what Kali was asking him. It didn't take a rocket scientist to know that if Kali even thought he was holding out, he'd kill him. And since he was not good at keeping secrets, he knew Kali would be able to tell by looking at his face.

"She asked me to get in touch with Arnold Recaro, who kidnapped her and Jace."

"What? Why?"

"I don't know…But she sounded like she was mad at Jace and wanted to get back at him."

Kali took mental notes. "That's all she wanted you to do?" Kali asked knowing Grand had already given him all the information he had. "She didn't say nothing about me?"

"No…She didn't mention you at all." He paused. "She only wanted to get in contact with Recaro."

"Cool…So what you doing later?"

Grand breathed a sigh of relief. "Nothing. Just 'bout to run grab something from 7 Eleven and then…"

Before Grand could finish, Kali hit him in his throat with the side of his hand catching him off guard. Then he took his hand and covered his nose and mouth. Grand tried his best to scratch and claw at him, but he could barely breathe from Kali's first blow and he was no match for the strength of a man who was crazed. Before long, Grand gave up his fight and died. Kali removed his hand, which was covered in spit and snot and smiled. Murdering to him was as easy and as pleasurable as fucking. He loved to do it and he loved to do it often.

When he was back in his car, he drove to Harmony's house to see her again. But when he pulled up, he saw her getting into Jace's car. So he went in and took care of her grandmother.

OUR LAST NIGHT TOGETHER
Harmony

When I jumped into his car, I wish I'd chosen another dress to wear to his party. But I didn't have time to change plus it was too hard finding anything with all of my stuff being in the living room.

"I'll take your bag," an older black lady said to me when I entered his house again. It was the same women I'd seen the last time I was over.

When I stepped into Jace's house, instead of the room off the side of the house where I'd been before, I knew I'd never be the same. His home was beautiful and I could see myself living here, making a home for us. This was the lifestyle I needed and always wanted.

Five minutes later, Jace walks up to me with the same blank look on his face he always had. I could never read his mind, but I know he was so cute. He was wearing blue jeans, his diamond chain and a black Versace shirt. He smelled good, too.

"You wearing that?" He asked holding a bag similar to the one I saw Tony bring to him the other day I was here. I know it was filled with money. "And what happened to your ear?"

I looked down at myself and said, "You want me to leave? Because my grandmother put me out for coming over here," I lied. "And I don't have anything else to wear."

"What happened to your ear?"

"It's a long story," I said touching the small Band-Aid on it.

He frowned a little and said, "Come up stairs with me."

When we got upstairs, and walked into his room, which was mainly empty I smiled. I remember when we use to sit on the porch of his house and talk, now he owned a house bigger than anything we could have imagined. Even though it was empty, it was still

y. A bed sat in the middle of the floor and I sat on the edge of it.
walked into a closet and came back out with a dress.

With the dress in hand, he looked at me a few times and said, "Stand up for a minute." I did. "Yeah...It looks like it'll fit." Then he opened the door and I saw a bunch of women's clothing and shoes. He had moved on without me already. "Put this on." He handed me a bag from Saks Fifth Avenue.

I stood up, accepted the bag and said, "Is this another girl's dress?"

"Yeah." He said sitting on the edge of the bed to put on his shoes. He placed the bag I knew was filled with money on the floor.

"I'm not wearing another girl's dress, Jace."

"Why do you always have to be so fuckin' difficult? Why can't you just bite your tongue sometimes?"

I sat back down and the bag slid out of my hands and to the floor. "Jace, what is going on? Do you have a new girlfriend already?"

"We weren't together no more."

"We ain't never not been together, Jace. We been with each other forever and your heart has always been with me. And mine with you. Right? Ain't that why I'm here?" I paused. "Do you want to be with me or not? You confusing me."

"How am I confusing you?"

"First you tell me you done with me, then you call me to invite me over here. But when I get here, I see a bunch of women's clothing in your closet. Can we at least talk about it?"

"No. Get dressed and meet me downstairs," he said walking out of the room, grabbing the bag off the floor.

I opened the door and saw him go into another room on the other end of the hallway. Then he walked downstairs. Still mad at him, I hurried across the hall and opened the door. Then I closed it behind me, found the bag under the bed and opened it wide. Inside was at least ten stacks of twenty-dollar bills, all dirty. I stuffed a few stacks under my shirt, opened the door and then dipped back across the hall. When I was done, I placed the money stacks in my bag. I couldn't believe I had just stolen from Jace but to me, it was all his fault.

While I was alone, I looked around his room. Then I walked into this large walk-in closet and saw perfume bottles sitting on a

dresser. I couldn't describe the anger I felt inside. Figuring I'd
able to drink tonight and forget it all, I slid into the one-piece dre
and had to admit, I looked good in it. I guess whoever she was, w
had the same body type. When the dress was on, I used anothe
woman's brush to fix my hair. Then I grabbed my purse, made sure
the money was tucked deeply inside and walked out the door. The
moment I opened the door, I saw Jace leaving out of the room I had
just been in, with the bag in his hand. My heart raced thinking he
knew I'd stolen the money. He stopped where he was looked at me
and smiled.

"Uh…You ready?" He asked.

"Yes." I said walking down the stairs with him. There was
something different in his eyes when he looked at me.

"We running late."

"Jace, can't we go somewhere else tonight? Just me and you?" I
said trying to avoid him getting hurt by Massive. "I mean…I really
want to be with you alone."

"Harmony, I got over two hundred people waitin' on me and
don't need this right now." He paused. "Now let's roll." He said as
we walked out the door.

We were in the car for twenty minutes before we reached a
mansion in Maryland. There were lots of designer cars and girls
who walked around looking how I wanted too, Rich. Jace got out of
the car and opened my door and I realized I didn't know what this
statement meant. Were we back together? Was I coming as a
friend? I saw a few girls from my school looking at me and I guess
they wanted to know, too.

"Don't they call her Miss Burns?" A girl said under her breath
as I walked past.

When I turned around to see who had said what, they all turned
away. My only comfort was that I was with him and they weren't. I
was on the top step of the mansion when a pretty girl in her early
twenties blocked our path. Stepping in between us she looked at the
dress I was wearing and then at my face. A few people stopped
where they were and watched.

"Hold up! Jace, does this bitch have on my dress?"

"Antoinette, go 'head with that shit. You and I both know everything in that closet I bought."

"Answer my fucking question, Jace! 'Cause I can't believe you chose this whore over me. After all the shit you said she did to you."

"Antoinette, you're a friend of the family, but don't make me forget that shit tonight. Calm down and enjoy the party."

He tried to walk away but she stopped him and said, "So you a pimp now."

"You really wanna do this?" He asked.

"Fuck you...Fuck this bitch and fuck this party!"

Jace gave one wave of the hand and two men dragged her away like yesterday's trash. Her red high heel shoe fell off and fell in my path. He kicked it out the way for me and I smiled.

"Fuck you, Jace! Fuck you and that bitch!" She continued to cry.

Jace looked back at her, shook his head and said, "Come on."

"So I know whose dress I'm wearing now."

"Don't start with me." He said. I feared being thrown out right behind her so I remained silent. We pushed past a few people and all eyes were on us. I guess so, after the scene that bitch made.

"Is she your new girlfriend?" I said asking and stopping in my tracks.

"If she was, do you think I'd carry her like that?" He paused. "Now come on, you ruining my night."

We moved past five men who nodded at us as we walked further inside. I didn't know when Massive would make a move, or even if he would. Whatever happened, I just hoped it wouldn't be tonight. I hoped Jace would be safe so that we could start all over.

When we get deeper inside of the party, I saw Kreshon, Paco and the rest of Jace's crew. I looked around for Kali too but didn't see him and I was a little relieved.

"Damn, Jace, where the food at?" Kreshon asked walking up to us, his eyes firmly on me.

Paco stayed behind but I saw the look on his face and I smiled. When he tugged at his ear, the same ear that Ebony ripped, the smile was removed from my face.

"It ain't here yet?"

"Naw? We don't have the liquor either."

Jace appeared irritated but stepped to another person and demanded that he get on it right away. He kept saying that the food

and liquor should've been there before he did since it was his par
Then he sent Kreshon and Paco to get some liquor to hold everyor
over until the big liquor and food got there.

After he was done with them he walked up to me and said, "We
ain't got no food, but you want some juice or somethin'?"

I wanted a little something harder. "You got anything else?"

Jace grabbed me by my elbow and moved me to a smaller room
off the living room. People were looking at me and a few jealous
bitches gave me evil looks. When we were in the room alone, he
closed the door and walked up to me.

"You said you pregnant right?" He asked staring into my eyes.
He was definitely mad.

"Yeah. Why you ask me that?"

"'Cause you don't act like it. And if you want me to be serious
about you and this baby," he paused, "I mean...You and my baby,
then you got to take better care of your body."

"What are you saying?"

"Don't let me catch you drinkin' no liquor at my party tonight.
Don't let me catch you drinkin' ever. You got me, Harmony?"

"Boy, please! What difference do it make if I drink or not?
People act like the baby gonna drink out of my glass or something."

"You sound dumb as shit."

"It's true! And what about you? It's not fair that I don't get to
drink and you do."

"Are you that fucked up in the head?" He asked looking at me
like I was crazy. "That you can't understand you fuckin' your...I
mean...*Our* baby up by drinkin' and shit?"

"I know plenty of people who drank while they was pregnant."

Jace got quiet and said, "You gonna be a fucked up mother. I
just know that shit."

"Jace...It's not that serious. I won't drink anymore okay?"

He just shook his head and walked out the door. Standing in the
doorway he said, "You comin' or not?"

"What about you, Jace? Do you still get to drink, too?"

He paused and said, "Naw. I'ma quit with you."

I walked slowly behind him and on our way back into the living
room, we ran into Kali. And he looked like he just came from murdering. His hatchet was on his back as usual and I got extremely
nervous.

"Fuck are you doin' here?" Kali said to me grabbing me by my arm. Everyone who was there stopped what they were doing and looked at us.

"Kali, what's up with you, homie?" Jace said prying my arm from Kali's grasp. Then he stood between us. "'Cause you trippin' hard right now." Jace said stepping in front of me.

"Move out the way, Jace," He said pushing him aside.

"Nigga, what the fuck is wrong with you!" Jace said pushing him to the ground. Kali bounced on his ass before standing up. He was preparing to rush him but ten guards hoisted him off of his feet. One grabbed him by the neck and the other ones had their guns out on him.

"Let the nigga down," Jace ordered.

When Kali was released, he brushed himself off, mean mugged the guards and said, "Jace, you shouldn't be around this bitch. She scandalous."

"This don't have nothin' to do with you, man. This between me and Harmony."

I knew he was about to bust me and tell Jace about us fucking so I had to say something before he did.

"Jace, he just mad because he wanna fuck me and I won't let him."

"What?" Jace looked at Kali and then me. "Is this true, Kali?"

"Come on, J. You and I both know that this bitch can't be trusted. This girl is dangerous. And she got plans for you, you don't even know about yet."

I wondered what he meant but didn't want to open up a whole new can of shit. There was no way Grand would betray me and tell him anything. At least I hoped so.

"I don't know about all that." Jace told him. "But you tryin' to fuck up a nigga's shit tonight and you gotta roll. We'll talk about all this other shit later."

Please let him just leave. I thought. *Please.* He'd already said one thing too many. He was almost at the door with the guards close behind him until he said, "While you all posted up with this bitch, make sure she tell you that I might be the father of that baby she carrying."

Jace looked at me and I couldn't say anything. I was stuck.

"Hold up, what you just say?" Jace asked stopping the guards.

"I said, she may be carryin' my seed." Kali said looking delirious.

"I'm not even tryin' to hear that bullshit. Tell this nigga he's lyin'." He said looking at me then at Kali. When I didn't answer he said, "He lyin' right?"

"Tell him the truth, Harmony!" Kali added. "Ain't no sense in leading this nigga on. 'Cause if you are pregnant with my kid, I'm takin' what's mine."

I felt like the room was spinning and had to get out of there. So I ran. I knew it made me look guiltier than anything but I didn't care. People created a pathway as they moved to get out of my way. On my way out the door, I bumped into the caterers as they were bringing in food and liquor. But there was something about one of them that stood out to me. He didn't look like a normal caterer. But my mind was so consumed with Kali setting me up that I didn't care. I had to get away. I didn't even know where I was going. I just ran and ran until I ended up on a dark street. It seemed like forever for someone to drive on the dark street but eventually a black man in a beautiful black Cadillac pulled up. When I looked at him I felt safe so I jumped inside and closed the door.

"Where you headed to?" He asked me.

"To the train station. Any one...I don't care." I looked at him as we headed up the road. "Thanks for picking me up."

"Not a problem, especially after all you've done for me."

I went through my purse and made sure the money was inside. When his words played in my mind. "What do you mean after all I've done for you?"

"Isn't your name, Harmony?"

I swallowed hard and nodded. "Who are you?"

"I'm the man who got your message." He smirked. "So the least I can do is give you a ride."

BIRTHDAY WISHES

Jace

Kali fucked me up with his bullshit. Even if it were true, why wait to tell me now? We were supposed to be boys. After the shit with the kid he kidnapped and then this shit with Harmony, I was through with him. The nigga was as good as dead to me.

"You want a drink?" Tony Wop asked. He didn't see the stunt Kali pulled earlier. "You look like you need one."

The liquor had only been there for five minutes and already it was half gone. Niggas ran to the table like they hadn't drunken anything in years.

"Naw, I'm good." I told him with my hand stuffed in my pockets.

"That ain't what Ericka and Tina told me." I looked over at them, although they were pretending to not be looking over at me.

"Man, some shit goin' on with Harmony and Kali."

"What…They fuckin'?"

"I don't know, but that's what he said."

"Are you cool with that?"

"We weren't together. But she supposed to be pregnant with my kid. Now this nigga sayin' it may be his."

"I wouldn't give that shit no more attention until the baby gets here. You also need to stay the fuck away from Kali. He too much trouble. I been told you that."

When Paco and Kreshon came back with the liquor I sent them for earlier, I was happy for the diversion, even though the caterers already brought in liquor. I just wasn't in the mood to talk about Harmony or Kali anymore to Tony. I was 'bout done with all this shit and the only thing on my mind was getting money. When they walked in, I could tell they were already drunk.

"I see ya'll started the party already." I said to them.

People coughing and complaining about pains interrupted thought process.

"What the fuck is going on around here?" Kreshon asked me

"You poisonin' niggas and shit?" He laughed.

"I don't know what the fuck is goin' on." I said looking around some more. My eyes scanned around to everyone else until Tony Wop said his arms were stiffening.

"You aight?" I asked him.

"Yeah, I'm good. I think." He said gripping his arm. "I'ma 'bout to go sit down. I think I pulled a muscle or somethin'."

"Do that," I said patting him on his back. Directing my attention to Kreshon I said, "What took ya'll so long?"

"Man, we was stuck in traffic up the street. Somebody in a Cadillac got into a car accident and blocked the whole road."

"Yeah. And after the nigga in the Caddy slammed into another car, some bitch got out on the passenger side and took off runnin'. The driver rolled out. The fucked up thing was, the only thing fucked up on the Caddy was the bumper." Kreshon laughed.

"Yeah, the other nigga's car was fucked up like shit!"

They put their half empty bottles of liquor on the table along with a six-pack of beer. Suddenly I wanted a drink so I grabbed a beer and looked around to see which bitch I would fuck tonight. I needed some pussy to get my mind off of Harmony. I would've gotten in contact with Antoinette but she was getting on my nerves, too. But once I put the call into her all would be forgiven.

"Sir, there's a call for you in the car," Kevin said walking up to me. I downed the rest of my beer and followed him outside. Once in my car, I picked up the car phone.

"Hello."

"How are things?" The man said on the phone. I was stuck because the voice on the phone sounded like Massive's. I recognized his voice from the clinic.

"Who is this? And how did you get my number?"

"You know who I am, son. And I do hope you're enjoying the food and drinks I supplied for your party. I wanted you to have a memorable birthday. Since it will be your last."

"Look, either you stop playin' games and tell me what the fuck is goin' on, or I'm hangin' up."

"You ever heard of Strychnine?" Silence. "Well by now I'm sure you can tell, if you've drunken any of the alcohol, that you should be in severe pain."

"Fuck is you talkin' about?"

"You're about to be a part of a major news story, son." He laughed. "I can't wait to tell Rick that I finally took from him what he took from me. My only child."

SIX MONTHS LATER

On The Run
Harmony

Angela had taken all of the money I'd stolen from Jace and now I was broke and expecting my baby any day now. The older I got one thing remained true, that all of the women in my life weren't shit. But the light at the end of the tunnel was that I got news that Shirley was murdered. The bad part about it was, they say it was a bloody death. The first person I thought of was Kali.

When I first got to this bitch's house, she couldn't wait to drop a bomb on me by saying she wanted to help me, but the place they were staying was too small. And that if I wanted to live with her, we had to get a bigger place. So she needed all of the twenty thousand dollars I'd stashed. Against my better judgment I gave it to her. And where did we move...Out of Fourth Ward and into Fifth Ward, the most notorious area in Houston, Texas, right off of Jensen Drive. I can truly say it was the worst place I ever lived in my life.

I was in the kitchen of the five bedroom run down house when my stomach started growling. Being pregnant, I was hungry all the time. Since her kids weren't home, I decided to make a pack of Oodles of Noodles I stashed in my room before they came back and started begging. My noodles were almost done until her oldest daughter came home.

"What you cookin'?" Tyisha, asked me walking through the door. She threw her keys down on the table and walked in the kitchen. Tyisha was one year younger than me and pretty but she didn't take care of her physical appearance. She reminded me of myself because we both liked to fuck all day every day but I still didn't like her. "I'm hungry."

"I ain't makin' too much of nothing." I said.

She stood behind me and I tried to block her eyes from seeing the noodles, eggs, onions and soy sauce I had placed in my pot because she wasn't getting any.

"Well it smells good."

If Angela bought food in the house on days other than the first of the month, I wouldn't have to hide my shit. "Thank you, girl. You know I gotta feed my BABY."

"Why you always sayin' somethin' about feeding your baby?" She frowned.

She knew damn well why I kept referring to my baby. I hoped that they would feel sorry for me and leave me and my food alone! But it never worked.

"Damn, I'm so hungry!!" She said. She was so close behind me that I thought she was gonna put something in my ass.

"Tyisha, do me a favor, go get me one of the bowls out my room."

"You gonna give me some if I do?"

I was trying to get her to get my bowl so I wouldn't have to leave her alone with my food. I wasn't allowed to use their dishes but I knew if I left, she'd be all in my shit. When I first got here, Angela made it known that I was not to touch her shit, so I started buying my own stuff. The funny thing is, the rule didn't apply to her. She felt she could come in here and borrow all kinds of shit, which I never got back. If I wanted to be able to feed myself, I had to get out of here and I had to do it soon.

"It's not enough for you," I told her. "I would if it was though."

She frowned and said, "Well, I'm 'bout to go back outside. You gotta go get it yourself."

The look in her eyes told me that the moment I hit the corner, to get my bowl, I'd be lucky if half of my food was left. So I took the pot into the room with me, poured it in my bowl and brought it back to the kitchen.

"Ugggghh!!! You so fucking petty!" She frowned. "Wasn't nobody gonna touch your food."

"I didn't say you were, but since you wouldn't get the bowl for me I had to do it myself."

"Whatever," she said walking her fishy ass out the door.

When she was gone I sat on the bed in the small ass room and ate my food. Then I looked at the small room I lived in and turned on a black and white TV in the corner. The only things in the room was a dresser where the TV sat, my closet which was jammed with a bunch of boring ass clothes since I couldn't afford anything nice and my food.

"Harmony, you home?" Angela yelled entering the house. "I have company so come out dressed! Somebody out here I want you to meet." She continued in her southern accent.

I belched a few times and put on something presentable. The sodium was killing me while I was pregnant but I needed foods I could cook quickly. When I was done I walked into the living room.

My aunt Angela was much shorter than me but still attractive. She didn't look like she was in her forties and could pass for her early thirties easily. But she wore the same thing over and over again. A pair of blue jeans and a brown button down work shirt from Central Parking Systems where she was a cashier. Her hair was pulled back into a ponytail so tight that the edges of her hairline rippled.

The guy who was with her was a known drug dealer in Houston and although he had a cute face, he always looked like he was up to something. He favored rapper Dougie Fresh greatly.

"Yeah...I ain't know she was that far along. She'll be perfect." He said before even speaking.

"Perfect for what?" I asked sitting on the couch rubbing my belly. "What ya'll talking about?"

"Braxton, this is my niece Harmony. And Harmony this is Braxton."

"I know who he is." I said. "Everybody in Fifth Ward knows him." He smiled. "That wasn't supposed to be a compliment."

He frowned and said, "I'm glad you know who I am, because we are going to be real close over the next couple of weeks."

"Why are *we* going to be close?" I asked. The baby felt like it was kicking me everywhere.

"I'll explain."

"Look...I'm tired and wanna go back in my room and get some rest. So get to the point."

"You always restin'." Angela said. "I need you to start helpin'."

"Well I am pregnant, Angela. What do you expect?"

She rolled her eyes and sat down on a chair across from me, but next to him.

"Braxton has a way for us to earn a few extra dollars. And since you not bringin' in no money no more, I need you to do what he needs."

"Why I gotta help? When my baby comes, I'ma draw welfare."

"That ain't enough money, stupid." She yelled.

"Well it need to be. Anyway, why I gotta help? Why can't you ask your oldest daughter? We're about the same age."

"Cause I'm askin' you." She told me. "Plus she ain't eighteen."

If I continued to go against her I knew she would put me out. I had to help her and it was as simple as that. "Doing what, Angie?"

"Tell her, Braxton." She was all excited and I knew it was because she had already counted the money she was going to make in her mind.

Before he even opened his mouth, I got up. "What are you doing?" She asked.

"Getting a beer." I grabbed one out of the refrigerator and had gulped over half when I caught the strange look Braxton was giving me. "What?"

"Hold up, you pregnant?"

I rolled my eyes, rubbed my stomach and said, "Yeah…So what?"

"Well you shouldn't be drinking."

"Nigga, I'ma grown ass woman." I could feel the baby kick in my stomach like it normally did when I drank liquor. I think it likes it or something.

"You can fuck that baby up with that shit."

I was feeling myself because I knew he needed me more than I needed him. "Look, me possibly helping you with your scheme and me drinking what I want is two different things. So stay the fuck out of my business."

I was finishing up my beer when he got up and smacked me so hard in the face, the edge of the beer cut my lip. The can rolled out of my hand and landed against the edge of the wall and beer drenched my shirt. All I could do was cry because I was so fucking angry.

"Like I said, you pregnant, and you ain't supposed to be drinking." He said sitting back down. He looked at me with an evil stare and then at Angela. "At least not in front of me anyway."

"I can't believe... You just hit me."

Instead of her asking him why he hit me Angela said, "Harmony, you know I told you before to stop drinkin'. You kinda had it comin'."

"Fuck you, nigga!" I yelled. "You say beer bad for me yet you'd hit me in the face." I continued. "So that's not bad for the baby, too?"

"'Cause you talkin' reckless. Now let's move past that shit and get down to business. You not drinkin' no more so enough said."

I was enraged.

"Angela I don't know what the fuck is going on but I don't want no part of this shit or him. So leave me out of it."

I moved to go to my bedroom when he said, "Bitch, sit your ass back down."

"Why so you can hit me again?" I turned around to ask him.

"You think you can talk to niggas any kind of way, huh? That's your M.O? Talking to niggas recklessly without consequences?" He asked. "Now if I ask you to sit down again, you gonna have a problem with your legs, too." I sat back down on the couch and he started, "Now...I need you to fly to DC and pick up a package for me. Then I need you to fly back with it the next day."

"What? You want me to smuggle drugs from DC to Texas?"

"Yes."

"I can't do no shit like that." I said looking between them, my face still burning from his touch.

I hadn't been to DC since I set Jace up and I wasn't in any hurry to get back there any time soon. I didn't have anyone I could trust to find out the status of things so I didn't know if he knew I was involved. After Massive tried to kidnap me, on the night of Jace's party for the second time, I punched him in the face so hard he crashed. I was able to get away on foot with my life and I was scared of going back.

"You can and you will do it," He said.

"If I get arrested, then what?"

"Then you don't talk." He told me. "It's simple. You take the rap and we'll make sure shit good for you when you come home.

You don't have a record so I doubt they'd give you too much time anyway."

"Well I don't want *no* time."

"Harmony, when your father was alive he took care of everybody. But he's gone now and we have to take care of ourselves. Now he's gonna give you twenty five hundred dollars every time you go and come back. That's a lot of money."

"And how much you getting?"

"I'm talkin' about you," Angela said, "and the fact that you not gonna have a place to live unless you do this. Everybody here has to pitch in and that means you, too. Don't think just because you're pregnant I'll let you pass."

"I don't wanna do this." I said to myself, knowing no one else cared.

"Harmony, ain't but one pussy can be in charge at a time and it damn sure ain't yours."

I had heard that saying before from my mother, and I wondered who stole it from who. In the end it served its purpose because it reminded me that I didn't have a choice. Bitches were scandalous especially when you had to live with them. I had no money, no place to go and if I moved back to DC, I would have to take the risk of somebody trying to kill me. Not to mention I was over eight months pregnant. My life was in her hands.

"When do I start?"

"Tomorrow."

●━━━━━━━━━━━━━━━━━━━━━●

Braxton had his brother Monkey drive me to the airport in his black Benz. Monkey was more attentive then his brother and I felt a little more relaxed around him. But I was still being made to do something I didn't want to do so I felt on guard.

"What happened to your face?" He asked me driving down the highway leading to the airport. Monkey was extra black and tall. Although he was a little darker than my taste, he was still very attractive.

"Your brother hit me," I paused looking over at him while the baby in my belly kicked wildly. I needed something to drink just thinking about it. Alcohol made me forget it all. "He ain't tell you?"

"Naw. He be off some dumb shit most of the time. Just do wha he asks you and it'll be fine."

"Can you tell me who I'm meeting?"

"I can't tell you shit but to be careful and be where you're supposed to be. The person will come looking for you." He paused. "When you get there you have the number you got to call right?" I nodded yes but was worried. "What's wrong? You gonna be on the plane and off before you know it."

"If it's so easy, why they have to come for me? Why couldn't they get somebody else to do it?"

"You pregnant so people won't suspect you as much."

"What about the other people who did it?"

He was silent and I already knew what happened. "How much time they get when they got caught?"

"Don't worry about all that. Just do what you got to do and play it safe. They went in there acting young and dumb and made a move that not only brought attention to themselves, but made them hot."

"What they do?"

"I ain't supposed to be tellin' you this but for some reason, I fuck with you."

I smiled. "I'm listening."

"We had two sisters doing it for us at first. One of them was afraid of airplanes and had to have a drink right before she boarded *every* time. On the day they had our last package, they went overboard and got hemmed up. The girl was actually talking about the weight she was carrying and how most police officers were stupid. They were being extra loud and dumb. Anyway, an off duty officer had them checked and found our product on their bodies and bags. They got late and we cut them off."

"How do I know an officer won't check my bag?"

"Because we playing it smarter by putting you by yourself. Just keep your mouth closed, meet the dude you have to in DC and come back home."

I never did anything like this before and I didn't know how I should act but it was all or nothing now. I was thinking about what I was facing when my baby started kicking again. I didn't have love for the baby growing inside of me like everyone thought I should. I felt burdened and couldn't wait for the day I could pop it out of me, and go on with my life.

"Ow!" I said when the kick got wilder.

"The baby kickin' your ass?" He asked me.

I laughed and said, "Yeah. All the time."

Silence.

"You still with the baby father?"

"Naw. We not together no more."

"You sounded sad when you said that…You still love him or something?"

"No…It's over for real."

"So you gonna raise this baby by yourself?"

"Yeah."

He smiled and said, "You too pretty to be raising a kid by yourself."

"So If I was ugly it would be fine?"

"Yeah." He laughed. "And I wouldn't give a fuck." I laughed harder. Spending time with him, in the car on the way to the airport was the best fun I had since moving to Texas. "Let's do this…If you don't get locked up, I'ma take you out when you get back."

"If I don't get locked up?" I said scared.

"I'm just fucking with you."

I calmed down and said, "Why you wanna take me out? I'm pregnant and don't have anything going for myself."

"Because I'm trying to get to know you. That's why. Give yourself some credit, Harmony. You got more to offer than you realize."

"You don't even know me yet."

"God favors the rejected sinners." He said looking into my eyes before looking back at the road. "How else can you give a testimony, unless you been through a hard life?"

I'd never heard anyone talk like him and knew I had to be around him, just to get uplifted. "You seem real smart."

He laughed and said, "Look, I'm no smarter than the average nigga. I just know something special when I see it. And I also know you hate being around Angela and her bad ass kids. You need a break. So what's up?"

"You gonna pick me up from the airport?"

"I'ma be there."

"Then I guess we have a date."

RAUNCHY BY T. STYLES | 190

Two Weeks Later

Monkey didn't have money like his brother Braxton, but he had his own house in the hood with a room for the baby when it was born. He took care of me, and made sure I ate and didn't mind me having the occasional beer if I wanted to, just as long as I didn't do it too much. There was a time when I wanted clothes, cars, and money. And to be honest I still did want those things, but staying with Angela made me realize that for now, I needed the basics so I could have this fuckin' baby in peace. Without worrying about somebody stealing the food out of my mouth.

Although I wasn't feeling transporting drugs from DC to Texas at first, eventually it was second nature. I did it so effortlessly that they started sending me back more often. The only problem was every time I went to DC, I met up with the same person. This dude name Domingo, who kept trying to holla at me. Just t like Monkey, he didn't care that I was pregnant. I didn't know so many dudes were attracted to pregnant females. Domingo would do shit like hold me up on giving me the package, if I didn't eat with him and shit like that. Eventually I told Monkey and he stopped bothering me all together. He told me I would regret telling Monkey though...And I never knew what that meant.

The only other issue I had with transporting was during a close call when a few cops were determined to help me grab my luggage off the belt. I argued them down at first but it turns out that they didn't want me lifting the bag because of my pregnancy. They had no idea that they helped me lift 7 kilos of coke in my suitcase. They even walked it to my car and Monkey was horrified when he saw their faces. I had to warn him silently with my eyes to take it easy. He didn't breathe fully until we pulled off without handcuffs being on our wrists.

A half an hour later, he was still looking in the rearview mirror hoping the cops wouldn't run down on us and lock us up. Even as nervous as he was all the time, with Monkey in my life shit was finally looking up for me.

I was cooking Monkey his favorite dinner when he called and told me he would be running late. He sounded worried and that kinda put me on edge. I always felt that any day now, something would happen and Monkey would leave me alone but so far he never did.

"What's wrong, baby?" I asked him.

"I can't tell you over the phone. I'll see you in a little while."

"Is it something I did?"

"Babes, there's nothing you can do to make me mad at you. It some other shit I'll rap to you about later."

I was a little upset because I was looking forward to spending some quality time alone with him. If he was upset, that would ruin the moment. We both knew the baby would be here any day now and that the freedom we had would be over. Even though I was pregnant, our sexual relationship was still good. Me and Monkey fucked every day since I moved in and it was the one thing I looked forward too. He didn't let my pregnancy stop him from pleasing me and I was starting to fall for him, even though I never fully got over Jace.

When he finally came home he looked like something was heavy on his mind. He normally came home happy but tonight was different.

"What's wrong?" I asked sitting his plate in front of him. "Everything cool with Braxton?"

"No." He said looking at me seriously. "He got locked up, Harmony. Now I gotta get in bed with them dudes from DC and I ain't feeling that shit."

"What…I mean…I thought you were in charge of the blocks and collecting the money. Why that got to change now that Braxton locked up?"

"Who else gonna run shit if Braxton gone? We don't trust nobody else like that." He told me. "Our main circle is small. It's just me, Braxton you and Angela. I'm next in charge so it has to be me. I already made the call to our connect." He paused. "Shit is going to be a little different, Harmony. I can't spend the time with you like I have been."

"But…For the first time in a long time, I'm happy."

"And we still will be happy," He told me pulling me to him. Then he rested his head on my belly. "But I want my little boy to come into this world not having to worry about shit."

I told him it was a boy and that I'd gone to the doctor. Truthfully I never went to the doctors. I just told him that so he could get off of my back about making sure that the baby was healthy.

"So...What does it mean to be in charge?"

"Well, for starters I got to meet up with our connect regularly. You might have to take trips back to DC more often too after the baby is born."

"You know I'ma do whatever I can for you." I told him.

"I know."

"Is that it?" I asked. "It seems like something else is wrong with you."

"Naw. Well...I think somebody was following me. At least I thought somebody was following me."

"When?"

"Tonight."

"Monkey, you always think somebody following you. You gotta relax, baby."

"It's easier said than done."

"How did Braxton get caught?" I said skipping the subject.

"I don't know. He was on his way to drop off a package because Angela got sick, when the cops picked him up. The only people who know about the drop was Angela, me and the connect."

"Why the connect?" I asked. It seemed suspicious that the connect would still be involved after a package was delivered.

"He asked us to make a special delivery for him. And gave us a few more packs to do it, too."

"You don't think Angela was involved do you?"

"I'm not sure." He paused not even touching his food. He loved my cooking. "Look, I gotta go wash up. I'ma eat that when I get out the shower, babes. I'm hungry as shit, too."

"Okay." I picked up his plate and put it back in the pot to warm it up again.

I hated that Monkey had to go through any of this shit alone. He was so good to me and sometimes I felt I didn't deserve him. He made sure I was safe and even went at his brother Braxton on several occasions when he disrespected me. Although I trusted him, I'd been burned so many times that I started stashing money just in case. It was my little nest egg so that when I had this baby, I could get on my feet, buy some new gear and even a car. But first I would have to lose this baby weight. If Monkey still wanted me after it was all said and done, I was gonna try to be monogamous with one dude. Something I'd never done before.

Monkey had washed up and threw on some new jeans, a plain white T-shirt and his chain. Then he sat in the living room and watched the football game. He ate his food but still didn't look like himself and it bothered me. Normally I didn't give a fuck about people but with him shit was different.

He was really into the game until we heard a knock at the door. He took a deep breath and walked toward it. For the first time ever, I realized he wasn't cut out for the drug game. I'd been around men who were ready before and he wasn't one of them. If I wasn't in his life, he probably would not have been bothered. He talked about working at the auto body shop working on cars. That's what he loved. But now, it was all about the drug game, and I preferred it that way.

Monkey opened the door and I saw him give a pound to someone I couldn't really see. I cut a couple slices of apple pie, and placed them on our plates as I waited patiently to see who came over.

"What are you doin' here, man?" Monkey asked. "I didn't know you were in town."

"I come at a bad time?" When I heard that voice, my heart dropped.

"Naw, wifey in the kitchen makin' apple pie. Come on inside and meet her." I knew that voice like I knew my own face. I heard it many, many times before. "Harmony, come over here baby." Monkey said to me.

I slowly walked over to the door and my legs felt like water underneath my body. I wanted to run but where could I go?

"How you doin', Harmony? Long time no see." He looked at me evilly. What really tripped me out was that I saw Nut and Cherry standing behind him. They looked strung out and not kept together like they normally did.

"You two know each other?" Monkey asked looking in between our intense stares.

"Yeah I know her, nigga. Very well."

"How?" Monkey frowned.

"This bitch carryin' my baby," he said before shooting Monkey in the stomach. "Now get the fuck outta my face."

"Oh my, GOD!" I screamed falling down to the floor to hold Monkey. His blood poured out of his body and drenched my shirt. "Why did you do that?!!!!"

Monkey looked scared as he gripped his stomach. He was still gasping for air when Kali said, "Nigga, die already!" And shot him in the throat.

I jumped up against the wall and Kali walked up to me, placed one hand around my neck and kissed me in my mouth. The hatchet he carried was still on his back and I wondered if he would use it. His breath tasted nasty and I hated him all over again.

"This some wild shit." He released me and stood a few feet away to observe me. "The moment I give up on trying to find you, you come right to me."

"What do you want?"

"My baby!"

Nut and Cherry walked inside and they both grabbed me by my arms and pushed me to the floor. When I was on the floor, Nut took Kali's hatchet off of his back while he held me down in her place.

"How did you know I was here?" I cried. "Why can't you just leave me alone?!"

"I found out when you dropped off the last shipment." He smirked. "I couldn't believe my luck when Domingo told me about this fine as bitch name Harmony. Who was pregnant..." He paused. "I thought to myself, 'Self, there can't be two fine ass pregnant bitches name Harmony in the world." He continued. "And you know what, I was right!"

"You're the connect from DC?"

"Yeah. I got my own operation now. Since you fucked shit up with me and Jace, I had to go off on my own." He said. "But once I found out you were working with them Houston boys, I moved heaven and earth to get to you."

"You had something to do with Braxton getting locked up?"

"What you think?" He said. "It took me all this time, and I finally found you."

"Kali, please leave me alone. We were supposed to be friends."

"And you are one of my best friends. Why do you think I killed your grandmother? And your uncle? And your dog?" He paused. "I killed everybody who has ever caused you a problem."

"Then what do you want with me?" I cried. "Why can't you just let me go?"

"Because I came for my baby." He said. "I told you that already."

Nut stood over top of me with the hatchet, lifted my shirt and lunged it into my stomach.

"Don't cut too deep." Kali advised.

Kali pressed his hand over my mouth and I could not begin to describe the pain I was in. It was totally unbearable. I felt them tugging and pulling at my body but didn't know what they were doing. Then out of nowhere, Kali takes the hatchet and slashes me across the face.

My face burned. My stomach burned and I wanted to die. After awhile I didn't feel the pain anymore. Just extreme pressure, before I passed out cold.

THE DELI

Jace

After five location changes I knew this was the place for us to be. There was a leak in my organization and I wasn't having any more excuses. I tightened down on my circle and now we were eight deep including me. After Massive poisoned and killed over twenty people at my party, which caused the cops to fuck with me every day of my life, I couldn't make money as easy as I could before. This change was necessary for the operation. We even tried showing him the same consideration he showed us by poisoning him, too. But every piece of food he ate, was inspected. Even the clothing he used was brought in by a special linen cleaning company.

When I got out of my limo, my bodyguards Kevin and Antony checked my surroundings thoroughly. When the coast was clear, I followed them into the Gee's Deli on Good Hope Road in Southeast DC.

"Hello, sir. Everyone's in the back waiting," said Paris, a neighborhood girl I trusted to run the counter. She was young and dedicated to moving up in the ranks. Since there wasn't a lot of places I could use a female, I told her to start with lookout at the deli. If she continued to prove her loyalty, I'm sure I'd be able to find her something else. There's one thing you can never have enough of and that was loyal people.

"Thanks. Is my cousin here?" I asked.

"No, he called and said he wasn't feeling well again."

Ever since the poisoning, Tony had been off. We were able to get him to the hospital in time for them to help him, but his mind had never been right since. Massive killed all those people to get to me and failed. And it was only because I had Kreshon and Paco get some beer from the outside, which I drunk instead, that's why I was still alive today. Mostly everybody else who drank Massive's poisoned liquor died.

As I walked toward the back, Antony stayed at the door to deter any customers from coming inside and Kevin followed me. We were closed until our meeting was over because I had a few things to discuss with my squad in private.

"Aight, if he calls come back and get me." I told Paris.

"Yes, sir."

I moved toward the back of the deli but before I walked into the room, he walked inside to be sure everything was okay. When it was he said, "Everything's good, sir."

"Thanks."

I walked inside and Kevin stayed outside at the door. Most of my crew was there and I was ready to tell them about the new direction we would be taking.

"What up, Jace?" Said Kreshon.

"How's it going, boss?" One of my new men said.

I sat at the table they were seated at, and folded my hands. I knew they wouldn't understand my reason for our next move but I was running shop and I was going to do what needed to be done.

"As you all know, we own pretty much all of Southeast DC." I paused. "We are the single source for the manufacture and distribution of crack cocaine in these areas. But by the end of the week, we will be the single source for the entire city."

"What?" Kreshon laughed. "I thought we were gonna move slow, especially after that attack from Massive."

"Fuck movin' slow. We moved slow enough and the money not comin' in how I want it. It's time to push."

"Don't you think we'll get some flack from the people we distribute to?" Paco said. "They buyin' from us but won't be able to move it if we take their territories."

"Yeah...We gonna catch plenty of flack. But they gonna catch more."

"Then why fuck with it?" Asked Paco.

"Because I got plans to take DC now, and Maryland later. Why move to Maryland if I don't even have DC yet? We need DC...I need DC."

"Whoa…This is a serious move." Kreshon added. "And a heavy one, too."

"But we can do it," I assured them. "I want what I want and what I want is DC."

"Kali know we making this move?" Kreshon asked.

Although me and Kali had our riff the night of my birthday party, I kept him on as muscle. He didn't need to come to our meetings and I never invited him because I still couldn't trust him, as far as I could see him.

"Kali and Tony Wop will be brought up to speed when its time."

Prior to my decision to change things up a little, Tony Wop handled our connect. But ever since he got poisoned I had a feeling he was the reason we were losing kilos of cocaine at a time. He'd claim he'd have a package delivered of a certain weight, but when our customers got it, it would always be short. And I'm not talking about a little short, I'm talking kilos short at a time. Tony would claim it was our connect and our connect would tell us to fuck off when we told him we needed to weigh each individual pack prior to money exchanging hands. So I found a solution for everything. And part of my plan was taking Tony off the weight.

"So now what?" Kreshon asked.

"For starters this is our new meetin' spot." I looked around. "And whenever we transport, we will transport using one of the five company delivery vans we've purchased out back. The only ones driving the vans will be Paco and four other drivers I just hired. People will think we're making food deliveries, when we're delivering something else."

"Sounds like what Grand did with the ice cream trucks." Kreshon said.

"Naw…We stop for no one but our customer." I paused. "We're also changin' our connect."

"What?" Paco said. "Why?"

"Because he had an issue when I requested that each kilo be weighed by one of our people before purchase. He claimed my pops didn't do business that way so he wouldn't handle shit that way with me either."

"So you think he was the reason supply was short?" Kreshon asked.

"It's either that, or mismanagement on Tony's part or..."

"Or what?" Paco asked.

"Or one of my men has been stealin' from me." I looked at all of them seriously. I wanted them to know what I was putting on the line for the sake of loyalty. They also needed to know with all seriousness that if I found out someone in my camp was stealing from me, there would be problems. I had come to the conclusion that I would be a far worst enforcer than my father ever could.

"What about Kali?" Paco said. "If we talkin' about trust, he need to be here, too."

"Come on, man. Don't start that shit." Kreshon said. "I told you to drop it earlier."

"Drop what?" I asked.

"We were talkin' about a few things before you got here." Kreshon started. "And I don't know if you know it, but Kali been out of town a lot lately. I know he your peoples, but I think he doing a few business deals on the side."

"That's a heavy statement, man. You better be sure it's true."

"I'm not, but if you want, I can find out for you."

"Yeah do that, and get back with me."

Muscle or not, if Kali was stealing from me, there would be serious repercussions.

"I also want to let you know that I heard a few dudes say that Massive is building shops in Southwest and Northeast DC. This is what sparked my reason for takin' over those areas. Not only do I not want this mothafucka gettin' money in my city, but if we continue to allow him to eat here, he will eventually move us out all together. And with the new whips ya'll driving, I know you don't want that." They all nodded in agreement.

"We moving on Southwest DC tomorrow night. With the other areas right behind them."

"What?" Kreshon asked as they all looked up at me. "That ain't enough time. Plus Porter Don ain't letting up off them spots that easily."

"Fuck Porter Don!" I told them. "Especially after I find out that this nigga's working with Massive." I could tell by the looks on their faces they didn't know that.

"Jace, you the boss and I respect that. But you can't go after Porter Don with the power we got by tomorrow. I'm all for takin' some shit but that's too soon." Kreshon paused. "We don't have enough man power."

"We got enough."

"How?" Kreshon laughed. "We only got about 100 niggas we can call on at any given time. The rest will have to be flown in from L.A. To fuck with Porter Don we gonna need at least five hundred niggas."

"We got more than that."

Everybody laughed.

"How many?" Paco said. "'Cause I'm with Kreshon give or take a nigga or two."

"We have access to one thousand men."

They all laughed again. "Boss, I don't mean to make light of what you sayin' and definitely on what you're tryin' to do because I know it need to be done." Kreshon started. "But we never had access to a thousand men."

"We do now."

"Well how did it go up from one hundred to one thousand in less than twenty four hours?" Paco asked.

"Because now we fuckin' with the Russians."

PART THREE

PRESENT DAY

Green Door – Adult Mental Health Care Clinic
Northwest, Washington DC

"Ms. Phillips, some of the things you did, don't seem to have been necessary." Mrs. Christina Zahm, said.

"Like what?"

"For instance, stealing the girl's earrings, or leaving the baby in the house by herself. It's almost like you enjoyed causing drama."

"Well I didn't."

"Do you think you're capable of love? Real love?"

"I can't say that I am. Nobody ever taught me love, except my father."

"What about when you were with Jace. Did you feel love then?"

"No…But I think I did when I was with Monkey. There was something about him that was unconditional. Even when I was with Jace, I always felt like if I did the wrong thing, wore the wrong thing or even said the wrong thing, love would be taken away. I guess he wasn't taught love either. His mother died, his father was not there and he was basically in the same shoes as me."

"What about your kids? Did you ever really love your kids?"

Silence.

"No. I can't say that I ever did."

TOUGH LESSONS

Three Years Later
Harmony

I had two three-year old fraternal twins I didn't want and I hated them for it. Turns out I wasn't pregnant with one but two babies. 'Cause of them, I went from living in a mansion, to living in a shelter called, *The Star of Hope* in Houston Texas, in less than twelve years. My face was slashed, my stomach was ripped to shreds and when people saw me they either gawked or ran. The only thing about me that I liked was the fact that my body was on par. So men didn't mind fuckin' me if I turned around and let them hit it from the back. It was the only way I could keep a little money in my pockets since I couldn't keep a job.

I was sitting on my cot, trying to get out of my chore for the day, which was helping to clean the kitchen. Everybody had chores and I hated bathroom and kitchen duty most of all. While I was going through one of the two bags I owned which included mines and my kids' clothes, one of my Spanish fly by night friends walked up to me. She stayed in the shelter, too. All though I never had a *real* best friend, if I was going to have a friend at all she was it. She knew all about Kali and Jace and my troubles back in DC and never told a soul. She was so easy to talk to that sometimes I forgot I barely knew her. We had plans to get an apartment together when we got jobs. Together with four kids between us, we were prepared to share a room if we had to.

"Harmony, we got some smoke," Marisol Hernandez said, in a thick Spanish accent. She was waving a baggie in front of me and smiling.

I looked around and said, "Girl, you betta put that shit down before somebody see it."

"Look at you bein' all scared," she laughed.

"Bitch, fuck you." I joked. "Jayden and Madjesty, go over there and play." I said referring to a small space a few feet over from our cots. My kids were nosey as shit and were liable to tell one of the staff members if they overheard us.

When they were out of earshot she said, "You wanna hit it with us? We goin' out back."

"Yeah. Let me get somebody to watch my kids for me." I said standing up. "Who watchin' yours?"

"Uh...I'm not sure." She hesitated walking over to her cot which was not too far from mine. "But school is out so you can ask any of the high schoolers."

"Stop lyin', bitch. I know you know who watching your own kids." I walked up to her.

"Harmony," she paused, "nobody really likes watching your kids. They too bad." She turned around, looked at me, and then looked away. The scar was hard for people to look at up close and sometimes I used it to my advantage to intimidate mothafuckas.

"And your kids not bad? Didn't Luisa and Rosa just get in trouble for stealing a kid's toy the other day?"

"Harmony, please!" She said walking around me. "Nobody's kids are as bad as yours."

I looked at Jayden and Madjesty across the way digging into Ms. Tami's bags and shook my head. Sometimes I felt like dumping them off but I didn't want shit coming back to me. And to think, the day Kali, Nut and Cherry stole them out of my body and left me for dead in Monkey's house...On the floor...I prayed that God would bring them back to me. Now I feel like they're nothing more than two bags of luggage God has burdened me with.

I didn't think I would make it out alive that night. But someone heard me screaming and saw three people running from the house with two babies. The witness called the police and the ambulance came and saved my life. It took ten blood transfusions but eventually I survived. And since I didn't have insurance and the focus was just on saving my life, they stitched my face up recklessly and sent me on my way. Leaving me scarred for life.

It took them three weeks to find my babies. The three of them were caught hiding in a Super 8 Motel. They said the babies had long umbilical cords still attached to them and they were smaller than they should have been because they weren't feeding them right. After they found them, they convicted Kali for murder and attempted murder. While Nut and Cherry were charged as accessories to his crimes.

The trial was in the papers nationwide, and for six months after, I was able to sell my story to writers for money. Now nobody cared and every day of my life I lived in fear, not knowing when or if Kali would ever be released from prison. Nut and Cherry were out already and I wondered where they could be. I never understood why they felt the need to help Kali, and I guess I never would.

After the trial, everywhere I'd moved, he'd find me and threaten to kill me when he got out. So I got tired of looking over my back and eventually moved to the homeless shelter where a lot of people were around me at all times. I'd been here for six months and although I wanted to move now, I couldn't find a place to live because I couldn't keep a job.

"Did you know I'm moving tomorrow? I found a place." Marisol said skipping the subject.

"Oh really?" How in the fuck did this bitch find a place? She didn't have a job either. "I thought we were moving together. What happened to that plan?"

"I didn't think you were serious." She said with a dumb look on her face. "Were you? I mean, we barely know each other, Harmony. You can come visit me though."

"Oh, but you know me enough to be in my business every day, huh?" While we were talking Jayden started screaming and I walked over to him and slapped his face. Sometimes for whatever reason, beating them made me feel better. It helped get some of the hate I had for the world out of my system.

"Why did you just slap him?"

"Fuck that! What happened to our plan?"

"I can't take you with me." She said in a low voice looking at my boys. "A good opportunity dropped in my lap and I got to take it."

"And what opportunity is that?"

"Do you know Mr. Ramsey, in the men's part of the shelter?"

"Yeah."

"Well he inherited a house. His mother died and he has an extra bedroom in a large house in Galveston, Texas. All I have to do is pay for the groceries and me and the kids can stay there."

"Mr. Ramsey?" I said confusedly. "I thought you didn't like him."

"I didn't," she said. "But you know how it is. He has the ability to help me and my family, and I need his help. You would've done the same thing."

She was right. "Who's staying in the house with him?"

"He has a son, He's about twenty four. He'll be there, too."

I knew immediately what my plan would be and it was all thanks to Marisol.

"Wow. I know you happy." I said nudging her. "But you know you gonna have to give up that pussy if you wanna stay there for good."

"Yeah," she said looking down at her hands. "I have to do what I have to do." She paused. "But he said he's going to marry me. So I won't be just some whore living in his house. I'll be his wife."

I was enraged.

I was jealous.

I was mad.

What gave this bitch the right to have a come up? Why her? Why not me? Someone who had been given a tough break from the beginning. Where was my chance at life.

"Where are your sisters going to go?"

Marisol's two sisters lived here too. They ended up at the shelter when their entire apartment complex was burned down, after her grandfather who also lived in the building, dropped a lit cigarette on the floor. He died and so did forty something people right along with him. Marisol and her sister's were a few of the only survivors.

"Look, we are about to hit this joint outside," she smiled. "It's a going away present from my sister Arial. If you want to join us, we'll be out back. But hurry. You know how they are."

"I'll be out in a minute."

When she left I thought about Mr. Ramsey. He was the one man in the shelter who kept telling me how attractive I was so I couldn't understand his sudden interest in Marisol.

The scar on my face didn't seem to bother him, and I hated him for it. I hated him for trying to make me feel like I was still attractive when I knew that I wasn't. It embarrassed me when he called me pretty or sexy. But now, he held the key to life out of here and I wanted to use it.

I walked up to Jayden and Madjesty and saw Jayden playing with a doll. "What I tell you about that?" I asked him.

"Not to."

"That's right! You play with cars not dolls! Okay?"

"Yes, mam."

"Look, ya'll stay right here and don't move. Do you hear me?"

"Why?" Madjesty said. "Where you going?"

"Look, don't make me cave your chest in." I yelled at him. "Stay right here!"

Out of both of my sons, Madjesty was the most rebellious. He wasn't as calm as his brother Jayden and it pissed me off. He seemed to hate the world as much as I did.

"If I come back and you've moved one inch, I'ma drop kick both of you."

With that, I walked toward the men's section of the shelter and had someone get Mr. Ramsey for me. Women weren't allowed on their side. It took about ten minutes for him to come outside and a smile spread across his face when he saw me.

I seductively walked up to him and said, "Mr. Ramsey, long time no see."

Mr. Ramsey was in his thirties and with me being only twenty-one, I was still considered a tender young thing to him. He had a lot of grey hair to be thirty-something but wasn't very clean or attractive. If he cleaned himself up though, he wouldn't be that hard on the eyes.

"Well, what did I do to deserve this visit?" He said walking up to me licking his dry cracked lips.

He placed his hands on my shoulders and massaged them oddly. It's like he knew I would come to him. Now that I think of it, I was starting to believe it was his plan all along. Maybe he knew Marisol would tell me that he had inherited the house, because he knew she told me everything.

"I hear you moving. And I'm wondering why you weren't going to say goodbye to me. What...You don't like me no more?"

He smirked. "Of course I do." He smiled. "But yes, I came up on some property in Galveston. So I'm leaving tomorrow."

"Well I'm wondering why you didn't invite me and my kids? And why you chose Marisol?"

"Because I didn't think you were interested in me, beautiful." The hair on the back of my neck stood up and I could see my ugly reflection in the browns of his eyes. I was nowhere near beautiful. "Whenever I walked over to you, you acted like I had the plague or something. Like you didn't want to be bothered, sexy."

"Well you were wrong," I said wrapping my arms around his waist. And then I looked around us and when I saw no one looking our direction, I cuffed his dick. "And if you let us move in with you, I'll show you better than I can tell you."

My plan worked perfectly and by the end of the day, he let Marisol know that she would not be moving with him and that I would be instead. Marisol walked around all day long with an attitude. I knew I had to leave because I couldn't fight and I knew she wanted my blood. I even asked Ramsey if he had a few bucks for me and my kids to stay in a hotel until the morning, but he said all his money was tied up on stuff for the house, and that I would have to wait. I wished he hadn't told her it was me who was moving with him, but now it was too late.

I was in the bed halfway sleep, with my kids in the bunk next to me, when someone grabbed me by my hair, covered my mouth and dragged me out a side door. I tried to kick and fight but there were too many of them. When I got outside, Marisol and her sisters jumped me. They kicked me in the stomach, head, and legs multiple times. Yelling stuff in Spanish, they wanted me dead and I knew it.

When they were tired, they stopped and Marisol stooped down.

"Perra! ¿Cómo pudiste robar mi hombre? Puta! Puta! Si no tiene hijos, te mataría!"

"Do you know what I just said, bitch?" Marisol asked me.

I wept and remained silent.

"I said, 'How you could you steal my man? And if you didn't have children, I would kill you!"

"Yeah! You're one lucky, bitch!" Arial said.

With that, Marisol took her foot and slammed it against my face. I passed out cold.

MS. BURNS

Harmony
Six Years Later

It was early in the morning and I was in bed with Ramsey when I saw the door open slowly. It was my nine-year-old son Jayden and he was creeping in slowly. Just like I taught him. Ramsey was snoring but that didn't mean anything. I had seen him wake completely out of a snore and jump out of the bed when he wanted to. So Jayden had to be careful. Very careful.

When Jayden got to Ramsey's jeans on the floor, he picked them up and grabbed his wallet. Then he opened it up and removed some money. When he tucked the money in his pocket, he put the wallet back undetected. I remained in bed for ten minutes before following him into his room.

If Ramsey wasn't so fucking stingy, I wouldn't have to resort to stealing his shit. Usually the best time to hit him up was after he'd had a long night of drinking. But lately he had been getting drunk outside of the house and when he came home, I'd be sleep. Between both of our alcoholic habits, it was tough keeping money around the house.

I walked into the twins' bedroom and took the bill out of Jayden's hands. I could smell the stench of their pissy mattresses because they never went to the bathroom at the right time and I got tired of cleaning behind them. If they wanted to live nasty then I decided to let them do that.

"How much you get?" I said opening the bill.

"He had two big two dollar bills." He said referring to a twenty.

"Do you mean a Twenty Dollar Bill?" I asked.

"I guess."

I shook my head and said, "Why the fuck you ain't take all the money?"

"'Cause last time I took all the money, you got mad because you said if we took too much, he'd know some was missing."

"Are you getting smart, bitch?" I asked.

"Naw, ma. He ain't getting smart. He just remindin' you of what you said."

I smacked the hell out of Jayden and then walked up to Madjesty and stared him down. I was sick of his rebellion when I was disciplining Jayden. Whenever I disciplined Jayden, Madjesty had to get involved.

"You know, I'm sick of you talkin' back to me."

"I'm not trying to talk back to you, ma. But you asked my brother to do something, and he did it. So why you got to hit him?"

I was just about to gut punch him when Ramsey walked into the room.

"You asked him to do what?" Ramsey said drinking out of a bottle of vodka he hid from me. Bastard! Where the fuck did he get that from? And when did he start hiding liquor from me?

"Nothing, baby." I said walking up to him. He put the bottle of liquor to my lips and poured it down my throat. "And why you hiding out on me? Where you get the bottle from?"

"You can't know all my secrets." He smirked.

"What you want for breakfast?" I asked tucking the money further into my pocket Jayden had just stolen. He liked to grope me a lot and I didn't want him to find his own money.

"Whatever you making." He said slapping me on my ass. "And hurry up. I'm hungry."

When he was gone I walked up to Madjesty and said, "You betta be lucky he didn't hear your ass. If you fuck this up for me, I'ma kill you. We live here rent-free and he pays for everything. The last thing I need is a loud mouth kid talkin' back." I continued. "I wished they never found your ass when they cut you out of my body."

He stepped back a little and then looked up at me. I wasn't sure, but something told me before it was all said and done, he would try to kill me.

"Ma, I'm not gonna be the one who fucks it up for you here. If anything, you are."

That was it! I had enough of him! Looking around the room, I saw an iron on the dresser. I grabbed it, plugged it up and Jayden started crying.

"Go close the door, Jayden."

"No, mama!"

"Close that fuckin' door!"

When he did I directed my attention back to Madjesty as I waited for the iron to heat up. Jayden's whimpers were getting louder.

"Shut the fuck up before I put it on his face instead of his thigh." When it was hot I knocked Madjesty to the floor and took the edge of the iron and placed it on his inner thigh. He normally screamed and tried to run but this time he didn't. Instead of screaming, a tear fell down his face as I pressed it harder against his leg. He wiped the tear away and smiled.

"You can't hurt me no more!" He said. Then he lifted the pants on his other leg and showed me burns I didn't place on his body. That meant he'd been burning himself.

I backed away from him and stared in amazement. If I couldn't keep him in fear, how could I control him? And then it dawned on me. I couldn't hurt him but I *could* hurt Jayden.

"Maybe it'll hurt more if I burn your brother instead."

The smile was wiped off his face and he said, "No! Don't...Don't do it. I'll do whatever you ask me to."

"Good. Then start by listening to me. I'm sick of your back talk, and I'm not gonna take too much more of it either. Do I make myself clear, Madjesty?"

"Yes."

I was losing control of Madjesty, and I knew it was just a matter of time, before shit hit the fan.

CUTER THAN YOU.

Harmony

Ramsey was always up under my ass. I couldn't go too many places without him. If I went to the store he took me. When I came home and cooked dinner he helped me. I couldn't get a break. But over the past month or so, things had changed. We weren't even fucking no more and I had to find a better alternative to fit my needs. That's where his son Dooway came in.

Dooway was two years older than me and a great fuck. The only thing about him was his temper. Unlike his father, he flew off the handle most of the time and it reminded me of Kali. When he got like that I left him alone. Dooway sold dope and had moved out of the house recently to stay in an apartment with his girlfriend in Houston Texas. So we couldn't see each other like we use to. I couldn't count the nights we'd sneak off in the basement, when everyone was asleep to get our nightly fuck on. After missing that good dick, he finally called and told me he wanted to see me tonight and that he had something to tell me. I wondered what it could be.

I walked into the bedroom to see Ramsey getting dressed. He pulled out his good cologne, his socks without the holes in them, new jeans and a new shirt. I was so excited about him leaving without me, so that I could fuck Dooway, that I didn't bother thinking about where he might be going. And at the moment he didn't bother telling me either.

"Where the boys?" He asked me.

"Over Renee's house. I think they might be spending a night." I said brushing his hair and dusting invisible dust particles off his shoulders. I stood behind him and looked at him through the mirror.

"You got me confused, Harmony. I mean do you like Renee or not?"

"Not. But she serves her purpose as far as the boys are concerned."

"I don't know why you even bother. Especially after the rumors that the boys are nasty started."

"It don't mean that it's her."

"Do you really feel that way, or is it just that you just don't care?"

"So what, you saying I don't care about my kids?"

"I'm not saying that, Harmony. I'm just saying you could be a little better mother if you tried."

"So wait, you turning all this on me?"

"I'm not turning anything on you. But what I am saying is that you could do a little better job as far as they're concerned. They be over there more than they be at home. You sure that's good?"

"Ramsey, you drink just like me all day every day. So please don't talk about parenting."

"You're right...And at the end of the day they aren't my kids are they?"

Silence.

"I'm not gonna let you bother me none." I smiled. He turned around and put his arms around my waist and pulled me to him.

"You know I love you right?"

"I know." I smiled.

"How come you never tell me you love me back?"

"Because it's better to show a person love than it is to tell them." Truth was, I didn't know what it was to feel *real* love. I was damaged. But again, I can say the closest thing I felt to love was when I was with Monkey. "Where you going?"

"Out with a few of my dudes. We getting some drinks. You wanna go?"

"Naw. I'm good."

"Okay. Well let me get out of here," he said grabbing his wallet. "I'll call you before I come home, to see if you need anything." He paused and said, "Hey, did you see an extra twenty dollar bill around here somewhere?"

"Naw."

"Okay. Well I'll call you later."

When he left I called Dooway again trying to figure out where he was. It didn't matter if he came when his father was there or not because after all, he was still his son. But when I called Dooway and he didn't answer the phone, I figured he was on his way.

Waiting impatiently, I went to the liquor cabinet and downed a whole lot of vodka. The warm feeling going down my throat felt good and relaxed me instantly. I was about to swallow some more when someone banged at the front door.

I quickly opened the door to see Renee, but my kids were not with her. Renee was short and brown skin with medium size breasts and a tiny waist. She wore a low haircut like a boy and had a cute face. Her boyfriend sold dope and he kept her fly and she loved showing me her new purses. Little did she know but I gave up chasing labels and stuck to chasing the bottle. It worked better for me.

"What is wrong with you banging on my door like that? Are the boys ok?" I asked looking behind her.

She bombarded her way inside and sat on the sofa. A sly look covered her face.

"I know." She said evenly. "I know everything."

I closed the door and sat on the chair across from her. "You know what?"

"You know what I'm talking about, Harmony. And the question is, what are you going to give me, to keep your secret? And I don't want to hear that broke shit either because history shows that when a nigga is caught in a bind, he always rises to the occasion."

When I thought about it long and hard, I knew what she was talking about but I wondered how she knew. My boys didn't even know so how did she?

"What are you talking about, Renee? You smoking or something? 'Cause you coming over here acting real crazy."

"Do you really want to play this game, Harmony? Or do you want to tell me what you are going to give me to keep quiet? And please don't tell me you don't know what I'm talking about because I know you do. Unless you're hiding more secrets than a little bit."

Silence.

"My kids couldn't tell you? Because they don't even know."

"They didn't tell me anything. Now I'm done answering your questions. What do you want to do? Pay me to be quiet? Or do you want me to tell Ramsey and everybody else who will listen?"

Silence.

"How much do you want?"

"Two thousand should be enough."

"TWO THOUSAND DOLLARS?!" I yelled. "I don't have that kind of money. If I did, I wouldn't be here."

"I know how you can get it." She smirked. "But you gotta be up to trying a little something different though."

"How?"

"Get Ramsey to put you on his life insurance policy."

"And then?"

"And then you kill him."

"What?" I said, not thinking I heard her correctly.

"Look, it's not even that hard." She said standing up. "I've done it before. All you have to do is convince him to put you on his life insurance policy, and when he does, you wait a few months before you kill him."

"You done this before?"

"Sure have, and if you tell somebody I'll deny that shit. Anyway, you don't know who I'm talking about." She paused. "Just know that killing somebody is easier than people think. If I realized it earlier, I would've done it more times than not."

"You a crazy bitch."

"Yeah...But I'm a rich bitch, too. Look how you live, Harmony. You gotta a slashed up face because you can't even afford a good plastic surgeon...Your kids smell like piss and you hiding a big secret. You tell me. Who's life is better?"

I guess I know who started the pissy rumor now.

"Even if I was thinking about doing something like that, the murder that is...How would I go about killing him? Unlike you I ain't never done no shit like that before."

"There's plenty of ways to make a murder look like an accident." She paused. "You cook his meals?"

"Yeah."

"Well does he have any desserts he like? Anything real sweet?"

"Yeah. Jell-O. Sweet Potato Pie...Shit like that."

She smiled and said, "What you do is go to the auto body store, buy some antifreeze and mix it in his deserts. Antifreeze is sweet and he won't taste it in his food." She continued. "Give it to him a little bit over a time and before you know it, he will get sick and die."

I couldn't believe what she was saying but what I couldn't believe even more was that I was considering murder. I walked over to the cabinet, grabbed some vodka and thought about what she was saying again. She had just given me an idea I never thought of, although I doubted she would benefit off my consideration. After all, I knew she would blackmail me forever if I went along with her plan, and Ramsey showed up missing. Naw, me and the kids had to move away from this bitch all together.

After she left, Dooway came over a hour later. He looked so sexy that I kissed him the moment he came in. I needed to cum after learning that Renee knew my secret because it was the only thing that made me feel better when I was upset. She really knew…A secret I had kept to myself for nine years.

I knew Dooway had a girlfriend and didn't give a fuck. I wanted him and he wanted me. When we made it to the basement, he leaned up against the wall and dropped his pants. I got on my knees and took his thickness into my hands. Then I looked up at him, he winked and I stuffed his dick all the way into my mouth. He got hard in a matter of seconds and he grabbed the back of my head pumping into me. Spit covered his dick as I allowed him to gag me over and over again. He had so much spit on his dick, that you could barely see the brownness of his skin.

"Get up," he told me. "And turn around. I want to get into that pussy."

From the back he banged me over and over in my wet pussy. It felt so good I came after the second thrust but didn't want him to stop. We fucked for twenty minutes straight until I came five more times to his two.

After we did us in the basement, we got dressed and he said, "I ain't gonna be able to see you no more."

"Why not?" I asked stopping what I was doing.

"I'm marrying, Diamond." He walked up the steps leading out of the basement and I followed him.

"Diamond?" I said not knowing her name. "Why you gotta marry her? Why ain't it enough just to live with her?"

"She's, my girl, Harmony. And I just came over here to tell you that."

"So you would fuck me first and then tell me you don't want to see me no more?"

"Naw, you fucked me remember?"

After we were dressed we went upstairs and I almost forgot we were in his father's house. I wanted him to tell me why he was cutting me off. I was tired of not having somebody for me. All my life I was second best, even when I thought I was first.

"So this is it, huh?"

"Yeah. We got us a place at Plum Creek Apartment in Houston."

I don't know what I wanted from him, but I knew I didn't want him to leave me. But that's exactly what he was doing, letting me go. He was at the front door when my kids came in.

"What's up, lil' niggas." He said taking Jayden's hat off and palming his head. Ramsey just got both of them fresh haircuts the other day. "Where ya'll been?"

"At Renee's. We miss you, Dooway." Madjesty said. "When you movin' back?"

"Never. I got my own place now."

Madjesty stepped back and appeared angry while Jayden put his head down in sadness. My kids both liked him a lot, and wanted the father figure I never allowed them to have. How could I? One out of four niggas could be their father and I didn't know which.

"So what this mean, you not gonna fuck my mother no more?" Madjesty said looking dead into his eyes. "Since you moving out."

Dooway stopped in his tracks and my mouth dropped. I don't know what shocked me more. The fact that Madjesty talked so recklessly, or the fact that he knew our secret.

"I'ma check you later, homie." He said softly punching Madjesty in the chest. Then he turned to me and said, "Harmony, I ain't supposed to be telling you this, but I fuck with you. And I fuck with your kids."

"What is it?" I said unable to handle any more bad news.

"You gotta get out of here. You not safe."

He walked out the door and I was right behind him, on his heels. "What do you mean I'm not safe?"

"Son." Ramsey said walking up to the house. We both didn't see Ramsey there we were so caught up in the moment. Everything was happening so quickly. First with Renee now with Dooway and then here was Ramsey. Did he hear us? "What's going on?"

Dooway looked at his father, and then at me, and walked to his car without speaking. There was something he was trying to tell me, but he wasn't trying to tell me in front of Ramsey. Ramsey and me both watched Dooway get into his car and pull off.

"What I miss?" Ramsey said walking into the house, with me following behind him. He palmed the boy's heads like he always did, and then stepped into the living room to take off his shoes. "He seemed to get out of here pretty quick. Did you two have an argument or something?"

"That's your son not mine." I said. "He came over looking for you, and then the next thing I know, he had to go."

"Wow. That's odd."

"But he did say I'm not safe here. Do you know what he's talking about?"

"I'm just as confused as you are." He was lying. "So…What are you doing tomorrow? I wanted to take you out to eat." He walked into the bedroom, took his pants off, threw them on the floor and sat on the edge of the bed.

"Nothing. Why…Where we going?"

"Nowhere big. I'm thinking of one of the restaurants in Houston. So you may want to put some nice clothes on." He walked into the bathroom, pissed with the door opened and said, "Oh yeah…And bring the boys, too."

"Bring the boys? You never want to go anywhere *nice* with the boys. You know they don't have any good clothes to wear."

"Well I do wanna take them now." He said giving me no real reason. Then he closed the door.

I took this moment to go through his pants while looking at the door periodically in case he came out. If I heard the toilet flush, I would stop what I was doing. But it didn't take long for me to find a piece of white paper in his pocket. There were two numbers on it. One was Marisol's which made me mad and the other caused my heart to thump. I looked hard at the number thinking I was seeing things. Or maybe he knew someone with the same name I knew all my life. And then it dawned on me, how many people in the world had the name Jace? I couldn't think of but one.

I took the piece of paper, ran into the room and grabbed the boys. We took everything we could grab by hand and got out of the house. I never saw Ramsey again.

THE MORE SHIT CHANGES

2003 Five Years Later
Harmony

My two-bedroom apartment was hot as hell and the fan I had in the window wasn't cooling off shit. Every window in my place was open and all it was doing was blowing more hot air inside. My life turned out to be nothing as I planned. Here I was, thirty-one years old, with two kids fourteen years of age. And I didn't have a pot to piss in or a window to throw it out of. I hated the world, I hated everyone and I was starting to hate myself.

I was sitting in the living room, trying to adjust the fan when someone knocked at the door. It was early in the morning so I knew somebody must've wanted to borrow something.

"Madjesty, hurry up and bring my plate and then go see who's knocking at the door," I told my son. He had just made my breakfast. "And, Jayden, bring me my coffee!" I yelled. My coffee consisted of one part coffee and three parts Brandy.

"Mam?" Madjesty yelled.

"I said bring my food, tell your brother to make my coffee and go answer the door!"

Madjesty pimped slowly towards me, gave me my plate and pimped to the door like he normally did. Once there he opened it wide.

"What up, Felicia." Madjesty said not really caring for her. Madjesty could be a snotty ass kid if you let him. "Ma, it's Felicia!"

I rolled my eyes because I already knew what she wanted, some liquor. Our friendship started as a, *'you help me and I'll help you'*, sort of situation, but lately it had turned into, *'I do everything for your ass and you don't do shit for me'*.

"Alright, let her in. And get Jayden and tell him to bring my coffee!" I repeated. "I'm tired of talking to him!"

"I'm right here, ma." Jayden said walking into the living room. He handed me my coffee and both Jayden and Madjesty grabbed their book bags and headed for the door. Their style changed a little over the years. Madjesty wore his hair in short cropped style and Jayden liked his hair long and braided to the back.

"I'll see you when we get back home from school." Jayden continued.

"Ma, you got some lunch money for us?" Madjesty asked.

"You know I don't have no damn money. Tell them people at the school to give you something to eat."

"But they said you already owe too much money." Madjesty continued. "And that you gotta start paying them back."

"Don't make me get up and fuck you up." I paused, looking at him seriously. "Now get the fuck out of here and get to school. I said I don't have no damn money!"

When they left Felicia sat in the living room with me and I poured a little bit of vodka into two glasses giving myself the most.

"Girl, your sons are too cute. They so pretty they look like little girls." She said downing all of her drink.

"Bitch, don't say no shit like that to me. I ain't raising no girls, I'm raising boys!"

"That was a compliment." She said frowning. "I wasn't trying to make you mad."

"Well I don't like it," I told her. "Would you want somebody calling you a man?"

"Fuck no."

"Then so be it."

"Relax, Harmony. I didn't mean it like that," she continued. "But I know you got so much to deal with, with the little girls calling here for them don't you?"

She then shook her cup for me to pour some more vodka in it. I looked at her glass knowing full well I wasn't giving her shit else.

"Yeah they call here all the time, and I give them young bitches the business, too. Especially Ivory, the little girl that likes Jayden. She relentless with her nagging ass. He ain't feeling her too much though. He not like Madjesty who loves the girls 24/7."

She laughed and said, "I heard that, girl. Uh…Can I have a little more?"

"Yeah…When you finally buy a bottle."

She looked a little pissed but I didn't care. "So you still fucking Diamond's husband?"

I laughed and said, "So I wouldn't give you some liquor and now you decide to ask me about your cousin's husband?"

"I asked because I heard they were moving again 'cause of you. Diamond said she think Dooway still fuckin' you and she gotta get her husband out of here."

"What?"

"Her exact words was that she wasn't gonna let Mrs. Scarface slash Ripped Earlobe steal her man."

I laughed because the ugly jokes couldn't hurt me no more. "Well we gonna do us. And that's all you need to know."

She laughed and said, "So, you got any smoke on you?"

"What you talking about?"

"Come on, girl. You know."

I had a twenty bag of weed but I wasn't giving her shit. "I got a little something but what you gonna give me for it?"

"What you want?"

"You know what I want. For you to testify against that bitch for me in court." I told her walking to the cabinet to get the bag. "I don't know why I got to keep asking you anyway. If you didn't tell me it was cool to go in when I did, I would have never known about the money or the smoke."

"She's my cousin, Harmony. Damn, you know I can't testify for you. You shouldn't have broken into her apartment."

"Nobody knows *I* broke into her apartment. Diamond just thinks it was me because she hates me. You the only one who knows for sure. But don't forget you smoked her shit up right with me." I continued. "All you got to do is tell the judge that I was with you that night. That's it. If I'm with her cousin, you know they can't pen this shit on me."

She was silent for a while but I knew I finally had her. The only person broker than me was her. And if she didn't have me as a friend, that meant she wouldn't have liquor or weed. I could supply my own high but she couldn't.

"Okay…Roll that shit up. And," she paused, "pour me another glass of vodka too."

I rolled my eyes and did what she wanted. We spent the next twenty minutes getting high and I couldn't wait to get this court shit over with. I hated court and had been in court for more things than a little over the past few years. I had been locked up for shoplifting, for fighting, for selling pussy and for robbery. If my father could see me now, I wonder what he'd have to say about me. He probably would be disappointed. But I checked out on life a long time ago and now I just did whatever I had to do to get by. It's funny how life can go a different way for you. I wonder where I'd be if my parents were still around.

● ─── ●

"Is it your sworn testimony Ms. Felicia Koone, that Harmony Phillips was with you on the entire night that Diamond Koone's apartment was broken into?" Judge Patricia Barksdale asked her.

I needed her to stick to our story and was confident she would. The only thing that gave me a little doubt was that I saw them talking to each other outside of the courtroom earlier. I hoped Diamond wasn't able to convince her to go against me. Diamond wanted nothing more than to have me arrested, especially since I was fucking her husband. We were even together earlier in the day and had plans to be together later that night. He could give a fuck about me breaking into her apartment and told me several times he'd made a mistake by marrying her. I wanted Dooway to be mine. I wanted somebody to finally love me and I was hoping it was him.

At first I thought Ramsey would love me, since he couldn't get a girl like me otherwise. But it turns out that he was setting me up for Jace to catch me. I didn't even know what Jace wanted. Was he after the kids? Or did he know I was involved in the attempt on his life? Not only did Ramsey try to set me up, I found out how he knew how to get in contact with Jace. He had gotten back with Marisol and they had gotten married while he was living with me. That's the day he got all nicely dressed. He was a married man and was going to deliver my kids and me over to Jace to get us out of his house. That whole thing he did by asking me if I wanted to go was to throw me off, and it worked. Turns out he never wanted me to begin with.

"Don't lie, Felicia! Tell the fucking truth!" Her cousin Diamond Koone yelled in the courtroom. "You know damn well this bitch was not with you!"

The judge banged her gavel and said, "Order in court! Order in court!" When Diamond was silent she said, "Now, Ms. Koone, I don't know how you handle things where you live, but in my courtroom you will maintain your composure." She demanded. "One more outburst like that and you will be in contempt of court and I will throw this case and you out immediately! Do I make myself clear?"

Diamond rolled her eyes and said, "Yes, your honor judge."

I was laughing like shit inside. I was going to get away with all of this shit and it was nothing that bitch could do about it."

"Now, Ms. Koone, is it your sworn testimony that Harmony Phillips was with you the entire night Diamond Koone's apartment was broken into?"

"Yes. She was with me and we were playing Bingo. So she could not have broken into her apartment. My cousin was mistaken."

The judge looked at Felicia suspiciously but things were out of her hands, I had an alibi. The judge ruled in my favor and me and Felicia was on our way out the door when Diamond came behind me and pushed me.

I fell face first into the cold dirty floor and turned around. I jumped up as fast as I could and we started fighting in the court building. I was flailing wild punches at her until a cop snatched me up, while another snatched her up and pulled her someplace else.

I was still fussing at her until I saw a familiar face staring at me. She'd aged a bit but it was still her all the same. It was my aunt Angela. If she was there, that meant it wasn't long before someone from my past found me. It could be Jace or it could be Kali. All I could think of was that I didn't want to die.

TWIN PROBLEMS
Madjesty and Jayden Phillips

Madjesty was in the back of the class looking at the cute little girl in the desk directly in front of him. The blue jeans he wore were ragged and the white T-shirt he had on was not too clean. Still there was a swagger about Madjesty that girls were automatically attracted to.

"Rocket." Madjesty whispered. Rocket was a cute girl whose boyfriend, Baisley, was on the football team. Even though Madjesty knew how deep Baisley and his crew was, it didn't stop him from hitting on his girlfriend. "Turn around, I gotta ask you something." He smiled.

"Boy, shut up!" Jayden who was also in the class with him said. "You loud as shit."

"Man, you shut up." Madjesty combated. "I wasn't even talking to you."

"But the girl don't want to be bothered."

Madjesty wasn't paying his brother any mind. "Rocket, let me get your number?"

"For what?" She flirted back. "You know I got a boyfriend."

"That ain't got shit to do with me. I'm trying to get to know you and I know you wanna get to know me, too."

Finally Rocket turned around and said, "You messing with me and I can't hear the teacher," she smiled. There was no denying that she really did like him. "You gonna get me in…"

"Madjesty Phillips, come up here right now and answer the question on this board. Since you want to interrupt my class with side conversations."

"What? I don't even know what the problem is about." Madjesty said pulling his cap down further on his head to hide his eyes. Madjesty always wore a cap and it acted as his safety mechanism against other people. Under his cap he felt no one could see how much he hated his himself inside.

"Exactly. Now since you want to disrupt my class, come up here and do it in the front of everyone."

Madjesty was so embarrassed but he reluctantly got out of his seat. On his way to the board, Rocket placed a piece of paper in his hand. He didn't look at it right away because he didn't want the teacher taking it from him.

Reluctantly he approached the board because school scared him in general. Like his brother, he could barely read. Harmony never bothered to teach them anything by way of education. Once at the blackboard, Madjesty stared at the math question confused. He didn't know where to start because it all looked foreign to him.

"Go ahead...Answer the question." The teacher persisted.

"I'm not sure how to answer it," he said looking at Rocket, who was trying to look away. She was embarrassed for him.

"Well you not being sure how to answer the problem, is not good enough for me. You interrupted my class and now I want you to answer this problem. And my pupils do, too." She said looking out amongst them. "Don't you class?"

They all agreed. It was settled, Madjesty was going to have to do an awful job of attempting to answer the problem until the teacher said, "Madjesty, are you okay? I mean...Did you cut yourself?"

"No. Why?" He turned around and looked at her suspiciously.

"Because you're bleeding. Go to the nurse's office right now!"

Madjesty tried to look at himself but he couldn't. The blood was in an awkward position.

"I'm going with him," Jayden said right alongside his brother.

The teacher knew better than to come in between the closeness of their bond so she allowed them both to leave.

Nurses Office

The nurse's office was cold and open. And Madjesty and Jayden sat as quietly as possible waiting on the verdict. When Madjesty first came into her office, the nurse's mouth dropped when she saw the amount of blood on Madjesty's clothing. Since she was not authorized to conduct a full examination, she immediately called the paramedics.

"Are you okay, son?" the nurse asked. "Are you in any pain?"

"No, I just don't know what's going on." He said holding his brother's hand.

"Me either, son. But we're going to find out right away," she said examining Madjesty carefully with a once over.

When the paramedics arrived, they took off his clothing and briefly looked over his file. A call was placed to his mother that went unanswered. They didn't realize that Harmony was locked up at court earlier that day and was unable to answer the phone.

Unable to wait on Harmony any longer, after some time Madjesty and Jayden were placed in the back of the ambulance and rushed to the hospital. After an examination, there were four or five doctors in the room who didn't understand the information the school nurse had on Madjesty Phillips', chart versus what they saw. Physically they saw one thing but clerically the chart said another.

After going with his professional assumption, the doctor decided to address Madjesty.

"Madjesty, I have good news," the doctor said in a concerned tone. "You are fine and there's nothing for you to worry about. But...But...I'm a little confused on what the nurse has on your health record as your sex."

"My sex? I'm not having none."

"I know. But...She has on your records that you are a...Well...Boy."

"I am," he laughed looking at his brother who hadn't cracked a smile.

"Have you ever seen the anatomy of a woman? In school?"

"The anatomy of a woman?" Jayden interjected. "What that mean?"

The doctor looked at the nurse in the room who put her head down. It was unbearable for her because she already knew what had happened. For whatever reason, someone had told these children that they were something that they weren't. She could tell with one look at Madjesty's low-cut hairstyle and her baggy clothing that the child believed in all her heart that she was a boy, when she was far from it.

"Anatomy means the bodily structure. In other words, a man's body is different from a woman's."

"Okay."

The doctor knew it was best to just come out with it. "Son...I mean, Madjesty, you are a not a boy. In fact, you are a girl."

"What?! No I'm not a girl!" she sat up straight on the bed. "Don't tell me that because it's not true! I want my mother! Where is my mother?!"

"Madjesty, you had your menstruation cycle today. That is why you had so much blood on your clothing. You are a girl."

"That can't be true! Because that would mean, I am too," Jayden said.

Unlike her sister she was secretly happy to hear the news. She always felt like something was off about her. Despite the short haircuts her mother made her get when she was young and the boy clothes she made them wear.

"I'll have my doctors examine you as well, but if you have the same anatomy as your sister, than you probably are also a girl."

Upon hearing the news Madjesty felt dizzy. Unlike Jayden she liked who she was or thought she was. She could never see being a girl and having to face people at the school. She hated the idea of her life changing in this way and wondered why their mother would have lied to them so viciously. Madjesty vowed then that no matter what, if it was in her power, that she'd make her mother pay.

GOOD NEWS & BAD NEWS

Harmony

There were hundreds of people walking around in the courtroom and I wondered which one of them had bailed me out. I didn't have any friends with money and even if I did, not one of them would waste it on me.

I had been in jail for two days and hated every minute of it. Bitches were on their periods and smelled like old fish and every time I woke up I had to smell someone else's shit. I didn't know how long I would have to be in there and couldn't get in contact with anyone to warn the kids to stay in the house.

I hoped my kids didn't get to begging for food and bringing attention to themselves. If that happened they could jeopardize my welfare checks if someone knew they were in the house alone.

I was outside of the jailhouse for five minutes, when I saw my aunt Angela sitting in a red Honda Civic at the curb staring at me. I was going to walk right past her, like I didn't see her until she said, "Harmony, I know you see me over here." I kept walking. "Can you please stop, I have something to tell you."

I stopped briefly and said, "Me and you don't have shit to talk about."

"I doubt that very seriously. Now do you wanna come over here or miss out on something good?"

"Something good, huh?"

I kept walking until she said, "I was the one who bailed you out, and the least you could do is give me five minutes of your time." She continued. "I'll even drive you to wherever you're going."

"I don't trust you, Angela." I said looking at her. "I can't help but wonder if you were the reason Monkey got killed. And how I know you not here to set me up? I know you the one who told Kali where I was."

"I'm not here to set you up." She leaned over and opened the car door. "Now come on and get in, Harmony. You are going to love what I have to tell you."

Against my better judgment, I got in her car. She kept looking at me and I could tell she was judging me already. My once long thick black hair was now scraggly, brittle and brown. I had lost so much weight that I knew she thought I was a crack head. And a slash in the form of a criss-cross rested on my face. Not only that, my skin was now cracked and dry and not flawless and youthful like it was when she last saw me. The streets were hard on me and life had taken its toll.

"I can't believe what he did to your face." She said examining me. "I'm so sorry."

"It's over and done with," I said not wanting to remember that day. "I'm fine so save your sorry-ness for yourself."

She cleared her throat and said, "So, how are the twins?"

"They're fine."

"I bet they're so pretty." She smiled pulling into traffic. "Just as pretty as you were when you were a little girl."

"Were?"

"You know what I mean?"

"Naw, I don't," I lied. "Anyway, I have boys."

"Boys?" She said. "But the papers said you had two little girls."

I told my lie for so long that I forgot who knew the truth. My lie lasted a while until Renee came over the house threatening to out me. When my kids were over her house that day, she walked into the bathroom while Madjesty was using it. When she saw her sitting down and her split tail showing, she tried to blackmail me. I don't even know why I really lied about their sex. It started as a way to escape from Kali if he was trying to find me. I knew he'd be looking for me with two little girls, when I had two little boys.

"Oh, I meant, little girls." I said angrily. "But stop beating around the bush and get to the point, Angela. What in the fuck do you want?"

"Okay, Harmony, there's no reason to get upset about it. I'm just asking because I haven't seen you in forever. And you are my niece." She paused. "So, where do you want to go?"

"I live in Plum Creek Apartments." I looked her over and then back out in front of me. "You can take me there."

"I didn't know you lived that close to me."

"Well how would you?" I paused. I was tired of the games and wanted her to get down to it. "Now, what's going on, Angela? I'm tired of being fake. Talk to me."

She sighed and said, "People have been looking for you for a while, Harmony." I looked at her. "But nobody has been able to locate you until now."

"What people?" I asked with raised brows. "Kali?"

"No! I haven't even spoken to Kali. And I didn't know he was our connect or that you even knew him until he murdered Monkey." She clarified. "I'm talking about your mother."

I laughed. "Bitch, my mother's dead. And I know you know that."

"I'm talking about your real mother. She got in contact with me about six months ago because she's dying and she wants to see you."

"What are you talking about?" I laughed.

"Your real mother lives in L.A and she's dying of AIDS. Her name is Irma Cruz."

"Irma Cruz?" Immediately I had a throbbing pain in my head. "You talking about my father's lover? The one who killed, mama?"

"No, the one who killed Estelle. Not your mama. Irma is your mama."

"You know what the fuck I mean!" I shot back. "I need you to explain to me what you talking about."

"There was a high stakes Poker game many years ago. A lot of money was at stake and people placed bets they couldn't honor. At that game was Rick Sherrod, Massive, your father and a few other people." She started. "Massive was in to your father and Rick for a lot of money that night. And in order to settle the bill, Massive offered to your father what he didn't even bid. His beautiful girlfriend, Irma Cruz."

"What does this have to do with me?"

"Listen, Harmony. You're finally hearing the truth." She paused. "Anyway, Rick saw how he looked at her whenever they were around each other, and he saw how she looked at him. I guess he figured it was easier to give her up in a card game when he needed her, then to have Rick take her from him for free.

"Now your father couldn't be with Irma publically though, because he had a life with Estelle. And although he didn't love Estelle anymore, he knew she could be vengeful if crossed. So they had to keep their love affair a secret for a while." I was so shocked I couldn't blink. "Are you okay?" She asked me.

"Uh...Yeah...Please go 'head."

"Okay, well, Rick didn't want a female, he wanted his money, and ended up killing Massive's daughter to settle the debt even after Massive paid him. I think to this day Massive has been trying to get back at Rick, by trying to kill his son Jace."

Now that was something I knew all too much about. "Go ahead."

"Well, your father and Irma fell in love after that game. But Estelle eventually found out and threatened to tell the police about his drug operation if he didn't leave her alone. But he had bad news for Estelle and that was that Irma was pregnant with his only child.

"Estelle had always wanted a child but couldn't bore one herself. And against Irma's judgment, Cornell convinced her to let them raise her baby as their own. Irma was devastated. She cried every day after he asked her to part with you. It wasn't until he convinced her that you would still be in her life, that she agreed."

"But why not just dump Estelle?"

"Because Cornell's drug operation was on the line and he needed to keep Estelle happy until he could find another way to deal with her. But his heart always belonged to Irma."

"But...I use to go with my father to see Irma all the time. I mean, why wouldn't she tell me that she was my mother."

"She was keeping your father's secret, and trying to spare you from any pain. It was for your own good."

"My own good?" I said in an evil tone. "Do you realize how much shit that bitch Estelle put me through?" I said gritting on her. "Do you know that Shirley made me lick her pussy everyday for the first five years I lived with her? And that her son raped me repeatedly? And you tell me it was for my own good?"

"I didn't...Know..."

"How could you? You never bothered to check on me. You were my flesh and blood yet you never cared. When daddy died along with is money, you died to me, too."

"I had my own kids, Harmony. Don't put this blame on me."

"Look at me. I had a fucked up life! I'm an alcoholic, I have two kids I hate and more than anything I hate myself. My family was supposed to be there to protect me and they didn't. Just like Irma, you tried to act like I wasn't there."

"That's not true!"

"When did you ever call to check on me?!" I yelled. "When, Angela?!"

"All I can say is I'm sorry now."

"Why did she kill Estelle?" I said irritated with it all.

"Because she loved Cornell and when she heard about what she'd done to him, by calling the cops, she vowed to get revenge. You have to understand that when Estelle called the police, she went against their arrangement. She broke the deal. She gave her only child up on the strength of a promise and that promise was broken." She paused. "When she killed her, she called me a few months later. She knew I was one of the only people she could talk to about it because I always hated Estelle. I asked her then why she left you, she said she saw in your eyes, for a brief moment, that you hated her that day. And she decided to never reach out to you again."

"I remember that. I wasn't looking at her like that, Estelle had just made me mad and I...I was...Everything happened so fast."

"She thought you hated her."

I laughed in disgust and said, "Fuck all that! Now what?"

"She wants to meet you before she dies."

"Well I don't want to meet her." I said waving my hand. "Anyway, I thought you said you had good news for me. Where is it?"

"I do have good news." She smiled. "Before Irma was diagnosed with AIDS, she was living in Concord with her two daughters."

"In Concord? The police didn't seize that property?"

"No...Cornell was smart enough to put it in Irma's name. He said he was renting it from her and the police couldn't legally hold the property. But now that she moved back to L.A, to be with her family, she wanted me to tell you that Concord Manor is all yours. If you want it."

"I have sisters?"

"Yes. And you also have a huge family in L.A."

The anger I was feeling was at its boiling point. I lived in a shelter, in places nobody wanted me and I didn't have to.

"Go ahead, Angela." I paused thinking about what she said. "I'm still not convinced I'm her child."

"Look at yourself...Clearly," Angela said. "Do you remember her face?"

Of course I did. I thought she was the most beautiful woman in the world when my father use to take me to go visit her.

"I remember."

"Well if you do, then I know you can see the resemblance. You are Irma's daughter. Her first born. And outside of having light skin like Estelle's, you two look nothing alike."

"But...Why...Why did she allow me to go through life alone?"

"When she killed Estelle, she was sure she'd get caught. But as time went on, it became apparent that no one was saying anything, especially you. And Shirley didn't see the murder to testify. So Irma realized she didn't have to be on the run anymore and came out of hiding."

I was pissed and I didn't give a fuck about Irma, Shirley or Estelle! All three of them bitches could kiss my ass. All I cared about now was that mansion.

"Do you have the person I can call, to get the property?"

"Yes. I have the number of the person you need to contact, Harmony."

"And it's really all mine?"

"The property was always yours, and was supposed to be given to you when you turned eighteen, but you got lost in the system. Since then Irma has signed over everything to you. And now that I found you, I can let you know that you can finally go home."

"What's in it for you?" I asked her. "Because I've found that through life, everybody wants something. So what's your thing?"

"I did my brother's only daughter wrong and I'm trying to make good. People do change, Harmony."

People don't change. Over time they become clearer on their stances in life. And my stance was that I hated the world, and everybody in it.

HOME SWEET HOME

Harmony

It had been a month since I found out I inherited Concord Manor. And the days leading up to this day were crazy. When I went to my apartment, someone from the office of Child Protective Services was questioning me about the girls. Telling me that it was wrong to convince my children that they were something that they weren't. By the end of the day, I had managed to convince everyone that both of them were lying and that Madjesty was exhibiting lesbian behaviors. They never bothered me again.

When the cab driver pulled up to the mansion many good memories flooded back to mind. I had everything when I was here and for the first time in a long time, it seemed that I was finally getting some of the things I lost back.

Angela ended up not being too bad after all. She bought me and my sons...I mean...Daughters, flight tickets and gave us cab fare to Concord Manor. Although good memories were waiting for me here, I also had a lot of bad enemies in DC who didn't want to see my face at all. And I didn't want to see theirs.

"That will be thirty five dollars, mam." The cab driver said.

I handed him forty, waited for my change and left the cab. I guess he wanted me to give him a tip but that wasn't happening. I needed all my money until I could find a way to get some more.

Me and my kids, with three suitcases between us, entered the manor's doors and it was as beautiful as I remembered. The same crystal chandelier hung about the foyer and the spiral staircase was as pretty as ever. Irma purchased new furniture and it was more lavish than I remembered.

"Alright, boys, this is the place I grew up in," I said to them. We put our suitcases down and walked deeper into the foyer. "And as you can see, I didn't come up in the ghetto like you think. I came up in royalty."

"Girls," Madjesty corrected me. This bitch got on my fucking nerves.

"You know what I mean."

She took her hat off her head and put it on sideways. Bruises covered her face and body and she looked older than her age.

"Naw, I don't. You had us thinking we was boys and then we find out we girls. Maybe you should do a little better job at keepin' up with your lies." Madjesty said, loving to challenge me.

"If you believed you were boys all that time then that's your dumbness not mine." I laughed. "I mean, didn't you bother looking at other boys when you were in the locker room at school? You don't know what a pussy versus a dick look like?" I paused. "I knew what a dick looked like at six years old."

"You didn't allow us to go to the gym remember?" Madjesty continued.

"What about the bathroom?"

"I knew something was different." Jayden said in a low voice with her head hung low. "I always knew. Something just didn't feel right to me." She said as if she wanted to cry.

"Well it is what it is! I had to lie to you to protect you from Kali. He was trying to kill you remember?" I said lifting up my shirt exposing my stomach that was ripped to shreds by Nut and Cherry's handiwork.

"You lied to us for so long that you really are starting to believe you were protecting us." Madjesty laughed. "You delusional, Harmony."

"So you calling me Harmony now? I'm not your mother anymore?"

"That's better than what I want to call you."

I was done with Madjesty and she didn't even know it. I found a few brochures on insurance policies for kids, and I decided to take Renee up on her advice by killing that little bitch slowly. She had her day coming.

"If I'm still calling you a boy now Madjesty, it's because you look and act like one. Even with knowing you a girl now look at how you dress." I said.

"What else are we going to wear? All the stuff you ever bought us is dirty and for boys."

"You do know I don't answer to you right?" I paused. "If you think you can do so much better, the door is right behind you."

Madjesty rolled her eyes and sat on the bottom of the step. She was frustrated and mad at me but I was that little bitch's mother, not the other way around. Unlike Madjesty, Jayden tried her best to dress like a girl using the clothes that she had. She would tie her T-shirts in the back and roll the tops of her jeans a few times so that they appeared a little snug. Jayden was very pretty like me when I was younger and always feminine, even when she thought she was a boy. I'm glad I went with my instincts by giving them names that could be for a boy or girl. Now I wouldn't have to change much.

"Why would you lie to us, ma?" Madjesty continued. "Why would you fucking lie to us about something like that? What would have happened if we would've stayed at the school? I couldn't face my friends being a boy one minute and a girl the next."

"You think just because you got a period you grown now?" I asked walking over to her. I wish there was something I could grab nearby because I would have went over her head with it. "Bitch, you not grown."

"Yeah, whatever," Madjesty said. "When do we eat?"

"We have to go to the grocery store first." I said digging in my bag. They both gave me looks because they knew what had to be done. "Do you remember how to run the plan?" Jayden nodded. "Madjesty, do you hear me talking to you?"

"Yes, ma. I remember how to steal. You taught us too well."

"Tell me how?"

She sighed. "We look for people who are shopping by themselves. When we find someone, we wait until they bring their carts out in front of the store and go get their cars."

"Good...And what else, Jayden?" I said, wanting to make sure she understood, too. She could be too fucking naive at times.

"Then we grab as many groceries bags as we can. And run over to you with the food."

"Good, now let's get ready to go."

"You see that man right there?" I asked them as we hid on the side of the Safeway grocery store. "When he goes for his truck, rush over there and grab the groceries out of his cart."

"Ma, I don't wanna do this." Jayden cried. "I'm scared."

"I don't give a fuck what you want to do!" I said slapping her upside her head. "I bet your ass wanna eat don't you?" Jayden nodded yes. "I know that! And since you wanna eat, you betta get your ass over there and get that food."

"Ma, I can do it by myself," Madjesty said. "She ain't got to go with me. She'll probably slow me down anyway."

She thought I was stupid. Madjesty never talked badly about her sister. She was trying to make me think she could do the shit by herself when I knew we needed two hands to pull this job off. The object was always to get as much food as possible.

"Naw, she need to go with you!" I looked at Jayden and smacked her in the face. "Now get your ass over there and help your sister!"

This is why I didn't want girls, they too fucking sassy and weak. If they didn't do what I wanted done, they were gonna pay for it dearly when we got back home. And I'm not even fucking around.

Once the man walked to his car, they ran over to his cart. I backed up further on the side so that no one would see me. Madjesty grabbed two bags and Jayden grabbed one.

"Bitch, get back over there and get another bag," I demanded from Jayden. "You got two hands, so use 'em!"

She ran back and grabbed another bag and they were almost by me when someone who didn't have shit to do with it yelled, "Sir, they're stealing your groceries!"

The man saw them stealing his bags and started running in our direction. And I was so caught up into making sure they did the plan correctly, that I didn't see the cop a few feet from them.

"Stop!" the cop yelled. "Stop right where you are!"

The man whose groceries they'd stolen followed the cop and my kids. They were all running in my direction. I didn't know what to do so I had to act fast. So I ran up to them and smacked Madjesty in her face and then Jayden.

"What the fuck are ya'll doing stealing from this man?" I asked looking down at them. They looked at each other confused at my reaction. "Huh...Answer my fucking question!"

"Ma," Madjesty started, "you told us..."

I smacked her harder and her lips bled.

"I asked you a fucking question!" I said looking down at her. "Why in the fuck would you steal from this man? Are you that fucking hungry you gotta steal?"

The cop and the man looked at me in kids in pity and I knew my plan was working. I hoped the cop would feel too badly for my kids to prosecute and the man would be too afraid of what I was going to do to them to make matters worse.

"Now I'ma ask you again, why in the fuck were you stealing from this nice man?" I asked Jayden.

"I don't know, ma" she said in a low voice. I could barely hear her because she was sniffling so much from crying. "But I'm sorry and it won't happen again."

"Sir, what do you want to do?" I paused looking at the man and then my kids with hate. "Because I'm perfectly willing to do whatever I have to do make this right, including marching them right down to the police station with you."

Madjesty and Jayden looked at me scared. The officer looked at them and then at me. Suddenly, he didn't look like he wanted to arrest them anymore.

"No...Mam, I think we can let you handle things from here," the officer said. "That is, as long as it's okay with you, sir."

The man looked at how frightened my kids were and agreed not to press charges. We gave him back the groceries and went home. Once back in the house I had no idea what we would eat. I hated them for putting me into this situation by getting caught. Once we were inside, we sat on the couch and looked at one another.

"So what are we gonna eat now?" Madjesty asked looking at me with a smirk on her face. "'Cause we did all that shit for nothing and we still hungry."

I can't explain the rage that came over me. I picked up whatever was next to me and it happened to be a lamp. Once it was in my hand, I cracked it over her head until it shattered at our feet. Blood gushed from the sides of her face and she fell to the floor. I knew I was wrong but the anger wouldn't allow me to apologize. These kids have taken everything from me. My dreams, my hopes and my life and now she wants to talk back to me?

Being tired of looking at her, I drug her by her shirt and threw her into the crawl space under the stairs. I used this crawl space a lot when I was younger. It helped me feel as if I was escaping whenever I was home alone with Estelle. Once she was inside, I locked it from the outside.

"I hate you! I hate you, bitch! I hope you die! Why did you bring us into the world if you hated us so fuckin' much?!!!!" Madjesty cursed me.

"Why don't you think about that while you spend the next five days in there."

"Mama, please," Jayden cried walking up to me. "Please don't put her in there. She doesn't mean to be disrespectful. She's just scared and hungry."

"Yes I do mean what I said, Jayden! I hate that bitch and I hope she dies!"

I once wished the person I thought was my mother died, and she eventually did. Thinking of that made me angrier.

"Madjesty, please! Stop! Ma is gonna think you're serious. Tell her you're sorry."

"Do you realize everything I gave up for you?!" I yelled at the crawl space.

"Yes, mama. I do." Jayden cried taking me by the hand. "And we love you for it. But please...Please don't do my sister like this."

"That's all you care about is your fucking sister! What about me?!" It made me mad that she kept talking about Madjesty. "Do you realize the life I had when I was here? I had a father who loved me, more than anything." I cried.

"I understand, mama. But...But...What can I do to make things easier for you?" When she asked me what she could do to make things easier for me, I felt an ounce of love in my heart for her. And then she said, "What can I do to make you not leave my sister under there?"

I could see the desperation in her eyes so I decided to push the envelope. It was obvious that they had each other and I was alone.

I wiped the tears off my face and said, "If you want that little bitch to come out, then go get me some money. As a matter of fact, don't want to ever have to worry about getting money ever again. That will be your job for now on."

"But...I don't know where we are." She whimpered.

"We are in Maryland." I said coldly.

"I know, mama, but I don't know my way around here. I'ma get lost."

"Maybe I will keep her there longer." I laughed. "It don't make me no never mine. I'm tired of seeing her face anyway. It will be one less mouth I have to feed."

"Mama, please don't. She...she may die."

"Well until you go out there and get my money, your ungrateful ass sister will stay under them stairs. And if I got to work extra hard to get some money myself, then you gonna go under there with her. Do I make myself clear, Jayden?"

"Yes." She sobbed. "Yes you do, mama."

"And I'm not talking about a couple of bucks either, Jayden. I'm talking about no less than one hundred dollars. That'll be enough to get us started."

She looked scared but I didn't care. I handed her a jacket because it was October and the temperatures could be frigid at night. I didn't want her to have any excuses for coming back broke. With the jacket in her hand, I pushed her outside of the mansion and locked the door behind her. I started fucking when I was twelve and she was fourteen. What better time to start than today?

REAL FUCKING WORLD

Jayden Phillips

Jayden walked a few blocks down from her house frightened. Although she grew up in the hood, she was sheltered most of her life. Despite what her mother was doing to her, she loved her, and she wished she could love her in return.

But she wasn't blind or stupid, she could see the hate in her mother's eyes when she looked at her. She was learning very early that if you wanted to survive you had to take care of yourself.

Jayden walked down the street with only her jacket in tow. Her beautiful long hair was tied in a knot in the back of her head and she looked loss. A few cars beeped their horns at her although she was wearing clothes that were boyish and hid her real figure. But anyone with eyes could tell that she was still beautiful.

After turning down a few honks, she decided to accept the next offer. Thoughts of her twin sister being in a dark hole horrified her. As far as Jayden was concerned, Madjesty was the only one she had in the whole world and she needed her happy and in the right frame of mind. Both of them had to be strong if they were going to deal with their mother. Harmony was becoming more and more irrational by the day.

When a white Hummer pulled up next to her, she smiled at an older man in his late thirties. She didn't know the first thing about being sexy, considering she was forced by her mother to hide her femininity most of her life. Now she had to call on her intuition to be what she was born to be...A girl.

"You want a ride?" the man said. Jayden didn't respond. "Aw, come on, cutie, I ain't gonna hurt you none. Where you going?"

"Uh...I'm not sure."

"Well let's think of that together. Because if you're out here alone then you must need a ride right?" He smiled.

"I guess so."

"So let me help you."

"Okay," she smiled oddly. "That'll be nice."

"Good, I don't want to see someone like you get hurt."

She hopped into his car and Ashanti's song 'Foolish' played on the stereo. It was perfect because she didn't know anything about the real world since Harmony had not prepared her. It was like Harmony wanted them to fail. But Jayden was smart enough to know that money ruled everything and if she wanted to have any sort of life, and if she wanted to help her sister, she had to bring it.

"Do you know where you going yet, beautiful?" He asked. The man was very attractive but she could tell he was at least twenty years older than her. "And why you walking out on this highway alone?"

"No reason." She said hunching her shoulders. "I guess I needed some fresh air."

"Fresh air huh?" He asked staring at her inquisitively. "So where am I taking you?"

"I don't know. Wherever you want."

He smiled. "Wherever I want?" He repeated. "Ain't you too young to be talking about wherever I want? I mean, an old fart like me could get the wrong impression. You wouldn't want me getting the wrong impression now would you?" He placed his hand on her thigh and rubbed it repeatedly.

"I don't understand your question."

"Come on, cutie. You know what I'm talking about."

"Actually I don't. But I do know this…Everything costs in this world." Jayden said feeling an ounce of boldness.

"Did your mother or father teach you that already?"

"I don't know my father but yes, my mother did teach me."

"I knew I liked you." He laughed. "How old are you anyway?"

He was starting to get disgusting with his stares and each time he looked at her, she wanted to run out of the car. But she thought about Madjesty and she pushed herself to be bolder.

"I'm old enough. If that's what you're asking."

"Old enough for what?"

"It depends on what you want."

The man looked at her knowingly and pulled over. Then he looked around the truck from the inside to be sure no one was coming.

"Is that right?" He asked pushing her seat back before doing his own. "'Cause I like the sound of that shit."

Then he unzipped his pants and pulled out his dick. All of a sudden things escalated real quickly and Jayden wasn't prepared for any of it.

"So what do you want to do and what do you want me to pay you for it?" He said licking his lips. "'Cause I don't mind paying a sexy young thing like yourself for the right services."

Jayden looked at him nervously. She knew she'd probably have to have sex with him, but was hoping things would go a little slower at first.

"Uh...I..."

"What you gonna do, girl?" He yelled yanking his ashy dick harder. He was growing annoyed and didn't want to miss a chance of having her wrap her mouth around his dick. "Come over here and get this money."

"Uh...How much...How much you gonna give me?"

"How much you want?"

"One hundred...One hundred dollars." She stuttered.

"Then you got it." He said reaching toward her. "That ain't no problem at all."

"Well let me see the money first."

The moment he was distracted and reached for his wallet, she bolted out of the door and ran as far as she could down the street. Even when she had gotten enough space between them, she still ran crying the entire way.

"Where are you going?!" He yelled at her. "Come back! I'll take you where you got to go!!!"

Jayden couldn't stop. She just ran and cried and ran and cried until she ended up back home, empty-handed. She walked slowly to the front door already knowing what her mother was giving. Scared, she mustered up enough energy, to knock on the door.

"You back already?" Harmony asked her standing in the doorway. "'Cause I know you know better than to come back without my money."

"I know better, mama. But...Things didn't work out right."

"I don't wanna hear excuses. You grown so be grown," she said placing her hands on her hips. "So where is my money?"

"If you can give me some more time, I'll…"

Harmony slammed the door in her face and Jayden broke down in front of Concord Manor's doors. She felt alone and the one person she could confide in, was under the steps in the house.

She had to be strong. So Jayden stood up, dusted off her jeans and walked away from the mansion. Then she walked up the road she was on earlier for about ten minutes. But unlike last time, no one beeped the horn at her. The quickness of her steps made her seem unapproachable.

After walking for about an hour, she ended up sitting in a McDonalds. With no money in her pocket to eat, she sat there and waited while everyone else ordered their food. She could taste the salt of the fries in her mouth and the softness of the burger on her lips. Her focus changed from getting money to getting something to eat first. She figured on a full stomach, she'd be more equipped to bring in some cash.

She was inside for twenty minutes when three girls walked in. They wore cute clothes, had fly hairstyles and were really loud. Jayden knew right away by the way they looked at her, that they were about to start trouble.

"Ya'll see that girl over there," a cute girl with the short curly hair like her sister's said.

They all looked at her and laughed. "Bitch, I thought that was a dude," one of them responded.

"Right! She dressed like a fuckin' man." Another one chimed in.

Jayden looked down at herself and the moment the girls left the restaurant, she took her hair down and allowed her long main to fall down her back. Then she took off the long sleeve shirt she had on exposing the dingy white tank top underneath it.

Although she didn't look as feminine as she'd liked, she did look more attractive. When she was finished dolling herself up as best she could, she waited. Waited for someone to talk to her. Waited for someone to say she was cute and waited for someone to give her some money.

Two minutes later, one of the three girls who was there earlier walked back inside. She stomped up to the counter.

"Sir, you forgot my fucking soda!" She yelled at the cashier. The other two girls piled back inside behind her. "And I know you heard me order one, too. Plus you charged me for that shit and everything!" she said throwing the receipt in front of him. "That's not right, sir!"

"Mam, if you are going to use that kind of language, what difference does it make if you call me sir or not?"

"Okay, BITCH!" She laughed, her friends laughing with her. "You forgot my soda. Is that better now?" She was really showing off since she had an audience.

The older gentlemen shook his head and went to get her drink. But in the process, she saw Jayden had taken out her hair and tried to appear more feminine.

"Let me find out she tried to transform." She laughed. "You still look like a boy, bitch."

"Fuck you," Jayden said under her breath.

"Oh shit! She said fuck you, Toni!" One of the girls instigated. "You got to go on her now."

Toni, followed by the other girls, walked up to Jayden. Jayden stood up and was going to do her best to defend herself realizing she was outnumbered. Before she could think of what to do, Toni smacked her in the face with the soda she'd just been given from the cashier. The cup busted all over her clothes and ice cubes clung to her hair.

Jayden angry, and fed up at the world, began throwing wild punches at the girl. But after awhile, the other girls jumped in and they all began to beat her so badly, a few customers got involved. One of the customers had just walked in during the end of the fight. He had two friends with him and they moved in on the girls like a couple of cops.

"Stupid, bitch!" Jayden said trying to get a hold of them again. "I'll fuck you up!"

But the seventeen-year-old boy maintained his hold on Jayden and his friends kept the other girls at bay.

"Why you always starting shit, Toni?!" the one who had Jayden said.

"Fuck that, Shaggy! She hit me."

"That's 'cause you threw a soda in my face, bitch!"

"Yo, get the fuck out of here before I call your peoples," Shaggy said to Toni. When she didn't move he said, "I'm not fucking around, Toni. Move." He pointed.

"You gonna see me again, bitch!" Toni said leaving out the door with her friends behind her.

"Go the fuck home," Xion added. He was light, tall and cute and had a rough edge to himself that Jayden liked.

When they left, Jayden tried to pull herself together by wiping the soda off of her drenched clothes and shaking the ice out of her hair. Shaggy, the one who helped her took a step back and looked at her fully. She looked familiar to him, very familiar but he couldn't place her face. Still, he hadn't seen her around the way before and wondered where she came from. At first glance, he thought she was into girls judging by the boyish way she was dressed.

"You aight, shawty?" He asked trying to feel her out. He was attracted to her immediately although he didn't know why. She was nothing like the girls he got down with normally. She was dirty and boyish instead of cute, clean and fly. "You can't be in here fighting and shit. These peoples call the cops quick around here."

"Well them bitches shouldn'tve put their hands on me." She said putting her hair in a ponytail. "I'm sick of this shit."

"I feel you," he said looking at her angelic face. "But they gone now. Ain't no need in you still bein' riled up." He paused. "You need a ride home?"

She was so caught up in the fight, that she forgot her mission and said, "No. I just want to be left alone."

"Aight, fam," he smiled. "Well, look, I'ma grab something to eat. Can I get you something?"

For the first time since he introduced himself, she calmed down and looked at his face. He was very attractive with his brown skin, a neat low hair cut and stylish clothes. Surely he had one hundred dollars on him. She thought. Now all she had to do was convince herself to be bold enough to ask him for it.

"Uh…Yeah," she paused trying to fix herself to ask him for something small before asking for something big. "Can you get me a Big Mac meal?"

"You got that," he said. He told his boys who were already at the counter placing their orders, to add a Big Mac meal to the order.

Then he said, "You sure I can't take you somewhere? It ain't a problem."

Ask him for the money, girl. She thought to herself. What are you waiting on? You see he a drug dealer.

"Look, can I ask you something serious?"

"Yeah...What's up?"

"Can you let me borrow two hundred dollars?" She remembered what her mother said awhile back. To always ask for more then what you want to get exactly what you need.

"Damn, you going hard ain't you?"

"Look, if you can't help me forget it," she said grabbing her jacket preparing to leave. Her food came right before she went out the door and he handed her the bag. "Thanks for the food though."

She went outside, sat on the ground against the window and tore into the food. But she was sure to leave half of sandwich and some fries for Madjesty. Whether her mother knew it or not, she would sneak her sister the food.

Jayden looked homeless and hungry and Shaggy felt for her. And although it wasn't his style, for some reason, he wanted to help her out. He didn't think she was on drugs because he'd been around enough dope fiends to know the difference. But she definitely had a hard life.

"What you doing, young?" Spirit, one of his friends asked watching him staring at Jayden. "I know you got the number right?"

"Yeah, nigga. She a little rough around the edges but she still a cutie." Xion added.

"Ya'll go wait for me in my truck," he said referring to the red Navigator in the parking lot. "I'ma holla at shorty for a minute."

"Okay...Just wanted you to know that one of your pops prowlers just passed by."

Shaggy hated the extra security his father put around him but dealt with it, knowing it was for protection. His boys went to his truck without relenting. Besides, he was the boss and in control of everything anyway. When he was alone, Shaggy walked outside and caught Jayden right before she walked away after finishing her meal.

"Come here, shawty," he said smoothly.

She turned around looked at him and said, "If you can't help me, fuck it."

"Aight then," he said about to walk to his truck.

Realizing she was going to lose her chance to help her sister she said, "No...Wait. Please...Don't leave."

He stopped and walked over to her. "How much you need again?"

"Two hundred," she repeated.

"Why you need two hundred dollars?"

"Why?" She said anxiously. "I just need it. Okay?"

"No it's not okay. You don't know me from a hole in a wall yet you ask me for two large. I need to know why, shawty. And since I'm in a position to give you what you need, you best be tellin' me somethin'."

Jayden sat down on the ground again and started sobbing. "My...My life is fucked up. My mother is a horrible person who is keeping my sister under the steps in our house unless I give her some money." She cried harder. "I don't have nothing to offer you in return, but if you give me the two hundred dollars, I promise...I'll do whatever I can to give you the two hundred back. Just please...Please...Help me help my sister. She's all I got."

Shaggy was moved by her sadness and sat down on the ground next to her. His friends couldn't believe what he was doing as they watched him out the window of his truck. He was the type of dude who wouldn't put himself out there for nobody. He had to be feeling her. They thought.

He reached in his pocket and handed her four hundred dollars. Her eyes grew big as saucers as she accepted the money.

"I'ma give you my number before I drop you off. I want you to call me if you need anything else."

"For real?" she asked wiping the tears from her eyes.

"For real."

"Ummm...Not that I don't appreciate it, but why so much?"

"Because I feel you and I got it to give."

She smiled, peeled off two hundred from the four hundred and gave it back to him.

"See, like I said, I paid you the two hundred back." They both laughed. "No seriously, thank you." She tucked the money in her pocket.

He took notice that she could have easily taken the four hundred dollars and never saw him again. He knew then that she wasn't on drugs and that she was a girl of her word.

"You paid me back the two hundred, but you still gotta pay me for the other two."

"Okay," she said hesitantly. "Well does it have to be cash?" She figured he wanted sex and she needed to be broken in anyway.

"Naw."

"Well what you want?"

"I want you to let me take you out. Since it's obvious you like to eat and shit," he laughed. She laughed too. "Where you live?"

"At Concord Manor."

"Wait, the mansion up the street?"

"Yeah."

"And you ain't got two hundred on you?" He continued.

"Everything is not what it seems."

"I heard that." He said. "But look, my folks is having a little somethin' at their house tomorrow. My mother is sick and goin' blind and she might not make it. So before she loses her eyesight completely, we want to do somethin' nice for her."

"I'm sorry to hear that."

"It is what it is." He said looking out in front of him. For a moment he disconnected. "But we been knowin' she might not make it for a while. If you want I can come scoop you. We can stay at my spot for a while, then go grab somethin' to eat."

"That sounds nice," she said. And then she remembered her mother. Making plans without knowing Harmony's moods could be a waste of time. "But can I call you first to make sure? I got to ask my mom first."

"Yeah…That'll work."

"What's your mother's name?" She asked figuring she could get her a card or something so she wouldn't go to the celebration empty-handed.

"Tracey Battles but everybody calls her Trip."

EVIL MANIFESTED
Madjesty

Madjesty was just let out from under the stairs when she entered her room for the first time. It was big and spacious and she couldn't believe she had a king sized bed and her own bathroom. The furniture inside was pretty and better than anything she ever had before. Since Harmony told her the room probably belonged to one of Irma's daughters, which was also her aunt, she wondered what kind of girl she was. Was she pretty and feminine, and did she like who she was? Because when Madjesty looked in the mirror, she saw a boy in a girl's body and she hated that about herself.

When Madjesty walked to her bedroom window, she looked out of it and imagined what people driving past the large gates thought about the family inside. She figured they'd think they were rich and happy, both of which they weren't.

Five minutes after getting into her room, Jayden came knocking on the door.

"Come in, Jayden." Madjesty said sitting on the edge of her bed.

"Are you okay?" She whispered, closing the door behind her. Although her mother's room was on the far end of the mansion, she wanted to be sure she couldn't overhear them. "I got the money as quickly as I could. Did mama let you eat anything?"

"Naw."

"Here," she said handing her the half of sandwich and fries. Madjesty downed the food quickly. When she swallowed it all she said, "How did you get the money? You didn't do anything nasty did you?"

"No...I didn't," she smiled. "But I did meet somebody. I like him and he kind of likes me, too."

"For real? Do he know your age?"

"Naw...But I think he's eighteen or somethin'. He's probably around my age."

"No he's not if he's eighteen."

Jayden laughed, "But Madjesty, he is so cute. I think he likes me."

"If he gave you one hundred dollars off the rip, he must be a drug dealer or something. I doubt if he like you though. You gotta be careful, Jayden. You kinda naive sometimes. That's why mama gets mad at you so much."

"I'm not naive."

"You are. Ain't no eighteen year old boy gonna give you no money unless you fuck him. Don't put yourself out there like that."

"Then what I'ma do? If she make me get money again how am I supposed to get it?" Jayden cried. "She put my sister under the stairs with nothing to eat."

Madjesty felt bad for going on her the way that she did, when she put herself out there for her. She gave her a tight hug, which was the only thing she could offer to repay her. Little did Madjesty know, the hug meant more to Jayden than anything money could buy.

"I'm sorry, Jayden. I just...I just want you to be careful."

"She told me I gotta be the one who brings the money in now." She said wiping her tears. "I don't have a choice, Madjesty."

"Man, I hate that bitch!"

"But I think I can do it. Instead of giving me one hundred dollars, he gave me four hundred."

"FOUR HUNDRED?!" Madjesty yelled by mistake. "YOU GOT FOUR HUNDRED DOLLARS FROM HIM?"

"No...Please be quiet," Jayden whispered looking at Madjesty's bedroom door. "We don't want mama to find out."

"He gave you four hundred dollars?" She whispered. "You sure you didn't do anything with him, Jayden?"

"I'm positive." She giggled. "But I gave two hundred back to him."

"Fuck you do that for?"

"Because I only needed one hundred. And I kept a hundred for us," she said handing her sister fifty dollars. It was more money than she ever held in her life. "It's for emergencies though. Don't use it unless you have to."

Madjesty stood up and hugged her sister again. She felt she should have been the person who helped her instead, not the other way around. After all, she was yanked from Harmony's womb before Jayden which made her the oldest and she was more aggressive. Yet her meek feminine sister had risen to the occasion.

"I love you, Jayden. I don't know what's gonna happen with us, but I want you to know I always got your back."

"And I got yours."

They were still rapping to each other when the doorbell rang. Madjesty and Jayden rushed into the hallway and looked down the stairwell. They saw their mother walk to the door and they followed her down the steps. As far as they knew not many people knew they were there. So who could be coming at that hour?

When Harmony flung the door open, a man was standing outside with a woman in a wheel chair. Harmony backed up and put her hand over her mouth. She looked scared and Madjesty took a little pleasure in her mother's fright.

"What are you doing here?" She asked backing up. "What are you doing in my house?"

The man walked inside, pushing the woman in the chair. "What, you not happy to see me?"

"How did you find me?"

"Come on, Harmony. How do you think I found you?"

"Angela?"

"Of course. You didn't really think she could change overnight now did you?"

Harmony looked at the woman in the wheel chair and said, "After all this time, I can't believe you're still with him, Cherry."

"You can't help who you love." Cherry responded holding her head down. "Now can you?"

"Where is Nut?" Harmony said.

"She overdosed and died." Kali said. "The stupid bitch took too much in."

When he looked behind Harmony and saw the children staring at him he said, "So Harmony...When are you going to introduce me to my kids?"

Hearing this caused the sisters to look at one another in confusion.

Harmony turned around slowly and looked at her daughters. "Madjesty and Jayden...This is Kali, and he may be your father."

VAN MUDERER

Jace

The ride was bumpy as I sat in the back of a white Ford Cargo Van. At thirty-one years old, I was getting too old for this shit. But it was time to make a move and I was taking shit to another level. These niggas wasn't feeling me when I said every corner in DC belonged to me. Back when I was coming up, there was a code. If a nigga had more soldiers than you, and was able to bark you off your blocks, then you bowed down with respect. But today all these niggas know is gun power so I was going to have to give these niggas what they wanted.

I had come up with a plan to handle these dudes who weren't trying to let up on some real estate I had on South Capitol St in Southeast, DC. From what my squad told me, they had about twenty niggas who were trafficking there and they even managed to one by one, kill off a few of my foot soldiers. So today I was coming with ten white vans filled with fifteen niggas each to send a message I knew they'd understand loud and clear.

"This is where the main crew be," Paco said to me from the driver's seat. "I see four or five of them out there now. The others be in the back of the apartment building over there on the right."

"Cool, dispatch the other vans to the other areas on South Capitol. I want all of them niggas cleaned out tonight. No more fuckin' around."

"I'm on it," Paco said.

"Cool, park across the street and let us out."

When he parked, they piled out and grabbed four of the violators but one got away.

"Get that nigga, Kreshon!" I ordered seeing the dude catching wheels, giving Kreshon chase. "Don't come back to the van without him."

Kreshon was already on it while my other men pushed the four into the cargo van unarmed. They tried to fight but a few quick jaw bangers put them in order. After they were inside we waited for Kreshon. He came back a minute later with the last man and we pulled off to a vacant area.

We resorted to kidnapping niggas and dumping their bodies. Out of all five of them, only one was armed before we took his piece. Paco drove as smoothly as possible to avoid detection from the cops.

"Which one of you niggas in charge? I asked them.

No one said a word. "Fuck it, kill all of 'em." I ordered.

One of them tried to break bad but Kreshon dropped his ass. "Sit the fuck down, you bitch ass nigga."

"I'ma ask you again, which one of you niggas is in charge?"

I waved to Kreshon and he was about to bust all of them until someone spoke up. "No! Wait," one of the men said.

"Nigga, shut the fuck up," one of his crewmembers interjected. "Why you punkin' out? If we gonna die at least die with some honor."

"Fuck honor, I ain't 'bout to die over no bullshit. Plus you know these niggas fuck with the Russians!" He advised. "He's in charge," he continued pointing to the man Kreshon had run down earlier. The last one in the van.

I gave Kreshon the look and he popped the one in charge in the head. Blood splattered all over my face and I smeared it off with the back of my hand.

The niggas moved a little like they were about to charge us when I said, "Somebody wanna go next?"

"Fuck is up, nigga?" One of them asked. The look in his eyes showed he was scared. "Why ya'll fucking with us?"

"You don't know who I am?"

"Yes…But I think ya'll got the wrong niggas."

"Naw…We got the right mothafuckas." I laughed. I decided to fuck with them a little. Just like my father, I started to enjoy making niggas suffer before death. "Which one of ya'll have a family at home?"

"Huh?" One of them asked. "What you gonna do, kill our family's, too?"

"I'ma ask you again, which one of ya'll got a family?" They looked at the slumped over body amongst them and then looked at me.

"Me. I just have a little girl and me and my shawty getting married next week."

"Prove it."

He went into his wallet and pulled out a picture of his girlfriend and I peeped at his address.

"Cool, that wasn't hard now was it?"

He looked with widened eyes at me. My men outnumbered all of them and it was hot as hell in the back of the van. I was done fucking around and it was time to get down to business.

"Since you got a family, I'ma let you live." I looked at my men and said, "Get rid of the rest."

There was a struggle at first but my men quickly got the situation under control. The violators never had a chance. With four dead men laid on top of one another, I looked at the last man standing. My men hovered over him just in case he made a move.

"You gonna let me go right?" He asked me. "You gonna let me see my family?"

"Of course. But you gotta do me a favor."

"Anything, man. I'm just trying to see my family."

"I feel you," I smiled. "I got a family, too." I said, not knowing if it was even true. It had been over fourteen years since I last spoke to Harmony and I didn't know where she was.

"Just tell me what you need."

I smiled and looked at Kreshon. "This guy's serious," I laughed.

"Yeah, he is," Kreshon added.

"I need you to do two things. Number one, tell your boss to stay the fuck off my blocks. If I catch any of you on my blocks again, I'ma let you get that money, while I run up in your houses and murder your families."

"Okay. I got it." He nodded. "And what else?"

"I'ma need you to stop breedin' kids." And with that I blew a bullet between his legs and we pushed him out of the van. He landed on the curb holding his hands between his legs and crying out in pain.

Me and my crew laughed at him limping away. Then we made one more stop and that was to the docks of Baltimore. A friend of mine had access to a trailer and we stuffed the other four bodies inside. Their corpses would be shipped overseas and never seen again.

Two hours later I was back in my Aston Martin with Kevin driving me home. My cell phone rang and it was Rick. Over the past five years, he had lost everything. Massive had changed his tactics from killing off the men in his crew, to killing off the family members of anybody associated with him. He couldn't get to me that way because outside of Paco, nobody working for me had a family. And we kept security on them night and day. We were loaners but Rick and his squad's families weren't protected. Before long, Rick was abandoned and now relied on me to take care of him.

The funny thing is, although I kept the money rolling, if I didn't call him, he wouldn't call me, unless he needed something.

"What up, Rick?" I said sipping on a cup full of vodka on ice.

"I need you to look out for me again," he said referring to sending him some more money to an offshore account. Lately he had been asking for a lot of money and I felt something else was up. I paid off his house in Mexico so I didn't understand why he was so broke.

"I got you. Is everything good with you though?"

"Uh yeah...I'm just trying to get my crib furnished. You know how it is, son. The ladies love a fly place."

"Fly huh?" I said. "You sure you ain't gambling again?"

"No, son." He laughed.

I heard him but there was a problem, he had already told me that he needed money the last time he called to get his crib furnished. What was he doing, furnishing it twice? Rick was slipping up and lying more and more each day. I decided then to make plans to visit him in Mexico. I needed to see him with my own eyes to be sure he was okay.

"Not a problem. I'll send you fifty."

"Well, can you make it one hundred?"

"One hundred grand?" I said shocked. "How much decoratin' you trying to do, Rick?" If he wanted the money, I wanted him to work for it. At least come up with creative lies for your bullshit.

He laughed and said, "Just send it, son. I really need it."

"Aight." When I hung up with him my phone rang again. It was Antoinette.

"Ann, I need you to book a trip for me to Mexico."

"Can I go with you?"

"Yes. But book the trip as soon as possible. I gotta go check on Rick."

"Everything cool?"

"I'm gonna see."

"Okay, honey. But I have to tell you something, Kali's home from jail and he wants to speak to you."

This nigga had a lot of nerve contacting me. After that shit with Harmony, he better be lucky if I don't send somebody to slump his ass. "I'm not fuckin' with that dude."

"He said he has some information that might be valuable to you."

Silence.

"Aight, tell him I'll meet with him at the end of the week. But book the Mexico trip now."

"I got you, baby, I love you."

"You already know what it is."

GO BACK TO KALI

Harmony

The air conditioning was on blast in my house and the bills were sky-high thanks to Kali. He managed in less than a week to cause more problem than he was worth. Him and Cherry came and went as they pleased and I hardly ever saw them. Yet when he was here, I could never get a good night sleep with him staying in my house. Was he gonna kill me? What did he want with me?

Trust, I had a plan to deal with him and Madjesty at the same time, and there would be no mistakes. It made me sick that he was threatening to tell Jace where I was and give his theory to him on what happened the night people were poisoned at his party. I knew there was only one way to get him out of my life for good. And that was to kill him but first I had to focus on bringing more income into this house. I had a plan to do just that, and it involved the porn industry.

I was sitting in my bedroom with Madjesty and Jayden and it was time to teach them what it took to earn money. Who would've thought, that the very room my father and fake mother slept in, would be used to teach my children the lessons of life? Sure, Madjesty brought in one hundred dollars last week, but what that showed me was that with the right guidance she could bring in much more.

"Ya'll sit down on the floor." They sat down with their backs up against the wall. I walked over to my table and picked up the three bright orange carrots that sat on my dresser. "Here take these."

"What's this about?" Madjesty rebutted already. She examined the carrot carefully.

"I'll tell you when we get to that point, for now, shut the fuck up and pay attention."

"You want us to eat them?" Jayden asked stupidly.

"Did I say eat them?"

"No."

"Alright then." I paused. "This is the first of many instructional classes I'm going to be conducting for you two. And I want you to pay attention because later on, we will be entertaining a special guest as a quiz."

They looked at each other in confusion. "Today the focus is on your gag reflexes. It is important that we work on them now if we're going to be bringing in the money necessary to live the life we want."

"The life we want, or the life you want?" Madjesty asked.

"It should be both." I smirked. "We need money, girls. And money can only come one way, and that is if it's earned."

"Ma, what about a job?" Madjesty offered. "I don't understand why we can't just get a job like everybody else."

"You don't understand because you're too young and mouthy. And if you continue to be disobedient, I'm stuffing your gay ass back under the stairs." I told her.

"Please stop, Madjesty," Jayden said. "Just listen."

Madjesty rolled her eyes and remained quiet.

"Now, I want you to take the carrots I've just handed you, and stick the entire thing into your mouths. I only want to see the butt of the carrot and that's it."

"But...They not washed," Jayden said.

"Exactly, and the dicks you'll be sucking won't be washed either. Now...Pick up the carrots and put them fully in your mouths."

They were slow at first until I said, "Either you two bitches do what I'm asking, or you can get the fuck out of my house. Unless you got someplace else to live I suggest you start sucking."

Slowly they picked the carrots up and put them in their mouths. Madjesty had the carrot only halfway in her throat and already was gagging, while Jayden seemed to do it with ease.

"Slowly, Madjesty. You must relax your gag reflexes first. Trust me when I say you won't swallow a dick if it's in your mouth, no matter how much you may feel like you will."

I looked back at Jayden and was still shocked. She was definitely going to be my moneymaker. She seemed to be a natural at this and before I knew it, the entire carrot was in her mouth and she was holding it steady. Tears rolled down the sides of her eyes and I didn't know if it was because she was controlling her reflexes, or crying, either way I didn't care.

"Okay, Jayden, that was pretty good, you can stop now. But Madjesty, you need to slow down." I said walking up to her snatching the carrot out of her throat. She wiped her mouth and looked up at me. "Here, open your mouth wide and relax."

"I don't want to do this." She said pushing my hand out of her face.

"And I don't want to do it either. But there's no way in hell there'll be three pussies in here, and only one of them bringing in money."

"Four pussies." Madjesty said.

"What?"

"You forgot about the gimp in the wheel chair downstairs. Don't she count?"

"You know what, I'm sick of your whining and shit. You're lazy, boyish and don't wanna listen."

With that I grabbed her by her shirt and pulled her down the stairs. Then I locked her back into the crawlspace where she would stay until I let her out. She was banging on the door but I didn't open it.

"Fuck is going on around here?" Kali said walking up behind me. I didn't even know he was here. "Why ya'll makin' all this noise in my fuckin' house?"

"Look, Kali. Either kill me or leave 'cause I'm sick of seeing you."

"You may get your wish soon enough," he said.

My stomach churned at the idea of Concord Manor being anywhere near his house. "I'm teaching her how to earn money, and since she wanna be disobedient, she got to learn the hard way."

"Well what you teaching her?"

"Why, Kali? This is my fucking house and these are my kids."

"Bitch, don't make me drop you. Why you got her under the steps?"

"I'm teaching her how to make money, the old fashion way! Anything else?"

He was quiet and I wanted to see if he gave a fuck. After everything he did to my body, by taking these kids out of my womb, now he had a chance to be a father and I wanted to see if he would take it or not.

"Well, keep that shit down. I'm tryin' to go to sleep."

When he walked off thoughts of shooting him in the back of his head danced through my mind, but I didn't have a gun or bullets, so I would have to wait.

Directing my attention back to the crawlspace I said, "You will stay in there until you learn to obey me."

After that I walked back up the stairs and saw Jayden crying. When she saw me enter the room, she wiped her tears away.

"I don't wanna see you crying no more." I said seriously. "It's time you learn about real life and its time you stopped being weak."

"I know...And you won't see me cry anymore, mama." She said. "I'm ready to do what I gotta do for me and Madjesty. Just teach me what you want me to know."

I smiled and said, "That's what I wanna hear."

After that I made the call to get our guest of honor and he came about fifteen minutes later. I met him while applying for welfare at the Department of Social Services last week. Even though he was in his early twenties, he seemed to be excited about my proposition. It didn't matter when I told him that the proposition involved my fourteen-year-old twin daughters. It's amazing how perverted most people are in the world.

"Jayden, this is Abdul and he's the guest I was telling you about."

Jayden looked me in the eyes and I could tell she knew what needed to be done. I had to be sure she was ready and I had to see it with my own eyes.

"Now, using what you learned today, I need you to show me...On Abdul." I paused. "Abdul, sit down on the edge of the bed please." He did. "Are you ready, Jayden?"

"Yes," she said in a confident voice. "Will you let my sister out after I finish?"

"Don't' ask me anything else about Madjesty. Madjesty made her bed and now she has to lie in it. Now, stay focused!" I said clapping my hands. "Using what I taught you earlier with the carrots, I need you to show me you got it down on Abdul. Suck his dick like a pro and don't stop until he cums."

Abdul tried to stand up and I said, "Stay down, Abdul."

Instead of looking like he was about to get broken off, he looked more nervous than anything and I hoped he would be able to go through with it.

With Abdul seated on the bed, she dropped to her knees in front of him. "Now, remove his pants." I instructed.

"I can do it myself," he told me. I guess he was trying to help her out. "It's not a problem."

"Abdul, when I invited you over here nothing about that offer included me wanting to hear your input. You are to sit here and remain quiet." I paused. "Now can you do that for me?"

"Yes."

"Good," I said redirecting my attention to Jayden. "Now, take his jeans off." Jayden removed his jeans like he was a kid getting ready for bed.

"Look, everything you do must be a seduction. Everything! It ain't enough for you to do the act if you look like you're about to be hung or something. Every man must be made to feel like he's the only one. Because if he believes he's the only one, even when he's not, the money will flow. *Always.*" I paused. "Having sex and getting paid for it is all about the seduction." I continued. "Now, when you remove his boxers, be seductive."

"Seductive?"

"Yes...Have you ever had a crush on someone?"

"No," she shook her head quickly.

"Well, is there someone you like on TV?" I asked irritated.

"Yes."

"Good, use his image and keep it in the front of your mind always." I said. "Now...Remove his boxers like he's the one in your vision."

This time she did it a little better and I was pleased. I knew that in time, she would be perfect.

"Now, remember the carrot?" She nodded. "Good, think of the carrot with Abdul here." Abdul was already hard but Jayden wasn't confident anymore when she saw him naked. "Let it go as deeply in your throat as possible. Do you understand me, Jayden?"

"Yes, mama."

"Good, now put him into your mouth. *Slowly.*" She did what I asked with no gag. She was doing great, and I couldn't understand why. "Cool, now work the carrot back and forth but," I paused, "this time you want to take your other hand and cup his balls. Always make sure you give his balls some sort of attention."

"Okay, mama."

"Good...Now work your mouth back and forth and your other hand should be jerking the shaft. Do it with semi swift motions."

Abdul's head was leaning back and I knew he was almost there. "Good, Jayden! That's it. He's almost there."

In less than three minutes he came and Jayden jumped up to prevent his cum from getting on her clothes. "Jayden, you always and I do mean always swallow. Do I make myself clear?"

"But...It's nasty."

"Bitch, I don't wanna hear that shit! Always swallow. That one act alone will give us the ability to charge extra."

Now I couldn't be sure if it was her blowjob or if he was just a two minute brother. What I could be sure of was that she got him to cum, no matter how long it took. After we finished, Abdul thanked us a million times and rolled out. I told him I would be calling him for further lessons in the future and he said he'd be available any time. I bet, dirty mothafucka.

"You did great, Jayden."

"Thanks, ma." She paused. "But can I ask you something?"

"What?" I didn't want to hear anything about Madjesty.

"I was invited to this party later on tonight. The guy who gave me one hundred dollars is going to pick me up later. Can I go?"

"Yes."

"Thanks, ma."

"But, you don't go nowhere without bringing money into this house when you come back through them doors."

"Huh?"

"Huh?" I frowned. "Bitch, you heard me. Whenever you go on a date, I expect you to come back with money in your pockets. These boys ain't got no problem asking for pussy, so we shouldn't have no problems asking for the money. Understood?"

"Yes, ma."

"Good, now the going rate is one hundred dollars now, but as the weeks go by I'm going to expect you and Madjesty to be bring in no less than one thousand dollars a week."

"What? I mean...How?"

"I'm going to teach you everything. Just like I did tonight. Just prepare yourself mentally, because it is coming." I smiled. "Now what party you going to anyway? And who's throwing it?" I said on my fifth glass of vodka for the day.

"My friend is throwing it for his mother."

"Oh really? You have a friend already, huh?"

"Yeah, and he said his mother might not make it so they wanna throw her a nice celebration before she dies."

It sure would be nice if my kids threw something for me. I thought. "What she got...Cancer or something?"

"I don't know. But he said before long, her eyesight will be completely gone."

"Yeah...Well whatever. Just remember to bring my money back in here or don't come home." I paused. "What you wearing?"

"I gotta find something."

"Humph...Well before you leave, I need you to cut some onions for me. We went to the grocers yesterday and they're downstairs."

"Okay. How many?"

"Five."

"Alright, mama. No problem."

"Well, leave me be. I need my rest." I said walking to my bed to get in.

"Ma, I know you told me not to ask about her again, but how much do I have to bring in for you to let Madjesty out?"

Her love for her sister might be the thing I could use to keep her in line. Both of them for that matter. "You bring me back five hundred, and she's out."

She looked disappointed but said, "Okay... I'ma see what I can do."

"Either you do or you don't, it don't make me no never mind. But I will tell you this, she won't see the light of day until I'm ready to pull her out if you don't. That my dear is a promise." I paused grabbing my glass again. "And don't forget my onions."

LIKE ME

Jayden

Jayden sat in her room nervous about her first date with Shaggy. Had she had some nice clothes to wear, things would not have been so bad. But as it stood every article of clothing in her house was made for a boy. Her jeans were too baggy, her shirts were masculine and all she had was a comb to do her hair.

She tried to find the smallest T-shirt she had available in her closet so that it would show her budding breasts. Eventually she found a white Nightmare on Elm Street T-shirt, but it wasn't as fitting as she would have liked it to be. With her shirt on, she looked through her nothingness until she found the pair of high waist jeans she wore in middle school. Afterwards, she slipped on her only pair of shoes, a pair of dirty white K-Swiss tennis shoes. She hated how she looked and started to tell him not to come, but he was already on his way.

"Madjesty, you have company," Cherry screamed from the foyer.

Cherry didn't say much to the girls or to Harmony. She was ashamed for what she'd done to Harmony when she was pregnant. But expressing emotion, in her mind, would be disloyal to Kali. However there was kindness in her eyes and Jayden liked her, despite them not saying much to one another.

"Thank you," Jayden said.

Cherry was looking down at her legs and said, "No problem. Be safe."

Nobody ever told her to be safe, ever and she appreciated her words.

When Shaggy saw her come from behind Cherry, he focused on her clothing. But wouldn't allow her to see his displeasure. "You don't want me to meet your moms before we leave?"

"Not if I can help it." She said getting into his truck.

They drove a few moments in silence and Jayden tried to look at her reflection in the window. "You aight? You seemed fucked up about somethin'." He asked.

"I don't want to talk about it," she told him. "I hate always having bad news when I see you." She paused. "Tonight, she turned around, "I kinda wanna escape from it all. You know?"

"I feel you, but if we gonna be cool, I'ma need you to rap with me about what you thinkin'. I'm a big boy…I can handle it."

She laughed.

"I do have a question for you…"

"Go 'head."

"What is that smell?"

Jayden had smelled it too but tried to ignore it. "My mother made me cut five onions before leaving the house."

"Why?"

"I didn't even think about it, until I went upstairs to tell her they were done, and she was in her usual drunken sleep." She paused. "Told me to throw them in the trash…Turns out she didn't even need them."

"She knew you were going on a date?"

"Yes."

"She cold!"

"Tell me about it."

"You aight?"

"Why? I'd thought you wouldn't have time for shit like this."

"I don't know why, but before somethin' changes you might as well take advantage of it. I'm not normally like this with people."

Jayden sighed and said, "My mother is a monster," she shared in a low voice. "And for whatever reason I still love her. Although I wish I understood why. She makes me do stuff, that mothers shouldn't make their kids do."

"Wow…I ain't ever heard somebody sayin' some shit like that about their moms. Maybe she had a fucked up life when she was younger, too. I mean, it don't make it right but did she ever tell you somethin' about her past?"

"She never really goes into her past," Jayden said. "Just that she had a nice life before she had us." Then she looked over at him. "Anyway, I'm just happy to be getting away with you, even if this doesn't last too long."

"What you mean last too long?"

"Look at me...And look at you. Come on, Shaggy. I know you don't like how I look. And smell," she laughed. "You just trying to be nice."

"I don't know what you talkin' 'bout."

She smiled and figured she was being immature, although growing up with a mother as neglectful as Harmony forced her to be more mature than a lot of girls her age.

"Back to your mother, what's her price tonight?"

Jayden was shocked and embarrassed that he knew her already. "What do you mean?"

"If she lettin' you leave the crib, she must want somethin'. So what is it?"

"Five hundred dollars." She whispered.

"What the fuck?"

"I don't expect you to give me that much money, Shaggy. I'm just telling you what she wants because you asked."

"Where else you gonna get it from?"

"I don't know, I guess I gotta do what I gotta do," she said re-membering the lessons her mother taught here earlier.

"Man, fuckin' with you gonna have a nigga broke," he laughed. "But I'll see what I can do."

"Thank you," she said hopefully.

She felt like a party pooper. But so many things were going on in her young mind. She wondered if Madjesty was hurt, or if her mother would wake up out of her drunken stupor and beat her again.

"Now what's on your mind?" He asked. "I said I'ma work that money shit out for you. I ain't got no love for dope money. It comes and goes so for real, it ain't a problem."

"It's not that."

"What is it? Your clothes?"

"Come on now, Shaggy. You can't tell me you don't think I look like a mess."

"Then what you wanna do?" He said electing not to keep it too real with her at this time. He did notice her clothing but understood her situation enough to let shit slide.

"I can wait in the car for you until you finish your party. And then maybe we can go somewhere where people don't know you."

"People know me everywhere I go," he told her. "But how 'bout we do this, my home girl got a rack of clothes and she 'bout your size. I'ma call her up and see if she can hook us up. What size shoe you wear?"

"No! That's too embarrassing."

"Trust me, my home girl cool as shit. She ain't that type person. So let me call her. What's your shoe size?"

"I'm a size eight and a half."

"She a size eight. But I'ma see what I can do".

After Shaggy made the call, they pulled up to Greenbelt Apartments in Greenbelt Maryland. When they arrived at her door Jayden was surprised at how pretty and nice Olive seemed.

"Hey, Shaggy! Come on in," she said hugging him. "And this must be Jayden! You didn't tell me she was so pretty."

Olive wore her hair in natural curly red fro and her natural eyelashes were so long and pretty they almost looked fake.

"Thank you," Jayden said. "But I can say the same thing about you."

"Well we talkin' about you now, girl." She said smiling so wide. "A face like that can get you anything you want in life."

"Okay...Okay," Shaggy interrupted. "Both of ya'll pretty so let's stop with the girly shit. I can't be late for my peeps joint tonight."

They both laughed.

"I'm serious, Shaggy. Where you find her from? I ain't never seen her around the way before."

"Olive, I need you to hook her up right quick. Cut the small talk."

"You know I got you, boy." She said taking Jayden by the hand. Jayden liked her immediately and hoped they could be friends. "I was just picking something to wear for your party tonight myself." She continued. "Give us a few minutes, we'll be back and I'll have her real pretty for you."

When they walked into Olive's room, Jayden took note at how neat everything was. She had a screen TV that took up a lot of space and a large oak dresser and matching bed. You had to use a step stool next to Olive's bed just to climb onto the mattress.

"Before we go any further," Olive said. "What is that smell?"

"Onions. My mother made me cut them before I left tonight. She was trying to ruin my night."

"Humph. Well you're mother don't know me. I got some baking soda in my bathroom that will do the trick."

"Thanks."

"Okay, let me see what we have in here," Olive said opening her closet. Jayden was amazed at how many clothes she had, many of them still had the tags on them. "I like this for you," she said pulling out a cute red dress with a low cut in the front, "or this", she said pulling out a teal color one piece short set. "Which one you like, Jayden?"

"Anyone would be fine for me," Jayden said still embarrassed she had to go through someone else's closet.

"Do you like either of them?" Olive said turning around to her.

Silence.

Walking over to the bed she said, "Okay let's get rid of the elephant in the room. I know you may be embarrassed about havin' to do this, but I'm not that kind of person and neither is Shaggy. He don't do this kind of shit for anybody so he must be really feelin' you. But you gotta relax and go with the flow, Jayden."

"I know...But if you knew how fucked up my life was, you would see why it's so hard for me to trust people and take kindness. You wouldn't believe the type of shit I had to do today before even coming here. My life is some shit, Olive."

"I can look in your eyes and tell you have a hard life. But why let whoever's contributing to your unhappiness make things worse? Don't give them tonight, girl. Escape from all that bullshit and have fun."

"I wish it was that easy."

"Jayden, let me tell you a little something about life. People hate weak and whiny people. Not that your problems aren't real. It's just that you have the see the stars through the storm even when no one else does. You have to see the vision, even when there is no board. Other people won't do it for you. They'll just write you ou. of their lives and won't even tell you why. You get it?"

"I think so."

"Let me help you." She said opening her dresser drawer pulling out a bag of weed and some pills. "You smoke or pop?"

"Smoke or pop?"

Olive laughed and said, "I'ma start you off with smoke tonight. You need to relax."

Olive rolled a quick blunt and taught Jayden how to inhale and exhale and before she knew it, she was a pro. Within minutes Jayden was relaxed and hungry.

"Now…Which outfit do you want to wear?" Olive repeated.

"The red one." Olive smiled. "I think I'll look sexy in that one."

"I knew you would come around." Olive winked.

After Jayden got dressed, Olive straightened Jayden's slightly curly long hair and put some make up on her face. Then she stepped back to look at her work.

"Damn, Jayden, you look cuter than me in that dress!" She complimented. "Consider it yours."

"No…I can't take your dress."

"What I tell you?" Olive said seriously. "Relax. If somebody offers you a gift, accept it. That way doors will be open for more blessings."

"More blessings, huh? We getting high and you talkin' about blessings?" Jayden laughed.

"I'm talkin' the truth." She said walking up to her. "And I talk the truth whether I'm high or not. Now…Look at how pretty you look in my mirror on the door."

Jayden looked at herself in the door length mirror. The red dress hugged her tiny waist and presented her with a fat ass. Jayden looked like a rock star and finally she looked like the girl she always felt like inside. Even before her mother told her she was not a boy.

"Here, your feet are just a little bigger than mine, but I bought these Jimmy Choo sandals too big and I never was able to wear them. Try 'em on."

The shoes fit as perfectly as a glove. It seemed like everything was falling into place.

"And here's my number," Olive said handing her a piece of paper. "If you ever need a getaway, and Shaggy acting up, or even if he's cool and you wanna get out, you can call me."

There was something in Olive's voice that was seductive but Jayden couldn't place her finger on it. Olive gave her a hug and Jayden tried her best to prevent from crying. She was shown more kindness in one day than she had her entire life.

"You don't know what this means to me."

"I can see it in your eyes." Then she dabbed her tears away with a clean napkin. "Now stop it... You're gonna mess up my makeup job."

"Okay," she giggled. "I'm sorry. So what time you coming?"

"I'm waitin' on my girls so I won't get there until a couple of hours later. I'll see you soon though."

Jayden was hoping that she and Shaggy wouldn't leave before Olive got there but even if they did miss her, she had plans to call her later. When she walked out into the living room, and Shaggy saw her his jaw dropped.

"Stop looking like that," Jayden said feeling embarrassed.

"I knew you had a body on you, but this is crazy."

"Thank you... I think."

"You think right," he said looking at her again. "Damn, Olive, you should go into business for makeovers."

"Look what I had to work with." Olive said smacking Jayden's fat ass. "This girl had all this body under her dress."

"Good lookin' out," he said. "Maybe now she can loosen up and have a good time with me."

Jayden said, "I'll try."

"Remember what I said... The stars through the storm."

Jayden hugged Olive and rushed to the door to open it for Shaggy.

"Alright, homie. I'ma get up with you later." Shaggy said to Olive, wondering why Jayden rushed to open the door for him. It seemed like she was trying harder to be a boy, since she had the dress on. Unconsciously wearing the beautiful outfit heightened what her mother told her about not appearing feminine.

"Okay. I'll see you in a little while." Olive said to them.

When they walked to the car, Jayden unknowingly opened his car door and then ran around to the passenger side to open her door.

"Hold up... Why you keep openin' doors for me?"

"Huh?"

"I said why do you keep doin' that?"

Jayden was programmed so long to be a boy, that she didn't know how to be anything else. It was easier for her to walk like a girl, because she never fully grasped the concept of walking like a boy like Madjesty. So she over compensated by getting doors and things of that nature.

"I'm sorry."

"It's not about bein' sorry," he said in a soft voice. "I just want you to let me take care of you when you're with me. Got it?"

"Yes," she smiled.

"My boys don't even open no doors for me. And they niggas."

When they arrived at the party it was jammed pack. There were so many people inside their large house in Adelphi, Maryland that Jayden felt uncomfortable. But, what was unanimous was the nod Shaggy got of acceptance as he walked through the doors with Jayden on his arm. Beautiful couldn't even be used to describe her. She was breathtaking.

"Let me introduce you to my pops," he said loving the attention Jayden was getting.

"Your mother and father are still together?"

"Yeah...But he still steps out on her." He advised. "She cool with it now though. I think she know she's about to die so she wants to worry about what matters most. Me, our family and friends."

"What is she dying from?"

"Syphilis. She got it back in the day and didn't know it."

"You can die from Syphilis?"

"Yeah...When you get the late stages, you don't have any symptoms and then all of a sudden you have brain issues and you can barely move around. You can also go blind." He paused. "The doctors tried all they could do but nothin' worked to help her. Shit progressed and now she might not make it."

Jayden thought about Syphilis, and remembered what she was taught in school. If her mother was making her have sex for money, how did she know she wouldn't get something like that, too?

"Pops, I want you to meet somebody," Shaggy said tapping Paco on the shoulders. Paco was engaged in a conversation with a few

other people before he turned around and saw his son. "This is Jay-
den. Jayden this is my pops."

Paco stared her down like she was the last chicken on the plate
and he hadn't eaten a thing in weeks.

"Wow, son! You scored big with this one right here," he said
looking at her seductively. "You're very beautiful, young lady."

"Thanks, pops." Shaggy smiled. It was evident that he was still
trying hard to get his father's attention.

"No thank you," Paco continued, licking his lips.

"Dad, ease up." Shaggy said, slightly embarrassed.

"You know I'm just fuckin' with you," Paco joked. "But why
do you look so familiar to me?" Paco continued. "What's your
mother's name?"

Jayden did not want to risk somebody knowing her whorish
mother so she said, "Cybil."

"Cybil, huh?"

"Yeah."

"Well Cybil and your father did a beautiful job makin' you.
They should be commended."

"You are corny as shit, pops."

He laughed. "She knows I'm just playin' with her. Don't you,
honey?"

"Aight, it's time to roll before my pops tries to steal you."
Shaggy interrupted. Paco gave his son some dap and Shaggy
stepped off.

"Let me introduce you to my moms." He continued. "And I'm
sorry about that shit with my pops. I told you he can be over the top,
but we use to it now." Right before he reached Trip, Jace walked in
front of them. "Oh, this is my uncle," Shaggy said to Jayden. "Unc,
this is my new friend, Jayden."

Jace's mouth hung open. He couldn't move, and he couldn't
speak.

"You okay, unc?"

"Uh...Yes."

"Did you hear what I said? This is my friend Jayden."

"Shaggy, where did you meet her from?" He said seriously
without even addressing Jayden.

"What's wrong?"

"Son, where did you meet this girl?"

Jayden felt like she wanted to run and hide somewhere. Jace seemed hostile and it scared her. "At the McDonalds out Fort Washington…Why? Is everything cool?"

"Who's your mother?" Jace asked not getting the information he wanted.

It was the second time someone asked her that question tonight and she was starting to believe that they did know her mother. Did she look that much like her? Even if she did she had told a lie, and would now have to stick to it.

"Cybil. My mother's name is Cybil."

Jace's tensed body seemed to deflate. She didn't know if he was happy or upset with her response, although he did look at ease.

"Oh…You look like somebody I use to know. A woman name Harmony." And then he paused. "But…But you also look like…"

"You," Shaggy said seeing the resemblance. "That's crazy as shit! It's in your eyes, Jayden. I knew you looked like somebody I knew when I met you at the McDonalds."

"I'm sure it's a case of mistaken identity." Jayden assured him. "Where's your mother, Shaggy? I want to meet her." She wanted to get as far away from the man as possible.

"Aight, unc," Shaggy said sensing Jayden's nervousness. "Let me introduce her to moms. I'ma get up with you later."

"Alright, Shaggy. We'll talk about that other business then, too."

Shaggy worked for Jace which is why he stayed with money in his pocket.

Jace didn't trust the girl's response when he questioned her about her mother, and he needed Paco to find out where she lived and who she really was.

"Ma, I want you to meet somebody," Shaggy said walking up to her. "This is my friend Jayden."

Trip's eyes were wet from having to apply constant medicine drops to prevent them from drying out. She looked real frail and was sitting in her wheelchair when they approached. Trip could barely see anybody out in front of her, but when she heard Shaggy's voice she reached for his hand.

"Do you know I've never met one of my son's friends before," she smiled. "This is a first."

"Ma, she just a friend. It's not even like that."

"I know, Evan," she said calling him by his birth name. "But it's still a pleasure to meet one of your girl friends. Is she pretty?" she asked because she could barely see her.

"She sure is," Paco said from nowhere. "She's a sight for sore eyes."

"Dad," Shaggy said mad at his comment.

"Oh...Uh...I didn't mean it like that, son."

"It's okay," Trip said. "You know how your father is. But I do know one thing, if he says she's beautiful, than she must be beautiful. So, Evan, what do you have planned for tonight?"

"Shaggy, ma. I go by Shaggy not Evan."

"Boy, you know I call you by your birth name," she corrected him. "I leave all that nickname shit to you kids."

Shaggy laughed.

"Aight, ma. We can't stay long. I just wanted you to meet my friend before I left," he said kissing her on her cheek. "I'ma come by tomorrow. Call me if you need anything before then."

"Okay, I love you son," she told him. "And it was nice meeting you Jayden. I hope to talk to you again."

"Me too," Jayden replied, still feeling uncomfortable about meeting Jace.

Shaggy and Jayden were making their way out of the party when Olive, Toni, Courtenay and Cheryl walked inside the house.

"Ya'll leaving already?" Olive said. "I was trying to rush over before ya'll left."

"Bitch, if you woulda had your clothes out we would have been here on time." Toni said. "Instead of dressing one of Shaggy's bitches."

It was seconds before Toni and Jayden recognized each other. Toni, Courtenay and Cheryl were the girls who were in the McDonald's the other night.

"Hold up, bitch! Ain't you the one with all the mouth in McDonald's?" Toni asked. "Talk that shit now." She stepped up to her but Shaggy got between them.

"Bitch, I will crack your jaw if you start some shit at my mom's house." Shaggy said. "Olive, get 'em out of here before I hurt 'em."

"What is wrong with you, Toni? Why you always wildin' out?" Olive said.

"I'm gone anyway," Toni said. She rolled her eyes at Jayden and it was apparent that when they saw each other again, it wouldn't be nice. Then she and the girls walked out.

"I'm sorry, Jayden," Olive said. "And I'll call you later, Shaggy."

The girls left and Shaggy said, "Let's go."

Right before he walked out the door, Jace pulled him to the side and asked to speak to him in private. They stepped a few feet away from her so that she couldn't overhear their conversation. Jayden tried to appear uninterested, but she had to know what they were saying. She saw their mouths moving and judging by the way Shaggy would look in her direction between pauses, she figured they were talking about her.

When they were done, Jace gave Jayden one last look before walking away. She couldn't read his facial expressions but she had a feeling he didn't like her.

"Let's go," Shaggy said.

When they got back in the truck, she could tell something was on his mind. He wasn't treating her the same anymore. "Is everything okay?" Jayden asked.

"Yeah." He said short.

"Did I do something wrong?"

He paused, looked over at her and then back at the road, "I want you to be honest with me. 'Cause if we gonna kick it, I need to know you on the up and up about shit. One thing I can't stand is a fuckin' liar."

She swallowed hard. "Okay."

"If you tell me you're being truthful, I won't ever ask you about it again, but if I find out you lying to me, you ain't got shit to say to me no more. Ever."

"Okay."

"Is your mother's name Harmony?"

Jayden felt perspiration form on her forehead. Although this was their first date, she liked him already and didn't want to lose his friendship. Not to mention by giving her some money, she was able to save her sister from the hellhole she was living in. So she thought clearly, weighed her options and decided to answer his question.

"No, my mother's name is Cybil. I think your uncle has me confused with somebody else."

"It's cool," he said. "I told him that but he wanted to make sure."

"What...What did Harmony do so bad?"

"He said he was looking for her and that they have some unfinished business. I think she stole some money from him. But whenever I hear her name I never hear anything good about her."

"You know her, too?"

"You know, when he said the name it sounded familiar to me. Like I heard it before, but naw, I don't know her personally."

"Oh...Well I hope he finds her."

"My uncle sounds like he has every intention on finding her." He said looking at her expression. "So I know it won't be long."

"Oh."

Shaggy paused for a while, smiled and said, "I'ma drop you off at home, I have to meet my uncle later tonight." She figured he was lying and he sensed it. "I'm serious. That was the other thing we talked about. I work with my uncle and something came up he needs my help with."

"Okay. I believe you."

"Call me tomorrow though, unless I call you first."

"No...I'll call you!" She yelled realizing that if she was going to keep her lie alive, she had to keep him separated from her mother at all times. That included by phone.

"Alright," he said pulling up at her house. She still hadn't gotten the money he said he might give her but after the accusations of Harmony being her mother, she didn't want to ask him again. "Call me tomorrow."

Jayden tried to procrastinate, hoping he would remember to give her the money, or even tell her he'd give it to her later, but he didn't.

"Okay, I'll call you later." She closed the car door, and walked toward the house and he waited for her to open the door before he pulled off. Now how was she going to deal with her mother? The moment she opened the door, she saw Harmony standing before her drunk out of her mind.

"You got my money?" Harmony said. She was swaying and looked like she would fall at any minute. "'Cause I know you didn't bring your ass in here without my money!"

She figured it would be best to stall her until she could think of another plan. Telling her she didn't have the money was not an option. Glancing at the crawlspace where her sister was, she felt faint. She hated her twin sister having to go through so much pain.

"I got your money, but I gotta give it to you tomorrow."

"Tomorrow?" She repeated laughing. "I knew your young ass couldn't do no real woman's work." She paused. "You don't give your body to nobody and then wait for the money later. You get your money up front, little girl."

"I didn't have sex with him, mama."

Harmony paused for a minute and busted out laughing in her face. "Bitch, you must think I'm stupid! Don't nobody get rolled around in no nice ass Navigator and not give the pussy up." She said. "You fucked and sucked him for free! Tell the truth."

"I didn't. Just drop it!" Jayden said pressing buttons. If Harmony wasn't drunk she wouldn't be so bold. "He didn't want anything from me when he gave me the two hundred dollars either."

"Two hundred dollars? I thought you said he gave you one hundred?"

"I...I mean...I meant, one hundred."

"Are you lying to me, little bitch?" She said angrily. "And where did you get that dress?"

Suddenly, Jayden was tired of being the victim. "He gave it to me, mother monster! Somebody felt sorry for my life and decided to help me out!"

"Are you that fucking stupid? That you would believe that you can get something in this world for nothing?"

"I met someone nice. So who's stupid now?"

"Oh so what, you think you better than me? You think you're prettier than me? Well I was much prettier than you before I had this scar on my face." She pushed Jayden into the pillar by the door and she hit her shoulder. Her back was in severe pain and she realized now that she'd gone too far.

"I'm sorry, ma," she cried. "I didn't mean to be disrespectful."

"It's too late for that shit!" She screamed. "Take that dress off! Now!"

"Okay," she said walking toward her room.

"No! Take it off right here." Harmony was swaying so much now, she almost fell. "Since you wanna think you grown. Be grown now."

"But I don't think I'm grown, mama."

"Take it off!"

Jayden looked at her mother and knew there was no talking to her. So she removed the dress and it fell to her feet. Harmony picked it up and read the label. It was a BCBG dress.

"Who gave you this?" She screamed clutching the dress in her hands. "And don't tell me it was your friend!"

Jayden wiped the tears from her eyes and covered her vagina with her other hand. "I told you, mama. My new friend."

Just when she said that someone knocked at the door. "Who the fuck is at my door?"

Harmony walked to the door and opened it, leaving Jayden in the middle of the floor naked. It was Shaggy standing on the other side. Jayden tried to hide herself but Harmony said, "Don't move, bitch! Do you know this nigga?"

Shaggy didn't see Jayden at first and was confused at Harmony's drunken condition. He said, "Excuse me, mam, but is Jayden available?"

Trying to embarrass her, she opened the door wide. "Yeah...There she go right there." She pointed.

Shaggy stepped fully inside the house and he couldn't believe his eyes when he saw Jayden naked. He spotted the red dress Olive had given to her in Harmony's hands and wondered why she had it. Accessing what was going on, he immediately leveled a dark glare at Harmony.

"Are you hurt?" He asked.

"Sh...Shaggy." She said crying. "I'm...I'm okay."

"How come I don't believe you?" He said still looking at Harmony.

"I...I am," she sobbed. "Did...Did I forget something in your truck?"

He could tell she was trying to keep the peace and for Jayden's sake, he would respect that. "Yeah...I forgot to give you that thing you asked me for earlier," he said.

Harmony swallowed some more liquor and said, "You fucked her didn't you?" She thought it was funny for him to see Jayden humiliated but he ignored her.

Shaggy walked over to Jayden and handed her the money. She didn't know which hand to remove from her naked body so she used the one that was covering her breasts to accept it. With the money in her hands, he walked back to the door.

"Are you sure you okay?" He asked.

"Y...Yes."

"Aight," he said looking at Harmony again. "Call me first thing in the morning."

"Okay," she sobbed.

"I'm serious."

"I will," she said wishing he'd just leave. She was embarrassed enough as it was.

He took one more look at her and was about to leave until he said, "Fuck that shit, yo, Jayden, let's go."

"Excuse me?!" Harmony said. "My daughter isn't going anywhere with you."

"Jayden, go get in my fuckin' truck! Now!"

"If my daughter leaves out of here I'm calling the cops."

Shaggy snatched the money out of Jayden's hand and said, "Here, bitch! Take it!" Then he turned back to Jayden and said, "Go get in my truck, Jayden!"

Harmony scooped the money off the ground while Jayden ran outside and jumped in his truck.

"Bitch, you betta never come back either!" Harmony yelled in her driveway. "And your sister is as good as dead, too!"

Hearing this caused Jayden to jump back out the truck but Shaggy stopped her. "I gotta go! My sister's in there," she cried. "She's gonna hurt my sister!"

"You can't go back in there! She's drunk and trippin' right now. I'ma work some shit out." He said walking her back over to the passenger side of the car.

"No! She's gonna hurt her!" She screamed.

"Jayden, STOP IT! AND TRUST ME!" He yelled. "I'M GONNA COME BACK FOR YOUR SISTER, BUT WE HAVE TO LEAVE RIGHT NOW BEFORE THIS BITCH CALLS THE POLICE!"

Jayden wiped her tears and sat quietly in his truck. He walked around to his side and got in. Once in the truck he turned the heat on to make her feel comfortable.

"Here, put this on." He handed her a jacket out of the backseat. He looked at Harmony who was still cussing in the driveway and pulled off. "I don't know what's going on with your mother, but I don't trust her. Give me a day or two though, I'ma work somethin' out."

MEETING

Jace

I was in the deli with my bodyguards Kevin and Russian Antony, waiting on Kali to enter. Truthfully, I wasn't trying to be bothered with this dude but I wanted to hear what he had to tell me. Although Kevin had been with me since I took over DC, I hired Russian Antony because after all these years, Massive had still not been found. And he was going to have to come through both of them, to get at me.

When Kali finally pulled up to the deli, he walked inside and was patted down by Antony. "Sit down," Antony told him.

When he was seated I said, "What can I do for you?"

"Awe, shit. You all serious and straight to the point these days, huh? Let me find out you gangsta now. I heard about all the work you been puttin' in."

"You said you had some information for me, and since you been lyin' to me for the longest, I hope you come clean today." I said drinking the beer on the table. "Otherwise you can get the fuck outta my face. Feel me?"

"Where you want me to start?" Kali said with a grimace on his face.

"With Harmony. I'm still not understanding why you would do her like you did, when you caught up with her in Texas. And I wanna know where you get the product from."

"I told you, man. I saved up some money and was able to buy a package."

"From who?" I investigated. "And if you were going into business yourself, why you ain't let me know? I had to put Paco on you to find out what was up. And then the next thing I know, you get locked up."

"Man, it wasn't nothin' but a little bit of money. Shit wasn't even that deep."

"I betta neva find out you were stealin' from me, nigga."

"And what you gonna do?" He threatened. His old attitude was coming back.

Antony and Kevin cocked their weapons and aimed at him. "Do you really wanna know the answer to that?" I asked.

"Man, I'm just fuckin' with you." He smirked. "But that little bit of weight I was sellin' them Houston niggas wasn't nothin'. Trust me." He paused. "As far as Harmony's concerned, you act like she was still your girl or somethin'."

"That ain't the point, but at one time she was. Not only that, there's a possibility she has my kids."

Kali looked away and said, "I wish you get over that shit, man. 'Cause I never lied to you when I said me and Harmony fucked." I swallowed hard. "But I also know I'm not the only nigga she fucked either. I keep telling you to stop worrying about that pussy cause them babies could be anybody's."

"Don't tell me 'bout no Maryland niggas again."

"I'm talkin' niggas in your crew."

"Who?"

"Paco and Kreshon. So you see, truthfully, Jace, any of us could be the father."

I could feel Kevin and Antony's stares at me upon his revelation. "So you tellin' me, niggas who I broke bed with, fucked my girl?"

"That's exactly what I'm sayin'. It wasn't just me."

I looked away from him, clenched my fist and said, "Do you know where she is?"

"Naw. I ain't seen her since that shit happened in Houston."

"How you get out?"

"Let's just say you never saw me."

"I'm still lookin' for her, so I need to know if you know them kids names."

"Naw, man. But if you want, I can find out for you. I got you."

There goes his favorite phrase again. "Naw, I got some people on that already."

"I know you wasn't feeling the reason I went to jail," he said skipping the subject, "but I've been working on my temper and I'm a little more relaxed now."

"You being relaxed ain't my problem no more."

"So what you sayin'?"

"I'm sayin' it ain't my problem. And I know you know what I'm sayin'. Our business together is done."

"Why? Couldn't nobody bust a gun like me before I got put away." He said. Look, man, you need me. Plus I can deliver somebody to you, you want."

"Who?"

"Massive."

Kevin and Antony looked at me and smirked.

I shook my head and said, "You act like I haven't been tryin' to find this nigga already. We've searched high and low for this dude and still can't get at him. And now you think you can come home and find him off the rip?"

"If I find him, and deliver him to you, will you let me back in the crew?"

"If you find him and deliver him, I'll give you half a million dollars. Fuck a crew. I want this nigga dead."

"Well let me do that for you," he smiled as if he knew something I didn't. "Trust me, you ain't got to be lookin' over your shoulders no more."

"Seein' is believin'" I told him. "So where you layin' your head?"

"I got a place out Maryland. At this mansion." He paused.

"You came up like that?"

"It ain't take me no time." He laughed. "But I'ma get back on my side of town. I gotta go get my hair cut at Rod's. I'll let you know when I find him."

"Bet that."

When he left Kevin said, "Fuck that nigga, boss! I don't trust him."

"Tell me somethin' I don't already know." I said. "Look, have somebody follow him to Rods. And then bag some of his hair."

"His hair?" Antony asked.

"Did I stutter?"

"No...No sir."

"Aight, then. Ya'll ready?" I asked them.

"Whenever you are, boss."

"I'ma give Paco a few more minutes and then we out."

After ten minutes, I stood up and was getting ready to leave, when Antoinette called. She had been acting weird ever since she set up my trip to Mexico.

"What's up, Ann? I'm jive busy right now."

"I know, but when are you coming home? I thought we were going out tonight?"

"Maybe later. I gotta get up with Paco soon." I looked at my black Audemars Piguet watch. "He should've been here by now."

"Okay...Well I'll see you when you get home. Let me know if you coming early, I wanna cook you somethin'."

"No doubt."

After hanging up with her, I decided to call Paco because I hated niggas keeping me waiting. Although our meeting wasn't paramount, it was important enough to deserve my attention.

I had asked him at Trip's to get some information on that girl I saw Shaggy with. If she was who she said she was then so be it, but if she wasn't I needed to know that, too. Because I swear she looked like Harmony did when we were younger. She had the same eyes, same hair and same smile. It seemed like every time I found her, she got out of my hands.

I got in contact with some nigga Harmony was keeping time with in Houston, a nigga named Ramsey. But right before I got there, they were gone. The nigga she was staying with said he didn't know where she went. But I didn't believe him, so I had my men murder him and his girl. Some bitch name Marisol.

When I called Paco his phone rang one time before he answered. "Man, I'm sorry I'm not there. But you gotta get down here to Spring Grove. Your cousin Tony might not make it tonight."

"He might not make it?" I said. "Drive me to Spring Grove," I told Kevin as I kept the phone to my ear.

Kevin and Antony checked my surroundings outside of the deli, and then we dipped into my limo.

"Yeah, man." Paco finished. "They were trying to get a hold of you but said your line was busy. He's worse than ever, Jace."

"What happen?"

"They said...They said he...He...Took a hammer to himself."

"Took a hammer to himself?"

"He beat himself in the head with his hammer. The gash is so thick, he cracked his skull and punctured his brain. They don't know if he gonna make it this time, man. I'm sorry."

"I'm on my way," I said hanging up. "Push it, Kevin!"

BLACK HOLE

Madjesty

Madjesty hadn't eaten any food or drank any water in two days. Her stomach growled often and her mouth was severely dry. What she didn't know was that Harmony stayed so drunk, that she actually forgot she was under the stairs.

When Madjesty heard a constant rolling sound approaching the crawlspace she was in, she moved deeper into the hole frightened. But when the door opened, she saw Cherry in the wheelchair with a bowl of soup and green gelatin on a trey.

"Are you okay?" She asked peeking inside the darkness. The space was not big enough to stand up or to move around. And Madjesty didn't move to the right, because she had defecated on that side. So the places she could move were limited. "Can you hear me, Madjesty? Are you okay?"

Madjesty not trusting her slowly said, "Yeah...I...I think so." She then looked around from the inside, to see if her mother was there.

"Did you want to come out for a little while? Your mother is gone to the bar with Kali."

Madjesty crawled out of the space and the bright lights hurt her eyes. She couldn't believe that her mother went ahead with life like nothing mattered. After crawling out of the hole, Madjesty sat on the couch and devoured the hot soup and Jello. The smell from her body was sickening as Cherry held onto a cold glass of milk.

"Eat slowly, Madjesty, I don't want you to hurt your stomach." She smiled weakly. "When was the last time you ate?"

Food hung from the sides of her mouth as she said, "Two days." Madjesty saw the sadness in her eyes and said, "How do you know my mother? I mean, why is she so mean?"

"Your mother grew up alone pretty much. She didn't have a mother to tell her she loved her, or even a grandmother for that matter. When the streets raise you, it is what is is."

"It is what it is?" Madjesty said evilly. She knew Cherry was not the one to take her frustrations out on but who else could she do it to at the time? "My mother locks me under her stairs and you tell me it is what it is?"

"I'm telling you that's life. You need licenses for everything else in America, but how to be a parent." She said. "She can't love you because she don't know how to love and she don't love herself."

When the silence was too uncomfortable, Cherry shifted around in her wheel chair a little. She hoped she didn't make a mistake by bringing her the food. But unlike Kali and Harmony, who had suddenly been fucking nonstop for the past few days, she alone thought about Madjesty being trapped under the stairs.

"Here, drink this, too," she said handing her a glass of milk.

Madjesty held the cup with two hands and downed all of the ice-cold milk. Some of it poured out the sides of her mouth, and damped her shirt. Her stomach rumbled and she figured milk was probably not the best idea after not having anything to drink for days.

"So now what?" Madjesty asked. She was becoming mean, cold and heartless the more she saw how life went on without her. "What's your plan now?"

"My plan?"

"Yes. You fed me and now what?"

"Well, I haven't spoken to your mother since I've been here. So I'm going to do it today. Hopefully I can talk some sense into her, but I can't make any promises."

"How do you talk some sense into someone who could care fucking less? Please let me know."

"I know, Madjesty, and I understand why you're upset. All I can say is that I'll try."

"Well that's not good enough!" She yelled. "And where is my sister?"

"She left here a few days ago, with her new friend. She hasn't been back since."

"So she gave up on me, too, huh?" Madjesty thought out loud. "I really am in this shit alone."

"I'm sorry."

"Yes you are," Madjesty said more enraged now than ever. "But you never answered my question, how do you know my mother?"

Cherry was growing increasingly uncomfortable with how Madjesty looked at her and was starting to feel that she made a big mistake by opening the door. "We grew up around each other. I was only four years older than her, but the streets raised both of us. And, when I was high one day, I did something I should not have. I...I took you and your sister out of her womb, when you were just babies."

"It was you?" Cherry nodded her head. "I always thought my mother was lying about that story."

"She wasn't."

"And they let you out of prison?"

Although she was released, Cherry didn't understand how Kali got out so quickly. There wasn't any articles about him so she didn't think he escaped.

"Yes. They let me out."

"The way I feel, I wish you would have killed me. It would be a whole lot better than staying here."

"Don't say that, Madjesty. I'm fucked up because of the lifestyle I led. I won't ever be able to walk again and I have Hepatitis...Which basically means my liver is almost fucked." A tear fell down her face but Madjesty could give a fuck. "But when I see kids like you and your sister, who have a chance, I wanna tell them if I can. And I wanna say I'm sorry for what I did to you."

Madjesty stood up, looked down at her and laughed. "Bitch, please. The only reason you helped me is so that you can rest easier at night." Cherry moved a few times in her chair not knowing if Madjesty would hurt her or not. "If you allow that bitch to treat me like this, then you no better than she is. How can you be?"

"That's not true. I do care about..."

"No one! You care about no one but your own self, GIMP!" She spat. "All of you are fucking crazy! And the moment I turn eighteen, and can take care of myself, I'm done with this shit. But ya'll just betta hope I don't kill a few of ya'll on my way out the door."

"Madjesty," Cherry said in a soft voice, "please. I want you to understand. If I could do anything to help you I would, but I can't. This is out of my hands."

Madjesty wiped the anger off of her face, smirked and walked back to the crawlspace. "Thank you for the food. But personally, I hope all of ya'll rot in hell." Once inside she said, "Do yourself a favor, and forget about me like my mother."

Cherry wheeled her chair up to the crawlspace and locked the door. But she thought long and hard about what Madjesty had to say...And she wondered what if there was anything she could do to help her.

INTO HER OWN

Jayden

Jayden was sleep in the Holiday Inn in Laurel, Maryland until she heard a knock at the door. She jumped up, looked out the window and saw Shaggy outside. Always sleeping naked, she grabbed the sheet off the bed, wrapped her body up and let him inside. When he walked in, she flopped back on the bed.

"Please tell me you've left out of this room at some point." He said bringing in a McDonald's bag filled with two hotcakes and sausage meals. He placed the bag on the dresser next to the bed and sat down. "I gotta know that you didn't stay in here an entire week, Jayden." When he saw the money he gave her for shopping still sitting on the dresser, in the exact same place he left it, he had his answer.

"I'm not hungry, Shaggy. I don't want to do nothing but sleep and die."

"Why would you say some shit like that?"

"Because it's true."

"Don't wish nothin' into your existence you not ready for." He said seriously. "'Cause that shit most definitely can happen."

"And how do you know I'm not ready to die?" She said crying as usual. "My sister is probably still in that hole even though it's been almost a week. I'm scared to death for her and don't know what to do. I feel all alone."

"You not alone."

"How you figure? You come by every two days which leaves me with nothing to do but think."

"Look, I'm just tryin' to help you get on your feet, but I ain't never say we were together."

"I know that," she said. "You keep telling me the same thing over and over again. I know we not together, trust me. Can't you have friends without it being anything else?"

"Yeah."

"Exactly, so just because I say I want to see you, doesn't mean I want to see you like that."

"That's how you carry shit when I don't call you back. I still gotta work, Jayden. This paper I be droppin' on you don't fall off trees."

"Then why do you help me? If I'm such a burden why bother?"

"I hate when you ask me that shit. You need to toughen up and stop actin' like a kid. I hate that shit about you."

She hated the weakness part about her too. "Well answer the question? Why do you help me?"

"I don't know yet. But I can tell you this, you better get all you can out of this situation while it lasts."

Silence.

"Understand this, Shaggy, you don't have to do any of this if you don't want to. I'm not looking for a boyfriend or your money. Right now, all I give a fuck about is my sister."

Shaggy thought about what she said and replied. "This is what we gonna do. We gonna take you shoppin' for some new gear, and then I'ma have Olive go with you to get your hair and toes done. Definitely them toes because them things ripped up these sheets." He laughed. "I can't get down with girls with banged out feet." He paused.

"We only friends right?"

"Right, and I don't like my friend's feet lookin' fucked up either."

"Whatever," she said hitting him playfully. She really was glad he was there because already he made her feel better.

"Then I'll take you by your mother's house to check on your sister."

She jumped up and wrapped her arms around his neck. "Thank you soooo much! Thank you!"

When Jayden knocked on the door, she looked like a million bucks. The angels were with her because after being out on her own for only a week, she had already made a major come up. Secretly the life she fell into, was the life her mother always wanted.

Before she knocked on the door she could feel her heart racing and thought she was going to pass out. Her mother could be loud, confrontational and embarrassing and she wasn't sure if she was tough enough to handle her, although she was desperately trying to. The problem was, she didn't have a plan, but seeing Shaggy parked in the driveway waiting on her, made her feel slightly more confident.

So she swallowed, took a deep breath, exhaled and knocked on the door. Her mother opened it wide and Jayden was surprised to see her looking like a new woman. Not to mention the smell of alcohol on her breath was non-existent. Her hair was even combed and she was wearing the red dress Olive had given to her. That part fucked her up but there was no way in hell she wanted the dress back after her mother's rotten pussy had been all in it.

"Come in, baby," Harmony smiled hugging Jayden. "You look so beautiful."

Jayden almost fell over at her mother's show of affections and she wanted so desperately to believe that she was finally changing. She savored the moment of a mother and daughter embrace and gripped her tightly. Suddenly, the years of physical and mental abuse didn't matter anymore. She was at home. But when she walked fully into the living room, the white lady sitting on the couch brought her back to a grim reality.

Harmony grabbed Jayden by the hand and led her to the couch. "Jayden, this is Mrs. Katherine Sheers and she is a caseworker with the department of child services. She's just stopping by to make sure you're both okay."

"So you're, Jayden," she said shaking her hand. "You don't look too much like your sister."

"Well we are sisters. Twins at that." Jayden assured her.

Jayden's eyes roamed to her sister Madjesty who sat quietly in a floral patterned dress which she looked uncomfortable wearing. Madjesty's homely look was completed with a tired pair of patent leather shoes. She looked like a light skin-boyish Celie from the movie The Color Purple.

"I know. Twins are the best. I was a twin you know," Katherine said. "Before my sister died in a car accident at the tender age of ten."

Jayden didn't respond because she didn't care.

"Well...I was just telling your mother that I hope you and your sister like attending Friendly High School this year. You'll both be enrolling next week. Right Mrs. Phillips?"

"Oh of course," she said as fake as hell. "My daughters both are looking forward to the new school. Aren't you?"

Harmony gave them straight-faced stares. She would not hesitate to rip them to shreds if they fucked this up.

"Yes I am," Jayden said. "As a matter of fact, mama has already been preparing us. Tell her about the lessons you taught us recently, mama. And how they will lead to better opportunities. You know, ma, the lessons with the carrots."

"The lessons with carrots?" Mrs. Sheers repeated. "I don't understand."

Harmony gave Jayden another evil glare and Jayden returned it. With the stranger in the room she felt bold and she didn't care. She wanted Harmony to be as frightened this moment as she was all of her life.

"I was using carrots to describe the value of money, Jayden has it a bit wrong."

"Oh really?" Jayden said. "Because I don't remember it that way. What do you think, Madjesty?"

"I think ma got it right," Madjesty said, as it was clear to Jayden that she was mad at her.

"Oh...I see," Katherine Sheers said. The sisters continued to stare at one another in silence. "Well anyway, I will be in contact with your family periodically to make sure things are in order."

"Can you tell me why?" Harmony asked. "I mean, we'd love to have you but I'd like to know what sparked this visit."

"Oh...We got an anonymous call, so we like to make sure things are in order when this happens. But as I can clearly see, everything here is fine. I wish you luck on your job search, too. But I must say that you are lucky to have a home which is rent free."

No one knew that Cherry placed the call after the confrontation with Madjesty.

"Yes I am, lucky. I will be even better when I can find a job."

Katherine stood up and said, "Well I better be leaving now."

"Okay, well let me walk you to your car." Harmony said rushing behind her before taking one more look at Jayden and then Madjesty.

When she was gone Jayden used the opportunity to talk to her sister. She sat next to Madjesty on the couch. "Madjesty, I miss you so much," she said throwing her arms around her. "I thought about you every day. Are you okay? Are you hurt? Mama is so fake isn't she?"

"Get off me, Jayden." Madjesty said pushing her off.

Jayden backed up and said, "What? Why?"

"You're the one who's fake."

"What...Are you mad at me or something?"

"What do you think? You're gone for a week, you don't bother to call and check on me and then you show up looking like a model while I'm living in hell? I thought you said that we're all we got. What happened to that, huh?"

"I...I couldn't call you, Madjesty. I didn't think mama would let me talk to you, but I think about you every day."

"Fuck that! Fuck you and fuck life!" Madjesty said standing up. Then she held her stomach and doubled over. She was in severe pain. "I'll see you around at school. I'm out." She said walking up the stairs.

The hate festering inside of Madjesty was all over the place and Jayden didn't know how to react. She was changing and it was obvious that she was changing for the worse.

When Jayden walked outside, she walked right past her mother who was standing in the driveway talking to Katherine. Then she jumped in Shaggy's Navigator and it was the first time that Harmony had really laid eyes on Shaggy while she was sober. She knew that kid. And although she'd only seen him a few times, because whenever she was hanging with his mother they were on their way out the door, she could never forget his face. He was always very attractive even as a little boy.

"I'll see you later," Harmony said to Jayden. "You kids have fun."

She was being fake in front of the caseworker and Jayden was upset. Especially after the way Madjesty treated her. She believed that it was all Harmony's fault, because in actuality, it was.

"You'll be home in time for dinner right?" Harmony said pushing her luck, thinking she still had Jayden under control.

"You'll see me when you see me," Jayden said. "Shaggy, pull off on this bitch."

Shaggy threw up the fuck you sign with Katherine watching. And the caseworker looked at Harmony wondering what could have possessed them to act in such a way.

"Kids," Harmony shrugged. "You can't live with them, and you can't live without them."

Since Jayden wanted to play hardball, Harmony had plans to hit her where it hurt. And she would start with Madjesty.

MEXICO

Jace

Mexico's weather reminded me of being in L.A. In fact everything about Mexico reminded me of L.A. The palm trees, the water and the people dressed in less than nothing.

I just pulled up in front of the ten million dollar villa I had bought my father. He relocated here, because after Massive had killed off his entire crew, he felt he wasn't safe anywhere else. But when I got there, something seemed off balance because an unfamiliar car sat in the driveway. Me and Kevin got out of the car we rented and knocked on the door. No one answered.

"You want me to check around back?" Kevin asked.

"Naw, we'll come back later."

We were just getting ready to go back to the hotel where Antoinette was waiting on me, when a white man in a pair of tight ass blue swim trunks opened the door. I could tell he had recently been out of the pool because he was wet and had a towel in his hand.

"Can I help you?" he asked dabbing his wet face with the towel. "Are you gentlemen lost?"

"We're not lost but you can help us."

"Okay, and how can I do that?"

"I want to know where's Rick? This is his house right?"

"Rick?" He laughed. "You mean Bad Lucky?"

I looked back at Kevin and said, "Who the fuck is Bad Lucky?"

"I'm sorry, man. But around here we call him Bad Lucky because whenever he places a bet he loses," He joked. "As a matter of fact, that's how I got this house."

I gave Kevin a knowing look, took a step back and watched him drop him to the floor.

"Let me tell you something, mothafucka, this is my house!" I said yelling over top of him. "I own the deed to this property and it's paid in full. Now I don't know what deal you had with my father, but that shit is dead. Do you hear me? I want you out of my house by morning."

Blood was everywhere and I could tell his nose was broken. I was just about to have Kevin hit him again when I saw four Doberman Pinscher's staring at us growling from inside the house. With the dogs as his guards, he stood up and used the towel to cover his bloody nose.

"The only reason you're still alive is because they can't see my face. But dogs are great in that they can sense danger," he continued looking back at them. "Now if you want to stay alive I'ma make it simple," he said slowly. "Leave *my* property and never return."

"I already told you I own this house."

"And I told you Bad Lucky placed a bet and lost. He owed me three million and I considered my debt paid in full by taking over the deed to his house. Now if you'd like, I can reverse our bet and have him tortured every day of his life, until he gives me my money. And since you're his son, I'll leave that up to you."

"Where can I find my father?" I asked feeling like dropping this nigga myself.

"Bad Lucky hangs out in Cancun, at a resort called Riu Caribe, about fifteen miles from the Cancun National Airport. You can probably find him there."

I backed away from the door with my eyes on him. Keeping in mind that with one wave of his hands, those dogs would be on full attack. When we made it back to the car I started thinking. All of this drama, including never being able to lead a full life because Massive would forever haunt me, and the death of my mother was all a result of Rick's gambling addiction.

When we pulled up at the resort, I asked a few people about Bad Lucky. It fucked me up that they all knew where and who he was. And that meant if I could find him, Massive could too. Maybe he knew where he was and wanted him to kill himself slowly.

When we went out back to the beach, I saw him involved in a small card game. A bunch of ones were on the table and I knew he had fallen hard. My father never played with anything less than one hundred dollar bills.

"Son," Rick said standing up from the table. Five Mexicans who were involved in the game didn't seem too happy to see me. "What you doing here?" Then he addressed the men who all had serious expressions on their faces. "Amigos, este es mi hijo."

I knew Spanish from going back and forth to L.A so I understood him to say, 'This is my son, Friends'. They all grunted and mumbled under their breath.

"Tengo que hablar con mi padre en privado. Esto sólo le tomará un momento." He continued.

In English he said, he needed to talk to me in private and to give him a few minutes.

One of the men stood up and appeared angry about my father having to leave the game. "No trate de correr de nuevo, Bad Lucky. No vamos a tener un problema de matar a usted oa su hijo."

I understood him clearly, too. He said, *'Don't try to run again, Bad Lucky. We won't have a problem killing you or your son.'* Rick smiled at the men and walked off.

"How's it going, Kevin? I see you've been keeping my son safe after all these years." Kevin just nodded, even he was losing respect for him. "You mind giving me and my boy a few moments in private?"

Kevin looked at me and I said, "It's okay." Kevin stepped a few feet away and turned his back to the conversation. But he was still close enough to jump in, if something happened.

"Rick, what's going on?"

"What do you mean?" He said looking half drunk. "We're playing cards, son. I'm out here enjoying the beautiful weather." He said putting his hand on my back as he looked at the beach. "Open your eyes, beautiful girls are all around us."

"You know what I'm talking about."

"I don't." He said removing his hand. "What do you mean?"

Before we went any further, I needed to know if he would lie to me or not. He didn't know that I had been to his house and he also didn't know that I understood Spanish. I never tried hiding my fluency from him, we just weren't close enough for him to know. Still, whether he would lie to me or tell the truth would help me make my decision about the future of our relationship.

"How's the decorations goin' at the house?" I asked. "I figured you'd be stayin' there instead of hangin' out at some resort."

"How did you know I was here?" He asked out of nowhere.

"It's easy to find you. You're very popular amongst the ladies remember?"

"True...True," he smiled.

"Now...How are the decorations comin' along at your villa, Rick? And when can I see it?"

"Everything's going along fine. There's a lot of construction taking place right now, but I should have everything the way I want it by the end of the week," he said under his voice. "Then you can see it."

That was his first lie.

"Well I can't wait to see it," I said staring at him in his eyes. "And what did the man over there say to you in Spanish? And who is Bad Lucky?"

I squinted to see his face as the sun beamed against my skin and the birds flew around us in a distance. This was the moment that would change everything.

"Bad Lucky is a friend of their's. You don't know him," he paused. Even Kevin had to turn around to look at him on that part. "And in Spanish he told me he would wait patiently for me to reenter the game." He smiled putting one hand on my shoulder. "So, I have to go, son. I don't want to be rude."

"Okay."

"Are you staying in Mexico long? Maybe we can get a few drinks."

"Naw, I have to get back to DC. Money waits for no man."

"I heard that...Well give Antoinette my love."

"I will."

One look at the men that were waiting for Rick and you would know that they meant him harm, but I decided that he wouldn't be my problem anymore. I had to worry about my business back at home and as far as I was concerned, he was cut.

MY BLOOD

Jace

Paco said he had found some information I needed to know about the girl, and that he had to tell me as soon as possible. Since I was in Maryland on business, I decided to meet him in the parking lot in Greenbelt where they were holding a carnival. Paco showed up ten minutes after I pulled up and had a box of popcorn in his hand that pissed me off. I was here to talk business not fuck around.

"How was Mexico?" He asked sliding into my car. Kevin stood outside to make sure no one would walk up on me. While Antony stayed behind the driver's seats. Kids ran all around Kevin outside. "And how's Rick?"

"Everything is everything. What about the news I needed you to get for me?"

"I found out who the girl is."

"Who is she?"

"Her name is Jayden Phillips." He said throwing a few kernels in his mouth.

Irritated because I recognized the last name, I grabbed the box out of his hand, rolled my window down and threw it out.

"So she's Harmony's daughter?" I said rolling the window back up.

Paco seemed mad but saved face. "Yeah...And they live at Concord Manor."

"Concord Manor Mansion? In Fort Washington?"

"Yeah."

"How she get back there?"

"I couldn't find out, but she lives there. My source also said they saw some dude and a bitch in a wheel chair going in and out of the house, too. But they don't know who they are. What you want me to do?"

Silence.

"Nothing. I got to check some shit out first. Don't let anybody know that they're there."

Kali said he stayed in a mansion. But there was no way she would let him live with her after what he did to her.

"You know that ain't even in the talk."

"Keep it that way." I told him. "Is your boy still seeing her?"

"I think so. As a matter of fact, I think he put her up in a hotel somewhere out Maryland. They seem to be getting serious."

"Do you know which hotel?"

He seemed hesitant to give me any information at first, but he knew better than to keep it from me, too.

"Yeah…She at the Holiday Inn out Laurel, Maryland." He paused. "You want me to tell Shaggy to leave her alone?"

I thought about what Kali said about him and Kreshon fucking Harmony. And how they could possibly be the father of Harmony's daughters. If Paco did do me wrong, and fucked Harmony, and it turned out his son was fucking his own sister that would be on Paco not me. But if it turned out that Jayden was my daughter, I'd have to decide if I wanted to kill Paco instead.

"Naw. He seems to like her a lot, and I want to keep shit quiet right now." I paused. "But I'm 'bout to roll. I'll holla at you later."

"One." Paco said giving me a pound.

When he left I knew I had to finally see Harmony again. I told people she stole from me because I wanted them to think that was the reason I wanted her. Truth was, I never got over her and I wanted to know about my kids. But if she was back with Kali, I may have to leave both of them for dead.

NOT SO FRIENDLY HIGH

Jayden

Jayden stepped into Friendly High School looking fly. She had a Gucci bag which hung from her arm, diamond earrings in her ears and a silk blouse on her back. Shaggy had definitely looked out for her. Still, he always made it known that they were not together. He had lots of girls he fucked on the side, and didn't want people thinking the wrong thing about them. So they both agreed that she would act as if she didn't know him when she saw him in the halls. And she had so much on her mind that she didn't care. Besides, he put her up in a hotel, kept her fresh and let her have her own space. To top it all off, he still didn't get no pussy and she was quite the virgin. So what more could she ask for?

When Jayden walked to her locker, she looked a little further down the hall and saw her sister Madjesty. A group of girls surrounded her and they pointed at the same thrift store dress Jayden saw her in when the caseworker was at the mansion. Jayden felt terribly when she looked at herself and than her sister's clothes.

Going to her rescue, she rushed down the hall and pushed one of the girls confronting Madjesty. When Jayden looked at the girl she pushed, she saw Toni, the same girl she had a problem with at McDonalds.

"I swear, I can't shake this bitch if I tried." Toni said pushing Jayden back.

"Leave my sister alone!" Jayden said. "You always fuckin' with somebody!"

"Jayden, stay out of it!" Madjesty said. "I can fight my own battle."

"No!" Jayden told her. "She shouldn't be fuckin' with you! I had a problem with her when we first moved here from Texas." Now a huge crowd surrounded them.

"If this is your sister, how come you got her lookin' a hot ass mess?" Toni laughed, with her friends right by her side. "What kind of sister are you?"

Jayden was so mad at her comment, that she slammed Toni against the locker while Toni's friend's started jumping Jayden. Madjesty seeing them get out on her sister, grabbed a pencil out of her book bag and stuck it into the flesh of Toni's leg.

"Ahhhhh!!!! HELPPP!" Toni yelled.

Three security guards saw the incident and grabbed the sisters and took them to the principal's office. While Toni was taken to the nurses office.

"You two stay right here and don't move!" One of the security guards said leaving them alone.

Madjesty gripped her stomach and doubled over. "Are you okay, Madjesty? Did they hurt you?"

"They didn't get one lick off of me." Madjesty said clenching her stomach again.

"Then why is your stomach hurting? Every time I see you, your stomach is messed up."

"I don't know. But it's been bothering me a lot lately."

"You should ask mama to take you to the doctors. Something could be very wrong and it's been going on too long, Madjesty."

"Jayden, I see your life has changed, but mine is still the same." She said with an attitude. "When have you ever known Harmony to take us to a doctor?"

"Can I do anything, Madjesty? Maybe I can get Shaggy to take you for me. He's really cool and will do anything for me." Silence. "Madjesty, please talk to me. You're shutting me out and I'm not the one who hurt you."

"I want you to stay out of my life. Me and you aren't family anymore."

Her words hit Jayden like a sack of rocks on her heart and caused her to cry. "But...I...I don't understand why. You're my sister."

"And I hate you for it! You left me alone. You left me by myself to deal with her on my own. Do you know what it's like to live with a mother who hates you?" Madjesty cried for the first time ever. "We said we'd never leave the other's side, Jayden. And you broke your promise."

"I'm sorry. But...She put me out. She told me to leave."

"You lying!" Madjesty said. "Mama said that boy told you to go with him and you paid mama five hundred dollars to let you leave." She cried harder.

"That's not true!"

"You didn't stop one time to think about me."

Before they could continue their conversation, Mrs. Crimply, the school's principal came into her office.

"I don't know how you two behave in Texas, but this type of behavior will not be tolerated at my school." She said picking up the phone. "What's your mother's number? I need her to come get the both of you today."

⚫━━━━━━━━━━━━━━━━━━━⚫

Jayden's stomach turned the moment she walked into the mansion. Unlike Harmony, Jayden didn't have fond memories of Concord Manor.

"Madjesty, go to your room," Harmony said with an attitude, as if she was a good disciplinarian. "I'll call you when dinner is ready. And don't bother turning on that TV since you're suspended from school, you're going to be suspended here, too."

Then she walked to the kitchen as Jayden stayed in the foyer. "Jayden, come here."

"I'm about to call Shaggy to come get me. I'm not staying here with you."

"Come here now. I'm not asking you, little girl, I'm telling you."

Jayden followed Harmony into the kitchen while Harmony took a can of spaghetti out of the cabinet, opened it with a green electric can opener and put it into a pot.

"I see you've been taking care of yourself," she said turning the eye to the stove on low. The heat hit the pan and the spaghetti crackled quietly inside. "That's good." Then she opened the cabinet over the stove and twisted a bottle of vodka and took two gulps. She didn't bother using cups anymore.

"I'm fine. If that's what you're asking."

Harmony downed some more vodka and said, "Looks like you're doing better than fine to me. I sure wish I could buy Gucci purses and stuff. Life has served itself to you on a silver platter, huh?"

"What is this about? And what do you want with me?"

"Money. I want money, Jayden. You are still my underage daughter, and you don't get to do what you want."

"I'm not scared of you and you can't run my life. Because I finally understand that you are nothing but a jealous old bitch!"

"You know what, at first I may have denied that accusation, but maybe you're right. Look at me and then look at you. You have my face."

"And yet you hate me the most." Jayden combated. "Maybe that means you hate yourself, too."

"I've hated myself since my father died," Harmony said stirring the food.

Then she reached into the cabinet and pulled out a knife. "I wonder how pretty your face would be, if I sliced it? Then we could have matching faces. Wouldn't that be great?"

Jayden's heart banged loudly in her chest and she backed away. "Don't worry, I got something better planned for you."

It was obvious that Harmony loved playing mental games on Jayden. Then she put the knife back in the drawer and reached under the cabinet to pull out a bottle of antifreeze. Then she took a spoon and stirred it into the food on the stove.

"WHAT ARE YOU DOING?!" Jayden screamed.

"Shhhhhhhhhhhhh." Harmony said with a finger over her mouth. "You can stop this if you want to. You really can."

A tear ran down Jayden's face. "Why are you doing this?"

"Because I can." Harmony said drinking more vodka from the bottle. "I brought her into this world, and I have the ability to take her out of it."

"Mama, you're killing her. Don't you care?" She sobbed. "She is your daughter."

"I know."

Jayden hated herself for crying when she saw the pleasure in her mother's eyes. She really was, mother monster. Not wanting to give Harmony any more satisfaction, she wiped the tears from her face. "How long have you been doing this? How long have you been putting stuff in her food?"

"For a while." She said. "But enough small talk. Let's talk about what you can do for me, for a change. I expect you to give me a thousand dollars a week to allow you to live where you want to, and to allow Madjesty to stay here."

"You want me to pay rent even though I don't live here?"

"Exactly."

"Mama..."

"If you don't give me the money," Harmony interrupted. "I will kill her. Slowly. It's as simple as that. And if people blame me, I will put the blame on Kali instead. He's not supposed to be here anyway after what he did to me, so it'll be easy for people to believe me."

"What if I tell them you poisoned her?"

"Then I'll use this instead," she said opening a drawer in the kitchen with a key, removing a gun. Then she dished out a bowl of spaghetti and placed it on the counter. "But be clear, if you tell anyone about this, anyone at all, including your little boyfriend, there will be trouble for you." Having made her point, Harmony placed the gun back in the drawer and locked it.

Jayden put her hand over her mouth in horror while Harmony laughed. Then Harmony yelled, "MADJESTY! COME GET YOUR FOOD!"

Jayden and Harmony shared quiet looks, as Madjesty removed the poisoned food off the counter and went upstairs to eat it.

"I hope you know how serious I am." Harmony said. "My money, or your sister's life. What you wanna do?"

L.A.

Kali

Kali walked and pushed Cherry through the gates of Massive's mansion in L.A. It was quietly tucked into a part of city not many people knew about. Massive liked it that way. But Kali was quite aware of where he lived, considering he'd been working with him for many years. Jace and his crew didn't know that Kali was responsible for every murder in Rick and Jace's crew. He was even responsible for conducting the hits on Rick's crew member's family. Kali's hands also killed both Herb Dayo and Sick Sense and their bodies would never be found. But lately Massive had been putting the pressure on Kali to kill Jace but he needed to weigh his options first.

"Kalive, it's nice to see you," Massive said to him after giving his doorman the authorization to let them inside. "What brings you here?" They shook hands and Kali pushed Cherry inside of the living room, next to a couch. Then he took a seat and Massive sat across from him.

"I wanted to talk to you about a few things. That is if you have a few minutes."

"Sure." Massive said drinking a glass of very expensive bourbon. "Can I get you some liquor? Or coffee?"

A maid sat a cup in front of Kali and Cherry without waiting on their responses. When she poured their coffee, Massive began speaking.

"So what can I do for you?" Massive eyed Cherry carefully and then the large Gucci purse that was nestled in her lap.

"First, I wanna thank you for lookin' out at the prison. I didn't believe shit would go so smooth."

"It's easier than you realize to fake a death and escape. Money rules everything."

Massive had orchestrated someone else to be killed in prison by fire, who was Kali's same body type. The man was burned so badly, he was unrecognizable. Then he had the same guards involved, help get Kali out of prison. Although the other man was listed as an escapee, Kali was listed as deceased.

"Yeah, well I appreciate it."

"Outside of your lady friend here, you didn't let anybody see you back at home have you? You don't want too many people knowing you are alive."

"No. Nobody knows I'm back," Kali lied, looking at Cherry from the side of his eyes." She knew like he did that everybody knew he was back, even Harmony, the one person he wasn't supposed to be around. "I did have to connect with Jace though. So I can get him for you."

"Good, I needed one of my best men free. It's good to know you're keeping a low profile."

"I am."

"When can you deliver him to me?"

"Well now I have more access to him, which means I can finally hand him over to you like you've asked. I'm just going to need more help to do it."

"Are you sure this time, Kalive? I don't want any more mistakes."

"Yeah. I'm sure."

"And how do I know I can trust you?"

"Haven't I gone over and beyond the call of duty for you already? Wasn't it me who took out most of Rick's men and their families and half of Jace's crew?"

"This may be true, Kalive, but one may think because you went so far to prove your loyalty to me, that you aren't loyal to anyone."

"I'm loyal to the right people as I am to you."

"I hear you, but it's difficult to vouch for you."

"What does that mean?" Kali shifted a little.

"There's nothing worse than a man who betrays the one he was originally loyal too for someone he doesn't know. He's the lowest of scum of the earth as far as I'm concerned. At least the young man, Jace, has some loyalty."

"Don't fuck with me?" Kali said standing up.

Massive laughed. "So what did you think you were coming here for, to kill me?"

"What?" Kali said surprised at his question.

In actuality his plan was to see how much more he would give him to kill Jace. If it was less than five hundred thousand dollars, he was going to put a bullet through his head, no questions asked. And the gun he would use to kill Massive was nestled comfortably under Cherry's ass. When Massive's men checked them for guns, they didn't bother to lift her to check up under her body.

"You heard me, Kalive."

"And stop callin' me Kalive! It's Kali!"

Massive laughed and ten men appeared from within the home. What was weird was that Massive didn't appear to give them any sign.

"Kalive, you're out of your league." Then he focused on his men. "Take them downstairs. I'll give orders later on what to do with them next."

Four men manhandled Kali and a fifth man took Cherry's purse out of her lap and pushed her toward an elevator within the mansion.

"Get your hands off me, mothafucka!" Kali yelled. "Get the fuck off me!"

Massive's laugh could be heard until they made it to the elevator and the doors closed. Cherry was scared and didn't know what would happen next. She just hoped that they wouldn't lift her up and find the gun under her lap.

"You don't know who you fucking with," Kali yelled at them.

The men remained silent as they put them into a dim room within the basement. When the door was shut, with a closed fist, Kalive banged on it repeatedly. When he was tired, he turned around to look at her and smiled.

"What? What's so funny?"

"Just wait."

What Cherry didn't know was that he planned everything up to this point. Lifting her up, he pulled the gun out from under her seat and looked at his black Chopard sports watch and waited. Ten minutes later, loud noises could be heard from upstairs. He only hoped *they'd* know where to find him. But the moment the thought entered his mind, someone kicked in the door.

"Sorry, I'm late, homie." His cousin Vaughn said coming inside. "But we had to take care of the situation upstairs first."

"I can't believe this shit really worked." Kali said.

"I did…I told you he didn't have no respect for you. He thought you were dumb." Vaughn continued. "Now you 'bout to make a come up. And all of them wet boys, including Jace gonna learn to respect you."

"Exactly," Kali said. He walked out the room and pushed the elevator button.

"Kali," Cherry yelled, seeing them at the elevator from the room. "Bring me over there, too."

"Wait a minute," he said pushing the button again when it didn't light up.

"Fuck is up?" Kali said looking at his cousin.

"I don't know. Maybe we should take the…"

Right before he got the words out, one of Massive's men came from out a side door and blew Cherry's head off. He then aimed at Kali and his cousin, fired and missed.

"OH SHIT!" Vaughn ducked and caught the dude in the chest with a hot slug.

Kali ran up to the shooter and fired two more shots in him before the elevator opened. He couldn't even look at her body. They got on right away and Kali was beyond hurt. Cherry's murder was fucking with him seriously.

"The linen vans we hijacked are outside," Vaughn said as they ran from the elevator, through the living room and out the door. It was his idea to steal a couple of vans from the company Massive trusted to wash his linen. His one obsession at not getting a taste of his own medicine caused him his life.

"Did ya'll look for money in the house?"

"Yeah, we got everything we could find," he said when they walked outside. "It looks like a little over a million."

"Aight," he paused. "Where are the vans?"

"On the side of the house, next to the service entrance."

In the driveway, the two linen trucks that were stolen months back waited on Kali. One of Kali's men opened the back door and hopped in, Cherry's blood still on his body. Hogtied in the middle of the van was Massive. He was bleeding and the white gag over his mouth was drenched in his own blood. Also in the back of the van were two of his men.

"What you want us to do with him?"

"I got it." Kali said still stewing over Cherry's death. "Where's Dino?"

"Here you go, man," Vaughn said handing Kali's his Silver hatchet in the brown leather strap.

Kali removed it from the leather case and without saying a word, swung and chopped Massive's arm off. It partially hung off his body before he took the next swing at his neck. Vaughn and his crew knew how violent he could be, but didn't think he was so disgusting. Then as if he was cutting a slab of beef, he chopped off his head while everyone stood in silence.

"Take me to my car," Kali said wiping the blood off of his mouth and eyes. "And burn this fucking van with the rest of his body."

RUNNING GAME

Jayden

Jayden walked into the school after a week of suspension with a new attitude. Toni was still out sick but said the pencil stabbing was an accident and neither Jayden nor Madjesty knew why.

After the conversation with her mother, Jayden decided to do what she had to, to take care of herself and her sister, even if Madjesty didn't want her to. The moment she got to her locker, she saw a familiar face. It was Xion, one of Shaggy's boy's and he was looking at her hard.

"Are you gonna keep looking, or come over here and speak to me?"

"I wasn't sure if that was you at first. The last time I saw you, you were at McDonalds and looked...I mean..."

"Fucked up," Jayden laughed. "It's amazing what a little money and backing could do for a girl."

"No doubt." He said. "But the difference is crazy."

"Girls change." She said leaning up against her locker flashing him her pretty smile. She saw her sister Madjesty walk past her, and did everything in her power not to look in her direction. She made a decision that if Madjesty didn't want the relationship, she wouldn't force it on her.

"So...You still with my man Shaggy?"

"Shaggy?" She said as if she didn't know him. "Who that?"

He laughed and said, "Yeah okay. He the nigga who fed your ass the day I met you."

"Oh, that nigga!!!" She joked. "I was so busy looking in your face that I didn't even notice him." She smiled.

"Don't be sellin' me wolf tickets."

"What the fuck is a wolf ticket?" she laughed. Jayden was enjoying his conversation greatly.

"It's a joke my mom's say all the time."

"Well trust me, I ain't selling you nothing you don't wanna buy," she said seductively. For some reason, being responsible for herself gave her more confidence. "I didn't know you went to Friendly."

"It's my last year. And I'm just goin' now 'cause I make money here."

"Doing what?"

"Selling weed." He boasted.

As they were talking, Jayden saw five girls walking up the hall in their direction. They wore real raunchy looking clothes and were loud. Immediately a light bulb went off in her head.

"Well, I gotta go. What's your name again?" Jayden asked.

"Xion."

"So, Xion, you said you sell smoke. But what else you got?"

"Ecstasy, too. Why?"

"I wanna buy some weed and some E pills off of you." She said keeping her eyes on the girls. They were real loud at their lockers and it was clear they were trying to get everyone's attention. She hoped they didn't walk away before she had a chance to introduce herself to them.

"I ain't know you get down."

"There's a lot of stuff you don't know about me. Yet," she smiled looking into his eyes. "Now, Mr. Xion. can you help me or not?"

"How much you need?"

"As much as you can give me."

"I can give you whatever you need."

"If you keep talking to me like that, you gonna make me think you wanna take care of me or something."

"Maybe I do."

"Let's do this. Bring the weed and the pills by this hotel," she said writing the name and the address on a piece of notebook paper from her book bag. "Tonight at about 6:00 pm. Let's talk about it then."

Xion got excited and said, "I'll do that."

When he was gone, she walked up to the girls and said, "Excuse me, would ya'll happen to know where I can get some pills from?"

The main girl of the group had a tattoo on her wrist that said Passion. She said, "Damn, how you gonna just walk up to us and ask us some illegal shit like that?" She laughed.

"Yeah, what we look like?" Another girl said.

"Ya'll look like ya'll like to have fun. And not all stuck up like some of these other bitches around here."

Passion looked at her friends and said, "Sounds to me like you got us down pack."

They all laughed.

"I figured as much." Jayden said.

"Well, new girl, you were just talkin' to the nigga who could hook you up with some pills. At least that's where I get my shit from."

"Damn, I shoulda asked ya'll before he tried to holla." Jayden said trying to push her naivety deep inside. She wanted to seem as real as possible to them.

"The way that nigga was smilin' all up in your face, you not gonna have no problem gettin' what you need." She said giving one of her friends a five. "You shoulda pushed off on that for real. Xion's cute ass is paid."

"The way he was acting, I'm sure he's gonna be sniffin' behind my ass later. But I ain't 'bout to chase no nigga." She paused. "Anyway, the name's Jayden." She said extending her hand. Passion shook it along with the other four girls. "What's ya'lls?"

"I'm Passion, this is Foxie," she said pointing to a cute girl with short gold hair, "this is Na Na," she continued pointing to a girl mixed with Asian and African American, "this is Gucci," she added pointing at a girl with a long stringy black weave, "and this is Queen." She ended, speaking of a girl with a scraggly looking bob.

What Jayden noticed immediately was that they all looked like she use to. Like they needed something and somebody. She didn't know why she could pick up on such insecurities, since she just made a come up herself, but she did.

"Ya'll live around here?" Jayden asked.

"Yeah...We live up the street."

"And you?" Gucci asked, with a slight attitude. Jayden knew she'd be the toughest to get through to.

She wasn't going to tell them she was living in a hotel. So she decided to use the house she hated to her advantage. "I live in Concord Mansion."

The girls' eyes widened and they seemed to be excited that someone so fly was keeping conversation with five wanna-bee's. When she saw the gleam in their eyes, she knew she had them exactly where she wanted them.

⚫━━━━━━━━━━━━━━━━━━━━━━━⚫

When Jayden got back to her hotel, she saw someone sitting in a car waiting on her. She saw his face before and tried to run into her motel room but Jace had Kevin and Antony catch her.

When he walked up to them he said, "Let her go." They did. "I'm not gonna hurt you. But we need to talk. Can I come in?"

There was something about him that comforted her, and she allowed him inside her room. Kevin went in with them while Antony guarded the front door.

"Don't be afraid, I said I'm not gonna hurt you." Jace said. "And if I have things my way, nobody will."

"Well what do you want with me? You kinda scare me."

"I want the truth." He paused. "Are you, Harmony Phillip's daughter?"

Feeling like she didn't have anything to lose, she told the truth. "Yes. She's my mother."

Jace swallowed and said, "Who is your father?"

"I don't know. I mean...My mother said it might be this guy named Kali who's living in our house now."

"So Kali does live in the house with you?"

"Yes. Do you know him?"

Jace looked at Kevin and said, "Yes. I do."

"Can you tell me what you want from me? Did my mother do something wrong to you? And now you wanna take it out on me?"

"I don't know about Kali but I might be...I might be your father."

"How?"

"Me and your mother use to date back in the day. She told me she was pregnant, but my life was heavy back then and we lost contact." He said feeling bad for not being in their lives even if it wasn't his fault. "But I need to know if you and your sister are my daughters. And I need you to help me find out."

"But why? Why do you wanna find out?"

"Because you and your sister," he paused, "what's her name?"

"Madjesty." She smiled.

"Could have a much better life. And I'm in a position to give you a better life. But I need to know first."

"What do I have to do?"

"Will your sister consent to a test?"

"I don't know," she said. She was considering telling him about her mother poisoning her with antifreeze. The only thing was, if he was not their father, and she told him Harmony's evil secret, the plan could backfire in her face. And Harmony might kill Madjesty anyway. She'd been seeing Madjesty at school and could tell she wasn't sick anymore and that was because she'd been paying her off. "But we're twins. Is there a way to use just my DNA?"

"I'm not sure. But can you get some of her hair anyway? Off a brush maybe? I just don't want to start the process and they tell me I don't have enough DNA."

"Yeah. I could probably get some of her hair." She paused considering how it would be to have a real father. "If you are my father, are you going to be around?" Jayden asked hopefully. "Like in my life and stuff?"

"I can show you better than I can tell you." He said.

Jayden smiled.

"But how are you? Do you need anything?" Jace continued.

Remembering what her mother said, to always ask for more than what you want to get what you need she said, "Yes. Some money."

"Okay. How much?"

"Fifteen hundred dollars."

He gave Kevin a look and he reached into his pocket. "Are you living here?"

"Yes. Me and my mother got into it." She said, her head hanging low. "I'm not going to be here long though."

"How is Harmony?"

Jayden frowned a little. "She's okay. I guess. Just mean and hateful."

He didn't want to waste their time talking about her so he said, "Here's some money to tie you over. If you need something else," he wrote his number down on a pad in her room, "call me." Then he handed her five thousand dollars. "But get the hair from your sister for me. And I'm gonna come back to check on you both."

"Okay." She smiled looking at the wad of cash.

"Alright, Jayden. I'll talk to you later."

●━━━━━━━━━━━━━━━━━━━━━━━━━━━━━━●

When he left Jayden waited for Xion to get there. They went out and got something to eat and had a good time together. She was surprised at how much she liked being around him. She was having more fun with him than she was with Shaggy. They immediately fell for each other and could not deny it.

When they got back to her room after hanging out, Shaggy was there. He didn't let them see him, but it fucked him up that Xion got with somebody he was keeping time with. And then he remembered, he never told anybody he was with her. Anger covered him when he thought about all he had done for her. If she wanted to fuck with Xion so be it, but he decided he wasn't taking care of her anymore. He knew Xion's money was okay right now, but he had plans to cut him out of the business. Then he'd be broke and Jayden would come running back to him. But he wouldn't clean her up so quickly this time...Unless she came back begging on her knees.

A NEW CREW

Madjesty

Madjesty and her friends skipped school and were at her friend Wokie's house smoking weed, drinking and getting high. These days Madjesty was different. She was angry, she was violent and she didn't care if she lived or died and that made her extremely dangerous. Shortly after being suspended from school, she started feeling slightly better and wasn't sick anymore. With her newfound health and energy, she decided to be the menace she always wanted to be.

One thing she taught herself within a matter of days was how to shoplift big items. She stole everything from designer jeans and tennis shoes, to food and liquor. Just like her mother, she'd taken to the bottle but she favored Hennessey. And with a person already on the edge brown liquor did nothing but made her evil.

On top of everything she was the leader of a gang of five kids from her school who were outcasts like her. The five of them were already together and after seeing how she stabbed troublemaking Toni, they brought her into their pack. The gang consisted of three boys and two girls. The boys' names were Kid Lightning, Wokie, Krazy K and the girls' names were Glitter and Sugar. And with Mad's leadership, they called themselves the Mad Max. Madjesty dropped the last part of her name and went by Mad and anybody who failed to call her by her nickname had problems.

Unlike being home with her mother, she felt love for life when she was around them and as a gang they made themselves stronger than ever.

"Why you mad?" Kid Lightning asked.

Kid Lightning had a honey colored complexion. He was lanky with arms like twigs. But his outspoken behavior made him a favorite amongst the crew.

"No reason." She said laying on the floor smoking.

"You sure?" Krazy K persisted. "'Cause I felt like something was off, too." Krazy K had feet as big as shovels and a permanent scowl on his face, but out of all of them, he was the nicest.

"She said she don't wanna talk about it," Wokie added. Wokie was short, dark and often more quiet than the rest.

"Why you always taking up for Mad? She can take care up for herself." Glitter interjected. Glitter had deep-set chocolate brown eyes and she wore her hair in braids. She always had weed and liquor which made them love having her around even more. And over time, Glitter was quickly becoming Mad's girl.

"I said I'm fine. I don't know why ya'll don't believe me."

"Stop lying," Sugar said. Sugar had a very small mouth and wore her hair in a curly ponytail. Large red glasses rested on the bridge of her nose and she had a squeaky voice. "I know what it is."

"What is it?" Mad asked.

"You saw, Jayden. And you always get like that after you see her."

Sugar was right, Mad was still stewing over the fact that her sister had come over to the house to give her mother some money and didn't bother speaking. Even though Mad told her she wasn't her sister anymore, she was angry that she didn't at least try to reach out to her again. She wanted a relationship with her twin, but she'd been hurt so much, that she wanted to know that she wanted the same.

What bugged her out the most was the fact that she swore she saw Jayden going into her room. When she asked her did she invade her privacy Jayden said no but Mad knew she was lying. So what did Jayden want? She couldn't be stealing because it was obvious she had more money than she did, judging by the designer labels she wore. And then there was the relationship Jayden had with Harmony and money exchanging hands between them. Mad was full of suspicion of those around her, even her gang members.

"Ya'll know we have to do something together to make our gang stronger right?" Mad suggested. "It ain't enough for me to hear ya'll say ya'll got my back. I need you to prove it."

"What can we do?" Glitter asked kissing her in the mouth.

"The ultimate, baby."

"And what's that?" Wokie questioned.

"We need to do something that will bind us together forever. Something that if somebody ever found out, we'd all go down for."

"The only thing I can think of that would bind us like that is murder." Glitter said.

"That's exactly what I'm thinking,"

"Who we gonna murder? Some random person?" Krazy K asked.

"I got somebody in mind. But once we do this shit, we can never turn back." She said looking upon her crew. "Ever."

RAW MEAT
Jace

I met Kali at the Deli to see what he had to tell me. He seemed excited and I hope he had news about Massive. When he pulled up in a minivan and his cousin Vaughn got out to open his door, I knew he had started his own thing and that this meeting had to be about the money. I never fucked with Vaughn and he knew it. Antony let Kali inside alone after searching his pants. He had an extra bop to his walk and I knew he was feeling himself.

"What's up, Jace." Kali said walking in fully, revealing the hatchet on his back.

"You can't come in here with that, man." Antony told him.

"Here," he said handing it to him. Then he set a box on the table. "Because today, ain't nothin' more important than what's in that box right there." Kali said pointing at it.

"What's that?" I asked.

"That's for you," he winked.

I opened the box to see Massive's mutilated head inside. Antony and Kevin looked at me and for the first time in a long time, I smiled.

"You really got this nigga." I said. "I can't believe after all of these years, you put this nigga down."

"I told you. I don't know why you ain't believe me."

I quickly got suspicious and said, "How were you able to get to him so easily? What's up with that?"

"I dedicated 24/7 to finding this nigga, not the other way around."

"What you mean?"

"He wasn't looking for me, Jace. He was lookin' for you. It's easier to hunt somebody if you not being hunted."

"I feel you."

"So when can I collect my money?"

"What happened to you being a part of the crew?" I asked fucking with him.

"Naw, I decided to start my own thing. No offense, but your way of leadership clashes with mine at times."

"Is that right?"

"Yeah."

"Where you layin' your head these days, Kali?"

"I'm here and there...And everywhere."

I looked at him and thought about the games he ran on me. And how he fucked my girl and even to this day, shacked up in her house. The thought of the kidnapped girl ran to my mind too, and how we never found out what happened to Herb Dayo and Sick Sense, two niggas who couldn't stand him.

Thinking of all of that I said, "I'm not payin' you."

"What?" He asked leaning in closer to me. Kevin adjusted accordingly.

"I said I'm not payin' you, nigga. After all the problems you caused me and my operation? You owe me this shit."

"You can't be serious, nigga?"

"Very."

Kali looked at me like he wanted to rip my throat out and Kevin and Antony closed in on him.

"I hope you realize what you're doin'. You just had me get rid of a nigga who hunted you down all your life, and traded him in for a worse one. Nigga, I'm the devil come to life. You sure you wanna tell me, you ain't givin' me my money?"

"I ain't repeatin' myself, now get the fuck out of my shop."

"I got you." He winked.

Kali walked outside the deli and we looked at each through the window. I knew he'd be mad, but it wasn't until we exchanged glances in silence, that I knew how mad he really was.

When he walked off and got into the van Kevin said, "I'll never question your authority."

"Then don't start now." I said.

"I won't. But I just wanna make sure you ready for what's getting ready to go down."

"Even if I wasn't, it's too late to turn back now ain't it?" I said looking at Kevin then at Antony. "This nigga has been obsessed with me...Since we was kids. Even if I did pay him, I wasn't going to get rid of him."

"So what's the plan?" Kevin asked.

"He doesn't know I know where he rests his head. So I'ma hit him where it hurts."

"And then what?"

"And then I'ma kill his ass before he can kill me."

THE SINS OF A MOTHER
Harmony

I hadn't seen Kali and Cherry in a while and I would not have cared, except for the fact that they would come and go as they pleased and that made me nervous. I hated not knowing when he was going to be in my house. Were they gone for good or what?

When I walked into my house after coming from the bar, something didn't feel right. My instincts told me to turn around, but I didn't go with them. Instead I walked deeper into my house, and was struck over the head by what I'd describe as a two by four. When I looked up, I saw Madjesty standing over me, with five other kids.

"Madjesty, what…What are you doing?" I asked rubbing my head.

Without answering me, she hit me again and I felt off balance. "Pick her up and take her to the basement." She ordered.

They drug me by my hair to the basement and the kids held onto me. I was in the middle of the floor waiting on what would happen next. Madjesty walked slowly down the steps and all I could see were here legs until her full body came into view. Although they held onto me, I was in so much pain I couldn't move anyway.

"Put her in the chair," Madjesty said.

Using duct tape, they taped me to the chair in the middle of the floor. Next to the chair was a table with a George Foreman grill, knife, two hats, an extension cord, refrigerator and a video camera.

"Madjesty, please. I'm your mother."

"Plug up your camera, Sugar." Madjesty said. "And Wokie, plug the grill up."

A girl with red glasses placed the video camera on a tri-pod in front of me. And a dark skin short boy placed the grill at my feet and I was fearful. When they were done setting up, Madjesty took her baseball cap off and put a ski mask on. Then she stood next to me. Everybody else moved out of the camera's view. Then she placed a piece of tape over my mouth and a hat over my head.

"Hit record, Sugar."

I heard a small beep before Madjesty spoke. "I'm Mad and this is my whore ass mother. She's a mother who has for every day of my life, tortured me. And for the next thirty days, I'm going to torture her back, before I kill her."

I heard her walk in front of me before she grabbed my feet. Then she pressed it on the grill and they sizzled. The pain I felt was unbearable. She left my feet on the hot grill for five minutes and I tried to scream but the tape covered my mouth.

"Cut!" She said.

She took the hat off of my head and I saw the camera was off. Tears ran down my face but she didn't care. "This is your mother?" Sugar asked.

"Yes!"

"But why would you wanna do this to your mother?" Wokie said.

"Do you think the fact that this is my mother makes me more or less loyal to the gang?" Madjesty said. "I'm killing the woman who brought me into this world to prove my loyalty to this gang. How many of you would do the same?"

The kids looked at each other, then at Madjesty and back at me. When the decision was made to go further, they took me out the chair, stripped me naked and threw me to the floor, the tape still on my mouth.

"Wokie, you fuck her first," she said. "And I want ya'll two to fuck her next."

"What?" Wokie said.

"Listen, the next time one of ya'll questions me, I'm gonna think our gang ain't as tight as it should be. Now I'm telling you to fuck her." She said pointing down at me.

They didn't argue anymore and one by one the boys climbed on top of me and raped me. I couldn't believe what was happening, and more than anything I couldn't believe the hate in my daughter's eyes. For the first time ever, I realized what I had done to her. She was ruined and now I would have to suffer for it.

THE PAPERS

Jayden

Xion took Jayden to Concord Manor because Jace said he had something to tell her, and he needed to see Madjesty, too. Judging by the urgency in his voice, she knew it couldn't wait. He kept asking was Kali there and that if he was, he would meet them someplace else. But she told him he wasn't.

Jayden and Xion had been spending more time together, since Shaggy decided he wasn't going to put her up in the hotel anymore. She ended up renting a room in Xion's aunt's house and it worked out better for her because she could save money.

When Shaggy flipped out, and told her she was on her own, and gave her no reason, she knew then that she had to get her own paper. And together with Passion and the girls she found hanging around the school without a cause, she started Thirteen Flavors. A babysitting service for kids, with a special division for their lonely and horny fathers. She decided her mother was right about some things after all, pussy made the world go 'round and it was time she got with the program.

"You want me to wait out here for you?" Xion asked Jayden as she grabbed her Louis Vuitton purse out of his car. "I ain't getting into too much tonight. Especially after for whatever reason, Shaggy cut me off."

Jayden sighed and said, "Do you think it had something to do with me?"

"Do he know about us?" Shaggy asked.

"Not that I know of." Jayden said. "Plus me and him were never together. He told me that shit over and over again."

"Aight, well, I got some other shit goin' on anyway. You sure you don't want me to wait though?"

"Naw, I'ma call you when I'm ready."

"You sure? 'Cause I don't want you to have to call nobody else to do nothing for you."

"I know you not talkin' about Shaggy."

"Yeah."

"Xion, were you not listening to me?" Jayden giggled. "I'm done with Shaggy and he done with me. Just be by the phone when I call you." She said giving him a kiss.

"I got you, ma."

She got out and walked up to Concord Manor's doors and knocked. The moment her knuckles hit the door, she noticed it was open. She waved to Xion and he pulled off.

"Madjesty," Jayden called her name. She closed the door behind herself. "Harmony!" No one answered. "Madjesty, I need to talk to you. Are you in here?" She walked to the crawlspace hoping her sister wasn't inside. She wasn't.

When Madjesty didn't answer, she walked upstairs to her room and saw she had lots of tennis shoes lined up against the wall. And when she went into her closet, she saw about ten pairs of new jeans, twenty new shirts and eight baseball caps. She smiled thinking that maybe Harmony had done right by her daughter after all by buying new clothes. But where was Madjesty? She saw her house keys on her dresser and knew she was inside somewhere.

"Madjesty," she said moving out of her room and toward the basement.

Before she touched the basement's door, Madjesty appeared from inside with a New York Yankees baseball cap covering her eyes. Her jeans were baggy and she looked more like a cute boy each day. Jayden heard some noise downstairs but didn't know who was causing it.

"What's that noise downstairs?" Jayden asked trying to walk down the steps. "Is mama here?"

"No…And that's the TV on." She said closing the door behind her.

Jayden followed Madjesty into the foyer before Madjesty threw her an evil glare.

"Where's mama?"

"She gone. Now what are you doing here?" She asked. "Why you not posted up in the hotel with some nigga?"

"I have something to tell you," Jayden said grabbing her sister's hand. Madjesty snatched her hand away. "I'm sorry, sister, I'm not trying to invade your space. It's just that...Well...Jace has something to tell us. I think it may be good, Madjesty."

"Mad."

"What?"

"I keep telling ya'll not to call me Madjesty no more. I go by Mad now."

"I'm sorry."

"And who the fuck is Jace?"

"Mama, use to be with him back in the day. And I think...Well, I think he may be our...."

Right before she finished her statement, Jace pulled up to the mansion and walked through the doors. He had Kevin and Antony behind him. Through the open doorway, they saw ten vans parked in the driveway.

"Is Kali here?" Jace asked Jayden.

"No. I don't think so?"

"Is he?" He asked Madjesty.

She shook her head no. "Who are you?" Madjesty asked him. "And what are you and all these vans doin' at my house?"

"You must be Madjesty?"

"Mad. I go by Mad now." She said looking at him and then Kevin and Antony who were standing behind him. "Now who are you and what are you doin' in my house?"

Jace looked at both of them sadly and dug in his pocket. Then he pulled out a little piece of paper and said, "I have some news for you girls. It's the paternity test." He paused.

Mad shot Jayden a dark glare.

"Don't be mad at Jayden," Jace said spotting the look, "I had her bring me some of your hair out of your brush. For the test."

"When was that?"

"It was a while back. I came into your room real quick and left back out."

"I knew it," she said rolling her eyes. "You tried to say you weren't in my room when I asked you."

"Madjesty, please!" Jayden said.

"Mad!" She yelled. "I told you to call me Mad!"

"Girls, this is serious." Jace said. "I have to tell you something. Both of you."

He unfolded the paper awkwardly in his hands and said, "Jayden, I'm...I'm your father." Jayden was so excited about the news that she wrapped her arms around him. And even Madjesty...For the first time in a long time, smiled.

"So...So you our father?" Madjesty said with a tinge of excitement. "So that means you gonna help us now right?" Suddenly she wasn't so angry anymore.

Jayden and Madjesty hugged each other but Jace didn't seem so excited. Then Madjesty hugged Jace and he hugged her back. She didn't know what having a father meant for her, but at least she didn't have to go at life alone anymore. She had someone who she could tell wanted to be in her life, even though it was her first time meeting him.

"I'm going to do whatever I can for you girls," Jace said. "But, Madjesty, you're not my... You're not my biological daughter."

The smiles were wiped off of the girl's faces.

"What are you talking about? You said Jayden's your daughter and we're twins." She corrected him. "So I have to be your daughter, too?" She looked at Jayden. "Right?"

"Honey, you aren't my biological daughter."

"How is that possible?! It doesn't make any sense." Mad said stomping around the foyer. She was upset and embarrassed that she allowed herself to celebrate without hearing all of the facts. Normally she was more careful, but now she'd gotten so caught up in the moment, that she lost her control.

"I didn't understand it either. But before coming over here, I talked to a doctor about it." He paused. "When you're mother was pregnant, she had a condition called, hetero...hetero...."

"Heteropaternal superfecundation." Kevin helped him. As always he was with the doctor when he got the news.

"What the fuck is hetero...Whatever the fuck?!" Madjesty said.

"It's when your mother had different sexual partners...At the same time."

Madjesty and Jayden looked at each other. "What?" Madjesty said confused.

"Ma, fucked two niggas at the same time, Mad. She was a fuckin' slut!"

Madjesty looked at everyone in the living room with wild eyes. Once again, her mother succeeded at making her feel like an outcast. She didn't want another father. She wanted the father her sister Jayden had. She wanted them to be connected. Always.

"Do you know, who my father is?" Madjesty said wiping the last tear off of her face.

"Yes."

Jayden and Madjesty looked at him hanging onto his every word. "Who is he?" Jayden asked.

"Kali."

Mad backed up from them, and leaned against the pillar in the middle of the floor.

"How do you know?" Jayden said as Madjesty frowned.

"I had somebody pick up some of his hair from the barbershop. I sent it in with our hair. Just to make sure."

From a far, anyone looking at how angry Madjesty was all the time, and how dangerous Kali was, could easily see the family resemblance. And the same thing rang true for Jayden. Already, it was evident that she and Jace were cut from the same cloth because they both went after the all mighty dollar.

"I want to be by myself." Madjesty said evenly. "Please leave."

"Madjesty, we can take another test to be sure," Jace offered.

"Please leave," Mad whispered.

"I got you and your sister. You don't have to worry about shit."

"I'm not a fuckin' charity case!" She screamed. "YOU DON'T HAVE TO TAKE CARE OF ME!"

"Mad, when you comin' back downstairs?" Wokie asked coming out of the basement's door fixing his pants. Seeing everyone in the foyer he said, "Oh...I didn't know you had company."

"Go back downstairs, Wokie. I'm coming."

Wokie walked back downstairs and Madjesty said, "Please leave. Now. I need to be alone with my friends."

Knowing there was nothing else they could say to her at the moment, Jace and Jayden left the mansion. When they were gone, Madjesty walked down the stairs with the weight of the world on her shoulders. She dreamed of how hard she was going to make life for her mother over the next thirty days before she finally decided to take her life.

"Put her on the chair, and tape her down," she ordered.

Everyone jumped to take care of the chore, seeing the anger in Mad's face.

Madjesty stooped down in front of Harmony, grabbed a knife that was on the floor and slid the tip of the blade up and down Harmony's inner thigh. The members of her gang didn't say a mumbling word.

"I found out who's my daddy today, mommy," she said angrily. She adjusted the baseball cap on her head and said, "I guess the saying's true. Like father, like son."

She lunged the knife slowly into her flesh the same way Kali did many years before.

PRESENT DAY

Green Door – Adult Mental Health Care Clinic
Northwest, Washington DC

"What happened to you next?" Mrs. Christina Zahm asked.

"Too much to tell you about. All I know is, for thirty days I was tortured like you couldn't imagine."

"After the thirty days, is that when all those people got killed?"

"Yes."

"So what happened to your children after that?"

"They took on the personalities of their fathers. In fact, they started spending more time with them. Madjesty with Kali and Jayden with Jace."

"And then…"

"Oh my God…And then…That's when all hell broke loose!"

Although Raunchy is a fiction based story, The Cartel Publications would like to offer you some facts about the STD 'Syphilis'.

FACTS ABOUT SYPHILIS

How do people get syphilis?
Syphilis is passed from person to person through direct contact with syphilis sore. Sores occur mainly on the external genitals, vagina, anus, or in the rectum. Sores also can occur on the lips and in the mouth.

What are the signs and symptoms in adults?
Many people infected with syphilis do not have any symptoms for years, yet remain at risk for late complications if they are not treated.

Primary Stage   The primary stage of syphilis is usually marked by the appearance of a single sore (called a chancre), but there may be multiple sores. The time between infection with syphilis and the start of the first symptom can range from 10 to 90 days (average 21 days). The chancre is usually firm, round, small, and painless. It appears at the spot where syphilis entered the body. The chancre lasts 3 to 6 weeks, and it heals without treatment. However, if adequate treatment is not administered, the infection progresses to the secondary stage.

Secondary Stage   Skin rash and mucous membrane lesions characterize the secondary stage. This stage typically starts with the development of a rash on one or more areas of the body. The rash usually does not cause itching. Rashes associated with secondary syphilis can appear as the chancre is healing or several weeks after the chancre has healed. The characteristic rash of secondary syphilis may appear as rough, red, or reddish brown spots both on the palms of the hands and the bottoms of the feet. However, rashes with a different appearance may occur on other parts of the body, sometimes resembling rashes caused by other diseases.

<u>Late and Latent Stages</u>   The latent (hidden) stage of syphilis begins when primary and secondary symptoms disappear. Without treatment, the infected person will continue to have syphilis even though there are no signs or symptoms; infection remains in the body. This latent stage can last for years. The late stages of syphilis can develop in about 15% of people who have not been treated for syphilis, and can appear 10–20 years after infection was first acquired. In the late stages of syphilis, the disease may subsequently damage the internal organs, including the brain, nerves, eyes, heart, blood vessels, liver, bones, and joints. Signs and symptoms of the late stage of syphilis include difficulty coordinating muscle movements, paralysis, numbness, gradual blindness, and dementia. This damage may be serious enough to cause death.

What is the treatment for syphilis?
Syphilis is easy to cure in its early stages. A single intramuscular injection of penicillin, an antibiotic, will cure a person who has had syphilis for less than a year. Additional doses are needed to treat someone who has had syphilis for longer than a year. For people who are allergic to penicillin, other antibiotics are available to treat syphilis.
How can syphilis be prevented?

The surest way to avoid transmission of sexually transmitted diseases, including syphilis, is to abstain from sexual contact or to be in a long-term mutually monogamous relationship with a partner who has been tested and is known to be uninfected. Condoms lubricated with spermicides (especially Nonoxynol-9 or N-9) are no more effective than other lubricated condoms in protecting against the transmission of STDs. Use of condoms lubricated with N-9 is not recommended for STD/HIV prevention. Transmission of an STD, including syphilis cannot be prevented by washing the genitals, urinating, and/or douching after sex. Any unusual discharge, sore, or rash, particularly in the groin area, should be a signal to refrain from having sex and to see a doctor immediately.

THE END

COMING SOON

RAUNCHY 2

MAD'S LOVE

The Cartel Collection
Established in January 2008
We're growing stronger by the month!!!
www.thecartelpublications.com

Cartel Publications Order Form
Inmates <u>ONLY</u> get novels for $10.00 per book!

Titles		*Fee*
Shyt List	_____	$15.00
Shyt List 2	_____	$15.00
Pitbulls In A Skirt	_____	$15.00
Pitbulls In A Skirt 2	_____	$15.00
Victoria's Secret	_____	$15.00
Poison	_____	$15.00
Poison 2	_____	$15.00
Hell Razor Honeys	_____	$15.00
Hell Razor Honeys 2	_____	$15.00
A Hustler's Son 2	_____	$15.00
Black And Ugly As Ever	_____	$15.00
Year of The Crack Mom	_____	$15.00
The Face That Launched a Thousand Bullets	_____	$15.00
The Unusual Suspects	_____	$15.00
Miss Wayne & The Queens of DC	_____	$15.00
Year of The Crack Mom	_____	$15.00
Familia Divided	_____	$15.00
Shyt List III	_____	$15.00
Raunchy	_____	$15.00
Reversed	_____	$15.00

Please add $4.00 per book for shipping and handling.
The Cartel Publications * P.O. Box 486 * Owings Mills * MD * 21117

Name: _____

Address:_____

City/State:_____

Contact # & Email:_____

Please allow 5-7 business days for delivery. The Cartel is not responsible for prison orders rejected.